Wednesdays Were for Dying

A Secrets of Salomé Novel

August Keller

Published by August Keller

Wednesdays Were for Dying (A Secrets of Salomè Novel, Book 1)

Ebook ISBN: 979-8-9910695-1-9

Paperback ISBN: 979-8-9910695-0-2

authoraugustkeller@gmail.com

For those who've tried and failed to outrun their minds.

You are a force.

CHAPTER ONE

Ezra

SEPTEMBER 1848. LONDON, ENGLAND.

Memories cut like knives and every time Dr. Ezra Talbot stepped into the Thames Police Court, he bled.

The familiar, musty scent of papers and stale tea hung in the air as Chief Inspector Roland Hugh exhaled a puff of cigar smoke.

Ezra took a half step back, enough to dodge the haze yet restricted enough so the man across from him wouldn't notice.

Desks littered the station in no particular order. He was thankful one rested between himself and the ratan-backed chair Roland reclined in. They weren't alone here. Ezra wasn't sure whether to be grateful for the milling constables or annoyed by their hushed tones.

"What do you want?" The inspector's smirk lines deepened as he attempted to meet Ezra's gaze.

Eyes were wretched, necessary things and staring into another's was a discomfort he tended to avoid. There were better things to look at—perhaps the speckled mole trapped between the man's upper lip and graying mustache, or the sliver of a scar that marred his ear. Ezra grimaced and stared at the man's unkempt brows instead.

A bit of crumbling ash fell from the cigar's end and tumbled down Roland's gaping vest. If Ezra were lucky, he'd burn. Just a bit, nothing he'd be forced to tend to of course.

Roland rocked his muddy boots on the desktop and Ezra heard the granules pile on the surface. Later, someone would sit in this space and drag their tin cup through the soil.

Shifting closer Ezra brushed it to the floor with an errant paper.

"Ezra." Roland's mustache flared.

The bronze bell above the door gave a familiar clang. For some it may be considered a pleasant sound, they'd hear it once or twice at most, but for Ezra the clang reverberated in his mind, sharp and piercing. If he were alone, he'd cover his ears and the inability to do so now set him off. The hum of conversation elevated and the tick of the timepiece in his pocket made his jaw clench with every mark. Wooden-soled boots approached from behind, warning of further unpleasantries.

He was a quiet man in a world of endless noise. With noise came suffering. Had Ezra been a few moments earlier, he'd have procured the body he wanted and avoided this conflict altogether.

"We have an arrangement," Ezra ground out, pushing his hands into the pockets of his plaid trousers. The slacks were worn enough that the inner lining was soft but not enough that it had begun pilling. This mattered.

"Ah, yes we do—did." Roland shrugged with false nonchalance.

"I am here for my physical, sir." An auburn-haired young man puffed up his chest, entirely ignorant of the way the other Bobbies clung to the edges of the room with feigned indifference.

"Not now!" both men barked.

"Who was it, and what did he pay?" Ezra leaned in closer. He wanted the cadaver nearly as much as he wanted more distance between himself and the Chief. He hadn't competed for the dead in years and had no intention of starting now.

"Jeffcott something or rather." Roland drummed his fingertips on the desktop. "I gave it to him for free as it were."

Jeffcoat? The man was an asinine doctor and Roland was playing a fool's game. What a pity the inspector knew him more than he'd like.

A trail of sweat trickled down the back of Ezra's neck, attracting the cold air to his too-warm skin. He'd shudder if he weren't being watched.

"Jeffcoat is a nobody. What game do you play?" he spat out.

"I have a string of physicals for you along with a stack of medical files. You haven't tended to your duties, and thus, I gave away your body."

Roland was correct—Ezra hadn't been to the court in over a month's time. He'd been busy, but not so busy he couldn't have made things work. He simply hadn't wanted to. Nonetheless, the toe of his boot jostled restlessly, and his jaw clenched.

"You know my address. Have these things delivered."

Roland rested his cigar on a tray and crossed his arms over his chest. "Have you heard from your father?"

Mm, there it was. Ezra laughed a humorless little burst of air. Roland didn't care that he hadn't tended to physicals. The man only cared to stick his nose where it wasn't welcome.

"Send me your physicals and paperwork," Ezra bit out, turning to leave.

"Oh, but you're already here and so is my first recruit." The inspector's chair scraped against the floor as he stood. "May as well begin now."

"Very well." Ezra swallowed the acid rising in his throat. "Send him to the back."

He needed to get away from the muffled whispers of comparison between himself and his father.

"Here will do." Roland cocked a brow.

Years of working together had given the man ample fuel for targeting him. Roland enjoyed walking the unpredictable line between ruffling Ezra's feathers and sending him spiraling.

Ezra forced himself to focus on the recruit as the young man held out his document for a signature.

"Shirt," Ezra muttered, tugging the slip from his outstretched hand.

"Pardon, sir?" The constable's pale, freckled cheeks pinkened a bit beneath his rounded spectacles.

What a pity. A man who blushed was pathetic.

"Name?" Ezra gave a resigned sigh and clicked open his medical bag for his Piorry stethoscope. He gestured to the constable's clothing. "Take it off."

"Finnian, sir. Finnian Bulcroft, sir." The constable's fingers fumbled as he struggled over the wooden buttons.

Ezra conducted his evaluation quickly, doing his best to ignore the way his hands began to itch. Chances were, he'd be unable to wash them until his next appointment. His swallow was dry over the mere idea of waiting, and the discomfort burrowed deeper beneath his skin.

Making quick work of the routine, Ezra returned his tools to his bag and dragged his palms across the thighs of his pants. It wasn't as effective as washing his hands, but it distracted his mind from feeling the linger of skin on his.

"If there is nothing else," he said, fastening the bag.

"Papers," Roland grunted, bringing his cigar back to his lips. "Pay attention to the ones on Bethlem Royal Hospital. I've left something special there for you."

Roland pushed a thick stack of papers toward him.

Ezra eyed them warily. Generally, he saw to simple details between the police and the coroner, or decomposition studies, not paperwork. Sliding his tongue over his teeth, he gave a jerk of his head before bending to slip the stack into his arms.

"I am sending a body to the morgue—it resembles human soup. I thought you'd enjoy it," Roland called after him, an obnoxious laugh echoing behind him as Ezra exited onto the street.

September had begun slipping a hesitant chill in the air, and while it lessened the stench of London, it seemed to turn the world gray. He needed to tend to a house call in the West End and chances were he would be tardy, not because tardiness was his nature, but because he despised the West. The population there was inherently whiny and stupid to near pity's sake.

Ezra opted to take a growler to the edge of Hyde Park before disembarking and walking the rest of the way. Wind rustled the stack of papers tucked beneath his arm and he tightened his grip on them. Turning up the collar of his frock coat, he ducked his head into the wind that whistled past. Despite the inclement weather brewing, the park was bustling. Water from the Serpentine River churned, turning it a muddy brown. He watched as fallen leaves caught in the current.

A sound above him caught his attention and he paused, looking up toward the bridge. Laughter? Only drunken men made such a sound in public, but this was a woman.

Ezra ducked back into his collar. Her volume irked him, that was all.

"Fly with me, Hazel!" Her words tore through the wind as she clambered to the rail and stepped between the rungs. The woman's boots were slick, offering little in regard to protective friction, and the water below seemed to reach longing waves toward her.

The shrillness of her tone grated on his nerves and his jaw tightened. All he'd wanted was a quiet walk in the park, some time to forget about the Inspector and bury the history they shared.

Ezra stepped briskly along the cobblestone path, weaving between the golden branches of weeping willow trees as he hurried to escape the sounds.

"Magdalena, get down!" A woman shouted just as the scream of a second companion tore through the air.

Magdalena? A vise closed around his lungs, and Ezra turned, his eyes darting wildly until they settled on her. She wore a simple navy cloak, and a crooked bonnet rested on her wild golden hair.

No, it's not her. Too young, too tall, too improper, he determined with relief.

A pedestrian grunted at him to move from the path, and Ezra stepped aside, losing her in his line of sight.

He looked up again just in time to see someone collide with her from behind, and the woman lurched forward.

No.

Ezra's fingers tightened around his papers, rumpling them. He watched as she tipped over the rails, suspended between bridge and water far longer than logic permitted before disappearing beneath the murky surface of the Serpentine.

"Magdalena!" The two horrified companions shrieked.

Panic and chaos unfolded in a flurry of activity. Menfolk shed their overcoats and passed their top hats to those they escorted, scanning the waters below. Bystanders stared beneath the bridge in vain.

Idiots, the lot of them. Had they no concept of wind patterns or currents? Were not these two things practical knowledge?

Ten seconds.

A tormented groan escaped his lips as the decision was made.

Triggered by instinct he hurried along the path beside the river, pausing at the water's edge. He observed a simple man who stared at the waves in silence, his own hands pushed into his pockets. Nondescript, plain, perfect.

Forty seconds.

"Do you swim?" Ezra set his stack of papers and medical bag on the rocks.

The man turned toward him, nodding. "I am a Navy man."

Wonderful, he hated the Navy.

"Have you any understanding of distance and directionality?"

Ezra removed the man's top hat as he spoke, earning him a bewildered expression.

"Yes, sir." The man faltered whilst Ezra jerked his coat off his shoulders and tossed it beside his bag.

"You will swim southeast and meet a woman in the waters at approximately forty yards. Bring her to me."

Ezra didn't give him any further opportunity to consider what this meant. He simply grasped the man by the waistband of his trousers and dumped him into the river.

The man sputtered as his head rose above the waters and kicked to stay afloat.

Sixty seconds.

"Move!" Ezra bellowed.

Whether out of confusion or surprise, the man obeyed, using strong strokes toward the direction he'd been instructed.

Ezra watched with bated breath, unaware of the throng gathering behind him higher on the banks or the way his papers scattered in the wind.

The young man ducked beneath the water in his search, staying below the surface for a moment.

Eighty seconds.

The man resurfaced, pulling the woman with him and tilting her chin toward the sky as he lugged her to shore.

Well done. Though Ezra would never say it aloud. Compliments weren't his nature.

One hundred seconds. Time was running out.

The man staggered beneath the weight of the woman and her petticoats as he carried her through the shallows and lowered her to the ground at Ezra's feet.

Ezra knelt beside her and pushed an ear to her chest. Her bodice was cold and the dampness nearly too much for him to bear.

Onlookers' whispers distracted him, and he glared them into silence. The heart was no longer making its rhythmic pattern. Her face was void of color and her bow-shaped lips purpled with the combination of water temperature and lack of oxygen.

The coal miner who asphyxiated, from the article he'd seen in *The Edinburgh Medical Societies*. Ezra had long been interested in testing the ideas of artificial respirations himself, but doing so meant far worse than simply filthy water gracing his ear.

Distance yourself. It would be simpler had he not heard her name.

With a tilt of her pale chin, Ezra opened her airway and used one hand to pinch her nostrils. Then he lowered his mouth to hers, forcing air within her.

Her lips were wet and cold, but terribly soft against his. He shuddered and attempted to rid his mind of how filthy she likely was.

No time to gag while saving lives.

In a curious sensation, her chest rose in response to the forced air. He used the heel of his palm pressed firmly on the sternum to create an exhale.

Everything was still—the onlookers, his nerves, even the wind for a moment.

Again, he lowered his ear to her chest. No change.

Three more artificial respirations and three more forced exhales.

Closing his eyes, he considered the interior of her lungs and the contents of her stomach. Both would contain water, which she couldn't independently expel. To remove it was impossible, though perhaps with enough pressure it could be forced out.

One hundred and twenty seconds.

Ezra crossed his arm over her body, gripped her sopping wet shoulder, and leveraged his weight across her chest. Perhaps he should have felt poorly when a collection of her ribs broke from the action, but he hadn't the time to dwell on it.

Ezra failed to anticipate one thing—that the maneuver would indeed force the water out.

And he was the only thing in the way of its release.

A gurgling built up in her throat and there wasn't enough time for him to raise an arm or jerk away before the fluids within her became the fluids on him.

His heart pounded. Get it off. Get it off. Get it off!

His clothes hung damp on his body and trickles of water dripped from his lashes in a frigid path down his stubbled cheeks. Both hot and cold at once, he knew he hadn't much time before he lost his composure.

Ezra hardly noticed when desperate gasps shuddered through her and her fingertips came to life, clutching at the lapels of his coat.

Don't touch me.

He couldn't get the words out, they remained trapped in his throat, suffocating the air from him.

Somehow, it seemed she heard the unspoken plea, and her fingers curved into fists, pushing him away. This was enough, just enough of the unexpected to keep him from fraying further.

Ezra should be pleased, and the parts of him that held firm to logic knew he was. It worked.

It worked. And for a fraction of a moment, he regretted that he had no one in his life worth telling.

"Magdalena!"

Another woman, one several years younger, pushed through the crowd toward them.

In a daze, Ezra glanced toward the bridge where the other companion still stood, sobbing and wailing—how helpful.

Magdalena. Her name turned over in his mind, his attention shifting back to her dripping frame. Her steel gray eyes met his, full of— accusation? Eyes, the wretched things, it seemed an entire language existed inside them and he'd never learned how to translate their unspoken words.

She didn't seem happy with having been saved. Or had he only imagined it?

Time to leave. Quickly.

His tidy stack of papers had strewn about the shoreline and a handful had blown into the river. Of course.

He scowled at the documents before stooping to gather them, soiling himself all the more in his pursuit. The name "Bethlem" was scrawled across the top of one in runny, mottled ink. So much for Roland's preferred subject matter.

"Doctor Talbot, congratulations." An acquaintance clapped a broad hand on his shoulder.

Ezra's shoulder lurched defensively toward his ear. Don't touch me.

"However did you determine such a method?" The man continued in free oblivion.

Frozen in place, Ezra felt the turn of too many faces angling toward him with this declaration of his name. No less than fourteen pairs of crawling eyes studied him like a circus creature.

It's what he was in the end, an oddity, a peculiar thing unlike the rest.

"Education is one's greatest asset," Ezra muttered before shrugging away and completing his escape.

The panic he held at bay only increased the closer he came to his laboratory.

You will get it off. You will wash off this feeling. You are not dirty.

It was a lie, a poor one at that.

Chapter Two

Ezra

Shifting the papers and his medical bag to one arm, Ezra's fingers fumbled with the corner of his coat. The little hem was far more worn than the rest of the fabric on the coat, well used from opening doors as he did then.

He let out a soft groan before stumbling into the warmth of the flat.

Mrs. Keene, his secretary, sat at her desk delving into a novel and chewing on a crust of bread.

"Oh, dear," she murmured, rising to throw open cabinets in search of a towel.

He hated it, the pity in her eyes and the way she tried to tend to him. Mrs. Keene's aid would make things quicker, though he wished he didn't need it.

She retrieved his papers and medical bag and set them down before wrapping the linen around his shoulders.

"Let's set the water quickly." Her fingers tucked and poked at him but never brushed against him as she took his coat.

Ezra's chin jerked stiffly before turning back through the door he'd entered. One more flight of steps upward and he reached his flat.

Together they made quick work of setting a bath.

"Mm," he murmured, taking the kettle from her hands and pouring it into the tub.

"You're welcome," she simmered. "You ought to use your words, Dr. Talbot. Even children are taught not to mumble."

A child? He hadn't gotten the privilege of being one of those, not in the ways that counted.

Mrs. Keene didn't dawdle and clicked the door behind her with a grunt.

There were few he could tolerate for any length of time. Mrs. Keene, though prone to calling him by his true name when she was displeased with him, was one. The buxom widow had no living children of her own. She kept her graying hair tidy, avoided errant conversation, and aided in speaking to his patients when he had no desire to.

Undressing quickly, he sank into the water and lathered his lye soap. It was a harsh cleaner but the lasting tingle of it made the lingering, invisible imprint of the events wash off his body. Once was rarely enough. He'd frequently wash twice, three times if he were truly filthy. Ezra knew average men did not bathe midday if at all in London, and he only cared when forced to endure their scent.

Mrs. Keene knew ritual well; she'd have prepared tea and porridge.

After dressing, he locked the door behind him and took the steep, narrow staircase to the laboratory below. Wordlessly he sat in the wooden chair behind his desk.

His secretary quietly set a tray in front of him and left, as if she sensed how entirely done he was with mankind.

A log popped in the hearth and he rubbed his ears until the sting of noise ebbed away. Gradually, he settled.

Mrs. Keene tsked when she returned to remove his tray. "You've got a house call in nearly half an hour. Take care to avoid being tardy and mind your words."

Blast it, a house call. With the woman in the river, he had forgotten the one in the West End. Ezra pushed his fingers through his damp hair.

"They sent word," she said about his missed appointment, tossing over an accusatory glare. "I have rescheduled them for tomorrow."

Ah, yes, he'd be sure to make the drowned woman aware of how inconvenient her near death had been.

Magdalena. He turned the name over in his mind, letting it fall noiselessly over his tongue. Ezra hadn't heard that name in quite some time.

"An apprentice sir, would benefit you." Mrs. Keene repeated their familiar argument.

If only he could bring Mrs. Keene on his visits, though they'd discovered years ago that she had neither the stomach for blood nor any other bodily fluids.

"Mrs. Keene, I've no intention of gaining an apprentice. I've heard they require ample sunlight, interaction, and even need to be fed on occasion. I am ill-prepared for that variety of commitment." He frowned. "Given time it would feel neglected and I've no time for its emotions."

This was the greatest number of words he'd strung together all day, he realized.

"You speak of an apprentice as though they are livestock." She sighed and nodded in her silent though disapproving way.

He didn't correct her. Man was much like mammal and thus, there was nothing to argue.

Tugging on a dry coat, he pulled his top hat from a bronze rack and prepared his medical bag before slipping into the hall.

A growler accepted his coins in exchange for transportation toward Whitechapel. Not every driver wanted any part in how far east he was traveling. The further east one went, the more it reeked and the less presentable everything became. The structures, the streets, and most assuredly, the people.

"Here." He tapped the roof of the carriage and waited impatiently for it to slow enough for him to step out.

Fire, people, cold temperatures, and needlessly waiting were Ezra's least preferred encounters. The growler slowed but had not yet stopped when Ezra opened the door, clambered down, and much to the driver's irritation, slammed the door rather abruptly behind.

"Gah." The man flung up his arms in displeasure before clicking the reins and leaving him there in the rank, ankle-deep mud.

Streets were narrower there in the east, the buildings far closer together and stacked precariously. There was less civility. Yet while the filth disturbed him,

Ezra rather preferred the lack of facade the people presented with. In the east there was no fanfare, fewer patient complaints, and limited social expectations. In any event, it was easier to tend to patients who experienced true life versus those with petty upbringings and higher opinions of themselves.

Ezra peered up at the building. Situated across from the Mansley Foundling Home for Boys and Girls, the exterior of the tenement house was covered in a thick layer of dust and littered with notices of public health concerns.

He pulled a handkerchief out of his pocket and held it up to his nose before slipping in.

An infant patient resided two stories up, the third door on the left. Each interior wall was nearly paper thin and the goings on inside each dwelling were easily known by neighbors. Likewise, the exterior walls were fragile, and one could feel the autumn air seep in through its cracks. The entire structure nearly swayed in a stiff breeze.

There was a cough across the corridor, the sound of which slipped out from beneath the large gap between the bottom of the door and the flooring. The beginnings of a marital dispute sounded at the far end of the hall.

Ezra hurriedly knocked on the correct door.

"Doctor Talbot," he announced himself.

No more than twenty minutes later, his brows pinched as he made his way his way back down the rickety steps. His mind was on the babe he'd tended to, living there in squalor. A simple vaccination, yet he knew he'd dwell on it longer than he ought. Ezra wasn't one to conduct follow-up appointments, instead resorting only to checking the death columns in the paper to determine success or failure. But today, the thought itself made his stomach churn. He didn't look at infants often, they were a reminder of all the things he would never have. But this one—he wanted her to live.

A woman brushed past him in the stairwell and he flinched away from her. Don't touch me.

His eyes followed her as she tugged the sleeve of her dress down around her wrist to cover the newly forming bruises. Bitterness climbed in his throat at the realization.

Heavy boots stormed behind him, shaking the landing.

"You dare turn your back to me, Mara? Think of what's coming," a burly man shouted at her retreating figure. "I'll buy your madness if I must."

A shudder rippled through Ezra having little to do with the cool temperatures. He slouched further into his coat, tucking his hands into his pockets.

Early evening cast shadows across the alley, leaving Ezra to cling to the remaining shafts of light. He tried and failed to ignore the squelch and suction of filth under his feet.

Soon enough he would be alone. Warm, quiet, clean.

Safe.

Chapter Three

Magdalena

Magdalena Trudeau shifted uncomfortably in the soft down of the mattress. It was too soft, beautiful, and elaborate where it sat on the four-poster bed. Everything about the room was perfect and she had always held a peculiar disdain for perfect things.

It would be better if there were some small flaw that only she knew of, a tear in the curtains or a scrape on the pinstriped wallpaper. In the short time she had lived at her sister's estate, she'd found only one such treasure—a worn, imperfect charcoal depiction of a lilac. She had smuggled the illustration beneath her pillow, pulling it out when things grew dim.

They would likely not let her up from this idle, prone position until she developed a sore or found herself to be going mad. A wry smile tilted her lips. Madder, that is.

A physician would be called if one hadn't been already. The thought brought with it a fresh sense of dread. She had encountered many doctors in her twenty-six years, and none were any good. They'd let her blood or confine her for weeks to come. Both ideas made her nauseous.

She pressed a palm to her chest, feeling the flutter of life beneath her fingers. Aunt Salomé once told her that hearts were fragile things.

The older woman had pressed her rich brown hand over Magdalena's heart when she'd told her of it.

"What makes them that way?" she'd asked.

Aunt Salomé had bumped her nose with a weathered fingertip. "Why, secrets of course."

But Salomé is dead. Magdalena let her hand fall away to fist the rumpled bed linens. Goodness itself should be permitted to live forever. Why then was the best of life torn away in the wind like an exhale? Why couldn't Salomé have been different?

Gone. And Magdalena? She'd been left alone in their estate at Staffordshire Hall.

"Are you certain you wish for no pain relief?" a lady's maid asked from her bedside.

Magdalena forced a smile. "The greatest medicine would be a walk in the park." She rose to her elbows, unable to stop a crease of discomfort from marring her brow. She darted a hopeful glance at the open door. "Do you think you could slip me out unnoticed?"

"Trying to escape again, are you?" Her elder sister, Olive swept into the room.

"Always." A true smile tugged across Magdalena's face.

"With a great deal of investigating, we've placed a name with your rescuer." Olive's eyes sparkled as she sat at the foot of the bed.

Ah, yes. Olive had an infatuation with romance, and Magdalena had a hunch it was about to unleash itself.

"The esteemed Doctor Talbot." Olive sighed wistfully. "He offered you the kiss of life, bringing you back to us all."

Magdalena snorted and nudged her sister with her foot. "That is entirely ridiculous."

"It is not! I witnessed it with my own eyes." Olive pursed her lips. "You said so yourself—you did nothing but stay on that bridge wailing about until I was renewed."

Just as Olive clung to her tales of love, Magdalena clung to the solidity of logic.

"It was so infinitely tender that I saw it even from such a great distance. Can you not trust my words?"

"No, I cannot trust you. You who, out of all men, wed a widowed man twice her age with a hairline so far receded I can hear it pleading to be removed altogether," Magdalena teased.

"That was unkind!" Olive stood and planted her hands on her hips.

Her sister was right. Though terribly unattractive, her brother-in-law was a generous man and good to her sister. And, by default, to Magdalena.

"Forgive me, Olive." Magdalena blew out a sigh. "It is this bed—I simply cannot stay in it a moment longer."

"You find it uncomfortable?" Olive's forgiveness was apparent in the way she attempted to straighten her sister's wayward hair behind her shoulders. "We can have it replaced straight away."

"No." She shook her head sharply, then attempted to soften the words, reaching for her sister's hand. "That's not what I meant."

But it was the bed. It was the walls of the estate and the bustling city of London just beyond the window that Magdalena had traded for the vast rolling hills of South Gloucestershire. This wasn't home, it would never be home, and for all the beautiful things Aunt Salomé told her about hearts, she'd not taught her how to repair a broken one.

"... and Frank obtained his services for you. Despite your lack of affection for him, he holds you in high regard."

Magdalena realized Olive had been speaking but heard none of it save this last, small fragment.

Services?

The ladies' maid smiled at her needlepoint, and it was a near guarantee she smiled over Magdalena's confusion and not her craft.

"A Doctor Talbot has arrived for Ms. Trudeau," the footman announced from below.

At this, Olive paled and set about tugging the covers beneath Magdalena's chin.

"He is a physician is he not? He's already offered me such a profound kiss that my once-departed soul had no choice but to return to my body. Surely, he's seen a woman in a dressing gown on more than one occasion."

The sarcasm that dripped from Magdalena's surly tongue was not lost on Olive who gave her a final cautionary glare before pasting on a welcoming expression.

Magdalena dropped her head to the pillow; the action was too abrupt, and she groaned up at the ceiling. Footsteps sounded up the staircase and she attempted in vain to wish away the man of medicine. Her mood was far too poor to tolerate any examination or small talk.

Upon his entrance, the atmosphere in the room took an unpredictable shift, even for Olive who often soothed any social situation.

Magdalena turned, straining her neck to see the bearer of such a stifling apprehension.

Instead of speaking, the man surveyed the scene with an exploratory eye, his gaze landing on the drawn curtains.

With sure steps he crossed the room and thrust open the window coverings, sending a billow of dust into the room. Olive's cheeks flushed at the lack of cleanliness, but Magdalena smiled. There it was, an imperfection. Oh, how she loved simple, flawed things like dust.

Dr. Talbot flipped the window latch and pushed it outward, offering the room and the woman it held captive a cool breeze.

"Get up." He spoke with his back to her viewing the lawn below.

Magdalena watched him, knowing he'd not find a solitary weed in the gardens nor grass below. Frank was diligent in having hired a new gardener just before he'd married her sister.

"Doctor—" Olive's sputtering was cut off by his pivot.

In a swift snap of the bedclothes, he tugged them to the foot of the bed and reached for her gown-covered arm. It was an unusual manner of offering aid, but Magdalena presumed she should follow suit considering his no-nonsense tone and the entire avoidance of eye contact.

"You blessed man." She clapped her hand over his forearm, leveraging herself with his weight as she braced herself against the pain.

It met her with a vengeance, and she ground her teeth against the onslaught of discomfort. The fall breeze was far from comfortable in her thin dressing gown as he led her wordlessly toward a straight-backed armchair. Each step jarred her insides, and she glared at him.

"I take it back. You aren't a blessed man. You are malicious and I don't like you."

"Magdalena!" Olive gasped in horror, a response Magdalena tended to pull from her often.

Acknowledging her for the first time, Dr. Talbot seemed to truly look at her. It felt only fair she do the same. His dark brown hair fell naturally to the side in thick curls nearly to his shoulders. How the man could see at all through his shroud was rather impressive, and see he did with eyes such a magnificent brown they were nearly black. His square, stubbled jaw restrained full lips that were stiff and unsmiling.

Awkwardly his eyes slipped to hers for hardly a second's time before darting away.

Stop that, they seemed to say.

"Likewise," he mumbled, shaking off her grip on his arm as she lowered herself to sit.

The corners of the doctor's lips twitched at Magdalena's sharp intake of breath, an expression so fleeting that it would have easily been missed. Despite the chill in the room from the open window, sweat beaded on his temples while he conducted a brief examination.

Sure, firm fingertips pulled up her eyelids as he looked closely at each eye. He then moved on to her ears, nose, and complexion.

Even she wasn't bold enough to look at him as his fingers moved nimbly over her ribs finding precisely the three that offered the greatest discomfort. He lowered an instrument to her chest and listened intently while she inadvertently held her breath.

"Not breathing is precisely what brought you to this predicament in the first place," he admonished.

Olive's confused eyes darted between the pair of them as Magdalena burst out laughing. She realized Dr. Talbot hadn't intentionally made a joke, which had her giggling all the more. Her ribs ached from the effort, and the brief time of sitting hurt physically but eased her spirit.

Dr. Talbot wiped his hands on his trousers and backed away from her.

"No more lounging about, no restrictive clothing, and avoid heavy lifting." He studied her physique. "That shouldn't be a problem."

Olive pursed her lips and the maid coughed into a handkerchief as Magdalena's nostrils flared.

She squared her shoulders. "Lounging isn't my preference, and I can lift quite a lot when I set my mind to it."

"Then see to it you don't set your mind to it."

The doctor returned his stethoscope to his bag and snapped it closed.

In the ten minutes he had been in the room, nearly everyone within felt insulted. How refreshing. Despite what she told him, she liked him almost immediately. Perhaps she could overlook the small factor of him being a physician.

Just as he prepared to take his leave, a maid delivered the tea service.

At this Magdalena openly smirked.

"Have some tea, Doctor?" Magdalena met his void expression with a dare, taunting him to stay when it was evident he'd rather remove his eyelids than do so.

"I'd rather not."

"Whether you would rather or not is of little consequence." She smiled. "You saved my life, Doctor. Surely I can repay you in this small manner?"

The lady's maid gathered up her stitching and Olive's face flushed to an unworldly hue.

"Repayment ought to be of equal or more significant value. Your tea is worth nary a quarter-pence," he scoffed.

Olive, who abhorred confrontation of any variety, was nearly unhinged.

Magdalena freed her with a dismissive hand. "Olive, I suddenly find myself full of vigor. See to your other matters."

It took hardly any convincing and she fled, horrified, from the room.

The maid remained and set aside her hobby, crossing her hands in her lap openly watching the theatrical performance. The smell of the black pekoe tea wafted through the air, faintly cut with the scent of oranges. Just the way Aunt Salomé used to make it.

Magdalena readdressed the doctor. "Were you a military man?"

She wrapped her fingers around the fine China handle of the teapot, pouring two cups and adjusting them on their saucers. The simple action sent a sharp pain to her fractured ribs, but she masked the discomfort with a smile.

"Sugar?" She hovered the silver tongs over the cubes.

"Yes, no." Simply and in order.

"You rather resemble your tea preferences." She selected two cubes of her own.

Hand outstretched she offered him his fragile cup. There was a lengthy pause, and she wasn't certain he'd accept.

When he didn't readily do so, she hobbled to her feet and pushed it into his hands. He was likely still considering how one bore any resemblance to tea.

An average man would inquire at this point, and it bothered her more than it ought when he didn't. For the record's sake, she would've suggested adjectives such as tepid and bitter as the metaphorical comparisons. How unfortunate she'd not get to insult him.

Turning the dainty cup in his hands, he held it to eye level and brought it to his nose before inhaling. The refreshment having sufficiently passed his evaluation, he wiped the rim of the cup with a handkerchief, brought it to his lips, and emptied the contents in one gulp.

Perhaps tepid had not been the correct descriptor after all.

His cup clattered softly against the saucer as he returned it to the tray. Black medical case securely in hand, he prepared for his leave.

Magdalena found herself hesitant to see him depart. He was socially wretched, and she found it fantastic. If only everyone were so abysmal when it came to expectations, then they'd all be free to be real. And there were very few real things in this world.

"Most would now bid farewell." Magdalena plied him with the expectation.

"Mm, yes. Have life." He gave a curt nod, turned on his heel, and left.

She didn't have time to reflect on his odd parting before the footman announced another visitor. "Miss Hazel Morozov."

Magdalena studied the intricate floral pattern on the teapot before taking a slow sip of her cup, effectively and immediately burning herself on its contents. She sputtered, bringing her fingers to her lips, and returned it to its tray.

A curious man indeed.

The bustling up the steps indicated the arrival of her youngest sister.

In a flurry, Hazel entered and threw herself at her elder sister's feet.

"Will you ever forgive me?" Hazel dramatically wailed, laying her head in Magdalena's lap.

"We've discussed this already, Hazel, no less than six times." Magdalena's heart was soft towards the blossoming young woman.

"If only I didn't have such a fear of horses, I'd not have stumbled into drowning you," she wailed, then straightened and squared her shoulders. "But I am determined to master it. There is nothing I cannot overcome."

Magdalena patted Hazel's fine brunette hair, chuckling. "Master your fear of horses or drowning me?"

"What a terrible thing to say," Hazel gasped, and then snickered.

"In any regard, what's done is done. I am well. In fact, I met my hero just moments ago."

"I spotted him on his way out. He looks more like a mortician than a physician."

"He was insufferable!" Olive glided back into the room and took a seat beside the maid. "Did the matter improve at all after I left?"

"Absolutely not." Magdalena grinned, tucking her hair beneath her cap.

"You should not have encouraged him so," Olive admonished.

Magdalena was no longer listening as she looked out the window. The gardens, while not Staffordshire Hall, were beautiful and beckoned to her. Fresh air and a walk with her sisters were precisely the cure to having been trapped in this room.

She busied herself with dressing quickly, fingers brushing across each of the buttons of her blouse. Carefully, she counted five down and left it undone. No one noticed silly things like unfastened buttons, but the smallest things mattered to her. Magdalena wove a straight pin through the fabric to hold it closed.

"Charity is downstairs." Hazel used a straightened hand to block the loud whisper from Olive. "Shall we all pretend to be miserable?"

"Stop that," Olive chastised, but even she failed to hide her smile.

"Nervous—very, very dreadfully nervous I had been and am." Magdalena brought a dramatic hand to her heart while quoting the now rather famous Poe.

"Just what is so thrilling about near death and subsequent imprisonment in this room?" The sharp tone of their eldest sister, Charity, shrilled from the doorway.

The three looked at one another and erupted into a fit of giggles, Charity could make nearly anything dismal.

Instinctively, Magdalena's eyes sought Charity's cane. This was their new silent routine, to pass a walking aid like it was made of more than bronze and wood.

Magdalena took it from her wordlessly after Charity lowered herself to a chair. The cane topper had been created from a mold of Aunt Salomé's hand and she tangled her fingers with the wrinkled, upturned palm. Agony tripped through her chest, and she released it like a fiery brand, passing it quickly to Hazel who kissed it once before it made its round to Olive.

Magdalena attempted to bury her grief. Dr. Talbot should have let her die. It would have been easier to die, though thoughts like that made her feel terribly guilty. People like her weren't supposed to feel this way, not when she'd been gifted more in half her life than many experienced in all of theirs.

"Shall we?" Olive motioned toward the gardens beyond the window.

With cane in hand Charity pushed to her feet on crooked legs. Rickets were to blame for her sister's uneven pace down the hall and pain-filled trek down the curved staircase. How selfish Magdalena felt for her bleak thoughts and threatening melancholy. She was privileged far beyond her right, surrounded by love and family that should never have been hers.

Magdalena forced herself to view the beauty of the world around her—the fading green of an autumn garden, the colored leaves on sparsely dressed trees, and the dreary gray sky that mirrored her mind. A few late blooms of white flowers speckled the lawn in pinwheel shapes.

You are not alone. She reached out her hands and tucked them into the arms of Hazel and Olive, tugging them closer.

"I am glad you came to London," Olive said softly, leaning her chin close to Magdalena's ear. "I didn't think you would."

She nearly hadn't. Leaving Staffordshire Hall had been a loss in itself. She knew every creak in the wooden floors, every scar on the curved banister, every dent in the plaster walls, and their origin. Memories seemed trapped within its rooms and even when everyone else left and Salomé passed on, she could still hear the laughter and warmth of years gone by.

Olive translated her silence as discomfort and looked up at her, worrying her cheek between her teeth. "I should have requested pain relief when the doctor was here."

"I'm all right, I promise." The lie coated her tongue. "Or I will be now that I am with you all." She squeezed her sister's arm.

The city beyond the iron gates and hedges of the garden held its own memories. A childhood of running from physicians who couldn't possibly treat a mind as fractured as hers.

A smirk tilted her lips. If only Mother could see her now, with her bonnet willfully askew and her fifth button undone.

CHAPTER FOUR

Ezra

Ezra scowled as he climbed the steps to the facility. The central block of London Hospital in Whitechapel ought to be a disgrace to anyone who dared call themselves a medical professional. It was a voluntary hospital with such poor architecture that it physically pained him. No one wished to visit the sanatorium, not when it was the furthest thing from sanitary.

Surgeons bustled about with their bloodied aprons, mingling the fluids of one patient with those of their previous. Physicians and their apprentices scurried from patient to patient while the university students followed closely behind learning one hundred and one methods by which to kill those in their care and very few strategies by which to successfully treat them.

When scheduling himself here, Ezra bulked up his patients to complete the tasks in one day as opposed to stretching it out longer than necessary. Get in, get out, bathe, forget he had been.

Ezra found a wash station and used the last dregs of water to scrub his hands. Few cared to clean themselves until they were through for the day, considering it to be a waste of time.

He couldn't look too closely at the water he used. There were always foreign bits floating in it.

He smelled the group of men before he saw them. They reeked of iron and arrogance.

"Notice the lack of blood on this apron," an apprentice acknowledged pretentiously. He was a short, portly fellow with drooping spectacles and slicked-back hair.

So it would seem today's insults would be less discreet. Ezra only glanced at them as he finished his washing.

"Ahh, Talbot," Dr. Jeffcoat gloated as he willfully dropped Ezra's title. "I had the loveliest body to dissect just the other day. An absolute pig the man was."

The only swine in his autopsy theatre had likely been him. Dr. Jeffcoat sold out his theatre to citizens and medical professionals alike, offering seats like an opera for the sake of entertainment.

Dr. Jeffcoat and his students acknowledged Ezra's appearance and nearly turned up their noses. Their aprons were spattered with layers of bodily fluids—blood, saliva, phlegm, and worse. Several of the students had created the illusion that they were hard-working by marking their aprons intentionally or re-wearing the same one several days in a row.

Ezra dried his hands on a scratchy towel and dropped it in a bin. The housekeeping staff had a special dislike for him. His presence meant more work. It also meant less death, but they hardly seemed to notice that bit.

"Good day, Talbot." Dr. Jeffcoat offered a final smirk.

"Mm," Ezra imparted as his only response and stepped around the group. Dr. Jeffcoat was indeed, a nobody.

He continued on his way, receiving a few spatters of acknowledgment as he briskly passed through toward the surgical amphitheater in the attic. The wails of unmedicated patients, the coughs of the ill, and the soft hum of conversation echoed through the halls, enunciated by his rapid footsteps.

The amphitheater was particularly tidy, one of two expectations he had while accepting surgical requests. He viewed the tools laid out and ensured their cleanliness, completing the task just as his patient was wheeled in by an orderly.

"Make it quick," the orderly groused, clicking open a shiny new pocket watch. Clearly, he was paid better than Ezra.

Ezra scanned his chart. The patient before him was much like the variety he often saw at the voluntary hospital—rowdy, belligerent, and entirely mad. The other physicians had refused this particular man who fought with deceptive strength ill-suited to his average size. The young man of no more than nineteen years resided at Bethlem Royal Hospital, where he was most often restrained and in solitary confinement.

Ezra had a peculiar urging to look out for those struck by insanity, what with his own fractured mind and all.

His patient was strapped to the bed at uniform intervals, thrashing only his hands at the wrist as he grunted and shrieked like a trapped animal. He didn't pity the boy much. He had tended to his needs several times in the past month only to be kicked, and spat on, twice. Ezra had, however, written to the government seat when he'd seen the living conditions in that wretched place.

The cause for the man's surgical need was not outwardly apparent to the two nurses who awaited their instruction, and he knew they'd rather assist any other surgeon but him. He tended to expect them to know his plans and intentions without having voiced them.

The theater seats were empty, the second of Ezra's requirements. He wouldn't tolerate any snide comments or observations of his craft.

"Ether," he instructed.

The nurses looked at one another before one finally rose to the task and handed him the glass globe with an attached sponge.

"What procedure are we to assist with?" One nurse found the gumption to ask.

"Exploratory."

Ezra set the ether aside momentarily and stepped behind the patient's head. Most often, he was rather abrupt and poor at explaining. However, now he used stern, gentle fingers to close the patient's jaw firmly and leaned down closely to speak to him.

"This will smell rather putrid, perhaps a bit sweet to the nose and your taste. Do your best to take strong breaths so we can make things right."

He used one hand to keep the mouth firmly closed while reaching to the side and gathering up the ether.

The brave, or perhaps ignorant, nurse scoffed under her breath. "It isn't as though he understood you at all."

Perhaps. Or perhaps this man was simply trapped by a mind that sought to destroy him. Perhaps he knew things and saw things. Perhaps Ezra's words and the intent behind them had been understood. Unlikely, but there was a small possibility unlikely things could happen. He brushed off the peculiar thought.

No, not really. Again, logic won. Logic always won.

Ezra lowered the sponge over the patient's nose and the twisting hands slowed before falling still. He instructed the nurses to unclasp the buckles around the abdomen and then set to work.

Clasping back the patient's gown, he cleaned the filth from the stomach before using a straight razor to remove the few fine hairs at the site of the incision.

Then he retrieved a scalpel.

His hands were quick, sure, and efficient as he used a vertical, midline incision customary in a laparotomy. Upon a prior observation, the patient appeared to be in pain. He refused to eat or drink anything beyond tea and had taken to vomiting even that. It was likely he'd eaten something indigestible or that perforated his interiors. Appendix, though more likely in children, would be an equally justifiable ailment.

Ezra's mind was generally a revolving door of facts, though now, as blood began to saturate the white of his sleeves, he forced himself to remain focused.

Get it off, get it off, get it off. It was like a chant in his mind until he took a slow inhale through the nose and steadied his thoughts.

Once beyond the layers of skin and subcutaneous fat, the real work began. Exploratory was the correct word as he needed to pinpoint the cause.

It took but a few short moments before he discovered half of a bronze shank button at the opening of the small intestine.

He found it odd considering the patient's current dwelling and the limited clothing he was wrapped in. A blockage, just as he'd suspected. The young man must have swallowed it in his poor mental state.

Ezra cleansed the interiors and called for catgut sutures before stitching his way out.

Ezra left the nurses with their instructions before shedding his apron in a basket and making his way toward the surgical offices to obtain a change of clothing.

"What caused it?" The asylum orderly intercepted him in the hall, clicking his pocket watch closed.

"He ingested a button. Tell me, do you offer him food or is he expected to scrounge for anything to fill the gnawing of his hunger?" Ezra glared at him.

The scrawny, dark-haired attendant stilled the chewing of his tobacco as he saw the blood covering the doctor's hands. He took an instinctive step backward but gave him a testy gaze.

"Just be sure you sign the report and send it to Bedlam." The attendant shrugged with a nasty little sneer.

Bethlem, Bedlam. The two were used interchangeably to describe the hospital that offered a chaos so profound it was both noun and adjective. It was a wretched nickname of sorts, though it seemed fitting an employee would use such a moniker.

Ezra gave him no further thought and continued toward the washroom. He gathered a few appreciative glances at the sight of his once-white sleeves. He held his arms perpendicularly to one another, bent at the elbow, fingertips towards the ceiling.

No space for changing nor cleansing existed beside the theater, leaving the only solution down several flights of stairs, past courtrooms, committee rooms, more than 190 patient rooms, the laundries, and finally to the wash houses and cold bath in the cellar.

A true imbecile with no knowledge of medicine had inevitably been in charge of such architecture, and it was clear. Idiots should not build hospitals. Ezra was relieved to have surpassed the majority of such a stretch with no interactions and had just begun to let his guard down.

As luck would have it, he was destined for a lesser preference.

"Ezra? Ezra?" The familiar voice of Thaddeus Cain called after him.

He considered momentarily his options, making an unfortunate pause to survey where he may sidestep and avoid conversation.

This brief hesitation was all Thaddeus required to close such a space.

Thaddeus sidled up to him quickly.

"You can undoubtedly hear me, Ezra." Thaddeus panted slightly over his pace as he matched Ezra's footsteps. "You consider us friends, do you not?"

Women found Thaddeus to be handsome and charming. Ezra thought that of all the qualities a man could possess, being handsome was the least necessary. The coroner had thick sandy hair and a fashionable mustache that turned up ever so slightly at the corners. Women seemed to particularly enjoy the solitary dimple that graced his right cheek.

"Acceptably so." Ezra's pinched his lips together, taking the appropriate entrance, and entered the washroom where he kept several changes of shirt.

"Then I am particularly wounded that you would ignore me." Thaddeus had a flair for the dramatic. "After all we have been through."

He pushed back the hair high on his forehead exposing the gruesome scar he kept hidden.

"Come for dinner, would you?" He continued despite Ezra's ducking behind a half-wall division and proceeding to change from his soiled shirt and scrub a bit too rigorously with his preferred lye soap.

"No to dinner." He grunted.

"Why no dinner? Must we only engage in friendly matters within the autopsy?"

"Yes." Why was Thaddeus pretending they ever met for simple company? It sounded awful. Ezra gestured to the swatch of hair that covered his friend's scar. "Is your brain well?"

"My brain is functioning entirely too well," Thaddeus rolled his eyes. "Thanks to your expert surgery aboard the ship."

The Navy. Ezra shrugged away his annoyance. He and Thaddeus had served together in the Opium War aboard a naval ship. It was a season he tried often to forget.

The coroner lounged against the wall of the washroom. "If you are resistant to dinner, perhaps we could meet elsewhere? A friendly conversation and a drink would do us both well."

"You know I've no interest in either of those pastimes." Ezra shook his head while pushing his arms into the sleeves of his overcoat.

"Speaking of drinking, that body Roland sent to me? I have yet to thank you for it. Never has the morgue smelled so rancid. I've taken to dousing a facial covering in rum to tolerate it."

"What have you found?" While not fond of needless chatter, bodies entertained Ezra.

"I have no probable cause of death yet. Still trudging through the soft tissues."

"Mm, how was it brought in?"

"In a barrel of Spanish whiskey." Thaddeus winced. "It may well have ruined whiskey for me for a time."

"And the remains?"

"From what I can tell, and things have been particularly slippery, it's male. Lower class according to fragments of fabric. It has been a stretch since I last rifled through the sludge of decomposition, and I haven't missed it." Thaddeus, though disgusted, wasn't accusatory. "Ah, well. I'll give my best efforts for you. As you know, I quite truly owe you everything."

"I'll stop by to take a look at the bones." Ezra gave a dismissive wave of his hand. "I'll be off then, have life."

"So long to say hello and so quick to say farewell." Thaddeus stood from his reclined position against the wall, an exaggerated hand over his heart.

Ezra offered nary a grunt as he left the washroom first and took a side exit onto the street. If Thaddeus were a lesser man, he'd be insulted or frustrated with him. But as things were, the coroner was terribly wrong.

Ezra was no hero. He'd failed him, failed all of them. The guilt nearly had him turning around, prepared to suffer through a meal as friends with forced conversation.

Almost.

The British count for those killed in the war had been sixty-nine, which would have been seventy, had Ezra not removed a solitary bullet from Thaddeus's skull. It was sheer luck that the piece of metal had been slow-moving and shot from a great distance. In turn, Thaddeus was only a casualty who was now rather insistent on making Ezra less of a social catastrophe.

Luck indeed.

Ezra had been drafted most unfortunately into the Navy as a physician and opted never to carry a weapon. One physician per ship was all Britain had allotted, and they rather fancied keeping him alive. It was no wonder he opted not to carry a weapon, as once evaluated, he was found to be a horrendous marksman.

Outside Ezra quickly tucked his chin into his upturned collar and hid his hands deep within his pockets. Sunlight peeked through the afternoon clouds drawing out the crowds. In the streets lining the front of the hospital sat several food carts selling various goods, none of which were sanitary nor edible. Fitting. All those customers would soon be inside with their communicable diseases.

He hastened toward the main street to catch a growler, passing by the Mansley Foundling Home for Boys and Girls. Mr. Mansley could almost always be seen in the front courtyard surrounded by children as he instructed or sported with them. However, all were absent today.

Head toward his feet, Ezra ensured he wouldn't intentionally step in the sludge and waste covering the street. Because of this he failed to notice there was a set of eyes following him.

"Doctor?" A woman's voice called out.

Perhaps if he didn't look up nor address it, the voice would go away.

"Dr. Talbot, it is you. I'm certain."

The voice was faintly familiar, and he dared for a moment to pause and look up, searching for its feminine owner.

"Here." Just across the street a woman in a particularly impractical gown of soft yellow waved at him.

For mercy's sake. Anyone but her.

She held her cloak closed at the front in the same hand as a cotton sack and gathered up her skirts in the other before looking both ways and crossing the street. The roads were narrow this far east and there was nowhere to hide if he wished—and he did indeed wish it. There were only so many people he could pretend to tolerate in a day, and he had reached his limit.

"Ms. Trudeau," she reminded him and held out a glove-covered hand in his general direction, which he eyed with disgust. "Ah, that's right, you avoid unnecessary touching."

She lowered her hand and brushed it on her skirt.

It was likely many caught his avoidance though none were bold enough to address it head-on as she.

"You're on the wrong side of London," he opted to express.

Don't be curious, he warned himself. His greatest weakness was curiosity.

She sniffed. "I am welcome in the East or the West, thank you for your concern."

"You have mistaken indifference for concern." A wry smile tugged at his lips but he subdued it into a grimace.

"Then why say it?" She smirked.

He proceeded on his way without further discussion. Only when she met his pace in equal did he begin to sweat. He didn't run, avoided it at all costs really. There was little worse than willful perspiration. But Ezra would do quite a lot to get away from her.

"Could I properly thank you?" she muttered in exasperation, with winded breath.

"Go ahead."

Best get it over with. He could only hope the woman didn't begin crying. He despised tears.

"Well," she paused on the boardwalk. "Why did you save me?"

"That doesn't sound much like thank you." He stopped beside a decrepit tenement house.

"Why?" she repeated. Her gray eyes crashed into his.

He didn't have time to look away before they trapped him, and he saw things he didn't want to see. Pain, heartache, and darkness, wicked things with no cures. Yet there was more, something beyond the melancholy. It glimmered and shined, and he wanted to know what it was.

Stop looking, he demanded.

"So you would not die," Ezra rasped out.

"Why did you care?"

"I didn't." He shook his head.

"You lie."

"No." None of his words were a lie. He saved her selfishly for the sake of science and nothing more.

Ezra flexed his jaw and exhaled loudly before proceeding on his trek, leaving her standing solitary on the boardwalk. Just when he thought he had much avoided further conversation, she belted out behind him.

"You kissed me."

Whatever air had been in his lungs was sucked out into the street and the natural moisture of saliva one becomes accustomed to all but evaporated in that instant. Several passersby covered their snickers or in some cases laughed outright at her boldness. He had a hunch she'd never say such things in the West, and here, she used this society's lack of propriety to her advantage.

Ezra was still at an entire loss for words when she was once again beside him, smiling up at him with a cocky expression plastered on her face. She was a mystery. How could she laugh and smile amongst the things he saw in her eyes? Two conflicting powers that shouldn't mingle but somehow made her the most living thing he had ever encountered. Illogical.

"Don't say that," he hissed.

Heat built in the tips of his ears and he fought the urge to cover them.

Men don't blush, he warned himself.

"I would never," he choked out. "They are called—"

"... artificial respirations, I am aware."

"Edinburg Medical Societies—"

"... the coal miner," she finished his thought.

Now he was truly conflicted. A person with diligence to study, who already possessed some logic, was a rarity in London. Be it man or woman, he'd not before met anyone quite like her.

Thus, he did the only thing he could do. He looked at her. Mouth slack, eyes still avoiding hers, yet wondering and questioning.

She shrugged. "I was wrought with curiosity after I was told of your methods, and I set about to find answers."

"Then why did you say—?" He couldn't quite finish the sentence.

She grinned. "Ah. Men are all a bit alike in at least one thing. They entirely hate embarrassment."

She was right. He didn't find the feeling favorable. Yet there he stood with a peculiar appreciation. However unfortunate, Ms. Trudeau was clever.

"Let us agree to amiable conversation when we cross paths?" she requested.

"Amiable?" He hardly knew how to manage that.

"I'll model it for you most thoroughly," she offered.

"Mm," he grunted, turning away from her bright smile.

"Farewell," she called after him.

"Have life," he muttered under his breath, too confused over what transpired to do much else.

CHAPTER FIVE

Ezra

Rather unfortunate did his mumbled acceptance to her terms and conditions appear to be, as it seemed they crossed paths several times throughout the subsequent month that followed.

Ezra encountered her in passing outside the London Library at St. James Square. She was leaving and he was arriving when they crossed paths at the threshold where she held the door.

"Doctor," she acknowledged. "How good it is to see you."

"Mm." He nodded, entering through the door and leaving her behind.

"Propriety suggests you say, 'Good day,'" she called after him.

"Away, you moldy rogue, away," he muttered the Shakespearean insult.

"I do tend to grow on a person given enough opportunity."

He turned in time to witness her wink. He couldn't recall a time a woman had ever winked at him. It was unsettling.

Once inside, he searched the shelves for a particular text by Charles Mackay to no avail and found himself in a predicament. After some internal convincing, he approached the rather severe-looking library attendant and inquired after it.

"*Memoirs of Extraordinary Popular Delusions*, you say?" The attendant confirmed.

"Mm." He nodded.

"Appears to be a popular topic. I am afraid I've just checked out that particular text only ten minutes ago, along with a series of other odd publications."

He wasn't accustomed to having his preferred genre unavailable. In previous years, he'd not had any competition for medical texts as most physicians utilized university libraries or their personal collections.

"To whom?" His tone was a bit irate.

"The most unassuming and unexpected individual—a woman."

"Magdalena Trudeau?" Ezra's question was more of a statement.

"Impeccable. However did you know?" The library attendant looked much less severe, finding this to be a party trick of sorts.

"What ... else did you lend her?" He finally mustered the nerve to ask.

Confidentiality in a library was apparently of little importance as the man rifled through his records and pulled out a slip of paper.

"*Anatomy of the Brain*, by Charles Bell, William Harvey's *Anatomical Exercitations* ...." He paused while reading his scribbles. "Ah, lastly, *Every Man His Own Doctor* by John Tennent."

Ezra groaned after the last one was listed. "She'll kill all of London with that one," he muttered under his breath.

"I've not known any woman to find interest in such matters. I nearly refused to lend them, even after bribery." The attendant looked a bit sheepish.

"Bribery?"

"Yes, sweets. I've got a terrible knack for them."

Ezra left the library without searching for an alternative title, hands buried deeply in his pockets, chin tucked into his collar and thoughts swirling about in his mind.

The next week he saw her across Hyde Park and narrowly avoided an interaction by ducking behind a passing carriage and taking the bridge across the river. Never had he felt so punished for saving someone's life.

Ms. Trudeau didn't appear to care in the slightest that he offered her nothing but sarcasm and scowls and, once again, she sidled up beside him out of seemingly thin air as he was returning to the laboratory.

"What have you got?" She didn't offer a greeting but studied the bag held to his chest.

"You never appear to have a companion." He ignored her question.

"Utter bliss it is to be an orphan. As it turns out no one much cares for those."

She stood on her toes, trying to peek into the sack he carried.

Don't touch me. He jerked away.

"Have you finished my book on the mind?"

"Your book?" She asked incredulously. "I was under the impression it was a public library." She smirked. "Rather a dull read until I got to the diagrams. I have the need for hands-on learning, and there likely isn't a place I can obtain an addled brain."

"You could begin by investigating your own," he recommended with his version of a smirk.

"Yours would also likely be sufficient," she retorted.

She had no idea.

Ezra cleared his throat, the next words paining him. "You've been lent a particular text which, in the majority, is garbage."

"Pardon?" She paused, large, doe-like eyes blinking up at him, clearly a bit stunned he had any ability at a conversation starter.

"John Tennent." Disgust dripped from his tone.

"No need to worry." She waved him off. "Not once have I suffered an illness and felt urged to drink several quarts of whey."

"There are easier methods to induce vomiting," he agreed, ever so slightly relieved she'd not taken that volume seriously.

"Have a good evening, Doctor," Ms. Trudeau smiled softly.

"Have life," he murmured in her wake.

Why he often used those words in parting, even he didn't know. Perhaps in a dream or some plane of reality he had heard them, and so now, it was his manner of doing things—a manner deeply ingrained in his repetitious vocabulary.

CHAPTER SIX

Magdalena

OCTOBER 1848. LONDON, ENGLAND.

Magdalena spread the *Illustrated London News* across her knees and nibbled on a biscuit.

"Mags." Olive huffed.

She grunted a response and turned the page.

"Ladies do not read the paper," Olive whispered. Magdalena nearly snorted as her sister's eyes darted around the empty parlor.

"Then I won't tell your husband you've been reading over my shoulder." Magdalena bit back her smile.

Olive gasped. "I've done no such thing." She pressed a palm to her pinkening cheeks.

"Don't act so horrified, Olive. Aunt Salomé used to read the paper."

"That was in the countryside." Her sister shook her head. "This is London."

"How do you suppose one would treat cholera?" Magdalena scanned the paper with a furrowed brow. "Do you think turpentine does any good at all?"

"That sounds like a question for your physician." Olive grimaced.

"I don't think he cares much for me," Magdalena admitted.

"That is simply because he doesn't know you." Her sister ruffled her hair like a dog. "How can anyone resist the human embodiment of a Saint Bernard?"

Olive squealed and darted out of the way as Magdalena rolled up the paper and swung at her.

"Having fun without me?" Frank entered the room and swept his arms around his wife's waist to nestle a kiss against her temple.

Magdalena stood and left the newsprint on the lounger. A spark of irritation settled in her stomach, and she rebuked herself for it. She was a guest in his estate.

"Why, Frank, I wasn't aware you knew the definition of the word," Magdalena teased.

Olive stiffened and turned a glare toward her.

Magdalena swatted her traitorous mouth. "Naughty thing," she muttered. "That sounded a bit better in my head...so sorry, Frank."

"Quite all right, Magdalena," Frank gave her a pinched smile and straightened his limp, navy tie. "I do hope you are enjoying London."

He released Olive and crossed the room, gathering her discarded paper in his hands.

As much as anyone could be keen on filthy streets and noxious air. She had tainted feelings for this city, but he didn't need to know that.

"Of course." She smiled. "Three of my sisters and a brother reside in London... what's not to love?"

She hadn't been done with the paper, but it was clear he dismissed her as he settled into the seat and slung an ankle over his knee.

"Beautiful city," he murmured, face obscured by the print. "Any mail today, Love?"

He lowered the paper abruptly and dropped his foot to the floor, looking at his wife expectantly.

Olive nodded and lifted an envelope from a tray, "From the British Relief Association." She extended the missive. "We've been invited to join a fundraiser for Bethlem. Shall I have a dress made?"

He took it and tucked it into his vest pocket without opening it, then gave a smile that was far too sharp for Magdalena's liking.

"That won't be necessary." He shook his head, his brow softening when he heard the roughness of his tone. "We do not support the asylum."

Why? Magdalena knew better than to ask aloud.

As though he heard her unspoken question, Frank's face took on a guarded expression and he stared unblinking at a charcoal drawing on the wall. Just as quickly as his demeanor began, it fell away and he tucked himself behind the newsprint.

Nothing about Frank was particularly unkind. He simply unsettled Magdalena. She convinced herself Olive was the gentlest of Salomé's daughters, and her feelings were protective and nothing more. She had asked her sister once why she loved the man. Olive's eyes had gone glossy with revere as she explained his romantic inclinations.

Frank's absolute adherence to propriety irked Magdalena. Hang propriety—she preferred unfiltered truth. Perhaps Magdalena was shallow, but it seemed romance was a tactic used by unattractive men to lure in unsuspecting women.

"I'll be in the parks," Magdalena acknowledged abruptly. With her paper occupied, she tucked the copy of John Tennent beneath her arm.

"I thought he recommended you avoid that text?" Olive chided.

"So naturally I mustn't." Magdalena winked at her and slipped into the hall to collect her cloak.

"Take a companion," Olive called after her.

No, she wouldn't be doing that.

A carriage took her to Hyde Park as she read a curious chapter of the ridiculous book. Dr. Talbot had good reason to recommend against it. But it did spark a curiosity in the matter. If these were not proper treatments, what were and how did one discover them?

The movement slowed and the driver dropped down to open the door.

"Thank you." She smiled but avoided his extended hand as she prepared to climb down. Mother expected her to take those hands, and they felt to be an expense she couldn't afford.

She's been dead seventeen years, and she still controls you. The bitter reminder irked her, and Magdalena took the man's hand. Perhaps she shouldn't have come alone. Thoughts were worse when there was no one to distract them.

Smile slipping slightly she ducked past the driver and took the wide path through the park along the familiar Serpentine River.

Masochist, she smirked, settling on a bench close enough to see the gentle waves lapping at the shore, but far enough that she didn't feel compelled to do anything stupid.

Hands in her lap, she watched pedestrians explore the thinning grass and trimmed hedge lines. Carriages crossed over the bridge, and she recalled a more distant time and a different river.

A Wednesday, she recalled bitterly. She had an odd relationship with Wednesdays. How could she not when they kept trying to kill her?

Like tempting fairies, sunlight glistened over the peaceful waves of the river.

"Come in," they whispered. "Make it end."

A gasp stuttered through her, and she jerked to her feet.

"That's the end of that," she muttered, turning away from the river.

Food vendors littered the sidewalk, and she distracted herself with a treat as she walked. Further from the shore and closer to the East End, she settled onto a safer bench, counting passing mustaches.

"I never should have taken you out," she heard a man's angry tone snap. "Is your head for looks and nothing more?"

"I'm sorry." The response was soft and feminine. "Truly Peter, I—"

He kept his hushed tone, spitting words of fire that ignited a trail of ice down Magdalena's spine.

She spotted the couple on her left. The woman was small, lovely, and gentle beside a man nearly double her size. His meaty fists clenched at his side, and the woman flinched, clutching a paper sack of chestnuts to her chest. She'd not encountered either of them before, but there was something in her gut that made her perk up and pay attention.

He was a walking warning in his boots and a woolen cap. The parts of her that knew this wasn't her business were silenced by a soul-deep stirring she recognized, sending an eruption of goosebumps down her arms. The sensation ignited in her chest and, oh, how she missed being on fire.

"Hello fate," Magdalena whispered. "It's been quite some time, hasn't it?"

Thinking quickly, Magdalena pulled a coin from her pocket and stood.

"Pardon me, is that the paper you have there?" she called out, pointing beneath the man's arm. "Could I purchase it from you?"

The woman's hazel eyes sparked with worry as she chanced a glance at her husband's face. He curled his fingers around her arm and yanked her closer to his side. She met Magdalena's eyes and gave a minuscule shake of her head.

A sneer curled the man's full lips, and he looked around for some equally stupid man to share his disdain with.

"No," he scoffed.

"Peter..." his wife whispered.

He brushed off her words with a flick of a wrist like they were a gnat. "You wanted those chestnuts. You'd better eat every last one."

With embarrassment tinting her cheeks, the woman nodded and began chewing. Clearly, her appetite had vanished the moment his temper began.

"I'll pay you," Magdalena offered, holding the coin in her open palm. "You know how those vendors are when a woman tries to purchase. I'm meeting my husband, and I forgot his paper. We ladies are always forgetting the simplest things."

She ground her teeth into a false smile and gestured between herself and his wife.

Peter huffed out a laugh and gripped the petite woman around the back of her neck giving a sharp jerk. "Hear that, Mara? It isn't just you, it's the whole breed."

Peter shrugged. "You know, I don't think I will. I think I'll let your husband sort out his own woman." He tugged his wife around once more like a child's doll. "A little consequence always helps this one remember the next time. Doesn't it, Mara?"

He looked down at her, and his face blanched.

Magdalena had been so occupied getting her information that she'd failed to notice the woman's red face and purpling lips. Mara pulled her hands to her throat, lips parting in a soundless cry.

Fear sunk itself in the pit of her stomach.

"She's choking!" Magdalena gasped, turning on her heels looking for someone, anyone who could help.

Peter, the absolute dunce he was, tossed the woman about some more as though the lurching would set the blockage free.

Think, Magdalena, think. She tapped her forehead with a closed fist and paced. Was this similar to drowning? Would artificial respirations be effective? No, she shook her head answering her own question. Air couldn't get in, nor could it get out.

Removing the chestnut was key, but how? Her knowledge of anatomy was poor, but it made sense that if she used what was already in, she could push the bite out.

She stepped around Mara, wrapped her arms around her thin waist, and pressed a series of short, quick thrusts into her stomach.

Nothing happened. She'd be embarrassed if Mara weren't in the process of dying with a useless husband. The man wouldn't stop bellowing.

Frustrated, Magdalena used the heel of her hand and pounded on Mara's back.

A thin gasp sucked through Mara's body. The chestnut shifted.

She leaned Mara forward for gravity's sake and struck between her shoulder blades once more, sending the blockage hurling across the path.

Magdalena threw her arms around Mara and pulled her to her chest, stroking her head as tremors overwhelmed her.

"It's all right, you're all right," she said softly.

Mara leaned into her, and Magdalena knew in that moment that fate had destined for them to meet. If there were no other purpose for her to be in London, then in this knowledge she was content.

Peter pulled his wife away, but Magdalena clung to her and whispered in her ear.

"Meet me here tomorrow, same time."

She gave a parting squeeze and a heart-wrenching glance at Mara's tear-streaked face. "Keep yourself safe until then."

Dragged out of Hyde Park, Mara threw pain-filled glances over her shoulder and mouthed words Magdalena couldn't read as she went.

CHAPTER SEVEN

Magdalena

The atmosphere around her seemed to tremble with realization. She'd saved someone. In the face of panic, her mind found a logical solution and she'd acted. It was glorious. There must be more. More to life, more saving, more purpose—simply more. Here, in Hyde Park, she felt a changing perspective.

Magdalena wilted against the trunk of a tree, blowing out a shaky breath. With the way her heart raced in her chest, she felt a bit faint. She fluttered the neck of her coat to encourage airflow as an awkward laugh bubbled in her chest.

She looked up at the cotton October clouds. "Did you see that, Aunt Salomé? Tell me you did."

Only silence met her. Of course, that didn't come as any surprise. Her little corner of the park was empty, and clouds and women long since dead didn't speak to the sane. A pity really.

Somewhere behind her, a throat cleared catching her off guard to the extent that she shrieked and flailed against the tree.

Not funny, Magdalena glared at the clouds. Aunt Salomé had always been a fan of irony.

She straightened herself and brushed her hands over her skirt before turning toward the sound. Dr. Talbot stood on the path staring at her, mouth agape and knuckles white around the handle of his medical bag.

Of course, he'd show up now.

"How long have you been standing there?"

She casually went to rest her palm on the tree for support but missed it, and stumbled.

He had the nerve to smirk. Something felt amiss in the way he shifted on his feet but she brushed it off.

"I'm not an idiot," Magdalena blurted after righting herself. "I just … they …"

She trailed off, pointing to where Mara and Peter had just gone.

"Oh, for heaven's sake, you wouldn't believe me if I tried."

She blew the fallen locks of hair from her eyes.

"Common practice for choking is to slit the trachea," he murmured, cocking his head toward her as though trying to figure something out.

It was her turn to gape at him. "You mean to tell me you just stood there?"

Tongue in cheek, he looked away. "You did … ah …"

It sounded as if he was about to compliment her. She didn't imagine he offered many of those, if any at all.

"Well done, Magdalena. How brilliant of you," she offered in her best interpretation of his somber tone.

He coughed and the corner of his lips flickered.

The newsprint in his pocket caught her attention and she gasped, reaching for it.

"Is this the *Illustrated London News*? I had a question for you this morning." Magdalena pulled it from his coat and spread it across the bench in search of the proper page.

Dr. Talbot winced, and his nostrils flared. A dog barked in the distance and children ran past laughing. Both seemed to make him grow more tense.

She extended the paper toward him and thrust her finger into the words. "Which one works?"

In a jerky movement, one of his shoulders spasmed and he stepped away.

Awareness slipped in and her excitement paused.

"I'm sorry," she said softly. "I was terribly thrilled, and I forgot your—"

A muscle in his jaw quirked.

All right then, don't mention the peculiarity. Magdalena took a deep breath.

"Cholera," she said hurriedly, hoping he wouldn't turn and leave. She pointed to the article. "How does one treat it?"

"Mm?" He blinked at her.

"How do you treat—?"

He glowered. "I heard you."

Sidestepping her, he rolled up what was left of his paper and tucked it under his arm.

She rocked back on her heels, "Please? I don't think they have it correct."

He scoffed but walked on.

"In all of your life, Dr. Talbot, have you ever had questions that no one could answer?" she called toward his retreating form.

He froze.

"Do you have cholera?" he asked without turning. "A family member, perhaps?"

"No," she admitted.

"Then why does it matter?"

"Curiosity." She threw up her hands, rustling the single sheet of paper she still held. "How can I be all right knowing the news has treatments incorrect?"

Cautiously she caught up to him.

His eyes narrowed. "What makes you so certain?"

This felt like a test.

"The symptoms of cholera are cramping, irritability, thirst, vomiting, and diarrhea." She bit the inside of her cheek.

His silence hung in the air between them. "How do you know that?"

"I just do," she huffed. "But the paper states the treatments are vapor, mustard poultices, turpentine, sal volatile, hartshorn, brandy water, sulphuric ether—shall I continue?"

Dr. Talbot sighed. "You memorized it?"

"Why are you acting like you don't agree with me?" Her voice rose and a passersby looked on curiously.

He hissed out an exhale through his teeth.

"They are grasping at straws with these recommendations." She tried to calm herself, fiddling with her buttons. "What if people die?"

"People die every day."

There was a sardonic undertone to his words that made her pause. He was testing her. Why?

"What do the patients lose most with cholera?" he prodded.

Everything, their bowels, their stomachs. She felt helplessly ignorant. Magdalena traced the circular shape of her third and fourth buttons with her index finger, thinking.

When she didn't answer, he asked, "What are the fundamental needs to sustain human life, in order of importance?"

She pondered this for a moment. "Air, water, food, shelter." She ticked them off on her fingers. His first question had been what was lost most. "Water! That's it?"

He nodded. "Most perish from dehydration within the first day or two, some within hours."

She gripped her buttons until she feared they might pop off.

"Children?" She hated the gravelly way her question came out.

A flicker of pain flashed across his face, softening his features before he masked them. "Mm. They benefit from activated charcoal in some instances. But it cannot always be avoided."

Death, he meant death. Fear trickled its way down her spine and turned her stomach.

"How does it aid?"

"Activated charcoal contains zinc." He paused. "I don't know why that seems to be important. That is as far as I have gotten."

"As far as you've gotten in what?"

"Research." Now it was his voice that rose. "May I go? Or will you continue to chase me?"

He tugged the corner of his overcoat with panicked fingertips. The man had never been interested in conversation, but this was something else.

She flicked her eyes over him, searching for the cause. His muscles were stiff, and a sheen of sweat dampened his dark hair to his forehead.

"Here is your paper." She stretched it toward him. "Thank you for answering my questions."

For a moment he looked apologetic. He pulled off his top hat and ran his fingers through his hair. "I—" He threw a frustrated glance around the park. "I cannot answer any more questions today."

"Notice I haven't asked more." She tried to smile but his behavior worried her.

"You don't have to say them." He gestured to her face with a huff. "I see them in your eyes."

Magdalena clicked her tongue as a true smile crept across her face. "Why, Dr. Talbot, are you admitting to looking at my eyes?"

She fluttered her lashes at him and nearly snorted over his grimace.

"No." He sighed. "Everything you think is painted on your face."

Well, that was certainly false, but she could see the tension in his shoulders ease ever so slightly.

"What am I thinking now?" She rocked back on her heels and framed her face with her hands. Distraction was one of the greatest gifts one could offer another, and she sensed he needed it.

"I'm not playing this."

"Yet you are still here, and I dare say the longer you stay, the more pleasant your attitude is becoming."

Dr. Talbot scoffed.

"Do you know what I think, Doctor?" She stooped to scratch behind the ears of a park feline as it arched its calico back and wound itself around her. "I think you like my questions. If you aren't careful, you may even be beginning to like me."

He loosened his already wayward cravat but didn't respond.

Bolstered slightly by his silence, she crossed her arms and smirked.

"Now, if one were to have more questions, how would one find the reclusive physician in such a large city?"

This was likely a line he wouldn't cross, but the word "no" had never bothered her.

"Are you inviting yourself to a man's place of employment?"

She grimaced. When said like that ...

Magdalena pulled her book out of the depths of her pocket. "There is only so much I can learn from John," she shrugged, flipping through the pages with a feigned nonchalance.

"I told you—" Irritation flared in his eyes. "You are far too devious to be a woman."

Her eyes crinkled. "Correction, I'm devious because I'm a woman."

Dr. Talbot's sigh sounded much like giving up.

"Brick Lane." He gave a curt nod. "I don't like company."

"You'll hardly notice I'm there," she promised.

"I feel individual grains of sand beneath my socks. There is not a plane of existence in which I would not notice all of this." He gestured to her person.

"Careful, Doctor, I'll get the wrong idea," she said sweetly.

He smothered a cough in the forearm of his coat. "Must you bring your impertinence everywhere?"

Poor man, it looked like he already regretted the invitation.

"Audacity is my best feature." She glared at him.

His eyes darted across her so quickly she nearly missed it. "Your husband must be thrilled."

Husband? Ah, right, he'd overheard when she lied to Peter.

"Don't worry, Dr. Talbot." She raised a brow. "You'll be delighted to hear I'm not in possession of one of those."

"Shock and awe," he muttered sarcastically. "I'm filled with delight."

It stung, but not terribly. Besides, if she wanted a husband, she was certain she could fetch one. Controlling men had no problem marrying for money, and rumor had it her husband would inherit a sizeable amount.

She sniffed. "Don't worry, I won't ask if the untouchable physician has a wife."

A humorless laugh puffed out of him before the muscle in his jaw tightened and he turned away. So it would seem they both found a tender spot. She'd avoid it in the future.

"I'm sorry." She blew out. "I often bite before I think."

"Don't—" He held up his hand at her apology and molten disdain took over his face. "Don't say that."

"I don't really bite," she mumbled.

"Not that." His eyes shot briefly to hers, full of turmoil.

"I'm sorry?" She sputtered.

Dr. Talbot gave a sharp nod, dragging his tongue over his teeth and rolling his shoulders.

"You don't like apologies?" She blinked at him, absorbing this small detail that felt desperately important.

"No." He took a step back, pushing his hands in his pockets. "No, I don't."

Ezra

His laboratory was a sacred space. He kept it clean to the extent that it smelled of nothing but soap and the occasional medicinal herb. The times he felt particularly irate, he'd scrub the floors until they shined or organize his journals by content. London kept him occupied, and it was a rare occasion for him to have nothing scheduled in a day.

Ezra used a pair of tweezers to remove a partially decomposed ear from an apothecary jar and rested the appendage on a linen cloth before measuring it. He stooped for a closer look at the little beetles that ravaged anything he left in his jar. They scurried about looking lost and bored in the absence of their meal.

"I'll give it back shortly," he promised.

Carrion beetles were quiet, reliable, possessed a strong work ethic, and made for underappreciated domestic pets. He scribbled the rate of decomposition into a journal before returning the ear to its rightful place.

"Dr. Talbot?" Mrs. Keene stepped into the room, eyeing his jar warily.

"Mm?" He cleaned up after himself and washed his hands.

"There is a woman who wishes to see you."

"Send her away." He dried his hands.

"She says you invited her?"

"Blonde hair, inappropriately bold?" He sighed. It had hardly been a day's time.

She nodded. "I must say, Dr. Talbot—" A series of muffled words from the other room interrupted her. "My word, she's persistent."

"Mm," he cleared his throat. "Let's not say anything and simply let her in before all of London knows she's here."

"But …" She sputtered, desperate for further information. "Very well, but we aren't through. It isn't as though you have women coming for a social visit often, er—ever."

Indeed. Ms. Trudeau had already reminded him of how gross a misjudgment his initial acceptance of her self invitation was.

Mrs. Keene opened the door and gave a hopeful introduction of herself, as though the pair could be friends.

No, he ought to warn his secretary. This woman was a bit like an invasive tick. She fed on awkwardness and laughter.

Ms. Trudeau swaggered into the room. It seemed an inappropriate description of a woman's stride, but it was far from feminine and terribly obnoxious. Her hair was piled atop her head in billowing curls, and her hat irked him immediately for being crooked. A basket swung wildly from the bend of her arm. Offerings of gratitude were the worst. He hadn't the face for feigning appreciation.

Noticing his gaze, she stretched out the hamper in his direction. "Ah, yes. I've brought a gift to thank you, Dr. Talbot."

When he didn't readily accept it, she closed the distance between them and pushed it into his unresponsive hands. Twice now she had forced things into his hands and twice his appendages had betrayed him by accepting.

She's too close. He stepped away. Did she always neglect social distance?

"Well, go ahead." She plopped ungracefully into his armchair and looked at him expectantly.

"The doctor is quite particular about what he eats, though I can smell the delicious meat pies from here. I'm afraid he can't tolerate such textures."

Mrs. Keene sought to rescue him and flipped open the basket beneath his chin.

A gurgled sound of disgust slipped out of his throat as he dropped the offending hamper into his secretary's arms and turned to wash his hands.

"It's no matter, is it doctor? It's the heart that counts." Ms. Trudeau gave a dismissive wave of her hand.

He wasn't sure what the life-giving organ had to do with good intentions, but the longer she sat here the more his beat with regret.

As Mrs. Keene walked past her with the basket, the bold woman dared to reach in and snatch a pastry, nibbling at it with an expression of deep satisfaction. She was likely the most oblivious person he'd ever encountered.

Ezra watched as crumbs dropped onto her lap before bouncing to the floor. His floor. Meanwhile, she was carrying on an entirely one-sided conversation. On the bright side, she'd not care at all if he didn't speak. Unfortunately, this also meant he'd have a far more difficult time removing her if she couldn't pick up on the far-from-subtle clues that he wanted to be alone.

Why had he told her where to find him? Mm, yes, if he plied her with literature, she'd likely leave. He turned his back on her to select a few lengthy ones that should occupy her. A smirk threatened as he intentionally chose the dullest ones in his collection.

"—and then I said, 'thank you for the milk transfusion'—" she prattled on.

What? He turned back to her in confusion only to see her arms crossed over her chest, a smug grin on her lips, and a brow cocked.

"You are much like talking to a wall, Dr. Talbot." She stood.

"With the amount you go on, it is likely that that is not an uncommon practice for you." He wasn't sure if he was more uncomfortable with having been caught or having been played. He checked his pocket watch. "It took you four and a half minutes before you realized I was otherwise occupied."

"On the contrary," She shrugged. "I wanted to see precisely how many ridiculous things I could fit between the time I began speaking and you began listening."

Ezra scoffed. When had he last felt the urge to roll his eyes? Years, undoubtedly.

"Thirteen." She gave herself a checkmark in the air before her like it was some great accomplishment to spew nonsense.

"Thirteen," he repeated dumbly.

She took the word to be a question and began ticking off said comments across her fingers. Sanity help him, he'd let a mad woman into his laboratory and now she wouldn't leave.

"Doctor? Doctor!" A man's muffled call sounded from the entry followed by a pounding on the door.

Bless you, strange man. Ezra nearly dove for his coat and hat. Picking up his medical bag in the entryway, he stepped out into the hall.

Walking and listening, the man provided enough details for him to know a woman lay unconscious in the street below.

How dull. Couldn't someone have been stabbed? Surely that would occupy him until Ms. Trudeau found the common sense to leave.

They reached the patient quickly and he crouched beside her. Raising his fingers to her carotid he checked for a pulse. It was steady.

"Oh, poor Mrs. Langford," a voice piped up beside him. Ms. Trudeau mimicked his position, her skirts dragging in the filth.

"I thought you'd leave," he muttered.

"I did. To follow you." Ms. Trudeau reached out, taking the woman's hand in her own. "She's a storekeeper's wife, prone to such fits I'm afraid."

West End. Mid-forties, not the epitome of health and wellbeing.

"The usual ought to be sufficient." She stood abruptly, clapping her hands together like she had some great insight.

"The usual?" He scoffed at her feigned knowledge.

"Leeches. Doesn't a good leech solve a myriad of problems?" Her face gave nothing away, her brows were straight, and her lips pursed. "I'm joking. You know what a joke is?"

Her eyes twinkled. How did they do that?

You've looked too long. He turned away.

Ezra cleared his throat as he rifled through his bag and pulled out a small vial of smelling salts. Flicking the cap, he waved it beneath Mrs. Langford's nose until her eyes fluttered open and color blossomed in her cheeks. She sat up and he turned to leave. Ms. Trudeau would help her to her feet and he'd hurry on up and lock the door behind himself before she could follow.

"Mrs. Langford do come up for a thorough examination. Dr. Talbot is one of the very best in his field, you know?"

What? No, terrible idea. He turned to express just as much when he caught the slightest glimpse of Mrs. Langford's abnormally swollen legs beneath her skirts. Perhaps not the worst idea after all.

He trailed behind as Ms. Trudeau brought her up the steps and settled her into Mrs. Keene's desk chair. His secretary made herself scarce, likely unsure what care he'd need to offer and not wishing to witness anything gruesome.

Mrs. Langford's prattle was worse than that of the blonde, and he did his best to filter it out while completing an initial assessment. A woman's legs were never an easy extremity to view—just as many skirts as there was propriety. While he determined how best to proceed, he slid his palms along her waist, palpating the organs within.

When his fingers inched across the upper right portion of the abdomen she flinched and jerked away. Mm, yes. He considered the medical texts that could aid in his diagnosis before settling on it more solidly.

"How long have you experienced the swelling?"

Mrs. Langford sputtered in denial and Ms. Trudeau blinked at him in a mystified silence.

"As you wish. For how long, then, have you taken strong drink?"

"I don't know what you speak of." Mrs. Langford's face flushed a magnificent hue.

"If I enjoyed being lied to, I'd speak to a politician." Ezra got to his feet and brushed his hands on his trousers. "See your way out."

"Mrs. Langford," Ms. Trudeau sputtered. "His tact is ... lacking," She turned a glare toward him, "But he is remarkably bright. I have encountered many physicians throughout my years, and he ... he is the only one I would trust with my care."

Was she serious? Something flickered disagreeably in his chest. He found himself holding his breath, the anticipation nearly as uncomfortable as the patient herself.

Mrs. Langford sniffed, turning up her nose in disgust. "I have just a few sips each night to help with my pains."

Liar, a few pints perhaps. Ms. Trudeau's narrowed gaze held a silent warning, and he swallowed the words.

"You work with your husband. Long hours on your feet, I presume?" He gritted his teeth and reached to pull her skirts up a fraction.

Ms. Trudeau tugged at his sleeve mid-reach, and it appeared as though she were attempting to communicate with nothing more than glances and the drawing of her eyes. He didn't speak whatever wordless language she attempted.

"Oh, for goodness' sake, Dr. Talbot, ask the woman before you pull up her skirts." Ms. Trudeau's words were muffled, ground out under her breath.

Clearing his throat, he nodded. "Mrs. Langford, I need to view the significance of the swelling. I'll be brief."

He waited for her nod before proceeding.

The edema stretched from foot to knee, and the skin was taut and shiny with its pressure. Her stockings were scrunched around her ankles, resembling round sausages with split casings.

Just as he thought. "Your liver is inflamed from your excessive drinking. You need an immediate diuretic, and while you are not obese, you are far from the epitome of health. Coffee is my general preference, though I recommend you avoid it for fear of failing your heart. You must stick purely to a hot tea steeped with dandelion and ginger root, drinking it in a large quantity."

He scribbled the recommendations on a notepad and tore it off in a jagged swipe.

"No more alcohol of any variety for the time being or else the damage to your liver will become irreparable," he continued. "I understand your feet ache and the pressure feels extreme while you work. You must roll up your stockings despite the swelling. In time the tight stockings and the diuretic tea will reduce the inflammation in your extremities. Empty your bladder frequently. Your immediate directives are to return to your home, lay down, and elevate your feet."

She offered some feeble excuse about her husband requiring her at the shop.

"There is one other option." He rolled her stockings up over her calves with some resistance.

"And what is that?" Her eyes shimmered with useless hope.

"Death by Dropsy."

CHAPTER NINE

Ezra

Mrs. Keene dismissed Mrs. Langford with a more coddled repetition of what he'd already said. He didn't care a whit whether he saw this patient again. There were plenty ill in London and at least a handful who didn't closet their alcoholism.

Meanwhile, Ms. Trudeau made herself at home, taking herself on a jaunty tour of his laboratory.

Ezra didn't want her here. This was his space, his solitude. And now—now it was messy and smelled of lilacs.

Lilacs. His mind slipped to a place where they grew in the spring. It took him to a different time, a memory just as real as the room he stood in, one he begged to be free of. Ezra's heart raced in his chest and sweat trickled down his collar. He could feel the hands closing in around his throat.

He couldn't breathe.

You like lilacs. You've always liked lilacs. Don't let him take that from you too.

"Dr. Talbot?" Ms. Trudeau's voice was soft, warm, and grounding.

He swallowed back the panic.

"Mm," he managed.

"I like you," she stated simply.

His lungs inflated and the invisible band around his chest loosened. Ezra was accustomed to people spewing nonsense for self-gain. The only trouble was, he hadn't figured out what it was that she wanted and why she wasn't so simply run off.

She had a heart-shaped face with the faintest shadow of a cleft in her chin. It was her hair he noticed most, how tight curls slipped out of their confines, just as rebellious as she was. Her brows and lashes were darker than the rest of her hair, making her eyes seem all the wider. They challenged him as her chin rose defiantly.

The past spilled back into the present and he cleared his throat, looking away.

"I generally only lie to myself, Dr. Talbot. That's something you are familiar with, isn't it?" Ms. Trudeau didn't sound accusing, but sober and sincere.

He nearly choked on the accuracy of her words. People didn't speak like she did. They didn't pour out their thoughts like honey. They kept them confined. Now her opinions were out in the open, sticking to everything in a miserable skin.

Ezra needed something to do with his hands. It was as though this woman made things willfully uncomfortable.

He had never loved a woman, but he came close when Mrs. Keene chose that moment to enter with a tea service.

"Doctor." She shook an untouched plate in his direction. "Please do stop forgetting to eat your meals."

"How can one forget to eat?" They had no trouble overhearing Ms. Trudeau's whisper. At this realization, she spoke louder. "Do you know how much time I spend merely thinking about food? It hardly compares to the time I actually spend eating food. You truly are a perplexing man."

He cocked his head at her. "Food is nutrition and nutrition aids in life expectancy, of which the current in Europe fluctuates between thirty-seven and forty-three. Considering your only observed eating patterns, you should anticipate the earlier."

He sat at his desk and turned open a series of medical texts, searching for similarities in the treatment of arterial narrowing, a newer concept he desired to fully grasp. Mrs. Keene closed herself back in the front room.

"In this logic, you will undoubtedly live forever." He felt her smirk without seeing it. "That would most assuredly bring a swarm of people who'd wish to interview you at great length. You'd best eat whatever you like to avoid the interaction."

Ezra snapped his book closed with a sigh.

"If you intend to sit there all day, you will do so in silence. I've no patients in the medical sense today nor patience of the other variety for your noise."

To his surprise and dismay, she was unbothered by the concept and appeared to get all the more comfortable in his chair. Her arms crossed over her chest and that familiar cocky expression plastered across her face.

"You are an incredible physician to watch, though you have a deplorable way with words." She reached for a volume sitting beside the chair she rested in. "To be frank, it is nearly as entertaining to watch as your mind at work."

Shouts from the street below the window rose and distracted him for a moment. They were loud and sharp. He didn't like how the sounds crawled up his spine and settled somewhere in his shoulders with an invisible weight.

Flicking a glance to be sure she wasn't looking, he rubbed his palms quickly over his ears.

"John Tennant?" He turned to see her hold up a book in the light from the window. Confusion registered on her face. "You said this was rubbish, yet you keep it near?"

He dropped his hands. Evidently, they had very different views on silence.

"It makes me laugh." He gathered a bouquet of digitalis purpurea and began tearing the leaves off each stem, separating leaves from flowers in twin piles.

"You know how to laugh?" She looked at him dubiously.

In time she would learn he had a bit of a dark sense of humor, rare in its appearance and most often revealed while alone.

"Dead man's bells?" she asked, speaking of the decimated floral arrangement.

"Foxglove, digitalis, yes."

"Who do you intend to poison?"

The odds were becoming rather high that he had a person in mind.

"A poison in the hands of some is a cure in the hands of another."

"Tell me of it?" She returned John Tennant's publication to its place.

Had it been any other, he would have known they held no true interest, making small talk and attempting to draw him in. It was how she sat, elbows on her knees and staring up at him with an open intrigue, that convinced him she meant it.

"Used effectively it may treat angina pectoris, falling sickness (with a very scant dosage), arrhythmias, and some failures of the heart."

He took the leaves, rinsed them thoroughly, placed them in a stone bowl, and began using a pestle to obliterate the leaves into a dark green paste.

Magdalena stood, curious, and approached his workstation. He stepped backward as she took a cautious sniff, dipped one finger, and began to bring it to her lips.

He caught her wrist.

"Unless you wish for a leaky bowel all the way home, I recommend you do not eat everything you encounter," he growled, tossing her hand away and scrubbing off the feel of her on his trousers.

"You suggested it was edible," she shrugged, wiping her fingers on her fortunately sage-colored dress.

"Yet you know it to be a poison." He gave her an incredulous glare.

"Your irritation is valid." She looked only a smidge contrite.

Mrs. Keene entered the room to assess the tea service, which was still untouched.

"There's another caller," she muttered, giving the serving tray a disapproving look.

Ezra took the leafy paste and funneled it into an assortment of containers, pouring ample amounts of honey on top before properly infusing the mixture.

"Is it typical that you have so few appointments and many callers?" Ms. Trudeau remarked.

"It appears you are the catalyst by which misfortune comes knocking at my door this day," he said dryly, covering his medicines with a fine cheesecloth. "Let them in."

By his recycled red uniform jacket, it was clear the caller operated the horse-drawn mail van. His graying mustache twitched as he noticed the tea service.

"May I?" A smile quirked the mailman's mouth.

"Certainly," Ms. Trudeau offered.

".. not," Ezra finished.

The man opted to listen to the woman. Never had the sound of tea being poured echoed so, and in the most loud and prolonged slurp, he drained one cup, poured another, and repeated the pattern.

Even Ms. Trudeau looked a bit pained by the sound in the otherwise quiet room before tucking her lips into a straight line.

"Ah, yes." The mailman belched a hardly restrained rift, dusting his hands on his portly stomach. "You have a letter."

He dug into his satchel, scattering several across the floor as it overflowed. He stooped, gathered them up, searched some more, and finally found the correct correspondence. He extended it toward Ezra.

Ezra viewed the envelope with disdain, knowing the moment he touched it he'd be willed by his mind to immediately lather and wash his hands. This mail person was repellent.

Ezra refused to look at Ms. Trudeau whose shoulders had been shaking in silent mirth.

"It's from a detective." The mailman waved the postage when it was not immediately retrieved.

With a heavy sigh, Ms. Trudeau took the letter and thanked him, ushering him, in the most graceful manner, out the door. A true benefit of her nature, the man felt no offense and Ezra felt a small relief.

"A detective?" she asked. "What business do you have with a detective?"

"None." At her questioning he took the missive from her, tore it abruptly in half, and threw it in the fire.

Then he did indeed wash his hands—for two reasons.

CHAPTER TEN

Magdalena

One of her favorite pastimes was to watch people. They let things slip when they didn't realize they were being studied. Men especially tended to assume a woman couldn't uncover their secrets.

It was clear the doctor held many such secrets close, burying them beneath his gruff exterior and thick locks of hair that tumbled frequently into his eyes.

"Magdalena," Aunt Salomé had addressed her as a youth, "don't chase a secret. Let it unravel as all secrets do."

The issue was she'd never been a patient girl, and she'd grown into an even more impatient woman.

At first, Dr. Talbot maneuvered awkwardly with her in the room. His movements were sharp and his breathing almost pinched. Gradually, bit by bit, he seemed to forget she was here, then he nearly floated with precision. Every muscle, every step was quietly calculated.

He read often, scribbling notes in a leather-bound journal and turning pages with a reservoir pen. There were times he'd be set off by something she couldn't sense but knew bothered him. Dr. Talbot would scrub his hands until they were violently red and raw, or he'd leave abruptly only to return wearing a different shirt.

Now, he sat with a quilt wrapped around his shoulders and tapped his palms over his ears as he fed his wretched insects. Never idle for long, he'd leave her there as he tended patients or accepted a few into the laboratory—constables mostly.

He told her to leave once early on. She had, but only to see if Mara showed up in Hyde Park.

Mara hadn't.

When Magdalena returned to the laboratory, he simply ignored her. Being ignored didn't bother her, not when she got to see him for who he was. She'd enjoy more conversation, though, as it was rather dull to keep her mouth shut.

He cleared his throat beside her and clunked a stack of texts to the table.

"You've proven your stubbornness, now prove instead your affinity for knowledge."

He moved away quickly, seemingly uncomfortable to break the silence.

A fractal of hope sparked in her chest.

He added, "You are a mouth breather—perhaps try nasal breathing as you fill your mind with useful information."

Ah, yes, there was the sense of humility she'd nearly lost.

Magdalena shuffled through the literature he'd set in front of her. The majority was handwritten in a nearly illegible scrawl. His handwriting was so abysmal she was uncertain even he could read its contents.

"Queen Elizabeth," she muttered. "How am I supposed to read this?"

"With your eyes."

"Why, thank you. I hadn't thought of that." She offered the sweetest smile before opening one of the journals.

Whether he caught her sarcasm she couldn't be sure, not with the way his back was turned. In the past days, he'd spent any spare moments away from patients mixing various concoctions or prodding at his palm with the tip of a pair of tweezers. After each miniscule poke he'd jot something down in a notebook.

"What are you doing?" she'd asked.

"Cataloguing sensations," he responded.

Dr. Talbot only grunted when she asked why and that was the end of it.

Once she'd created a pattern in the scrawl of his l's, r's, and s's, she had found herself able to stumble through the notes he'd wished for her to read. Just as she'd finish one journal, he'd quickly replace it with another until she'd nearly read every bound or loose paper within the entirety of his laboratory. Even still, the drudgery of sitting and reading continued, but he was a mystery, and she wasn't content to let questions go unanswered.

It was on the third day after discussing an appointment with Mrs. Keene that Dr. Talbot asked something most curious.

"What are your opinions regarding children?"

His expression was blank, leaving her unsure how to respond. How did she feel about children in general, about having offspring of her own, or about their existence in a deeper sense? She settled for a half grunt, rereading through a stack of text while jotting a handful of notes on a notepad. A wisp of hair escaped its braid and tickled her face. She brushed it back with her knuckles and returned to nibbling on her fingernails.

"Specifically, a large number of children?" he pushed.

She set the book on her lap, legs draped over the side of the armchair she sat in, and gave him a pensive look.

"I have three brothers and four sisters living." That was all she cared to offer as he wasn't properly asking any questions at all.

"Nearly enough for a game of cricket," he muttered under his breath. "I am to vaccinate thirteen against the pox. Would you care to join me?"

She lurched upright. "Truly? In what capacity?"

Magdalena was giddy over the mere idea.

"Have you received your vaccination?" His prior question was forgotten, as this one clearly took precedence.

"Yes, my Aunt Salomé made sure of it."

"You'll be my assistant. I'll need someone to wrangle them well and hold them as I administer the vaccine."

"Let's go at once. Shall we stop for snacks?"

She was thrilled to participate in something remotely less dull.

Magdalena gathered her hat and cloak from the coat rack, pulling them on as she walked. Whether Dr. Talbot noticed her excitement or not, she couldn't tell, though he too prepared for the unpredictable fall weather and led the way down the confining staircase.

"Where are we headed?" Though her natural stride was generous for a woman, she was required to take two steps for each one of his down the board-walk of Brick Lane.

A question asked of him customarily took some time for a proper answer, and she waited for his response, watching him. The doctor's olive skin contrasted with the white of his linen shirt and cravat. She liked the almost boyish quality his dark curls took, tearing across his brow in a stiff breeze.

He'd be handsome if not for the discomfort his presence usually brought others, or for the expression his face generally carried. Both factors, along with his odd pastimes, were quite possibly why she'd never seen him with a friendly caller.

"A home for foundlings. Near Whitechapel."

He quietly hailed a growler.

As the ride paused before them, she waited for him to open the door. He didn't. Reaching for the handle, she slid in first, adjusting her skirts to make room for him. Still, he hesitated, studying the empty space with disgust.

"I haven't infected anyone with my optimism nor charm in several years," she encouraged cheekily, giving the bench seat a pat.

Dr. Talbot gave a huff of a cough. It wasn't a laugh, but she told herself it was awfully close. With a resigned sigh he stepped up beside her and used his medical bag as a barrier.

Magdalena smiled to herself, looking out the small window beside her. Things were about to get terribly interesting.

She wondered how he'd respond when he learned the caretaker of the foundling home was her youngest brother, Zebulun.

"Do you visit the orphanage often?" she asked. Did Zebulun know Dr. Talbot?

"Mm. I've been there a time or two."

His shoulder bumped against hers as he opened his black bag and looked within it once more, counting quietly before closing it again with its brass closure.

"Do children make you uncomfortable?" From what she could gather, all people made him uncomfortable.

"Children are … the only good," he said softly. "I don't like tears."

The second part was said in nearly a whisper. A bitterness seemed to overtake his features. She knew what it was. A secret. The kind that shouldn't exist but did.

"I'm sorry." Under normal circumstances, she'd reach over a hand in comfort but tucked it under her knees instead.

Though he didn't like apologies, this one didn't seem to upset him. "Mm. It's better than the pox, I suppose."

The growler lost momentum as the horse drew it close to the front gate of the foundling home.

As she often did, she found herself grateful for Aunt Salomé. This—a foundling home—had been what life intended for Magdalena. Yet over and over, fate had spared her, and she wanted to live in such a way that fate itself knew it hadn't been a mistake.

Children pushed their noses to the wrought iron fence as they drew closer, their small gaunt faces still smudged with filth suggesting they were new to the home.

Zebulun loved the children, protected them, and taught them. The numbers had grown chaotically but he could never turn any away. Salomé had always ensured he had more than enough funds to accept as many as he wished.

"How have you the finances for such a donation?" Zebulun once asked her.

"Oh, sweet boy." Aunt Salomé had patted his face. "Let's not worry about how we save the children, only that we do."

Magdalena waved at the unsmiling faces and offered a cheery expression. A small girl with twin blonde braids and rosy flushed cheeks sat in the dirt beside the gate, looking at her with tired eyes. She'd go quickly. She was quite charming, and the youngest were often the only ones chosen.

Zebulun had been the second-to-last and the youngest to ever arrive at Staffordshire Hall. Six years old and sickly he'd been, having lived a life at sea upon a fisherman's vessel. She remembered how, when he'd arrived, his clothing had held such a pungent odor that sitting near him had been a challenge.

He'd had little interaction with any women at all and viewed them with a wary eye. But Aunt Salomé didn't shy away from his scent nor his apprehension. She sat beside him at a distance until he tolerated her at a closer proximity. Before long, he'd crawled in her lap and settled in, taking a slumber that lasted such great length they'd nearly thought him dead.

Dr. Talbot tapped the side of the growler and nodded toward the fence, indicating she had been lost in her memory for longer than anticipated.

Magdalena slid out and stepped down independently. Any other woman may find Dr. Talbot's entire lack of consideration for others upsetting, but she was somehow aware that the concept of assisting her didn't cross his mind and wasn't intentionally rude.

When he didn't reach for the gate, she did so on their behalf, stepping back to let him go before her. He hesitated and shook his head, reaching around her to hold the gate with the corner of his coat so she would enter first. This, too, was not to be a gentleman but to sacrifice her to the heaps of children gathering in curiosity. She was fully aware he was simply using her to create an open walkway by which he could travel untouched.

Once inside, a handful of children familiar with her occasional presence offered shy waves before returning to their chores.

Ahead, she saw her brother.

"Good morning, Doctor, thank you for coming on such short notice," Zebulun Mansley said as he exited his office and fell into step beside Dr. Talbot.

His rich brown skin reminded her so much of Salomé's. Magdalena had once been jealous of their matching colors, but now it was a comfort.

"A ship arrived three days past and was wrought with a great illness. Many unfortunately perished, including both parents of these children. They arrived here yesterday evening."

Zebulun, having not yet paid his sister any notice with his one-track mind, didn't appear to see her trailing behind.

"We've set up a space for you in a storage room. I'll have a volunteer assist in bringing them to you one at a time."

"Where are the thirteen currently?" Dr. Talbot set about straightening a chair.

"You've passed many of them. They are playing in the courtyard."

"You mean to suggest you haven't quarantined them? They've just been passengers on a ship on which many died, and you didn't think to isolate them from the others?"

Dr. Talbot's tone was condescending.

Zebulun's jaw clenched. "We've no place for them to distance, Doctor. This is an orphanage; not a grand estate."

His warm chocolate eyes met Magdalena's for the first time over the doctor's head.

"This isn't a good time, Magdalena. Please wait for me in my office." Zebulun was the most tender-hearted of her brothers, but he didn't enjoy being chastised.

She opened her mouth to explain. "Actually, I—"

Zebulun cut short her explanation with a steady hand on her shoulder, which he used to turn her toward his office.

"Now, Mags."

"Do not," Dr. Talbot's voice turned to ice, "put your hands on her."

The words scraped out of his throat in a tone she'd not heard before. The doctor's fingers curled around her wrist and tugged her closer. Close enough for her to smell the lingering undertone of a foreign scent. Close enough for the heat of his chest to brush against her back.

He'll move away. This is too close for his comfort ... too close for your comfort.

But he didn't, and that was her cue. Introductions were evidently necessary, immediately.

Magdalena untangled herself from both and stretched out her palms in silent surrender.

"I'm afraid there's been a misunderstanding. Dr. Talbot, this is my brother, Zebulun. Zebulun, I'm here to assist Dr. Talbot today."

Just as two stray dogs may have a standoff in the street, the two stared at each other in silent assessment. If they had hackles, they'd be raised and ears pinned back, teeth showing.

In the end, Dr. Talbot stood down first, though the wheels of his mind began to spin in confusion.

"Half-brother, I presume." Dr. Talbot turned his questioning eyes toward her.

His eyes often settled on her nose, occasionally her brows, but now they met hers for the briefest, concerned moment.

Zebulun's lips twitched, his frustrations nearly forgotten. They were all accustomed to questions and poorly masked curiosity regarding their parentage.

"Not at all," Zebulun's eyes crinkled at the corners.

Dr. Talbot cleared his throat, and Magdalena considered whether to have mercy on his burning questions or to let him suffer. Opting to let him stew, she wrapped her arm around Zebulun's waist and tucked her hand into the alternate pocket of his vest in search of sweets. When it turned up empty, she gave him an accusatory glare.

"There's some hidden in the top drawer of my desk." He nudged her and gave her a squeeze. "The children have cleaned out my pockets today."

"You cannot possibly be fully related." Dr. Talbot looked at her like she was daft.

"And why is that?" She raised a brow.

"You are ... of fair complexion and he is ..."

"Shh." Zebulun covered her ears in a flash. "We never had the heart to tell her."

He shook his head in mock regret.

"That you are Black?" Dr. Talbot blinked in confusion.

"You're Black?" She yanked away from Zebulun's hands with a shriek.

"She's always had a covetous heart. Just wait until she hears I can vote." A smile quirked Zebulun's lips.

"No, tell me it isn't so." Her mock wail turned into a giggle.

The doctor turned a glare toward her, disgusted by their antics.

"We share an aunt who raised us. Our claim as siblings is by choice," Zebulun said firmly.

They both knew, they all did, that Aunt Salomé shared no blood with any of them. It was too late now to find answers to her endless questions. How did the woman come to possess an estate? An unwed spinster raising eleven orphaned children didn't seem odd until Magdalena was grown.

The doctor cleared his throat. "Ah. Well, perhaps another time we can delve into that. In the meantime, we've children to vaccinate and now to examine. Keeping the children outdoors for the time being as much as possible is beneficial if true quarantine isn't possible. I presume their sleeping quarters are close-knit?"

Dr. Talbot set vaccination vials on an overturned crate as he spoke.

Zebulun looked pained again. "Those who've newly arrived are bedding down in the carriage house in the evenings. It's not my preference, and I can't abide by it for long. They're grieving ..."

Dr. Talbot nodded slowly. "It's not ideal. There is a lot of straw in there, I presume?"

Zebulun shrugged. "It provides for cheap bedding while they're away from the bunk rooms."

"Be sure to keep the flame of a lantern far from any incidents." The doctor's response was so soft-spoken and sincere that Zebulun found no fault in it.

"Most certainly. Now to begin?" He called for an employee.

A young woman came in quickly with the first child, who was instantly wary. With an encouraging pat, she left just as rapidly.

Zebulun crouched to the boy's level and spoke in Gaelic.

After a prolonged silence, the boy squared his shoulders and nodded, sitting stoically in a chair and coughing awkwardly under the scrutiny.

Dr. Talbot studied the child, expression masked though she sensed a tightness in the way he maneuvered around, checking beneath the child's eyelids and his mucous membranes, looking within the mouth and observing his complexion.

Lastly, the doctor tugged at the child's shirt, pulling it from his trousers. The boy's eyes flashed momentarily toward Magdalena, where he must have determined if she were accepted by the doctor, she would be acceptable with him as well.

Magdalena bit back a gasp as a speckled rash came into view and Dr. Talbot stepped away. Something was wrong.

The boy sheepishly attempted to cover the exposed inflammation.

"We won't be vaccinating today." Dr. Talbot shook his head and paced the length of the room, collecting his thoughts. "I will give you a list and you will listen closely. I've no time to repeat myself. No one comes in or out of that carriage house without my permission."

It wasn't clear who he addressed, but Zebulun's posture had gone rigid, his expression full of concern.

"Whatever it is, it's not your fault," she said softly and tucked her hand into her brother's, offering a tight squeeze.

He didn't return the affection but stared blankly ahead, awaiting directions.

"Give me a job?" Magdalena asked Dr. Talbot.

He shook his head slowly, approaching the child once more. "Magdalena, my stethoscope and notebook."

He waved her toward his medical bag and withdrew a pocket watch, taking the cone-shaped device from her outstretched hand.

Hurriedly she retrieved the leather-bound paper and a reservoir pen, flipped to a vacant page, and hovered in wait for further instruction.

CHAPTER ELEVEN

Ezra

No, this wasn't in his plans, nor was he prepared for it. He came to vaccinate, not treat. And the majority of what he kept in his bag was useless for this.

Ezra took in a shaky inhale. "Write his name in a column on the left and follow it by his age, which both are?"

He chanced a glance up at Mr. Mansley.

"Mathias. Thirteen."

Ezra should have felt poorly that the caretaker looked so miserable, but he didn't have time for people's feelings.

"Follow it by the numbers one hundred and twelve bpm and twenty-one rpm. Make note of a flat red rashing on his trunk as well as," Ezra glanced over the child's shaggy mane of hair, "the presence of lice in great quantity."

Magdalena's eyes didn't rise from her notetaking.

He addressed her brother.

"We're in need of baths for the lot of them, and clean clothing. Remove the straw from the carriage house, and burn it along with their possessions as far from the home as possible. Gather enough kerosene to remove the lice on the females, and shave the boys to the scalp. They are all to bathe using a lye soap upon every surface—make sure of this."

Mathias shifted uncomfortably in his chair and Ezra tried to soften his expression. The child didn't deserve his frustration.

"What is it, doctor?" Magdalena lowered the journal.

The things he had wanted to do to Mr. Mansley when he'd touched her. It confused him just as much as the panic that momentarily clouded his judgement. Ezra didn't like it. He didn't like any of this.

The boy gave another small cough and blinked away from the light filtering through the window. Yes, however unfortunate, he knew what ailed this child.

"Typhus," he muttered absentmindedly, considering how best to treat him.

Typhus was a proven contagion, though no one seemed to know how it was transmitted. This was where he was forced by lack of science to combine logic with existing knowledge. He'd enjoy it if not for the infected children and all.

Mm, yes, an American physician had written an article on the subject.

"Dr. Gerhard," he murmured to himself.

"His nurse died." Magdalena blinked.

"Yes," Ezra admitted.

"Let us not jump so quickly to death." She set the notebook down and stepped closer to Mathias.

"Don't." He gripped her elbow.

She knew Dr. Gerhard? Surely, she hadn't recalled the study from a single read of text in his office.

"How?" He extended this small opportunity, testing his hypothesis on her. "Tell me how his nurse died."

Magdalena's lips pursed in thought. "She breathed in a patient's foul breath." Her nose scrunched up and she shook her head. "Gerhard suggested it was the exhale that infected her. That doesn't seem likely to you, does it?"

Remarkable. "No," he agreed pensively. "Nor does science aid us in knowing what did."

"So we simply do not breathe and we'll be fine," she joked.

He'd roll his eyes if she weren't onto something. Ezra tugged his cravat loose and unfolded it, wrapping the corners around his head and tying it as a mask over his mouth and nose.

"Clever," she acknowledged.

Turning, she undid her brother's cravat and tied it around him.

"I have another. I'll fetch it for you." Mr. Mansley ducked out of the room to retrieve it.

He returned quickly and handed it off to Magdalena, who pinched the corners behind her head and did the same.

Ezra felt some small relief in knowing they were partially protected. Distance would still benefit them all. He was good at distancing.

Mr. Mansley spoke to Mathias again in Gaelic and led him from the room, presumably to provide directions to both the children and the help.

Magdalena turned to him in her brother's absence. "In addition to the strategies you've suggested, what others will we be attempting?"

We. The word was small in both its verbal and written forms. But it weighed heavily in the air. She was giving him a choice. Since university, he'd not been required to justify his treatment. It should feel like an inconvenience, but it didn't.

It felt like an invitation—one he wanted to accept.

"I intend to gather various necessities. Frankincense, myrrh, quinine, sambucus, garlic, and honey."

She reflected on this list for some time, using her fingers to calculate information that was clearly well above her abilities.

"Sambucus, honey, and garlic you've deducted as the most natural defense to this illness, but I find those to be ... perhaps too simple?" This was both a question and a statement simultaneously, though she hardly paused for a response.

"I'm confused about your usage of quinine specifically, as you've clearly stated that you believe this to be typhus and not malaria." She frowned. "In addition, your journals have no mention of frankincense nor myrrh as a treatment for any, save topical use. Is your intention to treat the skin ailment? Are not these mild imperfections the least of our worries?"

Ezra's hands stilled on the worn handle of his medical bag. "How could you possibly know that information?"

"You gave me your literature. Did you not expect me to read it?" she asked incredulously.

This shouldn't impress you. Many people read. Knowing the information and applying the knowledge are two very different things.

"Now will you stop looking at me as though I've sprouted a third nostril and answer my questions?" Magdalena planted her hands on her hips and gave him a pointed look.

She truly wished to know? She shouldn't. This sort of thing bored the average person, yet her eyes addressed him openly as she awaited a response that would deepen her understanding and not pacify it.

Ezra rubbed the space over his chest that suddenly ached.

"There is no known cure for typhus. The rate of death may be between the teen numbers upwards toward sixty percent untreated. Because we don't know how the illness is transported, we increase the potential for an outbreak. I am limited by the lack of extensive research and by the experiments that have not begun to be theorized."

She seemed to hold onto his words like they mattered. Like he mattered.

"Malaria and typhus have ten or more symptoms in common, and quinine is easily accessible in the quantity we require," he continued before taking his notebook from where she left it to jot down the list required. "It is not a guarantee this drug will benefit them at all, though it gives them greater odds than no intervention at all."

"And the frankincense and myrrh?" Her eyebrows knit together.

"If this combination was good enough for Christ himself, wouldn't it be beneficial for orphans?" He wouldn't tell her all the things he used this combination for.

"This is not your justification." Her eyes narrowed at his lack of reasoning. The fact she didn't so simply let this pass made him smother a small smile.

"I've tested this combination on both animals and myself, and I've found it has internal healing properties. I have evidence suggesting it may reduce the length of illness and work to lessen the duration of one's cough. I have the experiment well documented in my flat if you wish to see it."

"Later perhaps." His response had apparently satiated her questions.

"I'll help you gather the supplies." She nodded toward the exit and stepped out ahead of him.

Chapter Twelve

Ezra

Standing in the carriage house entry, Ezra watched as early dusk began to settle its blanket across the sky. A bonfire filled with straw, and the children's meager possessions shot flames into the darkness. The smell was acrid and burned Ezra's nostrils.

That's not all it could burn …

He blinked away the thought. Thoughts did that sometimes, erupting in his mind in bits of panic.

Ezra stirred the experimental antidote in a tin cup and used the toe of his boot to shift one child's cot a bit farther from another's. Mathias had been brave; he was a good boy. It made sense for the eldest to be treated first, especially when Ezra wasn't sure of the after-effects. He gave them their dose of quinine to start, waited an hour, then gave the second concoction. It was a potent elixir that tasted far from pleasant, but the boy kept it down.

Ms. Trudeau worked hard as they'd distributed the medication from eldest to youngest along the rows of makeshift beds. The carriage house doors were open wide, letting the crisp autumn air cool the children. They'd all been offered a woolen blanket, though most were far too hot with fever to accept.

The scent of kerosene permeated the air as the children lay in an uneasy stillness amongst freshly strewn straw. An occasional cough echoed throughout the otherwise quiet. Nine of the children were feverish upon their examinations. Though feverless, Mathias was one of five who showed a rash along their trunk.

"My aunt, she used to say fevers fought battles no one could see." Ms. Trudeau sat on the floor with her hair wrapped tightly in a scarf to keep lice at bay. "But you must fight too," she whispered to a little girl who strangely resembled her. Straggly whisps of golden hair clung to the little one's damp forehead.

The child was three years of age and had refused to speak at all since her arrival at the home. Poor thing. He ought to remind Ms. Trudeau these children couldn't speak a word of English.

In addition to Ezra and Magdalena, only a female employee and Mr. Mansley had been exposed to the children. They'd agreed to take shifts resting with them throughout the night. No one was leaving tonight, and the caretaker sent word to his sister's home that she would be staying with him for a time.

Ezra ought to retire himself. It would likely be a long night. But his mind was restless, as if it knew someone was about to die. Life was far too fragile, and he'd likely fail to save at least one soul in the room.

His jaw tightened as he searched their small weary faces, wondering who it would be and what he could do to stop it.

When he looked at each, he saw percentages and survival rates while estimating the duration of their symptoms. He considered their demeanor and color, the severity of their temperatures and their overall responsiveness. Each child's probability fluctuated, but one was undeniably lower than the others'.

The one who looked like her.

Ezra stood abruptly to his feet and slipped into the night. He couldn't stay there a moment longer. His clothes were too tight, and they constricted around him even as he stood. He needed a bath, some vain attempt to wash off the unknown. Tearing the mask from his neck he pushed it into his pocket.

Part of him wanted to warn Ms. Trudeau of this early prediction.

You could be wrong. You've been wrong before.

"Dr. Talbot?" Ms. Trudeau's voice sounded through the dark.

He didn't turn. Instead he stared into the flames, shoving his hands deeper into his pockets.

"Come and sit with me?" she invited.

He glanced at her—she'd left the children and lowered herself to sit in the dry grass a distance from the flames. Shadows danced across her tired face, and she lowered her mask to hang loosely around her throat.

Ezra grunted a response and gave a curt nod, settling beside her.

"Thank you," she whispered.

Thank you? For sitting? For exposing her to typhus? For putting her to work?

"For this." She gestured to the children. "It makes me feel alive, and I ... I haven't felt alive for quite some time."

Silence hung in the air, and he watched as the peculiar woman moved to lay flat on her back in the dirt, staring up at the soft tendrils of smoke rising in the sky.

"Do you ever imagine living in a different time? A world where you can follow wherever fate leads you?" She didn't look at him. One would assume she spoke to the stars flickering overhead.

"No."

She chuckled, her hair tumbling from its scarf and haloing her head.

"I like you." She smiled.

She shouldn't say things like that.

Oddly enough, he felt he ought to lay back and look up at the dark himself. But it was dirty.

"You won't know if you like it unless you try."

He heard the smile in her voice.

Could she read everyone so simply or only him? What other things did she know of him?

He hesitated, inching back gradually until he lay prone on the earth. He couldn't recall ever doing something so peculiar. It seemed a comfortable position for contemplating things.

"So. Just how many ailments do you have, Dr. Talbot?"

He lurched back to sitting and glared at her. "What?"

She didn't say anything further. She simply waited. Of all the times for her to be silent and she chose this?

His pulse slowed and he barked out a humorless snort.

"No less than two. Likely three." He swallowed firmly around the tension in his throat.

"What names do they have?"

"I don't know," he admitted.

"What would you name them?" she asked.

Infernum, but it was already taken.

"I don't …." He lay back down to avoid looking at her. There was nothing further he could say.

"What is the first one?"

"I—feel things." Why was he entertaining this conversation? Perhaps it was the security that existed in the cover of darkness. Or perhaps he wished someone could know. "Things I shouldn't feel."

"You may want to rephrase that." Her chuckle merged into a yawn. "Describe it to me? You feel sounds, do you not?"

Unpredictably, yes, with little warning as to which would trigger him. How did she know this?

"Pain." He shrugged.

Noise often settled in his ears and gnawed through the muscles in his jaw. If it wasn't that it was the prickle of awareness running down his shoulders until it was all he felt, all he could focus on.

"And objects?"

"Their imprint lingers long after I've touched them." He sighed.

"So you wipe the feeling away on your trousers or wash your hands?"

"Mm." He nodded, because telling her he often wanted to unbutton his skin like a cloak and hang it in the closet wasn't a socially acceptable truth.

"And the second condition?" Ms. Trudeau prodded.

He didn't talk about the second one. Not to her, not to anyone. Ezra didn't answer.

"If you could cure only one, which would it be?"

The second. Always the second.

His chest ached again, and he rubbed at it. He wasn't used to questions like these. She couldn't possibly know he'd spent every day for the last fifteen years pursuing a cure like a mirage that bent and twisted the closer he got.

"And why are you the way you are?" Ezra asked. He needed to distract her.

"Stubbornness and spite mostly." He could tell she was smiling.

"Well." She stood and shook out her skirts. "I'm going to bed now. Don't stay up too late." She'd be rooming in her brother's office for now.

"Mm. Have life, Ms. Trudeau." He rested his palms on his stomach, keeping his position.

"Good night, Dr. Talbot." She stepped closer and looked down at him. "Don't think I haven't noticed you've spent all day calling me Magdalena."

She was smug. Smug and wrong, surely?

Ezra waited until he was certain she'd gone in before he stood and completed one more dosing of the children. He lingered over the youngest girl, brushing back her damp yellow hair and checking her pulse. It raced beneath his finger-tips.

Mathias had told his caretaker she'd fallen ill first. None of it settled him. Her fever must fall.

Ezra retrieved more ice and packed it beneath her armpits and around her core.

"Mathias may well not forgive himself if she passes on." Mr. Mansley's tone was hushed and tortured as he stepped closer to them. "He's taken it upon himself as the eldest to tend to them. In addition, he is her brother—his, as well."

Mr. Mansley motioned toward a boy who fell somewhere between the two in age. Moisture collected in his eyes as he looked away and cleared his throat.

Ezra couldn't deny the man's affection for the children.

"I've no guarantee that all or any will recover, you understand." It wasn't a question.

"You've expressed as much to Magdalena?" Mr. Mansley hedged.

It was an odd question.

"She's not ignorant." Ezra's tone was harsher than he intended.

Mr. Mansley didn't say anything further, but his expression suggested he didn't agree.

Ezra bid the man goodnight and slipped away to the storage room where a pallet had been made.

Sleep did not come easily, and even when he did finally doze off, he was quickly awakened.

A hasty assessment indicated another round of dosing for the children was required and several more grains of quinine were administered. This repetition persisted throughout the night, with the greatest stretch of rest equaling two hours.

The little girl continuously vomited up anything he presented, and her fever ebbed and flowed as though it were alive itself.

By the second morning, Ezra was alerted by greater news and was ushered in to discover that of the nine, the fever of four had broken. This was a significant decrease in the fevers often persisting with typhus, and these four demonstrated no further symptoms. He would re-evaluate in twenty-four hours and determine if they could be removed from quarantine.

Ms. Trudeau sat beside the smallest girl whose condition remained unchanged. Mathias sat beside her and taught her a short Gaelic nursery rhyme, which she attempted to repeat. She was by no means a natural talent in the art of song.

"Áine." Mathias touched the girl's hand.

Ms. Trudeau slowly pronounced the name until Mathias ducked his head with a shy smile. He had surprisingly not fevered at all, and his rash though not gone had stopped spreading.

Ms. Trudeau brushed the tangled hair from Áine's forehead and said the name again. In the first evidence of any form of recovery, the child's eyes flickered open and Ezra hurried around the maze of cots and crouched beside her. Áine babbled incoherently, regardless of the language, and clambered up from her position in a startling display of energy, throwing herself into Magdalena's arms.

Though surprised, she didn't turn the child away. Instead, she rocked her and attempted to soothe her. The girl's eyes darted wildly around, unfocused on any person as though she was somewhere else.

"Máthair?" A clear word from Áine's tongue. The girl struggled to pull the face mask down for a closer look at the woman she called mother.

Then, just as sudden as her initial energy, the child's hands stilled, and she was once again listless.

Ezra lifted her from Ms. Trudeau's arms and returned her to the straw where he examined her yet again. Her pulse was racing at one hundred and fifty-two beats, her breathing rapid and uneven. She was hot to the touch, and even though he packed what little ice the foundling home possessed around her, it didn't diminish.

Since he had arrived, she'd vomited any contents they administered, unable to keep down either quinine or any hydrating measures.

"She will recover." Ms. Trudeau spoke to calm herself. Her tone was too light, too optimistic. She was feigning comfort in the face of a grim reality.

The air in the carriage house was stifling, and Ezra couldn't render enough oxygen from beneath his mask, nor would he remove it within.

He took his exit, unintentionally creating a path in his wake as he paced the courtyard.

Her fever was too high, and regardless of whether the fever subsided, her brain may well be beyond repair. Confusion, delirium, and high fever were all symptoms that couldn't be relieved if she was unable to cease the retching.

Ezra sat beside a dry fountain and lowered his head into his hands, tugging his locks into disarray. Áine. She had a name which was perfectly suited to her person, and her beating heart was one he could not sustain.

In time, he knew, her interiors would fail, her body would undoubtedly seize, and he was certain there was already swelling on her brain. She had not the strength to bear the procedure to relieve it, and she'd likely perish before he was through.

This was a characteristic of the last phase of typhus before death. The science and knowledge of mankind didn't permit him to remove the agony that was her impending demise or his inability to stop it. He regretted most painfully that he could not save her and that she would part this life before a time more fitting.

It was then he determined her last moments would not be in pain, nor feeling the great discomfort of fever. She would not know the fear of her body giving out, nor the pressure in her skull as her brain began to swell.

While he couldn't spare her from death, he would most assuredly spare her from pain.

This, at least, he could do.

Quickly, he found Mr. Mansley and explained Áine's options with him. The man sent Magdalena away on some entirely unnecessary errands.

She wished all the children farewell, despite the majority's lack of response.

In some regard, he wanted her to stay, and in another, it was best she leave. This was the least preferred outcome, an outcome that Ezra despised yet couldn't prevent. His throat was dry at the prospect.

Mathias was outraged as Mr. Mansley explained their options to him. Ezra was most grateful that he couldn't speak Gaelic as Mathias screamed in a tone that began with anger and ended in pleading, neither of which would change Áine's circumstance.

Mr. Mansley gripped him in an embrace from behind and they both ended up in the dirt as the boy writhed in the despair of his choice, one which in a flawless existence he'd not have to make. His caretaker wept with him and the two clung to one another.

Though he was limited to bringing his young sister physical peace or a painful departure from this life, his choice, in reality, had already been decided.

When Mathias was entirely drained from all emotion, his face took on a rigidity that was all too familiar. He was distancing himself.

Finally the boy nodded, assisting Ezra in the entirety as he administered a dose of morphine into Áine's bloodstream.

The child's pulse no longer raced, her breathing slowed to a more relaxed pace, and the brows that had previously been furrowed softened as the medication soothed her.

Mathias held one of Áine's hands in his and Ezra held the other, gently rubbing his thumb across the back of her hand in slow, repetitive circles.

It would not be much longer. He would not allow her to be alone.

He wouldn't permit she feel the heaviness of solitude.

CHAPTER THIRTEEN

Magdalena

Zebulun had a simple sweetness to him that she lacked. While Magdalena loved out loud, he was devoted to quiet acts of service. It came as no surprise when he asked for her to run an errand.

"Get some treats for you and the children," her brother had encouraged.

With the cotton sack of sweets clutched to her chest, she slid open the latch of the wrought iron gate and stepped through into the courtyard of the foundling home. Mathias was well enough that he may enjoy a piece or two, and several of the other children were also feverless.

Between the children and herself, she knew the contents of the bag would be long gone by the time Áine was well enough to sample a piece. She paused to remove one from the bag and slipped it into her pocket. She would give it to the child later, when she was well.

The wind picked up and tore her skirts wildly around her knees.

She ought to close the carriage house doors.

Dr. Talbot's and Zebulun's backs were to her as she approached, their heads drawn together in quiet conversation. She found it peculiar the doctor so willingly stood close to another.

"I'll cover the cost, Mr. Mansley," she heard him say. "I have a friend who will do well by her and see to it she receives a proper burial."

Burial? From the entryway she could see a solitary empty cot.

No.

She shook her head. The words failed to register until her steps brought her closer. Tears in her brother's eyes. Tension in the doctor's shoulders.

Her fingertips went limp and the sack she clung to tumbled to the dirt, spilling its contents at her feet.

"Magdalena." Zebulun shushed Dr. Talbot, but it was all too late.

"No. No, no, no, no."

She shook her head, not registering the repetition that spilled from her lips.

"Not her," she pleaded.

Zebulun reached for her, but she pushed away his soft hands.

"You?" She knew her eyes held accusation as she turned toward Dr. Talbot, but she didn't care.

He had to have known. He was far too wise.

The doctor's face was grim, though not tortured. She didn't know why she expected his response to be more. More apologetic, more filled with pain, more detailed, and when it was not, she was struck by his fallibility. They continued to speak words to her, words that made no sense, and she backed away, hearing only sound fall from their lips and nothing more.

"No, this isn't fair," she choked out.

"Let me help you," Zebulun urged.

But he couldn't help her.

She saw memories flicker to life in front of her eyes like a horrific theatrical production she was forced to rewatch. Funny, wasn't it? How she wished to die more times than she could count but feared death with a consuming terror.

"She's too far gone now. We'll have to wait for her to come down," her brother murmured.

Magdalena fled.

Somehow, she boarded a growler and managed to get to Olive's estate as the faces of the dead stood in front of her eyes.

Mother and father ... she'd never cared for them, yet there was a certain tragedy in seeing their bodies pulled from the river.

Her twin sisters.

She choked on a dry sob. Why couldn't she cry?

Aunt Salomé.

The pain in her heart almost brought her to her knees.

No, she didn't want to cry—she wanted to scream. She wanted to feel something, anything else.

Shoving her coin toward the driver she hurried inside, up the steps and into her quarters. Sitting on the edge of her bed, her body trembled as curls fell into her eyes. She grabbed them in fistfuls, tearing them from their pins until cool hands reached for hers.

"Shh, I'm here, I'm here," Olive soothed. "Roberta, fill up a bath, dear."

She kept her honeyed tone but held tight to her sister's hands.

"I'm all right." Magdalena forced a smile. "I'm all right. I'm all right."

"Of course," Olive agreed, releasing her hands only when she was certain they'd not return to her hair. "Let's get you cleaned up."

Olive stood and gathered a clean set of garments and lilac soap.

Magdalena was already shaking her head firmly. "No,—lye. Lye soap," she urged.

Olive only nodded, sending a maid to retrieve it from the wash house.

"I'll be just outside the door," her sister promised.

Magdalena read between the lines—you're frightening me.

She'd pull herself back together in a moment. Perhaps tomorrow if she could.

She slipped out of her dress and into the water. The surface of her skin burned under the lye soap yet still she scrubbed until the skin was raw and red.

A moment. She'd give herself one moment. Not too long, just enough to make it stop.

Magdalena held her breath and let the water close over her head.

Stay, the water hissed. I'll take your pain.

"Magdalena..." Aunt Salomé's voice was muffled by the bath in her ears, and she watched as her hand lowered and yanked her to the surface.

Magdalena sat up from the water with a gasp. Aunt Salomé was gone, though the memory of her words echoed in her mind.

This wasn't the first time she'd lay under the water with open eyes burning.

After the twins passed from cholera, her mind thought of dark things. Perhaps she should have died with her parents and the young man who had pulled her from the carriage should have let her drown too.

Perhaps if she were supposed to die by water, she ought to do it herself.

Aunt Salomé had pulled all twelve years of her long legs into her arms and rocked her like an infant. In silence she'd sat with the woman crying into her sopping hair, brushing kisses across her forehead. Salomé's arms were soft and healing, like a balm that turned to an adhesive as it seeped into the shattered bits of her heart and put it back together.

Aunt Salomé's arms had turned rigid, and she'd arched away to look into Magdalena's eyes.

"Magdalena," she'd said almost sharply, "You are a force. You. Do. Not. Bend. You do not bend to pain. You do not bend to half loves or half-truths, and you especially do not bend to your mind."

She pressed her forehead to Magdalena's. Aunt Salomé's familiar citrus scent enveloped her, and Magdalena had nodded, not fully understanding what it all meant at the time.

The woman always buried clever little things into everyday conversation. In retrospect, every comment had been a clue pointing toward the woman Salomé had once been.

It hurt to live without her. It hurt to live at all.

"Magdalena, your pain can make you bitter or it can make you better." Aunt Salomé's accent was thicker when she said this, her heritage from the Islands more noticeable.

Magdalena didn't ask her then how she knew such words with familiarity as though they were human themselves … as though she had met the words, lived with them, partially become them.

Only now that she was gone did Magdalena wish she had asked. So many questions were left unanswered.

Once dressed, she climbed into bed, where she stayed. The days blended with sleep and failed words of comfort, but getting up seemed such a chore.

There wasn't anything left.

The door to her quarters opened and a rustle of footsteps sounded before it closed behind the silent visitor. It was likely Charity. Her eldest sister tended to sit in silence and glare as opposed to useless encouragement.

Magdalena would get up when she was ready. Tomorrow, when the autumn sun would shine brighter as she knew it would. The world was full of glorious tomorrows, and no matter what life took from her, it couldn't seem to take hope for long.

A body lowered to a chair, and papers rustled quietly. It was a familiar warm, woodsy scent with notes of licorice.

She knew immediately who it was. Him.

Someone had called the doctor, and they would answer for it later.

Magdalena wouldn't speak to him. He could sit there in his insufferable silence as long as he'd like. She'd out-stubborned him before, and he'd leave far more quickly from the room than she would from the bed. The absence of sound raged on, sinking into her mind like a perpetual scream. She didn't like the quiet.

"I have no cure for melancholy," he said after some time.

It wasn't in his nature to speak first, nor would he have come on his own accord. He was here to treat her, and he'd just been very up front with what she had always known—there was nothing that could put her back together this time. No peculiar resin built from an embrace or motivational words.

She'd have to dig herself out of this one alone.

"Why, then, have you come?"

Instead of speaking he tossed something in her general direction. His aim was nearly as atrocious as his penmanship, and it struck the headboard beside her ear. She reached for the item, but her fingers stilled, mid-reach.

Beside her lay a solitary peppermint candy. A lady's maid had retrieved it from the pocket of her skirt when she'd taken it for a wash. In hopes it would lift her spirits, she'd offered it to her, only to retreat when it brought a fresh and unexpected rage.

"It's time, Ms. Trudeau."

She looked up, noticing at once his somber dress, the black he wore from head to foot, covered in clothes of mourning.

"I can't go." Her voice sounded frail even to her own ears.

She hadn't gone to the twins' graveside. She'd screamed and clung to the door frames as her brother Patrick had tried to carry her out. She hadn't gone to Salomé's either, wrought with an unexplainable fear that rendered her frozen and panicked. It was the ultimate betrayal of her affections, and guilt rested heavily on her shoulders.

"Then you fail yourself." He stood, retrieving his hat in his hands.

Magdalena scoffed, the sound dripping with disgust. "Whatever the treatment for melancholy, I assure you, this is not it."

"How many ailments do you have?"

He stepped closer, close enough that it made discomfort roll across his features. Instead of moving away, he clenched his fists at his side and tightened his jaw.

"You asked me which one I would cure if given the chance." His breath was choppy, but he leaned in closer, inches between them as he met her eyes. "The second one. This is your opportunity, Magdalena, to cure something within yourself. I wouldn't waste it."

He stepped back and brushed a shaky palm through his hair.

The door clicked behind him, and she clambered to her feet. There was something about the unspoken things he shared that forced her to move. His moment of vulnerability changed everything.

Yanking a black dress from the armoire she stepped into it quickly. The reflection staring back at her in the looking glass was pale with eyes that looked like thunderclouds and matted curls that clung to her scalp. She grimaced and covered it as best she could with a black straw bonnet.

When she stepped from the room, she was immediately caught off guard by Dr. Talbot, who leaned against the wall, knuckles pressed to his lips. Lost in thought he studied one of Frank's many floral charcoal sketches.

"Ah yes. Shall we then?" He pushed away from the wall and cut her off, stepping in front of her and leading the way down the staircase.

Mid-stride he reached for a vase that Olive, in her romantic inclinations, kept full of seasonal flowers. He fetched several stems and extended them over his shoulder without turning.

"Tuck these wherever you may. Your scent is horrendous, and if I'm to bear your proximity in the carriage I require it be partially smothered."

Magdalena lifted an arm and took a steady inhale. While not her best, she didn't believe it to be nearly as dramatic as he suggested.

She set about tearing the flowers from their stems and tucked them into various pockets and the collar of her dress. She placed the empty stems back into their vase before hurrying in his footsteps.

Magdalena was bothered by the prospect he knew she'd follow him and awaited her pursuit in the hall just beyond her chamber door.

But he left no time for her to reconsider as he exited Olive's estate and hurried down the steps into the awaiting carriage.

Neither spoke, opting to watch out the window as the passing estates gave way to countryside. She didn't know where they were going, but she felt him beside her jostling his boot rapidly against the floor.

There was something wrong in the way he ducked his chin into the collar of his coat and his brown eyes reverted somewhere else.

CHAPTER FOURTEEN

Magdalena

"Nineteen." He shifted in his seat, fumbling out of habit for a medical bag that wasn't there.

"What?" He was so still, so solemn it made her want to ease this tension, not add to it.

"In my practice I have tended nineteen women over the course of thirteen years who have sought treatment for pinching in their arm or severe jaw pain. Within twenty-four hours, thirteen of them dropped dead."

He audibly swallowed.

"Why are you telling me this?" Her voice cracked, and she pushed a fist against her quivering mouth.

Dr. Talbot didn't answer as he stared out the window. The carriage turned down a narrow, less-traveled road with humble cottages set back from the winding dirt path.

"Upon autopsy I determined their cause of death to be angina pectoris." His hands encompassed his knees, gripping them until his knuckles turned white.

"I don't understand." She shook her head.

"Sometimes the pain is not the problem. Sometimes pain distracts from the origin. Death built this country, death mingles with the dirt beneath your feet, death simply is, yet you cannot accept it."

The silence between them was thick and heavy.

"It isn't fair," Magdalena finally whispered. "It hurts."

"It isn't fair?" he scoffed.

She wanted to kick him.

"It chooses victims by drawing a poor man's straw and leaving the worst to crawl the earth?" He blew out a sharp laugh. "Those are my reasons. Yours, Magdalena, are much simpler."

"Do not use my name when it suits you," she bit back. "Áine was a child."

The words clawed their way out of her chest in a growl.

"And your buttons that have always been unfastened at five are now at six. Is that her only farewell?" A muscle ticked in his jaw, and he dismissed her with a wave of his hand. "Tell me, do you hate death because you crave it or because it is solitary? We both know how you cannot bear to be alone."

Her breath caught painfully in her chest, leaving a dull ache in its path through her lungs. How could he possibly know that? And if he did, why would he say it aloud?

"You are being cruel." She slammed a boot into the wall, rattling the windows.

"I am being honest, and truth is pain." His volume rose.

"You are pain!" She lashed out so loudly the words rang in her ears, and he flinched.

They glared at one another for a moment, chests heaving and secrets spinning their way through their angry minds.

"You...." He chuckled darkly. "You have no idea."

It was then that the carriage pulled to a stop outside a humble country cottage dwelling. Another carriage was already there, and the short iron fence off in the distance partially obscured a familial collection of headstones.

They climbed wordlessly out of the carriage and into the soft soil. Ivy crept up the cottage exterior and a small barn was offset toward the back. While on the outskirts of London, the quiet street with ample property bounds felt familiar.

Instinctively Magdalena knew it belonged to him in some way. With his top hat in place, Dr. Talbot slid his hands into his pockets, for the first time looking oddly less like a man and more like a boy.

Magdalena's steps faltered as she saw the figures of a cloaked minister along with Zebulun, Mathias, and his younger brother.

She closed her eyes and clenched her fist around the peppermint candy in her pocket. She could not go and see the pit in the earth accompanied by a box that contained a child. Her vision clouded and her breaths tightened in her chest. Was it simpler to say farewell to someone you had loved for a long time or a short time?

"I'm sorr—"

"Don't." He jerked his chin. "Not here."

Here, like apologies were somehow worse in this location.

Magdalena stayed by the cottage as Dr. Talbot trudged on. She watched as he approached Zebulun and the other two. They spoke for a moment and Zebulun's eyes found her across the way.

He didn't hide his surprise. He'd tried his best to have her join them at Aunt Salomé's passing.

Zebulun offered a hesitant wave and turned back toward the graveside with a steady hand on each boy's shoulder. The minister, she presumed, said some words grounded in tradition before the group spent some moments in silence together.

To distract herself, she approached the cabin and looked through a smudged window at the interior. The contents within were covered with linen sheets and dust covered the window in a thick layer. Dense foliage around the door suggested no one had entered in quite some time. A home so close to London and he avoided living in it?

The cottage, set apart from direct neighbors but within shouting distance, resembled its owner.

Áine mattered to him, she realized, enough that he returned.

The small ceremony having passed, the others vacated the graveside to return to their carriage.

"You came." Zebulun beamed at her.

"I am as astounded as you, though let's not tell the others." Magdalena nudged him.

"I love you, sister." He tugged her close and kissed her on the forehead.

"And I you."

Magdalena wrapped her arms around him and buried her face in his chest. His scent was comforting, and they clung to one another for just a moment. The warmth of their connection eased their pain ever so slightly.

She pulled away to study her youngest brother. His eyes were moist with the sheen of unshed tears, and she raised her hand to his face.

"I'm sorry I abandoned you in your time of pain. Again."

"You don't owe me an apology." He said this, though she felt she did fail him. "Don't do this to yourself, Magdalena. We each have our own burdens to carry. You are no lesser for your struggles with death."

Knowing if the roles were reversed she would say the same, Magdalena offered a wobbly smile.

She hugged Mathias and his brother who shyly reached for her before they left in their own carriage.

Too easily, she expected Dr. Talbot would let her leave, but he didn't. When the others had not long disappeared out of sight, he cleared his throat and ducked his head toward the cemetery.

"Let's go."

"I can't." She shuddered.

"You can. Not without pain, but you can."

He was so troubled she was inclined to take a few faltering steps toward the fence.

"You don't understand." She shook her head, rasping out the words. "I have never..."

She hadn't ever what? Said goodbye? Moved on? Dr. Talbot was right—Magdalena memorialized them with her buttons like a pathetic apology for failing to see them off. She wished he were less observant, less wise, or that they had never met.

Liar, she blinked moisture back into her dry eyes.

"Their names?" Dr. Talbot nodded toward her buttons.

She hardly noticed gripping the buttons so tightly their imprint lined her fingers. He didn't call her silly or the act trivial—he asked their names.

He doesn't know the value you place on names, she chided her warming heart. But the soft feeling remained.

"Father was first." She traced the top button of her blouse. "Then mother a few moments after."

A grimace tugged her lips.

"You didn't care for them?"

"I hardly knew them." Magdalena shrugged halfheartedly. "Next came Ada and Alice ... Cholera took them."

"When you asked—" He tugged off his hat and pushed a palm through his hair.

"It's all right." She sighed. This was all too heavy.

"Fifth?"

"My aunt." Salomé's kind face swam in her memory. "She wasn't really my aunt, I don't know why she put up with me, with any of us—"

"Mm." He nodded curtly. "You were happy?"

"More than words can express." Her heart felt as though it began to tear in her chest, and she could hardly breathe.

"Áine?" The name sounded strained on his lips.

"Fate." She muttered like a curse. "She looked so much like ...."

Like me.

"You didn't want her to die, just like you don't want to die. Perhaps there was some wayward hope that if she lived, you could plant yourself in her life and exist vicariously through her. But now. Now she's gone, and you have to live for the both of you, alone."

There was that awful word again.

With his hands tucked in his pockets, Dr. Talbot swallowed and moved one of his elbows ever so slightly closer to her. In the time she'd known him, his avoidance of physical touch was entirely ingrained in his character. But she suspected he was offering, in his own way, his arm.

Stop feeling, she pleaded her heart. Just for now. But hearts were fickle things. They didn't listen to minds, and they certainly didn't listen to words.

She tucked her hand into the crook of his arm. In the moment her fingers closed around him, she felt his muscles flicker from relaxed to painfully rigid in no more than an instant. But he didn't pull away. This was the ultimate sacrifice—his comfort for hers.

He directed her through the fence before she'd fully come to terms with the sight before them—Áine alone. Her heart sped up and her stomach rolled, but Dr. Talbot waited. He ignored the clouds above that grew heavy with unshed rain, he ignored the cold air that she knew he didn't like. He simply waited.

There was something to be said about a person willing to pause life for someone else's cause.

When Magdalena finally gathered the gumption to lower her eyes to the ground, she saw a peculiar sight. The hole was far too wide for Áine. Instead, three caskets sat snugly side-by-side.

What other children had passed in her absence? What had she done in leaving them? Panic overwhelmed her.

"We found her mother and father." Dr. Talbot's voice was quiet. "Though they'd been buried prior, we transferred them here, with her."

He didn't say it, but she knew. He didn't want Áine to be alone either.

Flooded with immediate relief, an inappropriate chuckle escaped her lips. He had taken her hidden fears and relieved them. She'd not have known the complexity of his heart had he not given her limitless time to inch toward this place of realization. Where had he been when Aunt Salomé passed? Would his quiet, foreboding presence have helped her find boldness then? What a loss to have endured until this point without him.

To find Áine's parents was surely labor intensive. His exhaustion of all paths intrigued her, and she found herself regretful she'd not been there to witness and aid in his own process of grief.

"You have a token for her?" he reminded.

Reaching into her pocket, she felt the small, significant weight. Turning it over in her hands, she took it out and looked at it once more before pulling it to her lips. She kissed it before leaning over and dropping it into the ground atop the casket. While she could not pretend to know what happened after death, she imagined Áine painless and carefree, sampling this sweetness while holding the hands of both her mother and father.

Her eyes burned and warmth dripped down her cheeks. Tears. She couldn't think of when she'd last been able to cry.

Dr. Talbot seemed to notice at the same time as she, and he abruptly shook loose her fingers and walked away. Hands still in his pockets he ambled through the graveyard and sat atop a mausoleum some space away. His feet dangled as he lay backward. It was both disgraceful and disrespectful, and she would have let him know if it weren't for the relief she was feeling.

She crouched beside the pit and stared at the wooden toppers, the arrays of flowers, and the earthen walls.

"Goodbye, Áine," she whispered. "Goodbye, Mother. Goodbye, Father. Goodbye, Ada. Goodbye, Alice."

Her tears mingled with her snot. It was likely a horrific sight but, oh, how it soothed her soul.

"Goodbye, Aunt Salomé," she choked out. "I won't forget."

The rest of the conversation played out in her mind of all the things she would commit to memory.

Dr. Talbot still lay unmoving atop the mausoleum, his face tilted toward the sky and his eyes closed. A few beginning drops of rain clashed with his stubble and dripped down his face. She knew with a resounding certainty in this moment that something was stirring, something larger than she could imagine.

Magdalena searched for a nameplate on the mausoleum, spotting it covered in overgrowth and years of soil.

Eliana M. Talbot, beloved wife and mother.

Her year of death she estimated to be in direct correspondence with either Dr. Talbot's birth or very early years. His mother. Had he sought her out in this way intentionally? Did it bring him comfort to be close to her?

Clearing her throat, she slid a finger beneath her chin and loosened the bow of her bonnet.

"I'm ready."

"Mm. Goodbye, Mother." He sat up and slapped a palm on the stone top.

"You loved her?" she asked, unsure he was capable of the emotion.

"On the contrary. I've hated her every day of my life." He said it so flippantly it caught her off guard.

Magdalena was unsure whether he presented sarcasm to mask his truth or whether the bluntness was the truth.

Awareness crackled. He was familiar to her; she simply didn't know how.

CHAPTER FIFTEEN

Ezra

A knock startled him awake. "We're here, sir."

The driver stood beside the open door.

Ezra had fallen asleep long before Magdalena disembarked. He'd hardly noticed when she gave a hushed goodbye and slipped out, latching the door quietly behind herself.

Over a week had passed since he'd slept in his own bed. Even after the remaining children recovered well enough, he'd spent several nights in the laboratory. Could he have saved Áine, or was it too late the moment she'd arrived?

He ducked into the street and paid the driver handsomely for his service. Ezra was spent, his emotions particularly. He'd tried and failed to kill those pesky things long ago. It was to his benefit that evening approached, and Mrs. Keene had long since retired.

The old cottage had been just as he'd left it fifteen years ago. He could almost picture the lilacs blooming in the back acre every spring. Part of him wanted to go and see his old comforts in those woods. The other parts of him knew there was not a lick of goodness left in that house.

Arthur hadn't gone back either, Ezra noticed. Arthur likely hadn't stepped foot in the cottage since that very day.

Ezra had been twenty, and it had been his birthday. He rubbed his chest through his shirt. Death was too simple for men like his father.

I hope he suffers. Every day. I hope he dies slowly and with great pain. I hope there comes a time when he requires a treatment only I possess, and I get the opportunity to withhold it.

Ezra unlocked the door of his flat and began the rituals that kept him in some semblance of peace. Void of conversation, of unfamiliar sounds or scents, the single-room flat was his escape. He had one bed, one chair, one small table, and a bookshelf full of pathetic little memoirs of the methods he'd tried to repair himself but failed.

If only memories washed away as easily as dirt.

He dressed quickly after his bath, trying not to think as he often did, but his mind strayed.

Everyone felt the loss when Magdalena fled, as though she'd had an internal brightness that kept everyone warm. He shouldn't call her by her name, and he certainly shouldn't think of her when she was somewhere else. She was right—a wry smile tugged at his lips. Magdalena Trudeau was a bit like a mold, growing on him and spreading until it was too late to stop. Even this unkind thought had an undertone of something twisted and soft.

She looked terrible, and it was a wonder her family didn't send for him sooner. It confused him to no end how she could look so pathetic all while her eyes still sparkled. He hadn't known anyone else's eyes to do that. Magdalena was intelligent, and he'd not met someone with her ability to record knowledge in her mind after a single read of text.

Knowledge without technique is useless. He needed to stop his thoughts, as they'd begun to spiral. He wasn't accustomed to thinking in compliments or appreciation.

You could teach her. He scoffed. No, that would be reckless.

Enough thinking, enough wondering. He climbed into bed though the sun was only beginning to set. Fatigue made him weary to the bone, and the silence of his haven began its work of refilling what had been drained from him.

The next morning, she arrived at his laboratory shortly after he did, filling the place with her scent of lilacs and the sounds of happiness. He could feel her even when she was silent, how she made the dusty corners of his mind compelled to perk themselves up at attention and find the positivity in a rather bleak existence.

"Your ear is gone." Magdalena leaned closer to his apothecary jar.

Ezra frowned. Another experiment, unfinished.

Drying his hands on a towel, he slung it over his shoulder and looked at the beetles. It was difficult to be upset with the lads. They worked hard.

He retrieved a piece of dried meat from beneath the counter and fed it to them, pleased when they covered it in seconds.

She gagged beside him, and he muffled his own in response. It was a wretched sound. Still, it pleased him to know there was this solitary thing she couldn't tolerate. The petty part of him wanted to taunt her with it. Unfortunately for her, he liked to listen to that part.

Ezra removed the lid once more and selected a fine specimen and lifted it out with a pair of tweezers. Its little legs scurried in the air in confusion.

"Care to hold him?" He extended it toward her with a bored expression.

"I would sooner hold your hand than hold your beetle." She shuddered.

He choked. The insect slipped from the tweezers and dropped before scurrying across her boots.

In the only feminine display he'd seen from her aside from tears, she screamed and launched herself into the chair.

"Dr. Talbot! You did that on purpose!"

Her voice was breathy as she trembled on her perch like a little bird.

Ezra quickly covered the insect with a glass and used a piece of paper to return him safely to his home.

The sight of her there, standing in a chair, eyes wild and hair tumbling across her face, built such a chuckle up in his chest it was almost painful to keep in.

"Don't you dare." She sniffed, turning up her nose with a look of frustration, but her lips twitched. "I would rather my body be burned in a funerary pyre than be eaten."

She shuddered, climbing down.

The mirth died in his throat. No. Dead or not, he'd not relish the idea of his body being burned … not when the scent of burning flesh and agony was embedded in his mind.

He instinctively rubbed his forearms through his shirt over the memories.

Ezra was spared when a knock sounded from the entry in the front room, and Mrs. Keene opened the door. He could hear the deep timbre and self-invitations of Thaddeus Cain in the entryway followed by Mrs. Keene's open adoration of the man.

He rolled his eyes toward the ceiling. Perfect. He hadn't the faintest idea how he'd explain away Magdalena's presence, and Thaddeus would be sure to make things as uncomfortable as possible.

"Ezra, my good friend, have I quite the gift for you this day."

The baritone of his friend's voice rattled the windows and an assortment of glass test tubes littering the countertops.

His footsteps sounded across the floor and Ezra braced himself for a different sort of predicament. Women liked Thaddeus. Magdalena was a woman. She would like him, and it would be obnoxious.

Thaddeus stepped into the doorway, his ever-present Garrick coat flapping around him as he hurried. The man had invested in the changing fashions and had retired his top hat for a rounded bowler, complete with some sort of feather attached. Ezra found himself watching Magdalena's reaction more than his friend's. He felt an odd sense of disgust when her eyes widened, and her lips parted ever so slightly. She liked what she saw.

He pushed his hands into his pocket and sighed. He expected it, yet he didn't enjoy being right—not this time.

"Ezra," Thaddeus clicked his tongue in disapproval. "You've been keeping a secret from me I see."

He paused in the doorway, quickly removing his hat while giving Magdalena an aggravatingly slow appraisal.

"He's not one to offer introductions, I'm sure you're aware of this," Thaddeus spoke of Ezra as though he weren't present and tucked the bowler under one arm. Stretching out his other hand in greeting to Magdalena, a slow smile spread across his face. "Thaddeus Cain. What a remarkable pleasure it is to make your acquaintance."

"The only thing remarkable about it is your exaggerated reaction to seeing a woman," Ezra muttered the words, though at Magdalena's smothered snort, it was clear she heard it. Good.

"Ah, Ezra, you act as though it's custom for me to see you with any woman save Mrs. Keene. No offense." He winked at Mrs. Keene, who fluttered her lashes so frantically Ezra wondered whether she was having an affliction of dry eye.

"Ms. Magdalena Trudeau." She accepted the proffered hand.

The length she held it was professional, appropriate even, before she released it and stepped back, wiping her palm on her skirt.

"You aren't going to ask why I am here on a perfectly good afternoon?" Thaddeus wiggled his brows toward his friend.

"Because you like to suck the joy out of average weekdays by forcing me to socialize?" Ezra smirked.

"Absolutely," Thaddeus agreed with a cheerful nod before he bounced on the balls of his feet in a giddy little dance.

Then Thaddeus leaned in close, conspiratorially lowering his voice.

"We have an anomaly."

Chapter Sixteen

Ezra

An anomaly? The coroner needn't say another word before Ezra was pulling his coat and top hat from the rack.

Magdalena followed suit and, as an afterthought, he retrieved a text of skeletal structure and pushed it into her hands as they walked.

"Dr. Talbot." She hesitated. "Where are we going?"

"The morgue, of course."

Whether she followed or remained behind, he didn't care. There was an anomaly and those were one of the few, simple joys in life.

Thaddeus made to explain but Ezra stopped him, preferring to keep it a surprise as they climbed into his awaiting carriage. On rare occasions, the coroner needed his help, though it was more common for them to bond over irregularities. This was entertainment in its simplest form.

Once situated inside, Magdalena opened the well-worn journal he passed her and studied the systematic approach he'd created to best recall skeletal structure and their placement. She scrunched up her nose in evident disgust over the contents.

This he used as fodder to his previously reckless thoughts. See, she could never tolerate being an apprentice.

"You find this repulsive, I'm sure." Thaddeus leaned closer to her on their shared bench.

"I do not." She sat up straighter against the swaying of the seat. "I find his method of memorization difficult and unlikely. It doesn't suit me, and I'll find another option."

She ducked her head and continued reading.

An irritating bit of warmth made his chest throb and a smirk tugged at his lips. His own mouth was betraying him.

See? a rogue emotion whispered. He fiddled with the buttons on his overcoat as a distraction.

Magdalena began to hum a familiar though unplaceable tune, then whispered a little song under her breath before exchanging the original words for the names of leg bones. Carriage rides had once been the space for thinking. He couldn't think with her song of bones. How did he recognize it?

"Ha!" Thaddeus snapped his fingers. "I've placed your song. It is a shanty, is it not?" He chuckled. "How is it that a woman came to know a seafarer's tune?"

"My aunt used to sing it to us?" She said it like a question with puckered brows.

Thaddeus looked at her with far too much appreciation in his eyes. Ezra didn't know whether Magdalena would be considered attractive to others. He hadn't taken the time to consider it, but the coroner seemed to enjoy her. The way Ezra felt the tips of his ears flame up suggested he'd best continue to detour widely around that idea. She was Magdalena. She was ... he didn't know what else. But without a doubt, she couldn't be pretty.

"We've arrived. Are you certain you can handle this delicate situation?" Thaddeus' persistent gaze didn't stray from her.

"Oh, for the love of logic, stop your flirting and get out," Ezra groused, stepping around them both and into the street.

"If second-guessing my resilience is his idea of flirting, he has quite a way to go." Magdalena gave Thaddeus a consolation pat. "I like my flirting like I like my men, broody and sarcastic."

She blinked up at Ezra with an overly sweet smile before it turned into a huff of disgust.

"You are being rude," she muttered to him under her breath.

"I am being rude to a friend. It hardly counts." Ezra shrugged.

Thaddeus elbowed him and the two scuffled for a moment before Ezra stepped on the insole of his foot. He was as solid a friend as Ezra could have asked for. He had a knack for understanding when he could jab at him, but he was cautious of where he put his hands.

The coroner grunted before sheepishly unlocking the door. As the lock shifted, Magdalena brought a fingertip to her lips and tucked a nail between her teeth.

Ezra's eyes widened, darting between her mouth and her eyes. He could almost feel her teeth nibbling on his fingernails. Had she always had this habit? How had he not noticed before? Did she wash her hands? A gag threatened.

"If you were hungry, you should have brought a snack," he choked out.

Her lip curled in frustration, but she pulled her hand away with a sharp nod.

"I am nervous, Dr. Talbot," she hissed. "I predict there is a very dead person on the other side of this door."

"If you are nervous, pace, tap your foot on the ground, bang your head into a wall, I don't care. But do not, under any circumstance, bite your fingernails."

He tried to swallow his disgust, but another thought occurred to him, and a horrified gurgle sat in his throat.

"Do you eat them? Where do they go after you have chewed them off." He closed his eyes and shook his head. "Mm. I don't want to know."

"Point taken." She glared at him. "You are the worst. I don't know why I like you."

She muttered as Thaddeus held the door open and took her coat and bonnet from her, hanging both on the hooks in the foyer.

"Welcome to my house of death, dismemberment, and decay." Thaddeus offered a charismatic bow and then a wink. "May you come again but never grace my table."

This was unraveling in the worst ways. How could he have ever considered taking her on as an apprentice?

Thaddeus handed Ezra a candle and the two of them lit their way down the wide hallway and into the theatre.

They had been at this for years. At first the coroner would speak incessantly throughout entire autopsies. Ezra had sent him out of his own theatre many times over the years. It was difficult to think with the interruption of constant commentary.

Magdalena shuffled behind him as he finished lighting the last lantern.

"It's cold," she murmured.

Bathed in light lay the corpse, a sheet draped across its frame from head to mid-calf, leaving exposed the anomaly he wanted to see.

Magdalena gasped as her own eyes settled on it, and he froze when her fingers curved around his biceps and her forehead pressed between his shoulder blades.

Don't touch me, his mind begged. She's not, he tried to calm it.

For now, her grasp was barricaded by the thin material of his shirt. For now, she didn't know. How much longer could he hide all the secrets from her? There were so many, and one was bound to slip out, then another, until all were spoiled.

"You knew it was here." He sounded harsh, even to his own ears.

"I just need one moment. A small moment. Can I not have that?" Her voice shook.

"Ms. Trudeau, may I offer my own back? Ezra is oozing with discomfort."

Thaddeus sauntered over with a ghoulish grin, turning his back toward her. He exchanged a private glance with his friend. He'd always been good at keeping Ezra's secrets. The ones he knew.

"Well, he'll simply have to get over it presently," she muttered, her words muffled, and the heat of her breath made him sweat.

Ignore her. Distract yourself. She can't stay there forever.

He moved stiffly toward the cadaver as she shuffled blindly behind him. Slowly, he forced himself to breathe. If she stayed, sooner or later she would touch him, her fingers would brush against his skin, and he'd fall apart. It would likely be an accident, but then it would be too late. She'd look at him with pity when she found out. He hated pity. He'd tell her soon—it would be easier that way.

Ezra busied himself, studying the exposed calves on the table. Male, stocky, and well-muscled. An assortment of mild bruises in a linear pattern suggest he had once had an occupation moving crates or similar and frequently injured himself.

"Physical labor?" Ezra's words were absent-minded as his eyes traveled down the calf to the ankle and finally down to the anomaly.

"Fascinating, isn't it?" Thaddeus was across from him then, and they both observed the incredible deviation.

"Would someone please share just what is so captivating?" Magdalena's hands were loosening, and he could feel her head ease away from his spine.

Thaddeus began to share the details when Ezra gave him a sharp look. If she wanted to know, she'd have to look. If there was even the slightest chance she could make it as an apprentice, this would tell him. He felt a bit like growling. This was an idea he had no intention of pursuing, yet it kept circling back around like an obnoxious scent.

"Your curiosity will only be satisfied by your own observations, Magdalena." He tugged a handkerchief from his pocket and mopped at the moisture accumulating around his collar. "Stop touching me, I've had enough."

She released him, but he could tell she hadn't yet opened her eyes.

"You'll wear him down, I'm sure of it," Thaddeus stupidly encouraged.

Magdalena's chuckle was replaced by a gasp. "His feet!" She nudged Ezra further down the body and crouched low beside the table for a closer view. "Are those two toes ... connected?"

"Webbed." Thaddeus nodded. "Isn't it repulsive?"

"Not at all." Magdalena and Ezra spoke in unison.

Thaddeus's laughter rumbled out of him. "The pair of you are perfectly suited for one another's company."

"He was remarkably special." Her words were softly spoken as she gently used an index finger to touch the point of connection.

Ezra looked to Thaddeus, who nodded. "He's been well washed, as you always request."

Ezra gathered up the foot by its heel and pulled it closer for a clearer view. Rigor had retreated and it rose with little stiffness. Both the left and the right foot matched, though on the right one, which he held, the fourth toe was missing a nail. The damage was new, and no healing had taken place before his death.

Ezra returned the foot to the table with a sigh. The lack of any tissue changes indicated it occurred post-mortem.

"You lost his toenail?" A damaged cadaver always irked him.

Thaddeus looked chagrined. "You miss nothing, do you? It's on the cart, along with whatever else was washed off."

"You suggested he must have worked a physical position? What brought you to this conclusion?" Magdalena was inching upward in her perusal of the body, boldness growing.

Thaddeus leaned in closer to her, their shoulders brushing, and indicated the pattern of bruises across the shins.

"Would you be capable of watching the autopsy, or shall we build up to it another time?"

When Ezra realized he was holding his breath and waiting for her response, he ducked around her and snapped the sheet down around the man's hips. The exposure of everything aside from his unmentionables didn't give much time for consideration.

"Dr. Talbot, while you may be accustomed to seeing men in such a state, it is not something I am so readily prepared to do. I've got to build up to this gradually," she all but squeaked out. "I do apologize, sir. The doctor truly means well."

Her eyes were wide as she avoided looking at the man's abundantly hairy chest and acknowledged his face. Was she speaking to ... the cadaver?

Thaddeus had rolled a towel and placed it between the man's chest and chin, effectively closing the mouth while the eyelids were fastened with straight pins.

The man's jaw was round and covered in an auburn twist of facial hair, brows bushy and darker than his beard.

"Miss, he cannot hear you. I'm afraid he is very dead." Thaddeus snorted at his own dark humor.

She shuddered and stepped away, distancing herself from the morbid display that became quite real with the exposure of a face.

"What was his name?" she asked softly.

Thaddeus shifted on his feet and looked at him. A name? When had they last considered a body's name?

Even Ezra felt a bit bothered as he considered it. Dissection and experimentation were necessary evils. This was a void, soulless, and emotionless shell. Yet somehow, with her here beside them, it felt more human. Things were shifting in his mind. There was something about her that made him want to be better. It made him feel like the way he had been for so many years was no longer enough. She would change everything.

He couldn't let her.

Thaddeus shifted through a stack of papers with a grim expression. When he finally discovered the labeling title, he cleared his throat.

"William Drisdale."

He bent and scrawled the name across a slip of paper before placing it at the foot of the autopsy table.

Magdalena nodded her gratitude. "Thank you, Mr. Drisdale, for letting us see your feet. I'm sure they suited you well all your years." She paused as if thinking of something eloquent. "I am most sorry you are dead and that they will soon cut you open to determine why."

Her volume rose as though if she spoke louder, he would possibly hear her.

Ezra's lips pulled at the corners again as Thaddeus removed his vest and rolled up his sleeves. Ezra didn't do the same, not even in front of Thaddeus.

Then he cleared his throat. "Now that you have finished whatever that was, we'll begin."

Ezra looked at the assortment of tools Thaddeus displayed on a small table and selected a scalpel.

CHAPTER SEVENTEEN

Magdalena

The autopsy was one of those things that captured her attention so entirely, it was difficult to look away. She alternated between watching the incisions and peeking at Mr. Drisdale's expression. Thankfully, it hadn't changed.

Despite it being Mr. Cain's morgue, Dr. Talbot appeared to take the lead. She found it comforting to know he had a friend.

Magdalena backed herself into a chair and drew up her knees, wrapping her arms around them as she watched from a distance. The pair worked in silence at first, alternating tools to filet open the skin before sawing through the breastbone and cracking open the pieces like a walnut.

Exploring bodies likely happened in rooms throughout London, though it seemed to be a well-kept dirty secret. From where she sat, she noted that the procedure itself wasn't messy as the blood had been drained into a series of vats beneath the stone table. At first the realization made it all the more morbid, but she imagined it would have been worse if it splattered on the ground.

"If you faint, I'll leave you on the floor." Dr. Talbot didn't turn as he leaned down looking closely at each piece of this macabre puzzle.

The room may have spun for a moment, though she had no intention of admitting that to either of them.

"She's doing quite well, is she not? I recall my first theater experience. The amount of vomit that spewed across the floor from all the viewers did very little to improve the ambiance." Mr. Cain chuckled as he spoke to Dr. Talbot.

"Public autopsy theaters are not ones I have any interest in. This is much more suited to my taste." Dr. Talbot said as he scribbled an observation on a notepad.

"That is due to your affinity for silence and your craving to do things independently."

Dr. Talbot nodded slowly at Mr. Cain's words. "This is true. I do not care for the audience, nor the conversations that circulate. I will be the first to admit to objectifying the dead at times. I cannot abide by the remarks that are so openly stated about the bodies."

His words left much to read between the lines.

She listened to their interaction quietly, seeing how they worked in comfortable familiarity. Dr. Talbot would gesture to something every so often, and Mr. Cain would lean in close to respond.

"I'll see to it that I'm buried without any intrusion of my body." Dr. Talbot's jaw was stiff. "I don't wish to be touched or explored. Regardless of the cause, there will be no changing the nature of my death."

The idea of being touched, even postmortem, bothered him. Why?

"On the contrary, I wish they would find every peculiarity inside me," Mr. Cain said. "Particularly my brain. I have a spectacular mind and it ought to be kept in a jar in someone's possession."

He winked at her as Dr. Talbot shifted some things around, elbow-deep in the cavern of Mr. Drisdale's chest.

A bold red began to saturate the sleeves of the doctor's white cotton shirt despite most of the blood having been drained. She found it odd he hadn't pushed up his sleeves.

"I've got it." Dr. Talbot grunted as he held back parts and pieces.

"Already?" Mr. Cain went in for a closer look, snipping and clipping until an organ was removed entirely and released into his hand.

Mr. Cain dropped it into a bin beside the table making it easier for him to maneuver his hands in and explore what Dr. Talbot had found. They murmured together in quiet appreciation, and she considered whether her feet would hold her up at all or if her legs would go limp entirely.

"Come Magdalena." Dr. Talbot gestured to her with a jerk of his chin. "Put on an apron and push up your sleeves."

Mr. Cain stepped off into another room to gather further supplies. Standing tentatively, Magdalena stepped closer, rolling her sleeves above the elbow. The sight was one which, while sitting had been tidy and organized, up close seemed a mess. The worm-like pieces lower in the cavity were tangled up in such disorder she wondered how it all fit.

"Small intestine," Dr. Talbot answered the unspoken question. "Nearly twenty-two feet long I presume."

He was holding something toward the back of the body and ushered her to lean in for a closer look.

Doing just that, she could feel his strong presence beside her. There was no method to look without brushing against him, and she'd apologize if not for the fact she'd invaded his space no less than an hour ago.

"You'll have to reach in to feel it." Organs obscured her view, and he hesitated before taking her hand in his. It was odd, the way he blinked down at her fingers cupped loosely in his palm. Dr. Talbot's brows furrowed, and he sucked in a reedy inhale before straightening his spine and plunging her hand in beside his own.

Inching her fingers along his wrist, she used his limb as a pathway for her touch. Their fingers temporarily tangled as she blindly attempted to feel anything but the cool, slippery texture enveloping her hands.

As she did, she felt him spasm behind her, like the muscles in his chest convulsed and his fingers trembled beneath hers. There was something wrong.

She chanced a look over her shoulder.

"Don't," Dr. Talbot wheezed.

His hold on her hand loosened as he settled her fingers into the right space. He didn't move away, and she was trapped in the circle of his arms between the autopsy table as he held organs out of the way.

Should she ignore what happened? Was one supposed to ignore the pain of another so flippantly? It was pain she'd sensed, wasn't it?

But that was hardly logical. His condition was only one of discomfort, of feeling more. This wasn't feeling more. It was feeling everything.

"Congratulations, you've now met my second ailment." He remarked bitterly.

Magdalena didn't have the words to say, so she said nothing. Things like this weren't supposed to happen. He'd touched her before in assessment, and she'd seen him tend to patients. How could a man initiate touch but not receive it? What wretched curse had been forced on him?

Somehow grateful to have something to do with her hands, she gripped the rope-like structure he'd placed in them.

The rigidity of bone scraped against her knuckles from the back of the body, and she leaned over, straining on her toes to reach all the way in. She began to trail her fingers up and down along the cord gripped in her fist, looking for something that didn't fit.

"Feel carefully," Dr. Talbot's chest pressed against her. "Slightly north."

His voice was rusty and grave while she felt the rapid rhythm of his heart against her cheek.

Quickly moving her hands upward she paused, feeling something peculiar.

"A tear?" she asked as her index finger found its way into an opening that didn't appear to have an exit.

"An abdominal, aortic aneurysm killed this man." Dr. Talbot nodded and stepped away from the table abruptly.

Stepping back, she scrubbed her hands on a linen towel. Turning on him, her eyes roved over his features, looking for the secrets he'd buried and burdens he must be tired of carrying. One of his shoulders hiked toward his ear, appearing to be more spasmodic than willful. He looked like he wanted to vomit, or he couldn't breathe, she wasn't sure.

"At least it isn't syphilis." She shrugged.

They stood in a silence that would have been awkward if she were anyone but herself.

"W-what?" He blinked at her.

"The timing of your introduction was a bit off. You really ought to work on that." Magdalena raised a brow.

He expected a more substantial response, but she had no intention of giving it to him.

"You are … " He searched for the words.

"An absolute catch, I know." She winked at him and turned away, blowing out a pent-up breath through pursed lips.

He leaned against the table, toeing the ground with his boot, anything it seemed, to avoid looking at her.

Meanwhile, she couldn't stop glancing over at him. Curiosity flooded her. Filtering through every memory she had, she knew it to be true—she'd never seen someone touch him. Mrs. Keene would pass off a tray with caution. The coroner, even whilst wrestling on the path, kept his hands at a distance.

"Ms. Trudeau, are you interested in learning how to suture?" Mr. Cain stepped back into the theatre.

Blessed fate, a distraction. "Absolutely!"

Dr. Talbot removed himself from the work and disappeared down a back hallway.

The coroner made small talk mixed with what she was beginning to translate as a flirtatious though harmless personality. He showed her how to complete a few stitches before passing her the large needle and thread.

"You are lucky you can't feel this, Mr. Drisdale." She gave the body a reassuring pat.

The physician returned wearing a fresh ivory shirt minus the cravat. She'd always seen him formal, proper, and pristine, and this version was softer. He looked more approachable, even, dare she say, content?

"I'll show you where you are to wash your hands and arms. Be thorough."

He led her toward a small washroom where a pitcher and some lye soap were waiting. The lanterns were dim, and she scrubbed between each finger and up to her elbows as far as she could manage while he hovered in the background. A series of shirts hung in a corner of the room, and the bloody one he'd worn sat in a waste bin for disposal instead of for washing. She added her apron to the other basket.

She sensed this solitary secret was one of many, not the kind shared in hushed giggles, but the kind that tortured. They made their way back to the theatre.

"Will you take a look at the bones before you leave?" The coroner asked his friend. "The chief inspector is a bit pushy these days."

Dr. Talbot stepped toward a different table littered with skeletal remains. He didn't touch anything but studied the skull carefully before moving onto the pelvis.

"Have you noted the inconsistencies?" the doctor asked.

"Such as?"

"Cheap whiskey, a poorly crafted gray trouser and shirt, yet his structure was sound. This man was from the West End." He gestured to the pile beneath the table.

The bones were worn down and discolored by liquor, yet he called it sound?

"The teeth." Dr. Talbot seemed to sense her questions. "They indicate the practices of a barber-surgeon. There is no frailty or anatomical concerns due to poor nutrition, suggesting he was fed and tended throughout his life."

"You are much better with decomposition than I," Mr. Cain admitted.

"Where are the drawings?"

Mr. Cain gestured toward the counter where character renderings were spread about. Missing persons, she predicted.

"None of these." He shook his head.

Mr. Cain gave an appreciative chuckle. "How do you do that so quickly?"

"Here." He returned to the skeleton and gestured to a shadowy dip in its chin.

"A cleft chin can aid in the bodies' identification?" she piped up from her spot slightly behind them. This idea intrigued her. "And here I thought a dimpled chin simply existed for the sake of beauty."

Dr. Talbot snorted. "It isn't attractive. It is a defect. The lower jaw didn't fuse as it ought, and it's carried on through family lines. You have one." He pointed to her chin.

Magdalena stiffened. "You've just told me that not only do I have a birth defect, but that I am also unattractive." She cocked a brow. "Shall I delve into your features?"

He glared at her as Mr. Cain cackled with laughter.

"You haven't got a thing to worry about in that regard, Ms. Trudeau," Mr. Cain encouraged, his mustache twitching over another chuckle. "Ezra has never noticed a woman's appearance."

"I think it's time to go." She shook her head with an amused smile.

Dr. Talbot should consider himself lucky she wasn't prone to vanity. Magdalena didn't want to be beautiful, not when ugly things filled her head.

"Keep a foot for me, will you?" The doctor motioned toward a wall of glass jars in a corner.

Each held an anomaly of some variety, and her stomach roiled uncomfortably. Mismatched eyes, a misshapen heart, a hand with an extra finger to name a few, all swimming in preservative fluids. Some collect postage stamps. These men appeared to collect peculiarities.

The coroner paid his friend for the assistance and offered the use of his carriage, which the doctor declined. Dr. Talbot looked suddenly shy, an awkward characteristic for someone who'd just insulted her twice in a solitary sentence.

"Walk?" he asked. "The park isn't far from here."

He didn't look at her when he asked. She was growing used to it.

"I'd like that." She nodded, pulling her coat from the rack and tying the strings of her crooked bonnet beneath her chin.

CHAPTER EIGHTEEN

Magdalena

"You know," Magdalena began as they ambled through Hyde Park. "I wanted to die that day." She gestured toward the river. "I was a bit upset you didn't let me."

"Do you do that often? Want to die?"

"Only on Wednesdays. Those are for dying, didn't you know?" she joked.

He didn't tell her it was ridiculous, he didn't argue or attempt to dissuade her, but he did glance toward her with his head tilted ever so slightly and brows drawn low over his eyes. The moment he saw her looking back, he blinked away.

Something changed in the morgue. He seemed at war with his mind, torn between something he wanted to say but felt he shouldn't. For once, it seemed he'd share it in his own time.

"Your friend, Mr. Cain." She gave him a sidelong glance.

The doctor's shoulders stiffened at the mention of the coroner, and he said nothing.

"He made it clear that you do not make exceptions. You prefer to be alone." She watched him cautiously. "Why do you tolerate me?"

The doctor cleared his throat, and he relaxed slightly as he formulated a response.

"You were not as expected."

"In a positive way?" She raised an eyebrow.

"Not ... negative." The rigidity of his muscles returned, and she was fairly certain he was sweating. It served him right.

"You couldn't simply say yes, could you?" She smirked.

"Mm." His answer was enough. Evidently, he had something on his mind.

"Have you ..." He was a bit scattered, tongue in cheek, and he began again. "You have no likelihood of marrying, and you have few redeeming qualities. Have you ... considered any worthwhile purpose for your life?"

The remainder of his words flooded out in a barrage of staggered statements.

The number of uncomfortable pauses between each insult was astounding and coincidentally very disparaging. It really was fantastic, and she sputtered around her laughter.

"Such as?" She wiped threatening tears of humor from the corners of her eyes as he looked on in disdain.

"You could ... join me?" He stared at the trees, which were beginning to shed their leaves.

"And in what capacity shall I join you?" That sounded a bit obscure, but she'd not change it now.

"Professionally." His voice was strained.

"How disappointing," She smirked, knowing how this sort of comment made him choke.

"As an apprentice," he said slowly.

"That is unlikely, as you know." Despite her words, she smiled. His confidence in her was encouraging, but it simply wasn't possible.

"Why is that?" He stopped in his tracks and looked at her, irritation sparking in his eyes.

"Well, Dr. Talbot, I'm not certain you've noticed this." She fought back her laughter. "But I am, most regretfully, a woman."

Born a man, she'd have been free to pursue something as simple as interests. Now, she was forced to digest any fragment of knowledge in hopes they'd satiate an appetite for medical concepts.

He glared. "You are capable, or do you deny it?"

"I am denying nothing, especially my interest in the idea. But the fact of the matter, Dr. Talbot, is that is not the world we live in."

They walked in silence for a spell which gave her time to consider. Frank would be upset with her. Olive's interest would be for her happiness. Magdalena knew what she wanted, though it wasn't clear whether her choices would harm those she loved far more than she cared for herself.

"What if it were probationary?" he asked. "Six weeks and I will reevaluate?"

Why did he care? Why was he pushing something and why hadn't she said yes already?

Being raised outside London had many benefits, as did being an orphan. Magdalena possessed no notoriety, was easily overlooked, appeared to be entirely forgotten by society, and offered no contributions. She was neither publicly wealthy enough to have any place of social standing, nor was she too derelict to be a complete outcast. She was aware of the gift Aunt Salomé had handed her. She had a flexibility few were awarded and a curiosity for exploration that was so ingrained in her being that she'd never successfully shaken its pull.

Still, it was unusual.

"You think I can do this?" she asked hesitantly.

"Are you looking for me to call you a good girl and give you a pat?"

"Well ..." She tilted her head thoughtfully.

"Don't answer that." He shook his head, giving her a look of disgust.

This was unexpected. She liked unexpected things and unexpected people even more. Her stomach growled loudly, interrupting her train of thought. Dr. Talbot and she were passing through the most traveled portion of the park, littered with food vendors and their tempting scents drew her in. If they were a flame, she was their moth.

"There will of course be conditions to your apprenticeship." He began to walk again, his steps slow and relaxed.

"Yes, let's be clear so that you don't alter your stipulations later, when you've grown bored of my company."

"You are the most bizarre person I have ever encountered. I anticipate losing all of my hair before I grow bored," he muttered under his breath.

"Well, what are your expectations?"

"You are to wear simple clothing, dark is preferable, no ruffles or elaborate details, perhaps an apron. Your hair should not be loose but confined tightly and high upon your head. Bathe daily with soap, clip instead of biting your fingernails, and do not stink. If you stink, bathe—even if you have only just recently done so. It is that simple. Remember that."

Bathe daily? That was a little dramatic.

"Also, do not repeatedly wear the same clothing without a wash. You may wear your outer clothing one day only and then it must be laundered thoroughly before wearing it again."

She considered his requirements, and though they seemed excessive, none were too unmanageable.

"If you fail, I'll send you home on that given day. These are requirements, you understand?"

"I understand."

A vendor moved down the path beside them, their sign for smoked eel on display.

She gestured for Dr. Talbot to wait. Her mouth watered as she imagined the salted fish, flaky and chewy, soothing the hunger in the pit of her stomach.

"I'm sorry, will you excuse me a moment?" She stepped toward the cart, extending her arm to bring the vendor pause.

Dr. Talbot froze, his eyes darting between her and the eel vendor. His disgust was akin to her experience earlier in the day and not at all realistic considering her aversion was to a dead human body and his to an eel.

"You wouldn't," he whispered.

Certainly, she would. In fact, if it was the same vendor from a week past, his fare was delicious.

Mid-step he stopped her with a grip on each shoulder. "Watch."

He said this as though she were about to watch the grisliest of murders, and so she did. He narrated the situation in a whisper close to her ear.

"Watch as this man, shall we call him John, approaches the stand. I know you prefer naming your patients."

"Why John?" She was willfully pestering him at this point.

"Is not seventy percent of London's male population named John or William?" He shook off her comment and released her, splaying his fingers in a point as though just his index finger would not fulfill his need to draw her gaze toward this unassuming stranger.

"John has an appetite and he's reaching into his pocket for his pence. Might I draw attention to the variety of mischief on his clothing? Is that feces, or the decaying remnants of a meal he ate last week?" He took a slow sniff of the air. "I can nearly smell him from here. Ah, now this is my favorite part. John has paid his pence and is handed a bowl that contains the coveted smoked eel you so crave."

Magdalena tried not to notice the dirt encrusting John's arm nor the way he scratched at his head arduously while he lowered his nostrils to the bowl for an appreciative sniff.

"Note the yellowing of his sclera—the whites of his eyes," he clarified.

She recalled one of his numerous texts regarding the condition.

"A hepatic illness?" Her stomach rumbled and despite John's sickly nature, she was still famished.

"Mm. Do you see how John hunches over his bowl like a mutt, slurping and chewing his tasty treat?" Dr. Talbot's speech was unfiltered and bridled with glee.

John lifted the fish to his mouth, chewed hastily, and to her dismay some spittle and debris splattered into the bowl.

She swallowed hard and her stomach grew quiet.

The stranger returned the bowl to the vendor, wiped his greasy mouth on his sleeve, and walked their way. John offered Magdalena a beaming grin in which the majority of his teeth were broken, rotten, or gone entirely. She offered him a weak attempt at a smile in return.

"This, this right here, is what makes the earlier part my favorite."

Dr. Talbot returned his hands to her shoulders, certainly not aware he'd been doing so, further solidifying the idea his ailment was limited to others touching him and not initiating it himself.

A woman of slightly higher standing approached the stall and paid her pence. Without being told, Magdalena knew precisely what would happen next. She watched, appalled, as the seller used John's same bowl, added a serving of fish, and passed it to her, only for her to repeat the process.

"Now Ms. Elizabeth has received not only her share of eel but also John's share of hepatic illness."

Dr. Talbot erupted in a sound she had not considered him capable of making as laughter bubbled out of him, rolling over her in waves as his hands fell from her shoulders.

"Dr. Talbot, your sense of humor is horrendous." She scowled at him, feeling her nose scrunching up in disgust.

"Go ahead." He nudged her with his shoulder, hands once again shoved deeply in his pockets. "Have your eel."

He giggled once more, a boyish and endearing sound if not for the terrible cause of it.

"I'm no longer hungry." She lied, and he knew it.

Magdalena couldn't ignore her earlier considerations, and the near numberless times she'd visited a vendor's stall ran through her memory. She gritted her teeth as a gag threatened.

She understood now why the doctor ate nothing but porridge and a side of peas for every daytime meal. Though monotonous and bland, it was probably void of hepatic or other illness.

Dr. Talbot approached a different vendor nearby and paid double the price of eel, accepting straight from the coals into his pockets two baked potatoes. Potatoes were a greater expense with the blight.

"But you said—"

He held up his hands. "If one must visit a vendor, the baked potato is your safest option so long as you accept it directly into your own serving dish. My pockets are regularly laundered."

Magdalena's deceitfully wicked stomach growled loudly once more, betraying her.

Dr. Talbot sidestepped toward her and opened his pocket, revealing the delicious starch inside.

Reaching into his pocket, she took the fiery hot spud. Using her thumbs she split the soot-covered skins and took a bite.

It was entirely too hot, and she blew out her mouth to cool her tongue, holding the potato in the sleeves of her coat to avoid burning her hands.

This gift was considerate, and she realized that he had held a conversation (albeit far from civil), put his hands on her shoulders, and even laughed all within the past ten minutes.

He really was a strange man to have his temperament so altered by an autopsy.

Chapter Nineteen

Ezra

He was content. The feeling made him leery, anticipating when or how it might end. The space in his chest ached a little less, like warmth slipped in when he hadn't been looking and threatened to spark if he let it.

Ezra learned long ago that everyone played a game, only no one played the same one and they rarely shared the rules with anyone else. He wondered what hers was.

He was born with whatever his first condition was. For as long as he could recall, he'd been peculiar, but he'd been able to shake hands as a normal man or see a barber if need be.

Everything changed nearly fifteen years ago. His father was a terrible drunk, prone to rage and abuses under the bottle. Just when he'd thought perhaps his father had changed, Arthur came home drunk and nearly killed him.

Ezra could still feel his hands around his throat, taking the breath from his lungs. When he'd woken up moments later on the cottage floor, Arthur had been trembling and apologetic, but Ezra's mind was shattered. Arthur had reached for him, his fingers brushing against Ezra's skin as he muttered useless apologies.

The sharp suffering that followed was comparative only to burning. His mind mirrored the greatest agony he'd ever experienced and replicated it with a simple touch.

"What is on your hands?" Ezra unraveled under the pain, frantic to escape it.

"Nothing." Arthur shook his head and backed away. "There is nothing on my hands."

Still Ezra couldn't help but look at them, to confirm there was no visible disfiguration on the man's palms. Even now, the memory lingered with the sense of betrayal.

Nearly at the park's center with Magdalena beside him, Ezra shrugged off the memory. There was something on his father's hands after all—he was guilty. Arthur had always been guilty. The only good thing he'd done was leave London that day and never look back.

"I don't think I've ever seen you eat anything other than porridge." Magdalena folded up the skins of her potato and threw it into a bin. "Thank you." She smiled at him.

"The texture is consistent," he admitted, finishing his own snack and pulling out a handkerchief to wipe his hands. He'd offer it to her, but she'd already wiped her hands on her dress. Lovely.

"So which condition came first?" she asked, fiddling with the buttons of her overcoat as they ambled along.

Ezra chuckled. "The one I call first. And the second came—"

"—second." She rolled her eyes.

This felt right somehow, their new, simple banter. He was no longer hiding behind the worry she'd find out and be disgusted or treat him pitifully. If anything, she acted less concerned somehow.

He wondered what she'd do if she saw his arms. Would she run away? What if he told her of his childhood or the things that happened at Breton's?

These questions were another problem. He had far too many broken pieces and each was uglier than the last.

"How old were you?" she prodded.

"Twenty." He cleared his throat.

"Mm. Now nearly thirty-five." She nodded. "Those are good odds," she said under her breath, hardly meant for his ears.

"The odds are rubbish," he chastised. "You look at life through a lens of futile hope."

"I look at life like something to be beaten." She smiled like the words made sense, only they didn't.

"I won't be in the laboratory tomorrow." He remembered. "You may start the day after next."

"I'll cherish my last day as a filthy swine." She nodded soberly, her eyes sparkling.

They parted ways at the edge of the park. It made little sense for her to travel to Brick Lane when it was in the opposite direction.

He walked the rest of the way, making it up the steps just as the sky unleashed a torrential downpour. He wondered if she made it home before the rain fell. Ezra wasn't accustomed to thinking of other people. He didn't particularly want to begin now.

He slipped into the laboratory to complete a few end-of-day tasks. There was a handful of letters from the detective, which he set ablaze before settling into Magdalena's chair. He wasn't sure how it felt more hers than his now. He saw to a caller in the early evening before returning to the news.

The day's papers were filled with the ever-present discussion on topics of miasma and overwrought graveyards in the East. Bethlem Royal Hospital had a small touch of fame. It appeared they had failed to permit a complete survey of their properties upon their most recent inspection. A monetary fine was likely.

Curse them. He'd sent in an anonymous complaint and all they suffered was a fine? He blew out a sigh. This was the way of things.

Bethlem. Roland had been insistent about the hospital.

He stood and searched through the paperwork, finding the one with its blurred ink, now dried to the page. Ezra held it up to a lantern in an attempt to read its contents, but it was useless. He made out a handful of words, or were they names? Shadows parted and dread crawled up his spine.

This wasn't a document for him. This was a telegraph.

From what he could tell in the blurred text, the detective was returning to London. He couldn't make out the date, nor could he pretend he didn't care. This left his only option to return to Roland and see how much longer he had before memories came knocking on his door.

When Ezra retired for the evening, he saw to his routine and found the bed quickly, just as rapidly claimed by sleep. It was never the initial act of falling asleep that proved to be difficult, but the perpetual waking throughout the night that ailed him. The sound of thunder shaking the windows set nightmares into motion he couldn't escape.

An echo of heavy breathing followed stumbling footsteps. The sound of Papa's boots dragged across the floor as the wood beneath the boy's palms vibrated. A chair ricocheted across the floor and crashed into the wall.

Ezra's body trembled beneath the bed where he hid and begged himself to stay quiet.

The picture in his mind was distorted, as if he were watching it through a shattered mirror, creating several minuscule visions of the same image. It was worse than witnessing it through a solitary lens.

Ezra followed Papa's shoes with a fearful gaze as they came closer, the tips of them peeking under the bed, threatening to notify their wearer.

"Boy. Where are ya?" he slurred.

Ezra refused to answer.

Whether he answered or not didn't change the outcome. Papa sought only a target.

The man crouched beside the bed, bringing his face mere spaces from Ezra's. He didn't mean to, but a cry slipped from his quivering lips.

It was cold inside. Papa was never home to start a fire, and his liquor warmed him well enough he wouldn't notice until morning.

Ezra closed his eyes, clinging to his little stuffed dog until the beating stopped.

"Boots is on an adventure." The clouded memory of a story softened the blows.

"What's he looking for?" he'd asked.

"A bird. Boots is looking for a bird. And when he finds it, all will be right in the world."

There was no bird, he knew that, and nothing ... nothing was right in this world.

"I'm sorry, Ezra. It won't happen again." The words cracked and splintered as though the sound of them could be seen and not only heard.

With a start Ezra sat up in the bed, a flash of lighting needled its way through the curtains. Nightmares were as much a part of Ezra as the heartbeat in his chest. Despite the fire having long burned to ash in the hearth, he was moist with perspiration.

Climbing out of bed he sought a glass of water to soothe the burning of his throat and chest.

"Stupid," he said into the darkness.

The silver scars on his forearms glimmered in the bits of moonlight that slipped through the curtains. The flesh had grown taunt with age, yet even after the passing of time, felt as though it continued to burn, sharp with pain as if near the point of splitting.

He dabbed an oil of frankincense and myrrh on the scars and rubbed it in until the sharpness dulled.

He'd been ten when his father sent him to Breton's School for Boys. Just shy of eleven when he'd fallen asleep in the cellar with a medical text and a lantern settled unsteadily in the straw beside him.

Perhaps he ought to be grateful the nightmare hadn't been himself on fire, nor the sensation of the kitchen maids scraping away the blisters that developed on his arms.

Sleep would evade him then. It was better to remain awake than to fall into useless terrors. Reminders of a time that ought to be buried and forgotten, along with any of the men in them.

Quickly, he dressed and slipped on a coat. With light hardly in the sky, he went to the police station to procure the body they'd promised him. No one else was fool enough to be out so early. He needed this temporary distraction, and his experiments benefitted both him and the police. He'd take the occasional body free of charge, use it to create a series of decomposition studies, and later be called upon when they found a gruesome cadaver in need of details.

Body in tow in an undertaker's wagon, he and the corpse were delivered to the outskirts of town—the property of the empty cottage.

He set up at the edge of the yard, dismembering the limbs effectively from its torso before setting up the experiments. Generally, he used Thaddeus's field for his studies. After the nightmare, this somehow felt more cathartic. It was in his nature to clean as he went, leaving little more than blood behind with none the wiser.

A smile twisted his lips. He'd be sure to leave something in Arthur's bed.

Ezra littered the parts around the property. His favorite was the head, which he buried in a shallow grave, nostrils peeking out from a thin layer of soil in the garden closest to the front door.

He hesitated at the entrance with key in hand.

"He isn't here," he murmured.

Ezra inserted the key in its lock and gave it a shove, sending it backward hardly an inch or two with an eerie groan.

Sheets covered the furniture, and the stale air choked him. There were two rooms in the bottom portion, a washroom and a living space with a shabby kitchenette.

The familiar bed sat in a corner beside the crumbling fireplace. He hated that bed. This house, this floor, and the plaster ceilings with its gaping cracks.

He fought back the flashes of memory that threatened, urging his heart to slow its pace and the air to return to his lungs. A few chairs, a sunken couch, and the stove sat in places unsuited to their purposes, all pushed together years ago when he'd fled.

Ezra still stood in the doorway looking at pain and heartache and failures.

"Go on in now." He captured his lips between his teeth in an attempt to stop their child-like quiver.

Trunk of the cadaver in his arms, he trudged cautiously up the rotting steps and left it sitting in the sunlight of the attic. Downstairs he tucked one of the last remaining limbs on the bed and covered it haphazardly with a sheet.

That will do. He gave a satisfied nod as he carried the last arm toward the door. The barn would be a good place. Likely plenty of rodents had begun to accumulate in there.

A knock at the front door froze him to his place.

Wiping his bloody palms across the apron stretched over his chest, he waited.

Another knock sounded. Company? Neighbors on the outskirts tended to be ferociously nosy, as he recalled, reminding him why he preferred the anonymity of urban life.

He left the last appendage propped up on the wall behind the entryway.

"Mm?" He opened the door to reveal a pair of women, their hair done up in swoops and braids with visiting dresses flouncing across the cobblestone path.

"Good afternoon, sir, we are your nei—"

The speaker's voice trailed off as she caught a glimpse of his apron, and most likely the spatters that covered his sleeves and hands.

Ezra could feel his eyes pulling toward the nostrils in the garden and the fingertips peeking out of the rain barrel by the fence. He supposed if they were observed, the women may well avoid visiting in the future.

The second woman shuddered but extended a basket. "Your neighbors to the north. We saw the cottage inhabited a few days prior at the funerary services. We wanted to offer our condolences and welcome you to the neighborhood."

Ezra didn't say anything but accepted the basket with an extended index finger. He opened the door slightly wider to set it on the floor just inside.

"Appreciated," he nodded, beginning to close the door.

The first woman's eyes were wide as she glimpsed the sheets behind him and the furniture grouped together in the center of the room. He checked to confirm the foot he'd placed on the bed remained covered and saw a solitary toe exposed as the breeze from the door tugged at the sheet.

He sidestepped to block their view.

"A butcher?" she squeaked out.

That was ironic. He nodded. "Of sorts."

They quickly took their leave, whispering behind their hands as they went. Rumor would soon spread of his habitation there, though they would be sorely disappointed to realize he was a passerby with a gruesome hobby.

It was unfortunate there were no walls surrounding the property.

He took the last limb from behind the door and brought it to the barn, where he tossed it in some ancient straw, kicking a few blades over the top.

Tasks complete, he pulled water up from the well and washed quickly behind the cottage, changing into spare clothing. The morning and afternoon's majority silence was the recovery he had desperately needed from society. It was times of forced conversation that pained him, and any prolonged presence of others caused a nearly physical discomfort.

The carriage returned for him, bringing him back to town. He was a bit anxious to get Roland over with. Dates and times were important, and he needed to know when the detective would arrive.

The familiar bell tinkled above the door when he stepped in. A man looked up, the little auburn-haired one. Finnian Bulcroft.

"Good morning, sir." Finnian looked at the clock. "Er, afternoon."

Finnian stood and extended his palm.

Fabulous. Just what he wanted, a new Bobbie to train.

"Boy doesn't shake hands." Roland stepped into the doorway, his cocky little mustache turned at one corner as he lazily brought one ankle over the other. "Thinks hands are filthy."

"Oh, uh, sorry sir." Finnian lowered his hand and rubbed it awkwardly on his pants.

Ezra reached into the pocket of his vest and withdrew his folded piece of paper.

"I need a print of this document." He handed it to Roland who looked him right in the eye as he reached for the paper and willfully brushed his palm against Ezra's.

He fought the hiss of pain, catching it with his teeth and turned it into the fakest smile he could muster. Roland didn't know everything. He'd worked with

Ezra as a youth, years before this had begun, and there was not a doubt in his mind that if the chief inspector knew, he'd play with it.

Ezra's shoulder spasmed, but he masked it by reaching past Roland and adjusting a toppled clay trinket on the desk behind him.

Roland came around him and sat at his desk, smoothing the paper across the tabletop. "What happened to it?"

"I spit on it." Ezra met his eyes with a blank, unblinking stare.

Roland lifted it to his nose and gave it a steady inhale.

"No." The chief inspector shook his head. "It got all wet when you saved that woman."

Ezra stiffened. No. He couldn't know about her.

"Funny, isn't it. Another girl named Magdalena, after all these years?" A slow, wicked smile took over his face.

The room spun and Ezra steadied himself with the desk nearest him. "Silly coincidence, isn't it?" He was thankful his voice didn't give away the turmoil he felt.

"Or a curse?" Roland smirked. "I'll give you your paper, but you're not going to like it."

He stood and flicked through a roll of documents.

Secrets. So many secrets. He wished they were as easily destroyed as hopes and dreams. Secrets were the only thing that didn't die, not even when the people who harbored them did.

Roland handed him the paper, and Ezra willfully crumpled it and pushed it into his vest. If he wasn't going to like it, he wouldn't give this man the satisfaction of watching his displeasure.

Ezra gave him a sharp nod and ducked out into the street.

He felt the paper rustle against him all the way back to his flat. The way it sat in a crinkling lump against him made his skin crawl until it was all he felt, hyper-focused on it with every step.

Get it off. Get it off. Get it off. The mantra shrieked in his mind.

He hurried up the steps bypassing the laboratory and unlocked the door to his flat. Ezra tore the telegram from his vest as soon as the door closed, ignoring it as it fluttered to the floor.

A frustrated growl built up in his chest.

No.

Her face swam in front of his eyes, the face of a nine-year-old girl who trusted him but didn't know what he'd done.

He pushed his fists into the hollows of his eyes until they blurred, but then he could hear her voice.

"I do not wish to be called Miss any longer. Call me Magdalena or call me nothing at all," she'd demanded.

Ezra slammed the heels of his palms down over his ears, again and again as he lowered himself to the floor.

This wasn't why he had taken Magdalena as an apprentice. It wasn't. This wasn't purely the act of a guilty conscience. She was bright and full of potential. He wasn't making it up to a child he'd known for hardly any time at all so many years ago.

Liar! The word was like a hiss. It made him feel dirty, but it was a filth he couldn't be rid of, no matter how many times he tried to wash it off.

CHAPTER TWENTY

Magdalena

Once again, fate worked in her favor as Magdalena settled into her apprenticeship. Dr. Talbot was quieter lately but less hesitant to answer questions.

Now there was a giddiness in her step when she'd go on house calls with him, as though her steps knew that the more she traveled down this road, the easier it would be for women of the future.

Magdalena nearly memorized the bones of the body after putting it to song. There were a few, sparse auditory bones she couldn't seem to recall, as they didn't fit well into her little rhyme. When she'd shared this difficulty with the doctor, he'd referred her back to his journal and the numeric system he used.

It was likely the dullest way one could memorize anything. When she'd voiced the opinion, he sighed before rustling around in the armoire and withdrawing a complete skeleton, held together by strings and wires. He'd hung it up on the coat rack and gestured for her to sort things out herself.

"Rather tall, wasn't he?" she muttered, looking up at its toothy grin. "Happy too."

His back was to her as he fed his beetles strips of raw meat before washing his hands. "You believe it to be male?"

"Yes," She began mentally labeling the bones. It did help to see them in front of her.

"Simply because of its height?" He dried his hands on a linen towel and turned to face her, crossing his arms over his chest. Dark brows furrowed over equally rich eyes.

She knew he was challenging her, predicting that she had no further evidence to support her theory.

She studied the skeletal remains cautiously. Perhaps she'd missed some indicator of it belonging to a female. Carefully, she ran her finger over its hips and crouched nearer for a closer examination of the pelvis.

"He is assuredly male." She nodded slowly. "The weight and thickness of the bones suggest as much, though the pelvis is the best indicator. It is narrower than a woman's where these bones connect." She indicated the location.

He said nothing, so she forged on.

"This area on a woman would be more widely spaced for childbearing. In addition, his hips do not flare outward as a woman's would."

She stood and crossed her own arms, volleying her words. Was this pose intended to be threatening or defensive?

The corner of Dr. Talbot's lips turned upward slowly, a gradual falling away of his stern demeanor and rigid expression. He had a decidedly kind smile when it slipped out so rarely.

He loosened his arms and gestured. "This is John."

Magdalena had learned that nearly anything masculine was "John" to him and nearly everything feminine "Elizabeth."

As she turned away from the skeleton, a darkness on one of the ribs caught her attention, dragging her back for another look. Dr. Talbot kept everything within his possession tidy, and she confirmed as much by checking the rest of the skeleton. It was spotless, suggesting the discoloration and roughness in that particular space occurred before or at John's demise.

She rubbed a finger over the faint splintering of the bone. The evidence was undeniable.

"Fourth intercostal space on the left sternal border. You noticed?" His moods were ever-changing and flighty, one moment challenging her and the next offering his own form of hesitant appreciation.

Dr. Talbot lifted a knife from the tabletop near his experiments and loosely grasped the handle. In a swift movement, he brought the knife through the space and slid the sharp edge directly through the minuscule crack in the ribs. It was a near perfect fit, and she understood the implications.

"Murder is one I'll never understand." Magdalena shuddered and stepped away from the unfortunate John.

"He was a thief." Dr. Talbot shrugged and tossed the knife on the tabletop.

"Regardless, is it not up to the legal systems in our country to determine consequences?"

"You trust London with justice?" He scoffed. "The police will litter the staircase down to—"

He stopped himself, glancing at her. Rather abruptly, he turned and retrieved his top hat and overcoat from the chair.

"I've many things to show you today."

He didn't await any sort of response and slipped his arms into his sleeves.

Magdalena followed suit, buttoning her coat as she followed him.

His pace was impressive, and she imagined she would gain speed as time progressed. However, for now she was nearly panting as she pursued him.

By the time she caught up with him, he sat in a borrowed carriage impatiently holding the door.

"We'll miss something important if you don't hurry up." He let go of the door in her face.

Magdalena reopened it with a scowl. "If you'd provide more than eight seconds before switching from one task to another, I'd possibly be able to keep up."

She clambered in, latching the door firmly behind her as she sat across from him. "As much as I'd like to, I cannot read your mind."

"Small favors." Discomfort made him look away. "I dismembered a body three days ago and scattered it about my cottage to study the decomposition. It takes approximately forty-eight hours for insect eggs to be present on the body. Within twenty-four hours after being laid, the larvae hatch and immediately feed on the flesh. I don't wish for you to miss it."

Magdalena's stomach lurched at the thought of any variety of eggs present on a dismembered body, let alone said eggs hatching and subsequently feasting.

"How thoughtful," she said weakly.

He nodded, accepting this as appreciation.

She could hardly look at his jar of beetles and didn't imagine this would go well. "Dare I ask how you got a body for the sole purpose of dissection and dispersal?"

He chuckled. "Dispersal. I like that description."

Ezra explained his working relationship with the police court. She was only half listening as she thought of the vacant cottage.

"Why do you prefer living in town?" she interrupted.

For a moment, his face held no mask, and expressions shifted across his face like a deck of cards. He wasn't going to tell her. Not yet.

"I lived there long ago ... as a boy. I'd not been back in fifteen years before Áine's passing."

He said the words softly. Come to think of it, she'd never heard him raise his voice. He was mellow and patient despite how he smothered the characteristics with insults and sarcasm. One had to protect themselves as best they could, and those were clearly his weapons of choice.

"You returned only for Áine, didn't you?" Her gaze softened.

He gave a jerk of his chin, staring out the window.

"And your mother?"

"Passed on in childbirth."

"My parents drowned when I was nine. I lost them to the river Thames."

"Drowned?" His chin rose sharply, and his eyes met hers.

They stared at one another in silence.

"Magdalena?" He rasped.

His hand jerked through the space between them, twisting his fist in her coat and tugging her closer.

The doctor's chest heaved with emotion and her pulse sped up. Something about the dread in his eyes filled her with fear.

Ezra

No. Not her. Not like this.

Magdalena

"Dr. Talbot, are you all right?"

He swallowed and blinked away, releasing her.

"You have recovered well."

He leaned his head against the wall and inhaled through his nose, releasing it through his mouth.

Dr. Talbot's eyes, on the contrary, told a different story, a story darker than any history she held claim to. It was the kind of despair that infiltrated one's sleep and tormented them in the night, intertwining memories with the present in a battle for reality.

It was no wonder he didn't like eyes, she decided. Not when his showed a perpetual edge of fear and mistrust. What had happened to him? And why had the mention of drowning prompted such a reaction from him? She opened her mouth to ask, but the words didn't come. Perhaps this was simply a reminder of how he'd saved her from the Serpentine, or maybe the loss of his own mother played a role.

"There are many forces at work in this world, Magdalena," Salomé once said, "and something about life makes men want to die."

"And what force works against life?" she had asked.

"You," Salomé smiled. "You and fate."

She opted not to push the doctor, hoping it would encourage him to share more at will.

The closer they grew to the cottage, the more she noticed Dr. Talbot's knee bounce and nearly reached over to weigh it down.

The carriage slowed to a stop.

"Nothing develops human character more than trauma and misery." She clapped her hands together and clambered out.

"I've developed. Can it stop now?" Dr. Talbot groused, heading for the back pasture.

The grass was tall and dry, near knee high, and she hiked up her skirts to keep up with him. Clearly, he was through with further conversation.

When she caught up with him, he'd moved a large metal grate to the side and crouched low over a severed arm.

Her face flushed.

"Look!" The doctor took a dry twig and used it as a pointer, gesturing toward an invasion of maggots and other insects scattered around the point of severance.

She'd rather not, but his tone was so full of glee she gave it a quick glance.

Oh. Absolutely not.

A breeze swept up the scent and threw it in her face. This was a no for her. Magdalena gagged.

Realizing all too late what was happening, Dr. Talbot launched to his feet, grasped her by the back of the neck, and turned her head away just in time.

Magdalena wasn't one for blushing, but her heart raced and for once she was relieved he didn't spend much time looking at her. She couldn't recall the last time she'd been so thoroughly mortified. Clearly losing her breakfast in front of this man was just the humility she required.

Dr. Talbot covered his nostrils with his knuckles, his eyes widening as he did.

"It is a sympathetic response," he said, now gagging himself. "Could you?"

He gestured to the grate and backed away, every few paces stopping to heave.

"Are you serious right now?" She shrieked after him, using the corner of her apron to swipe at her face.

"I—really cannot."

He gave a last wave toward the metal grate. Then the infuriating man fled with eyes watering.

She gritted her teeth. A gentleman, he was not.

After she managed to heft the crate over the top of the arm, she found him sitting in the dirt, leaning against a stone wall of the cottage.

Lowering herself to sit beside him, she joined him in a puff of skirts and dust.

"Shall we agree to never speak of this again?"

"That would be kind."

She faked a gag, testing her theory, and his body involuntarily mirrored her.

He dragged a palm across his stubbled chin. "Stop," he chuckled, leaning his head back against the wall.

"So I cannot tolerate decaying bodies and you are undone by a gag?" She laughed. "I feel like I possess this great, hidden power."

She flexed her hand into a fist, shaking it like a boxer.

"Don't tell Thaddeus." He rolled his head to the side to look at her. "I take it you aren't up for the other pieces?"

His eyes were dancing, and she couldn't look away.

For once, he didn't either. He stayed just like that, unmoving, unblinking.

"I could manage," she fibbed, hoping she'd acceptably buried the breathlessness she felt. It didn't seem likely he'd pick up on it, even if she hadn't.

The doctor blinked and pressed his thumb and forefinger over his eyelids.

"Liar." He called her bluff and stood to his feet.

Dr. Talbot brushed his palm on his trousers before extending it to her. He'd never done anything like it before, and she stared at the hand to an awkward degree before wrapping her fingers around his forearm so she could avoid touching his skin.

"What was his name?" Discuss the cadaver, she thought. It was a clever distraction.

"Prisoner 214," he joked, "or—"

"—John." She cut off his words knowingly.

Magdalena shuddered at her own thoughts … to cut off.

Dr. Talbot finished his tour of the field of horrors on his own before stopping in the garden and shifting through the soil with a rake. She caught a few of his mutters before he leaned the tool against the barn.

"What did you lose?" She smirked.

"I didn't lose it." He paced a few steps, tugging a fist through his hair with a frustrated growl. "Something took it."

"Took wha—"

A bloodcurdling scream echoed across the fields.

They froze, eyes and bodies slowly turning toward one another as realization settled in.

"This is undeniably turning into a terrible day." She hissed the words as if the screaming woman in the neighbor's yard could hear her.

"Nonsense, things are finally getting interesting."

Skirts in one hand while the other held tightly to her bonnet, she hurried after him through the tall grass.

There, indeed, was a hysterical woman swatting a broom at a beast of a dog.

And there, in the canine's meaty jaw was, most regretfully, a severed head.

The earth spun a bit more quickly for a moment.

"Do something." She glared at Dr. Talbot.

"Consider this a part of your probation." He smothered a grin.

Magdalena looked him right in the eyes and gagged.

His face turned green, and his ornery expression sobered slightly. Palms held up in silent surrender he shrugged his shoulders, looking pitifully at his experiment.

She sighed, knowing full well he'd manipulated her into fetching the head with those soulful brown eyes. He was lucky she was easily charmed.

"Have you any dried meat?" She called to the woman, climbing over a dilapidated fence.

The woman nodded, her face pale as she dropped the broom and hurried into the house.

She returned with a fistful of jerky and pushed it toward Magdalena with shaky hands.

"What is his name?" Magdalena bent toward the mastiff and extended her exchange.

"Artemis." Aptly named.

"Artemis, darling!" Magdalena called to her. "I should have known. You are far too lovely to be a boy."

Artemis ignored her and lay down in the grass, slobbering over the maggot-infested remains.

Dr. Talbot looked like he'd stomp his feet if Magdalena couldn't wrestle the thing away.

This is ridiculous.

"I hope you know you are forever indebted to me." She flung the words at the doctor.

"I'll feed you," he called back, shoving his hands into his pockets and pacing.

The neighbor woman just stood there, eyes like saucers in her pale face.

Magdalena tucked the jerky between her teeth and clapped her hands, hurrying in the opposite direction.

"Artemis!"

Torn between sport and her snack, the dog stared at her a few moments before barking and taking off full pace toward her. She threw the meat a few feet away, and the dog settled down, forgetting all about the head.

Of course, Dr. Talbot made no move to retrieve it.

Frustrated, she untied her apron and jerked it over her head. Stooping, she wrapped the apron around the abandoned head and tucked it under her arm.

Don't think about it. It's a roast. She forced herself to breathe, in through the nose, out through the mouth. Her stomach flipped, in through the nose was a mistake.

Forcing a smile, she addressed the woman who remained frozen in place, watching them.

"Our apologies. We've recently buried some ... family."

"Poor Uncle John." Dr. Talbot's face was bland, but his eyes were alight with humor, and she feared he'd laugh outright.

Magdalena gave him what she hoped was a glare of warning. She nodded another apology, and they quickly took their leave.

The head weighed more than one would expect, and the moisture began seeping through her apron and into her armpit.

Halfway through the field, she pushed it toward the doctor's chest, ignoring his sound of displeasure.

"Take. Your. Head. Sir." She ground out.

She could not possibly change out of her clothes quickly enough, and her stomach was weak with the events.

He hesitantly took it, outstretched before him as though it were a serving tray, to prevent soiling his clothing as she had.

Back in the garden, he washed his hands, made a handful of notes, and made a mold of the canine imprints before adding a grate over the top of it.

"There is likely something you can wear inside." He jerked his chin toward the cottage.

He hesitated behind her as she stepped over the threshold, filling the door frame with his broad shoulders. Gripping the door frame, his eyes darted around to shadowy corners before he exhaled and followed.

After tugging back a sheet, he crouched and opened a wooden chest, shuffling things to the side as he looked for something she could wear.

These belongings must have been his mother's.

"Are you certain?" She could attempt to wash her own dress. It would be damp, but it would be clean.

"Mm." He nodded and pushed a dress into her hands before gesturing toward what looked like a kitchenette and washroom. "She means nothing to me. Soap is there, water too. I'll be upstairs. Let me know when you're through."

He stepped toward the stairs, looking unsure.

She waited until his footsteps sounded overhead before changing quickly into the rich burgundy dress with black lace trimming and fabric-covered buttons. Someone loved his mother, that much was clear. Aside from a few moth holes across the knees, the dress had aged well. Magdalena was taller than his mother must have been, and the dress fell to the tops of her boots and stretched a bit across her middle. Other than that, it fit decently.

Gently she reached to close the lid but stopped short. A stuffed toy, a dog perhaps, rested on the top. She withdrew its limp body, turning it in her hands. Had it been the doctor's?

"I'm finished," she called up the steps, holding the plaything carefully.

Dr. Talbot trudged down the stairs and paused on the staircase, his face cast in shadows and hands buried in his pockets. She wanted to ask if this was still okay, her wearing his mother's dress, but he hurried down the rest of the steps and brushed out the front door before she could.

"Put Boots back in the box and fasten the lid," he called as he went.

A dog called Boots. It was a precious thought—Dr. Talbot with a toy. Him as a child at all.

"You are indebted to me, don't you forget," she reminded him when they were back in the borrowed carriage.

"I'll feed you at the laboratory."

"No porridge?"

"No porridge," he agreed with a small smile.

Those smiles were beginning to slip out a bit more, she noticed. She'd file them away in a box if she could, only to look at them when things grew dim.

CHAPTER TWENTY-THREE

Magdalena

The first indication that something was amiss in the laboratory was the fact that Mrs. Keene sat fidgeting behind her desk even though her regular hours had long since passed.

"Who do we have waiting, Mrs. Keene?" Magdalena whispered.

Dr. Talbot backtracked toward the door.

"Tea as I wait?" A man's voice demanded.

"Yes, sir, I'll be right in," Mrs. Keene responded quickly.

"Who is that?" Magdalena's brows furrowed. She turned to the doctor when the secretary said nothing.

She could tell from Dr. Talbot's expression that the man in the other room wasn't welcome. His face had drained of its color, and he'd sucked in his cheeks as if gaunt. His lips were white and thin as a strangled sound caught in his throat.

Fear.

"Doctor," she whispered, catching the lapels of his jacket and raising on her toes to look him in the eyes. "Go upstairs."

She could almost hear what he'd say to her.

Don't look at me. Don't see this.

He nodded distantly, eyes flooded with moisture as he cocked his head in the hint of an acknowledgment. Then he shook her off and fled up the darkened staircase.

Mrs. Keene came and gripped her elbow, eyes full of worry. "I don't think you ought to go in there."

Magdalena gave a soft smile. It was the mask of a smile she wore when pretending to be all right.

"The things I ought to do, and the things that I do, are often two very different things. How about that tea?"

There was no one else here to save the day. No one was coming to Dr. Talbot's rescue. It was to her advantage that she was hungry. She was a lesser human when she hadn't been properly fed.

Heavy footsteps moved harshly across the wooden floor. He'd grown impatient.

Magdalena preferred the upper hand, and she took a deep breath before stepping into the doorway.

She didn't know what she'd expected. Perhaps a man of war or a hulking figure with a ghoulish face and beefy arms. He was neither.

His shoulders were broad, and a thick beard covered an olive complexion. There was a familiar square chin, though his was rounded by age, and dark brown eyes glared down at her.

A memory, faint and twisted by time, tempted her into recognition, but she didn't catch it in time.

"Em?" The tension in his eyes softened as he stared at her, and he gasped out a huff of pain.

He crossed the space between them with sure footsteps, stopping too close for comfort as he traced the black lace on her sleeve.

"Where did you get this?" He rasped out, his gaze hardening. He didn't wait for an answer. "You shouldn't have it."

"How may I help you?" She tugged her arm away.

The man straightened his shoulders and crossed his arms over his chest, looking her head to toe with nothing but judgment in his gaze. She wouldn't shift under his stare, no matter how much she wanted to.

"My son, Ezra Talbot. You know of him? This is his office, or so I've been told."

"I know him." So this was Dr. Talbot's father? She kept her expression neutral as she studied him.

She crossed the room and lowered herself into a chair before her knees knocked together. Obviously, she knew him. She wouldn't be in his laboratory otherwise. This man reminded her of her mother. He made her feel inferior without even speaking.

"'Son' is a loose term, wouldn't you say?" She'd mentally prepared for war, and now she would have it.

"Excuse me?" Mr. Talbot's eyes narrowed into twin slits with nostrils flaring.

The empty cottage. The tidbits she knew assisted in goading him.

"You're back in London?" She ignored his immediate defense and crossed a dainty ankle one over the other, settling back.

"I am."

"For how long?"

"As long as duty places me here."

She didn't know his profession, and there lay her first misstep.

"Arthur Talbot." He didn't put out an introductory hand.

She didn't offer her own name.

Mrs. Keene brought in a clattering tea service, her nerves having got the best of her.

Magdalena stood and took the tray from her, setting it on the small tableside.

"Tea?" she asked, grateful for the distraction. She didn't ask how he took his, nor did she care.

"Please." An irritating little smile tugged at the corner of his lips.

"How long have you been working for Ezra?"

With. "Some time now."

"You're a poor liar." He accepted the saucer she stretched toward him.

"I beg your pardon?" Magdalena took a slow sip of the scalding liquid, watching him over the brim of her cup.

Mr. Talbot blew his tea and returned his cup to the saucer upon his knee.

"Your hair." He gestured. "It isn't accustomed to being pulled back. It's as wild as its master."

He was right. Her curls still managed to find their way out, no matter how tightly she pulled them back. Magdalena fought the urge to tuck the wisps behind her ear.

"You've recently changed soaps, as well. This one is making your skin dry and red with frequent washings." He smirked, raising his teacup toward her. "And there is another problem."

She wouldn't play this game; he was good at it.

"You like him significantly more than he likes you." He took a sip.

Mr. Talbot's words stung more than she'd admit. The truth could always pack a punch. Fortunately for her, she knew how to dodge.

She knew he was goading her, backing her into a corner in hopes she'd lash out and share his son's business. She wouldn't.

"You do not know my occupation, which suggests you are not so close to Ezra as to know the details."

Magdalena tilted her chin and let an annoying smile flick the corner of her lips. It was just enough of an insinuation he could be wrong. He wasn't, but that sort of thing had always irked her mother.

Mr. Talbot's face reddened slightly. Perfect.

"I take it you are wearing my late wife's dress out of necessity, not personal preference. He got you into some sort of mess, didn't he? He's always getting into scrapes he can't get out of."

He took a smug drink of tea like he was a master of the game he played. Oh, how fiercely she wanted to beat him.

Magdalena said nothing, silently seething over each of his correct deductions. Somehow, she sensed in him too, something deeply burrowed between the lines of his words. He was bluffing.

"Lastly, he will never marry. You could not be his wife, but you look the variety who would easily be fool enough to believe a woman could become a physician's apprentice." He laughed, a humorless sort of sound.

Mr. Talbot stood, drained his cup, and set it on the serving tray.

"Where is he hiding now?"

"He has business to attend to." Magdalena matched his mood and gusto by gulping down her tea.

The cup clattered back to the tray as she stood. She wouldn't taste anything for a week, and the heat felt akin to drinking directly from a fire.

"His address," the man demanded.

Her eyes landed on the mail Mrs. Keene set beside the table for Dr. Talbot.

"It's no wonder he burned all your letters … detective." Magdalena chuckled, too, with equal solemnity. "Get out."

It made sense now, why he'd wash his hands after setting a detective's letters aflame. She wasn't sure she was right until the man flinched.

"A dutiful little guard dog he has." Detective Talbot gave a sad smile.

A small part of her wanted to dig through his pain and find its origin, but the way he spoke about her doctor irked her. The man was on his way toward the adjoining doorway when she spoke, her tone grave.

"Skunks." She stopped him with this unexpected word. "They make an awful stench, wouldn't you agree?"

The detective paused. He wasn't used to someone who didn't back down.

"Mm," he grunted.

Like father, like son.

"They become a bit bold in their endeavors. London's parks had a wretched problem with them a few years back, I do recall." Magdalena stared past him. "Few predators have any interest in eating something so pungent. In the end, nature did something rather curious as a solution—it increased its own population of great horned owls and red-tailed hawks. Natural predators of the skunk, as you would have it."

Mr. Talbot clearly did not see any sort of connection in this conversation.

"You are safe from me, Miss ..." He realized he didn't know her name, her first advantage. "I have nothing in common with predatory fowl."

He smirked, crossing the threshold into the entryway.

"That's correct." Magdalena followed, turning the full force of her glare on him. "You make quite a stink. Unfortunately for you, I am much like those birds. I have no sense of smell."

She reached around him and opened the door.

He stepped into the hall with an annoying laugh. "Perhaps I was wrong. Maybe Ezra does like you. He's always had a thing for fire."

She slammed the door in his face, locked it, and leaned against it with a shaky exhale. She could feel Mrs. Keene's eyes on her but wasn't ready to meet them.

"Do tell him I have need of him. It's regarding a case." Detective Talbot's muffled voice sounded from the other side.

Magdalena waited for a bit, seeing Mrs. Keene off, before she took a lantern and locked the laboratory behind her. Hopefully, she'd given him enough time. She couldn't go home without looking in on him first.

The steps creaked eerily beneath her feet.

Turn back, don't go, they trilled on his behalf.

She paused for a moment after knocking, allowing him to send her away, but the words never came.

She let herself in.

Dr. Talbot had left himself in the dark. Holding the lantern up, she searched the nearly empty flat.

This is all he has? She'd not seen a home that resembled its owner more so than this. A small table, single chair, and place setting for one offered a glimpse of his life.

There was a bite of chill in the air as the sun set and she started a fire in the hearth. He didn't like the cold. She didn't want him to be alone, Magdalena realized. She wanted to stay with him.

Life tended to distribute unequal measures. It poured out darkness into unfortunate hosts until they burst under the pressure.

When the fire crackled and the warmth reached out in hazy tendrils, he spoke from the edge of the room.

"Pathetic, aren't I?" He clicked his tongue. "The funny thing is … I knew he was returning to London. I had ample time to prepare."

Dr. Talbot sighed as she searched for him in the darkness.

She found him then, not sitting on the simple bed nor the chair but on the floor, back to the wall, knees to chest, arms wrapped around himself. Like a boy—one who was hiding.

"I believe that is called premeditation. It is generally illegal."

She crossed the room and lowered herself to the floor beside him.

"Why do you do that?" His smile was half reluctance, half grief.

"Because standing is tiresome." She tilted her head toward him and smiled.

He blew out a sigh. "Do you take anything seriously? Shouldn't you have run away from this disaster long before now?" He gestured to himself.

They were both a disaster. She was simply a very good liar.

"Would that make you happy?" She waited for the answer with bated breath.

"I don't think that is something I get to be." Dr. Talbot looked away.

"What?"

"Happy," he murmured.

Chapter Twenty-Four

Ezra

She didn't say anything for a moment, and Ezra wondered if she knew how to hold a mature conversation. It didn't seem likely, but he was tired.

Drained of civility, emptied of pretenses, and weakened from holding up walls, Magdalena seemed prepared to climb. He didn't like seeing her in his mother's dress. He had always hated the woman, and seeing something that belonged to her being worn by Magdalena made him despise her slightly less.

"I have enough." She leaned her head back against the wall. "Happiness," she added. "Too much really. It's a bit selfish of me to keep it all for myself."

She pulled an invisible thread from the palm of her hand and extended it toward him.

"You hold one end and I'll hold the other." She smiled. "Happiness is best shared, and my last person is dead, so there is that."

He felt ridiculous, but he reached for the non-existent fiber, wondering who had carried the other end before him.

"Wait!" She snatched her fingertips back and blew on them. "Awkward. There was a bit of dust on it."

She stretched it back across the space between them.

Ezra couldn't help chuckling before begrudgingly taking the strand. He tucked it in his vest pocket and gave it a pat for safe keeping.

"Why did he come?" She wrapped her arms around her knees and rested her chin on top of them.

He stood and shuffled through a stack of papers on his bedside table, retrieving a newspaper clipping and the telegram Roland had written to his father about the situation at Bethlem Royal Hospital.

His eyes darted between the chair and the space beside her.

The chair? When had his mind started presenting his needs as a question?

Hesitantly he sat back down on the floor. For now, his mind permitted it.

"I recall my brother-in-law fussing over this one." She scanned the news article. "They didn't allow a full inspection of the premises. Is that a police concern?"

Her brows scrunched as she reached for a report from the chief inspector.

"It ought to be, but no." He leaned in closer and pointed to the form she held. "The previous president resigned this past summer. This new one is a bit of a dunce; I don't think he'll make it much longer with these rumors."

"Frank mentioned rumors. I thought he was simply being dramatic." She frowned. "What are they?"

"Rumor has it that madness can be purchased at Bethlem."

"You cannot purchase madness." Worry flickered in her eyes.

"You can purchase anything for the right price." A shudder rippled through him. "I've got to visit a patient there tomorrow. I've agreed to look into things for the chief inspector briefly while I'm there. I shouldn't be long, and you can wait in the laboratory until I return."

He wouldn't take her with him. There were things in the asylum that could extinguish even her eternal optimism.

She was already shaking her head with a familiar, stubborn tilt to her chin. "I'm coming with you."

"Not there." He set his chin. "You shouldn't be there."

"Tell me, Dr. Talbot. Where do they send those with severe melancholy?"

The same place they sent men like him. He tugged at the cravat that was suddenly too tight. He didn't look at her but got to his feet.

"No," he repeated, fingers curling into fists beside him. "You do not belong there."

"It is likely the only place I belong," Magdalena snapped. "Do not insult me by offering your protection from darkness," she added more softly. "Not even yours."

He sucked in a fractured inhale.

"It is time for you to go home," he ground out, yanking his cravat off the rest of the way.

He despised confrontation. The way it made him sweat and his heart race. Mostly, he didn't like the way arguing with her made his stomach fill with dread.

The problem was he wasn't sure how one disagreed without hands flying or verbal assault. Ezra didn't want to do either—not to her.

The dread in his stomach turned to acid over the thought. No one would touch her. Especially not him.

"Dr. Talbot?" She stood, reaching for him.

An involuntary shudder rippled through him. Don't touch me.

Her hand dropped like she heard the voice of fear herself.

People entered asylums and never left. Every time he went, he wondered what they would do if they knew his mind felt things that didn't exist.

Perhaps this was why he didn't want her to see what lay within the walls of Bedlam—it would be a glimpse into himself. She shouldn't be exposed to what-ifs and painful possibilities.

Why won't you let her decide for herself? The futile remnants of past emotion tugged at him.

He stood in the darkness looking after her as she climbed into her carriage to return home.

She turned back to look at him before closing the carriage door.

"Goodnight, Dr. Talbot," Magdalena said, then held out her palm and tugged an invisible thread.

It wasn't logical, it was ridiculous even, but the little string he'd tucked in his pocket grew taunt in response.

He shouldn't have taken that peculiar little thing. For one, it wasn't real. For the other, if her happiness was connected to his, she'd chase it the rest of her life only for it to hang just beyond her reach.

So get her a ladder.

He scoffed at the ridiculous idea. It seemed like something she would think.

He turned around, slowly taking the steps back to his apartment. Part of him worried she wouldn't be back tomorrow. He'd said things she hadn't wanted to hear and there was nothing to keep her.

He froze there on the steps, gripping the rail to steady himself.

"You stupid man," he rasped. "You want to keep her."

That would never do.

***

Bethlem Royal Hospital lay stretched across St. George's Fields. The drive was large enough to fit two carriages side by side and sat situated between an expanse of orchards and gardens. The reform had brought positive changes to asylums, and many of the patients worked in the fields picking the last fruit and vegetables of the season.

"It's beautiful." Magdalena's forehead was pressed to a growler window as she watched the patients and the trees slip past. "Look at them—what are they doing?"

"Harvesting." His arms crossed his chest, and he couldn't keep his knee from jostling as it often did when he anticipated something unpleasant.

You shouldn't have let her come.

But what else could he have done? She'd climbed up into the carriage and refused to move like a petulant toddler. It was either that or drag her out, and he knew instinctively she would have made a scene if he'd tried.

"There are expectations if I bring you in." He pulled his medical bag from the bench and twisted his fingers around the handle until his knuckles turned white.

"Yes, sir." She gave the worst salute he had ever seen, which was saying something considering Thaddeus used to fail at them intentionally.

"You will not ask me any questions until we leave. There are things inside I will not be able to explain, things I disagree with but cannot change. If at any point things become too much, you are to leave and wait for me at the top of the stairs. Do you understand?"

Ezra met her gaze with an intentional sharpness and waited until she gave a hesitant nod.

The little spark in her eyes seemed to flicker. Was it fear? Doubt? He wasn't sure, but he didn't like whatever it was.

There was no further time to warn or prepare as the growler stopped in front of the hospital. Wide and ornate stairs led to towering wooden doors between massive pillars. Expenses hadn't been spared while building the asylum, as if in some vain hope it would be viewed as a sanctuary and not the bedlam people knew it to be.

Tucking his fingers inside the corner of his coat, he opened the heavy door and ushered her in.

"Welcome"—a man inside tipped a non-existent hat in their direction—"to chaos. May I check your coats, caps, or sanity at the door?" His teeth flashed with a caustic smile.

"Don't—" Ezra held up a hand to warn her.

Magdalena appraised him. "No, thank you, we'll keep them for—"

The resident blinked hazy eyes until they cleared, and as if seeing them for the first time, he smiled once more.

"Welcome"—he mimicked the lifting of a cap—"to chaos."

The same man, the same words, and the same pattern no matter how long one stood there.

Ezra sighed and tugged Magdalena along by her elbow as she cast curious glances over her shoulder.

"He's done that as long as I've visited. Wounded his memory in the Opium War."

Without a suspicious amount of luck, that could have been Thaddeus.

"Thank you," she whispered back. She may as well have shouted for how loudly it seemed to echo through the foyer.

The entrance hall was spotless with swept tiles beneath their feet and vaulted ceilings that seemed even taller with the grand windows towering above them. Affixed to the wall between every casement sat a bust of monetary donors. The sickly-sweet scent of medicines hung in the air.

Just get downstairs, see to the patient quickly, ask a few simple questions on Roland's behalf, and get out. That was all he needed to do.

The click of Magdalena's heels was loud.

Click. Click. Click. It seemed to resound in his mind until he clenched his jaw more tightly with every click.

You're spiraling. Ezra inhaled through his nose and read any sign he passed, attempting to distract himself. It worked, but only slightly.

"Psst." A whisper cut through the quiet as Ezra led Magdalena down the hall.

His hand was still on her elbow, and he dropped it, rubbing his palm across his slacks before returning his hands to his pockets.

"Psst." The whisper repeated more persistently. "Do not rouse the parrot."

Ezra spotted a woman hiding amongst the potted ferns.

"Keep walking," he urged his apprentice.

She stopped. Of course she stopped, she hardly listened to anything. But this—this directive he needed her to heed. The more times she paused, the longer it would take for him to get out.

A woman with graying sandy hair parted the ferns like the proverbial Red Sea and looked both ways.

"Lory is a naughty little thing," the woman whispered. "She says he doesn't speak, but if you listen closely, he says the most terrible things."

"There you are, Mrs. Lewis." A female attendant wearing a tidy gray uniform with auburn hair, swept from around the corner. "You are tardy for tea, dear. Do come along. How did you get out here?"

He was convinced this attendant must be a saint.

The resident muttered under her breath.

Next to him, he heard Magdalena gasp.

"Mara? Mara Spillman, is that you?"

Magdalena crossed the hall before he had time to grasp the back of her coat and threw her arms around the attendant.

Not a saint, a distraction. He glared at the back of his apprentice's head in hopes her thick skull wasn't enough protection from his irritated gaze.

"Good morning to you, Miss." Mara's eyes widened in surprise over Magdalena's shoulder.

Evidently, they weren't familiar enough to be caught in an embrace. Not that this seemed to bother Magdalena. He had half a hunch she'd cozy up to a pigeon so long as they'd been introduced at least once prior.

Feeling a bit obligated to keep her from making everyone else uncomfortable, he detached her arms from around Mara.

Magdalena gave him a sheepish shrug and took a few steps backward.

"It's me," Magdalena gestured to herself. "We met in the park. The chestnut?"

She made a gesture like she was choking and wrapped her hands around her own throat.

Ezra cast his eyes toward the ceiling and blew a forced exhale from his lips. He had undoubtedly hand-selected the most awkward woman to be his understudy. This would be his protege? Something in his gut stopped the insulting undertone of his thoughts and twisted it into feeling more complimentary, as though her nature was endearing. He cleared his throat, hoping it would clear his mind.

"Oh, yes!" Mara whispered, peering around them toward her superior's office. "It is good to see you. I never did properly thank you."

"Are you well?" Magdalena reached for her hand and squeezed it.

Ezra shuffled behind her, alternating his weight from one foot to another. He wasn't accustomed to waiting on others. If she were anyone else, he would simply leave her here. But he knew with it being her, he'd do so only to return and find her acquainting herself with the criminal lunatics in the rear wings.

"I don't want tea." The resident, Mrs. Lewis, stepped between them, tugging on Mara's dress. "I want something else."

"Perhaps a bit of lemonade after your tea?" Mara smiled gently.

"Give it to Lory. He likes tea." Mrs. Lewis spat on the floor, narrowly missing his boots.

Ezra shuddered. Managing to catch Magdalena's eye, he jerked his chin toward the men's ward.

Funny how her gaze didn't make his skin crawl as much as it once had.

"Rumor has it she once worked for the Queen. Lory has long since passed on, I've heard." Mara ducked her head with a soft smile, turning toward the women's ward with one arm looped around Mrs. Lewis's waist.

"Dead?" Mrs. Lewis screeched. She shook her fist, face flushed with intensity. "Good riddance, you wicked bird."

"Delusion," Ezra whispered low in Magdalena's ear.

Magdalena blinked with her glimmering wide eyes and smiled. "I like her."

Hadn't she said the same thing to him? Was it something she said flippantly? Something vaguely like jealousy pricked him. It was unlikely. The only thing he'd ever been envious of was when someone else got their hands on one of his cadavers.

Keep telling yourself that.

Ezra shook off the thought and pulled her along past the kitchen and down the men's ward.

The hall was long with a row of rooms on their left and windows on their right. The closer they came, the more his stomach swirled. It was one thing to go alone and another entirely to go with Magdalena. It seemed she could read him far too well, and he didn't wish for anything to be uncovered here.

Taking a left, they merged nearer to the criminal building in the rear. Even prisoners were treated better than the others. He tried to stop thinking.

She won't like this. He snorted over that one. No one liked this.

"Do you have a favorite?" she asked.

"Mm?" He blinked at her, wondering if he'd missed something.

"A favorite patient?" She gestured to the door he paused just beyond.

He scoffed. "Do you have a favorite mental illness?"

"Of course." Her expression suggested she did, in fact, have a preferred brain abnormality. She looked pensive for a moment; the corners of her lips slightly downturned. "But they are not their minds, Dr. Talbot. I would think you, of all people, would know that."

Yes, they are. This felt like a personal taunt.

"Mm." He nodded, tugging at his collar. "Why does this not surprise me?"

He didn't want to ask her any questions. Not about this. He just wanted her to stop talking.

Ezra sighed. "There is a door …"

"I see that." She rapped on it with her knuckles, raising a brow with a smirk.

"It goes to the basement." He swallowed the rising dread. How could one explain this?

"As doors labeled 'basement' often do." She gestured toward the sign.

Ezra growled, annoyance plucking at his temper.

"Very well. I will not warn you." He thrust open the door with the corner of his coat. "Keep in mind that I tried."

With every downward step, it grew colder, like the stone retained a chill that could reach far beyond the bones, and he saw her shiver. Ezra wanted to tell her he knew it was ugly down there. That they were dangerous, that he didn't have a cure for the madness beneath, but the words caught on a dumb tongue and stopped at his teeth.

This wasn't the space for the criminals. This wasn't where the mad still had mind enough for hobbies.

This was the place for screaming.

His pulse increased and he could feel it beating in his ears.

Whoosh. Whoosh. Whoosh. The madness upstairs was a child's plaything in comparison to what lay beyond this solid oak door.

"Dr. Talbot?" Magdalena tugged at his sleeve.

"Mm."

He retrieved a lantern from a hook before selecting a match from a tray on the landing and striking it on his boot. His fingers trembled, and he flexed his jaw. Perhaps she hadn't noticed. He didn't want her to.

"I am not afraid of the dark," she said softly.

"You should be," he murmured.

Eyes, they were his least favorite thing in the basement. He handed her the lantern, feeling partly guilty. The eyes always followed the light.

Ezra slipped the key into the lock, turning it before pocketing it. Slowly, like his hand had a mind of its own, he reached for Magdalena's arm and wrapped his fingers around her wrist.

It was safer for her if she stayed close. That's all this was.

Magdalena sucked in a sharp breath, "What ar—"

Her words stopped when he pushed open the door with the corner of his coat. It was either the blackness beyond that stunned her to silence or the immediate stench that coated the insides of their nostrils and slipped down their throats.

CHAPTER TWENTY-FIVE

Ezra

The door slammed behind them, trapping him. There was nowhere to flee. Between the iron rungs, reflective in the light of the lantern, three sets of eyes turned toward them.

"Fate be with us," Magdalena uttered.

He felt her shift closer to him. Shaking loose his hold on her arm, she wrapped her fingers around his elbow.

Not much luck that would do her. This was terrifying enough for a grown man—now he'd have to pretend it wasn't the thing of nightmares.

As if on cue, a shrill shriek and cry erupted down the hall, only to be passed from one cell to the next, growing louder as it came closer.

The sound made his ears ring, and he covered them, involuntarily tugging her hand up with it. She didn't let go.

The light glistened in the moisture that crept beneath the cells and along the walls. He didn't want to consider what the liquids were. The smell was enough to offer suggestions.

He stepped into the basement, and the door closed like an invisible draft had sucked it back into its notch.

"This way," he called over the uproar.

Her hand may as well have been sutured to his arm for how tightly she clung to him.

As their eyes adjusted to the darkness, a woman threw herself against the bars of her cell, hissing and baring her teeth.

Magdalena flinched away.

Send her upstairs.

But this was reality. This was the darkness she insisted didn't frighten her. Perhaps the only thing to keep her safe was the natural inclination of trepidation.

The procedure room door was cracked as they approached, and a bit of light and chatter crept around it. Two men held a conversation, and he heard the unmistakable sound of a swing twisting. Why couldn't they have simply shut the door?

He reached to pull it closed.

"Wait," Magdalena whispered, her fingers tensing on his bicep.

The crevice of light slipping from the door illuminated a line across her face as she peered within.

He knew what she would see. There would be a patient strapped to a chair suspended in the air by two ropes, which would then be twisted and released in a violent oscillation.

She gasped. "What are they doi…"

Her voice trailed off as he heard them release the swing and a sickening groan followed.

"Stop," she murmured.

He tried to tug her along, but she didn't move.

"I said, stop!" She shouted, heat flooding into her complexion.

The last word warbled ever so slightly as she let go of his arm and slammed the door against the wall with both palms.

The orderlies sputtered in surprise, and one flailed for a chair leg to stop its twisting.

A massive man sat in the chair, his head lolling to the side as drool trickled down his chin and onto his bare chest. It was cold. The man should have a shirt. But this wasn't something Ezra could fix.

"Who let you down here, Miss? You shouldn't be here."

The orderly grimaced, his light brown hair plastered to his sweaty head. Ezra could see a bruise forming under his left eye.

The second man Ezra recognized from the hospital. He was thin, of medium height, with dark hair and crooked yellow teeth.

He gestured toward Ezra and gave a tilt of his chin in some sort of silent instruction.

"This is prescribed, Miss. It's not your concern. Please close the procedure door on your way out."

The first attendant dragged the gray sleeve of his uniform across his brow.

Magdalena backed away, shaking her head, and closed the door with one last look toward the patient. His face, Ezra knew would be etched in her memory just as those before him were branded into Ezra's.

She paced beyond the door for a moment, as if attempting to rationalize or find a cure. Neither was possible.

"He is a man. How can they do this?" Her voice cracked. She gestured to the patients but didn't wait for a response. "Would you?"

Ezra was already shaking his head. This was not his doing. While he didn't have a cure, he knew what didn't work.

"No," he said simply.

"If he were not mad before the spinning, he likely is now."

She tugged at a loose curl so violently he wondered if she'd pull it out altogether.

He gestured to the solid door at the end of the hall with its barred cut-out at the top.

"Let's see my patient and be done with it."

There was a reason his patient was the only one kept behind a solid door. He was the embodiment of rage and fury. The man lashed out at both light and sound and required a firm hand with many restraints.

"What is your prescription for our patient?"

Ours. A softness slipped into that space in his chest, and he rubbed at it like it was tender and sensitive.

She wouldn't like his answer.

"There is no cure for his madness, Magdalena."

"What?" She blinked dread back up at him.

She wasn't understanding this truth. Magdalena, though touched by some of the pains of life, was innocent, unaware of how truly impossible things were. Life, real life, was pain. It shattered people into powdery shards until there was nothing left to puzzle back together.

Ezra was life. Ezra was pain.

It was this reminder that made him speak harshly.

"While I may be able to fix this man's body, I will not be able to repair his mind. Are you prepared for that? I am not this hero you have created me to be in your head. This reality is wicked and dark. There is. No. Hope."

He stepped closer to her until his chest nearly bumped into hers.

However little logic it may be, the thing that shined in her eyes seemed to catch fire in the wake of his words. Like it tasted the despair and feasted on it.

They stood there in the din of patient noises with chests heaving. Neither spoke.

"Touch me?" she whispered.

Don't. He flinched when the feeling of his thoughts resounded in his mind. But she hadn't asked permission to touch him—she wanted him to touch her.

He didn't understand. The way the air around them seemed to thicken, or the way the temperature increased when she reached for his sleeve and used it to lift his hand to her face.

He didn't understand any of it.

You've touched her before, Ezra reminded himself. Yes, he'd done an examination before, but this? This was different, like a longing built up in his stomach that begged to see if her skin was soft or how the faint cleft of her chin might feel beneath his thumb.

Ezra flexed his fingers, barely brushing against an errant curl. He imagined moving his hands through her hair and took in a shuddery inhale.

You want this? A part of him seemed to ask.

His mouth was parched, and he dragged his tongue over his teeth.

You do! It accused.

It had every right to sound incriminating. Only three people, including himself, knew what he'd done. Her name was enough reminder. She'd never forgive him if she knew … and he would never ask her to.

He dropped his hand and looked away, brushing his palm against his trousers.

Magdalena released his arm, letting her fingers slip off the hem of his coat. She didn't move, she didn't blink, she hardly seemed to breathe. How she knew when he was at war with himself, he couldn't understand, but she stepped away from him with a tempered sadness in her eyes.

"For a moment," she smiled softly, "I saw hope in your eyes."

Then she reached into his pocket and removed the key he'd tucked inside.

She's wrong.

"The thing about hope," she said, inserting the key in the lock, "is that it doesn't die. It simply goes dormant."

The door clicked and she pushed it open slowly.

She turned to look at him, "I'm going to wake that hope up."

Like a spider along his spine, the words made him shudder. The flame in her lantern swooshed wildly in the stagnant air of the cell before it stabilized and flickered safely in the dark.

She squared her shoulders and stepped into the room.

"What's his name?" she asked.

How had he nearly forgotten where they were?

"Franz." His tongue felt thick, and he cleared his throat.

Franz was suspended, arms extended over his head by two sturdy chains and rooted to the floor by foot locks. He'd lowered himself to his knees against the discomfort and fatigue.

Ezra felt sick. This was a wicked thing they'd done.

He took the lantern from Magdalena and hung it from a post, clearing his throat. "Franz."

His tone was brusque. He wasn't known for his bedside manner, and what transpired in the hall left him more shaken than he already was.

The young man, no more than nineteen, wore only a pair of linen breeches. They were saturated, and the pungent odor coming from him made it quickly known what the puddle on the floor was. He'd lost weight since his operation at London Hospital, and it wasn't for the better.

"Get in here." Ezra bellowed at the attendants.

Franz's head snapped up and he lunged to his feet, leaping forward only as far as his chains would permit.

Magdalena gave a stifled gasp.

"I am checking your wound," he told the man.

Ezra ducked around the chains and leaned in closely. Quick and sure fingers checked the area for heat and infection.

"Your position is no good for this," he muttered, using his shoulder to keep Franz from ramming into him with his chest.

The rustle in the doorway as the attendants entered made him even more irate.

"How many days?" He spat at them. "How many days have you left him to hang? Did I not give you sufficient instruction?"

He didn't wait for them to respond and surveyed the bed. It was no cleaner than the floor, but it was their only other option.

"Move him to the bed." His fists opened and closed at his side.

"A bed? He hasn't earned his bed." The dark-haired orderly switched a wad of chewing tobacco from one side to the other in his mouth.

He could feel Magdalena's anger rise, but he held up his palm.

"It is prescribed. Do your job and get out."

The two unlocked Franz's feet, which he immediately began thrusting and kicking toward any in proximity. The chewer trapped the flailing legs between his knees while his friend unlocked one hand and trapped it under his arm.

Panting, the friend tossed the keys to Magdalena.

"Make yourself useful. The doctor is going to have to help us."

Magdalena caught the keys and darted around the sea of tangled arms and legs to unlock the last limb.

As she did, the chewer leaned in a bit too closely and took a hearty sniff of her hair.

"Pretty little thing," he whispered, brushing his lips against her ear.

The fury already swirling in Ezra's gut began to boil, threatening to erupt.

Get Franz to the bed. Then you can take out the rubbish.

"Pretty kind? Pretty intelligent? Or just pretty?" She jutted her chin, but Ezra caught the unease in her words.

"Just real pretty." The orderly licked his lips, eyes flickering over her body in a way that made even Ezra shudder.

Ezra struggled against Franz's weight as they wrestled him to the bed.

"Go upstairs, Magdalena."

"Not without you." She shook her head. Her eyes shifted around the room before landing on the bed void of linens and heavily stained.

"Now, Magdalena!" His tone rose.

If she stayed in that basement and either man determined to do something unpleasant, Ezra would be very little protection. She deserved more than that. He was hardly a man; he couldn't keep her safe.

With Franz on the bed, the quieter attendant restrained the ankles with a leather strap.

"She wants to stay and play with me. Don't you, princess?" The chewer looked at Ezra and winked.

His blood was ice in his veins and his jaw ached from grinding his teeth. Why wouldn't she just listen? Didn't she understand he was trying to protect her? He shouldn't have brought her in the first place. She should have simply waited at the laboratory. His frustration mounted as ire found its way into the fibers of his tense muscles.

Ezra inconspicuously tucked the toe of his boot behind the attendant's foot as they cinched one of Franz's wrists to the cot.

"Perhaps if she were only pretty, she'd be happy to linger in your filthy presence," Ezra said coldly. "Unfortunately for you, she has a fully functioning mind."

Releasing Franz's arm, Ezra shoved his knee into the back of the attendant's leg and shouldered his weight against his back sending him sprawling across Franz's chest.

With a grunt, the orderly scrambled off him, ducking away from the unrestrained limb.

Franz swung.

Ezra wasn't quick enough and the unexpected connection of Franz's fist against his jaw sent him staggering backward.

Everything stopped.

Get out.

Now.

Mounting panic rose before him like billows of blackened smoke. Ezra was swallowed whole by the plague of terror.

The lingering sensation of Franz's fist was fire on his jaw.

It's all in your head.

None of this is real.

Just Breathe. The demand lacked authority and he couldn't obey.

"Doctor!" Magdalena gasped, anchoring Franz's arm to the bed as she quickly latched the strap.

Memories snaked their way through his mind like a twisting serpent, constricting until all he could see and feel was another man. Another fist. Another time.

Somehow he gathered his scattered medical bag. Left the room, the basement, the asylum, everything behind.

"Dr. Talbot!" Magdalena panted. "Dr. Talbot, wait."

She tugged at his sleeve.

The air was too sharp, the sun too bright. His vision seemed to constrict, creating a tunnel of panic. Things looked farther away, yet he could feel them entirely too close.

You're spiraling. She'll see it.

It didn't matter. Let her see what her mistake caused. Let her know he was no host for hopes and dreams.

These moments, these fits of panic, always felt like watching himself, much like a critic observes a painting. He could see his actions, see the pain etched on his face and the choices he'd make, but he held no control over them.

Panic was the solitary thing logic couldn't fight.

This is Magdalena, he tried to tell himself, begging himself to show restraint, to bite his tongue.

Yes, and you should have forced her away long before now.

This, he knew, was true.

"You're bleeding." She reached for him.

Don't hurt her! The vise tightened once more around his lungs and the earth spun beneath his feet. Her fingertips were cold, yet still they burned. There was no rhyme nor reason for the torment he felt. Just that he needed it to stop.

His fingers jerked up to stop hers and she caught them in her own, swiping at the split in his lip with her thumb. His skin crawled, and his shoulder buckled toward his ear. She may as well have broken his fingers.

"Magdalena." Her name on his tongue was like a shattered plea, gruff and harsh with pain. "Stop."

He tugged her wrist and pulled it away, shaking her off before finding a bench and dropping into it. Lowering his head into his hands, he tried to reduce the frantic spinning of the earth. Rotational therapy must feel much like this.

His breathing was forced, and he gasped for more.

"He didn't do it on purpose," she said softly.

He. Did. Not. Do. It. On. Purpose. No, this was no longer about Franz.

Ezra laughed a dark and bitter laugh, catching Magdalena off guard.

"Shut up," he growled, head still in his hands. His chest heaved against the depth of emotions that swirled out of control. He braced himself with the back of the bench and swayed to his feet. "Don't be so naive. They all mean it."

"What?" She kept her voice even and steady as she met his eyes.

"You heard me," He rolled his shoulders, tongue in cheek. "There is no goodness in this world. You will die alone and cynical just like the rest of us."

"You don't mean that." Hurt seeped from her eyes.

Had he not been made of half pain, half panic, he may have been capable of stopping there, but this was a train full of momentum that couldn't be stopped.

"There are generations of trauma and madness in this world you cannot even begin to touch. There is a depth to the darkness that would put your own pathetic melancholy to embarrassment."

He jammed his hat on his head and wrenched his bag from her hands.

"You have forgotten one thing." She turned up her chin defiantly.

Do it now. Break things off before you truly hurt her. The apprenticeship was a mistake. It all was.

"Hope." Her eyes were full of it. Perhaps it was what he'd taken to searching for in them. The thing that made them sparkle and shine.

"Hope? Hope is for children, Ms. Trudeau."

She stepped away from him, wrapping her arms around her waist.

He wanted to reach for her, to say pitiful words he didn't believe in.

No, this was for the best. She didn't belong with him, and no matter how much he had foolishly begun to believe the possibility, he didn't belong with her either.

"Well then," she said softly. "I find myself thankful for having never grown up."

Ezra abandoned her there, in front of Bethlem Royal Hospital. He walked aimlessly, passing shops, lost in a sea of sound and pain until numbness settled into his bones.

When the panic leached out of him, he felt sick with guilt.

What have you done? The thing you should have done long before now, his mind rationalized.

But if that were true, why did he feel like he'd lost something important? Something that made life worthwhile, bearable … brighter?

It was with every confidence he knew himself to be irreparably broken. Hope didn't exist for people like him, nor should it. Hope was for people like Magdalena Trudeau, who were kind and pure and good.

The space in his chest throbbed, but when he reached up to rub away the discomfort, he opted to leave it there. This was a most deserved pain. Dread took root in his stomach.

You are your father after all, aren't you?

Had she made it home? Had he made her cry? How long until she forgot him?

No. He didn't get to worry about her any longer. That sort of thing was earned.

There was likely not a man in all of London who more personified the Bedlam basement than he.

Chapter Twenty-Six

Magdalena

November 1848. London, England.

Aside from the time you emotionally ate an entire roast duck, this is quite possibly your most impulsive decision, logic warned her. But, well. Food, the fun part argued.

"Ms. Trudeau." A bank teller stood in an open doorway. "Mr. Lee will see you now."

She smoothed her sweaty palms on the skirts of her elegant dress. No matter how many years it had been since the death of her parents, she would never enjoy mimicking what they intended for her.

She crossed the room, remembering to count her steps as nearly endless governesses had once instructed. Step, dip, step, dip. Or was it dip, step, dip? Oh, for goodness' sake, what did it matter anyway?

"Please have a seat." Mr. Lee indicated the luxurious green velvet chair across from him. "What can I help you with today?"

She stared at the desktop, tempted to nibble on a fingernail.

An unwed woman doesn't look into the eyes of a man, she reminded herself. Whyever not? So she wouldn't see the cobwebs behind them? Well, where else was she supposed to look?

Frustration prompted her eyes upward.

"I have an account." She pushed a small card across the desk toward him and clasped her hands in her lap.

He picked it up and studied it, nodding slowly as he turned and sifted through a few ledgers before selecting the proper one. His eyes widened ever so slightly at the numbers, and while he'd been the picture of professionalism, he chose now to call his secretary for a tea service.

"Have you set about to be married?" He steepled his fingers with a congratulatory and pleasant smile.

"Goodness no." She waved her gloved fingers with a little chuckle.

You are a respectable and grown woman, calm yourself. She ducked her head and averted her eyes.

"As you know, this estate may only be released to your husband." He had the decency to look a smidge contrite.

"Of course. Whatever would I do with such a sum?" She ground her teeth against the threatening eye roll. She didn't know the numbers herself, nor did she care.

Magdalena cleared her throat and sat up straighter in the overstuffed chair.

"I have an annual allowance as permitted in the document." She pointed to his ledger.

"Yes, I see ... and you have withdrawn precisely ..." He coughed to clear the awkward tension. "Nothing in seventeen years?"

"Correct." She nodded. "Which I wish to remedy today—in full."

She pinched the seam of her glove to distract herself.

"All seventeen years? In full?" His eyes darted toward the doorway. "Miss, that is an awful lot for a young woman."

"Yes sir." She nodded casually. "I need it."

"Whatever for?" His professionalism slipped as he planted his palms on the desk, leaning in closely.

"That is not your concern." She attempted to mask her frustration.

He exited to collect the notes.

She busied herself sipping his fancy tea while she waited. It had been the dullest week of sitting in Olive's grand estate reading endless medical texts and entertaining the revolving door of callers the family tended to. At one point she'd brought up Bethlem, much to Frank's displeasure, and her brother-in-law had even raised his voice for a small moment.

"You will not go to that place. It is dangerous." He glared over at her. "It hides secrets you could never understand."

Frank had stalked away from the table as if the conversation were through. It was like the man didn't even know her. Nothing tempted her to do something more than being told not to do it. So she simply misled him into believing she was still conducting her apprenticeship with the doctor.

Mr. Lee handed her a satchel puckered with bank and promissory notes and leaned in closely.

"Have you a guard?" he whispered, standing in the doorway as she signed the paperwork.

"I shan't need a guard." She stepped over the threshold and into the lobby, turning to pat his arm. "I have held a detached human head in these hands. Very little frightens me."

Mr. Lee's face blanched, and he quickly closed the door after a respectful parting.

She shrugged as she headed toward the bank exit, tugging on the scratchy sleeves of her dress. *It is not every day I masquerade as a lady. How should I know to do it properly?*

For a moment, in the shadows, she thought she saw the doctor watching her, his hands pushed in his pockets. But by the time she turned back around, the figure had disappeared.

Magdalena stepped into the chilly November air and accepted the hand of the footman who helped her into the carriage.

She sat, satchel across her knees, and unclasped it.

My word, how much money did mother and father have? She gasped, fisting back in the things that spilled out.

She was a wretch when it came to money. She'd never needed much with Aunt Salomé, and it felt like an unwanted responsibility. Part of her wanted to open the carriage window and shove the bills out just to watch them scatter.

Instead, she moved a portion of the notes to her pockets and left the rest in the bag as the carriage pulled to a stop before an expanse of wide steps.

Here so soon? With a shuddery inhale she allowed herself to be helped from the carriage and asked the footman to return in a few hours.

Taking the steps quickly, Magdalena made her way through the tall, ornate doors and into the tiled foyer.

"Welcome," the patient at the door began, "to chaos." He offered a dramatic pause. "May I check your coat, cap, or sanity at the door?"

This time, however, Magdalena stopped and squinted at him. "What is your name?"

He only blinked at her before repeating his same question.

"My name is Magdalena Trudeau. I'll keep my coat and cap as it's a bit cold where I'm going." She leaned in closely and quirked a small smile. "Sanity is relative, isn't it?"

Some distant part of himself seemed to respond to her introduction, and he tipped his chin, offering a more subdued smile.

"Walker, Miss. Matthew Walker."

With the duck of his head, she saw the scar that spanned from his right ear across the top of his skull.

She gave him a gentle pat. "Perhaps you ought to say, 'Welcome to Bethlem Royal Hospital. My name is Matthew Walker. May I take your coat and cap?'"

It didn't bother her that he didn't have a response. She promised to practice it with him as often as she could.

However, at the moment she had an appointment with Bethlem's president, Mr. Fallon.

Magdalena followed the signs toward his office.

It was a bit unnerving, gross even, how the separation between her fingers tended to sweat when she was nervous. Her gloves grew damp.

No matter, she told herself. If she couldn't beat the man to a battle of wits, she'd leave him baffled and confused by her request, simple enough.

She knocked on the door and heard a rustling on the other side before a voice welcomed her in.

"Ms. Trudeau."

Mr. Fallon cleared his throat, gesturing toward the chair across from where he sat at a desk.

She'd never met him and had gone as far as to set up the appointment via courier so he couldn't say no.

She studied him, taking a seat. The hair at his temples was stark white and the remainder a reliable gray. He had a full mustache, stained at the lips with coffee, of which he took a steady gulp before returning his cup to a coaster.

Magdalena caught the muted undertones of whiskey in his mug as tendrils of steam wafted toward the vaulted ceiling.

Behind him on the wall was a massive painting of his likeness. It was quite possibly the ugliest artwork she'd ever seen. In the portrait, he sat in a plush chair with bronze buttons covering his coat and shirt sleeves. Depicted in the background was a muscled, rearing steed and a waving Spanish flag. It was so hideous she could only marvel at the narcissistic catastrophe.

Mr. Fallon puffed up his chest. "Had that commissioned just after I began here at Bethlem."

"It is ... quite something." She could only hope her shallow attempt at tact was not as obvious as it felt.

"How can I help you, Ms. Trudeau?" He steepled his fingers on the tabletop.

She cleared her throat, eyes scattering around the room. "Well, good ... sir?" She grimaced. "I ..."

The man's eyes narrowed, sensing her uncertainty.

Keep him talking. Most men of any standing adored speaking.

"Tell me about your busts," she blurted, gesturing toward the plaster heads affixed above the arched windows.

"Pardon?'

"Your busts, sir." She forced a doltish smile. "There is nothing I enjoy more than privileged men fastened to walls."

Too far, she pinched herself beneath the table.

"Ahh, yes." He shrugged. "Previous presidents of Bethlem, including my predecessor, a brother through marriage. May my sister rest in peace." His brows furrowed. "You scheduled an appointment to discuss my ... busts?"

Her eyes roved over the generous facial structures of the men on the wall. Their stern features and blank, unforgiving eyes seemed to stare at her in judgment. She cocked a brow at the one with a dimpled chin.

You have a birth defect, you know. Not much good that information did her now.

"Miss?" The president rapped his knuckles on his desk.

She supposed her purpose had been postponed long enough.

"Mr. Fallon." Magdalena folded her fingers tightly in her lap. "I wish to purchase the basement."

The words spilled out of her like a drunken confession.

Mr. Fallon sputtered into a fit of such coughing that it drew Magdalena to her feet and around the desk where she clapped the heel of her palm between his shoulders until it subsided.

He dismissed her uncomfortably with a shooing gesture.

"Pardon?" His eyes watered and he wiped the collected moisture with a handkerchief.

"I wish to purchase the basement."

A hearty laugh developed deep in his chest, erupting out of him and blanketing the room with the insult.

Magdalena pursed her lips and stared directly ahead until his humor paused, at which point he looked back at her, and the laughter began again.

She turned her steel eyes to meet his when there was finally a reprieve in the obnoxious sound.

"Are you through?"

"You wish to purchase the basement or reside there?" He chortled, slapping a hand on his rounded knee.

Magdalena stood and began emptying her pockets onto the desk, banknote after banknote piled in a tantalizing and tempting stack.

His chuckling trailed off, and finally, he studied her.

"Why?"

"I want to make a difference." She had squared her shoulders so much for one day that they were beginning to ache.

He blinked. "Then we will happily accept your charity, but I cannot in good conscience permit you to purchase any part of Bethlem Royal Hospital."

"Then do it in poor conscience."

He sputtered. "It is not for sale."

"Then I would like to rent it."

"But I have nowhere to place those patients."

Magdalena smiled at that. "I wish to keep the patients."

"What?" His soft jaw flexed.

"It is the patients there, that space which I need." This was nearly impossible to explain.

"I'm sorry." He stood, hand extended towards the door.

She stood as well. "One month." She edged the money across the desk toward him. "I want to do what I wish with the basement, no arguments and no intrusions unless I request it. I need four attendants. If you do not notice a difference in one month's time, I will leave you with your banknotes and I will vacate the premises."

"I would not ..." He hesitated.

Ahh, there it was.

"One month?" He repeated softly, likely confused as to why he entertained the idea.

"One month."

"Two attendants," he bartered.

"Three."

"Two, or I will not consider it another moment."

Magdalena sighed. She'd seen what Franz was capable of. It had taken three men to subdue him and even that was not sufficient.

"Two. But not the current two. They're terrible." She blew out a frustrated sigh before stretching out her hand to seal the agreement.

"That is not up for discussion." He shook his head.

"Fine," she clipped.

Mr. Fallon swallowed hard, looking between the money and her gloved hand before clasping her fingers firmly.

"You will fail," he acknowledged, retrieving his palm.

"Oh, Mr. Fallon." She clicked her tongue. "That is not something I do."

She turned to leave, shoulders drooping only when she was out of sight. How tedious it was to be a proper woman. She wanted to do something awkward just to get rid of the feeling.

She'd memorized the steps to and from the basement during her previous visit with the doctor. How a place like it could exist enraged her. The stairs were steep, and the cold began to infiltrate before she reached the door.

Magdalena gathered up the lantern, tucking a few spare matches in the recesses of her pocket before using one to light the lamp and take the key from its hook.

She pushed open the door with minimal hesitation. It was different this time, to go in alone and knowing only partially what her intentions were.

The smell immediately took her breath away. It was so thick and foul she could nearly taste it.

With heart pounding in her chest, she held up her lantern. The first several cells were empty, and she passed them quickly until she came to a woman. Looking beyond the shrieking and agitation, she searched through the filth and the baring of teeth into vacant eyes. The woman's pupils were dilated in the light, and her olive skin was flushed beneath the tangle of graying black hair.

If eyes were the window to the soul, this woman had lost hers long ago.

"Hello," Magdalena whispered. "I am Magdalena. It's a pleasure to meet you." She gave a hesitant smile. "I'll be back."

Further down the hall was a man, massive, tall, and beefy, restrained to a chair by leather straps. His chin rested on his chest, and Magdalena recognized him as the patient who had undergone the violent rotational therapy.

"Hello." She introduced herself once more, unphased by the way he didn't look up.

The same two orderlies stood in the procedure room, mopping up water from the floor while engaging in simple conversation.

"Good morning, gentleman." She stepped into their lantern light. "I will tend to the mess. Please check in with Mr. Fallon. I'll not need you for two hours."

The one who had boldly flirted with her before scoffed at this. He dropped the mop in the puddle and stepped toward her.

"I don't think so, princess. This is my basement."

Princess. The name slathered her in disgust, dripping with meanings she hated and ideals she never wished to be.

"Delusion," she muttered under her breath. "Even the orderlies are plagued."

She waited, watching him, and bit back a smile as he finally stormed from the room.

"Do not think for a moment that I won't be back with answers," he shouted as the door slammed behind him.

"This is a mistake, Miss." The other orderly paused, looking a bit hesitant. "Be careful down here."

He ducked out, leaving her alone with the patients.

The silence itself seemed to reverberate as the key turned in the lock. She held her own key in her pocket, yet the sound held a certain sort of threat. For a moment, she wondered if she had, in fact, dug herself into a hole she could not easily climb out of.

"It's a bit late for that, now, isn't it?" She spoke to the puddle as she mopped it up. To her relief, it didn't respond.

Unfortunately, this was where her plan ended.

With the mopping completed, she finished her tour of the basement, stopping just beyond Franz's door. From the barred cutout at the top, she could see him locked to his bed, just as he had been a week prior. Had they moved him at all?

"It's all right, Franz," she murmured in his direction. "I'll help you find yourself soon enough."

A whisper was all it took in this cavernous hole. It echoed from one end of the prison to the other, bouncing off moist stone walls and ricocheting around in the mind.

The woman at the end of the hall and Franz began a boisterous shrieking back and forth. What could one do with this caliber of madness? Magdalena was made of two parts, logic and an insurmountable heart. Those spectrums warred with one another as she stood there in the darkness with her solitary lantern illuminating a haze around her.

"Salomé?" She closed her eyes and spoke into the void. "Salomé, what would you do?"

But Magdalena already knew. Salomé would sit with her, bearing witness to the endless pit of her mind, and love her still.

"Is this too much? Is it too dark? Are they too broken?" The hushed whisper of fate slipped through the cracks in these stone walls.

The sickly, manic laughter of life itself seemed to respond: "I've done it, I've done it! Onto the next I go!"

Without a doubt, Magdalena knew. If she left, if life won and not fate, these patients would be gone, none the wiser. Forgotten. Alone.

"No." The word was sharp. "You can't have them."

Magdalena stormed through the basement, stopping just outside the large man's cell, and plunked herself into an ungraceful heap on the floor. Anyone who entered would well think her to be mad, and perhaps she was, just a touch. But here in this wretched space, she had an entirely unhinged conversation with the thing called life.

"I'm here now." She directed her words toward the sleeping man. "And I will do my very best to remind you all that you are human."

Then, emboldened by her little speech, she lifted the lantern toward her face and blew out the flame, thrusting the four of them into blackness.

It was, perhaps, a very poor decision.

Breathe. She obeyed the command of her mind. Even the sound of her labored inhales seemed to fill her ears, and she strove to steady them. The darkness of night was brighter than this, what with the stars and the moon to soften its realities.

She sat as time trickled past, and the silence made the sounds of the basement come to life. She felt them then, the tickle of the creeping things in the dark. The patter of little feet and the brushing of rodents against her legs, causing her to shriek and clammer away.

Her palms scuffed against the floor, searching for the lantern, but she couldn't find it. Insects scurried over her hands, and she shook them off, bringing her fingertips to her lips as she attempted to still their trembling. The sounds of the woman's chains created a rhythm that was enough to turn her mind into madness as the chair in the cell nearest her scraped across the floor. Terror seized her, and she heard as much as felt the thrum of her rapid heartbeat in her ears.

She clapped her hands over her ears to dull the sounds, but still they echoed through.

Dr. Talbot.

Dr. Talbot's mind was like this, and she'd not been able to help him.

Find the lantern, logic reasoned with her.

She crawled across the floor until her knees sent it clattering.

Light the match.

Her fingers frantically searched through her pockets. The first two were broken and the last, when she attempted to strike it, snapped beneath her fingers. Frustrated, she cried out into the abyss.

Then her mind settled on Salomé.

"Hope, Magdalena, is like a muscle," Salomé had taught her. "The more you use it, the stronger it becomes. At first, it's a bit puny and easily shattered, but hope is best built from the broken pieces of yesterday."

Magdalena picked out the longest of the splintered matches and brought it to the heel of her boot. Striking the match and shielding the spark with her hand, she lit the lamp, scorching her fingertips in the process.

In the shallow glow, Magdalena closed her eyes, gasping for breath with her back pressed to the damp wall behind her. When she opened them, the large man's face was pressed to the bars of his cell and a grin covered his filthy face as he laughed a disturbed and toothy chortle.

"Quite the wretched place, this basement." She laughed in relief with him, resting her head on the wall. "I'm sorry, I couldn't bear it for even twenty minutes."

Were they listening? Did they understand? Some part of her believed that even if they didn't, speaking to them was important.

"I think we need a cat." She stood, brushing off her skirt. "A very large one with a fantastic appetite if possible. We shall also need many, many lanterns, and to remove these bugs will be an arduous chore."

"*Acta non verba*." The voice hissed through the basement.

Magdalena jumped, muscles taut, as her head snapped toward the sound. In comparison to the earlier darkness, the light from the lone lantern felt it could illuminate the entire basement. She left it behind and hurried to the woman's cell, grabbing at the bars.

"That was you? You speak?" She gasped.

"*Acta non verba*," the woman growled again, deeper from her chest.

"I don't—I don't speak Latin."

Magdalena berated herself. Salomé had offered language to them all, yet only Olive had use for the romantics of Latin.

She searched the woman's angry eyes. "You're in there, aren't you? You can come out now, I'll look after you."

The woman's eyes seemed to roll around the room as she physically circled round and round the chain keeping her to the floor. She didn't speak again, but it was hope.

Hope was alive in the Bedlam basement.

CHAPTER TWENTY-SEVEN

Magdalena

It took nearly a week to cleanse every cell from top to bottom. Each bed was disposed of and replaced. And indeed, she did find a cat. The feline was massive with a ferocious appetite and aptly named Samson.

The large patient, she discovered, had been dropped off at the asylum with only the surname Ellington, so this is what Magdalena called him. Ellington was immediately enthralled with Samson. When the attendants were available to help, Magdalena would hold Samson up for a pat which he was able to conduct with a particular gentleness. He was by far the sweetest of the three and her heart ached to know he suffered because he couldn't speak.

The woman was far more distrustful. She had been left without a name, found wandering the streets and frightening others.

"My aunt, she always said that a name is what makes a person feel like a person."

Magdalena sat outside the woman's cell, legs crossed beneath her, an array of Shakespearean texts scattered across the floor.

The patient seemed to hate nearly every name she suggested, stomping and shrieking until Magdalena stumbled across Luce, which was met with only silence.

"Now there is something most important about this name," Magdalena leaned in conspiratorially. "Salomé also used to say that calling someone by their name was just another way of saying, 'I love you.'"

Magdalena began collecting all the books as she stood.

Hesitantly Luce stretched out her hand toward the books.

"Oh ..." Magdalena looked down at *The Comedy of Errors* and held it up. "Would you like to see this? Your name is here."

She set the other books on a shelf and hesitated before sliding the lock in the key to her cell.

Luce was still restrained. Magdalena hadn't found a way around that yet.

She held her breath as she stepped closer to Luce and held the book in her outstretched hands, pointing to where her name was written.

"*In absentia lucis, tenebrae vincunt.*" Luce snatched the book from Magdalena's hands and turned her back on her.

Luce, it appeared, spoke only and entirely in Latin phrases.

Magdalena left Luce with the book, which she sat holding clutched to her chest. It was doubtful she could read, but this concept of a name, her name inscribed within, was a powerful thing.

Franz was not so easily reachable. While the other two tolerated her presence, he did not. Often, she sat in silence with him in his cell while he was heavily restrained. He didn't tolerate her speaking often, though she still tried, daily and without fail.

She noticed early how he would use his toes to trace images on the floor of his cell. When she realized he was drawing, she hastily brought in papers and charcoal. Perhaps it was ignorant of her to loosen one of his arms and permit him this small pastime.

He was still unkind, he still frightened her, but now he scribbled across the papers in silence and stillness. She had tried to offer paints, but he had only taken to the color blue, slashing it across page after page. It unnerved her, and she took the paints away.

A mere two weeks it had been, yet already they were hers and she was theirs. "Good morning, Franz."

She unclipped the top buckle of his restraint and lifted his head to offer a sip of water.

Franz drank heartily. The last gulp he used as he often did, and spat it toward her in a forceful stream. If she were not mistaken, there was beginning to be a small smile in his eyes. Besides, she was getting better at dodging.

"Franz," she sighed.

His eyes followed her around the room as she prepared for the attendants to arrive. The orderlies weren't happy with her frequent requests or the changes she made. These things meant more work and they were accustomed to the bare minimum.

But she was pleased. The patients were no longer relieving themselves into the open air or their clothing, which had meant frequent changes and daily bathing. The scent, though still musty, was more reasonable, and she brought in flowers and light to help.

Nights were difficult with no attendants or lanterns present until she arrived each morning.

"You ever going to get tired of your little charity?"

The prickliest of the attendants, Lawrence, the tobacco-chewer, wandered down before his partner and stood just inside the cell. He clicked open his fancy pocket watch and glanced at the time. He was early.

Magdalena forced a smile as she unclipped the next two straps over Franz's chest. He didn't like this attendant much, and his fists opened and closed as he bared his teeth. In truth, the patients had just begun to tolerate her.

"I have a sister named Charity, so it's unlikely."

Magdalena stooped to unbutton Franz's nightshirt in between the clips while they waited for the other attendant.

"It's all right, Franz," she whispered, pushing his blond hair away from his forehead.

"Still acting like they understand you, huh?" Lawrence pushed away from the door frame and ambled closer to her.

She could smell his chewing tobacco as he hovered over her head. "That's close enough," she said sternly.

"You get awfully close to them." He ignored her, stepping closer and closer until she was effectively trapped with her back against the wall. "Do you know how difficult it has been to make this job even remotely bearable? The things I have done to have a little ... fun?"

Magdalena gripped Franz's change of shirt in her hands, twisting it around her fingers. Unfortunately, her confidence was mostly bluster.

The man's hand crawled up her neck and cupped her chin, gripping it harshly in his fingertips.

A bead of sweat trickled along her hairline. "I'll scream."

She tried to turn her head, but his chest pushed her further into the wall while his knee pinned her legs immobile.

"Go ahead, princess. These walls were made for screaming." His mouth began a descent toward hers and she flailed her trapped arms between them.

A roar erupted from behind him. Franz.

Before she could blink, Magdalena watched as the attendant's body was dragged backward and weightlessly tossed aside.

Magdalena shuddered, looking down at the attendant sprawled across the floor. She realized then what had happened— Franz, his buckles loosened, had somehow managed to unlock the remainder and escape his confinement.

Lawrence clambered to his feet, cradling his unnaturally positioned left arm in the other hand.

Franz stalked him up against the wall and had it not been entirely terrifying, she'd have felt the pleasure of revenge.

"Franz," she gasped, tossing the shirt on the bed and stepping between the pair. "Franz don't. Please, look at me."

She patted her shaking hands across her body.

"I'm safe, Franz. See?"

He ignored her and raised a fist just as the other attendant came running into the room. She blew out a disgruntled huff. Five minutes ago would have been nice.

The other attendant was larger and stronger, and he delivered a fierce blow to Franz's abdomen, sending him reeling.

"Stop! Stop this!" Magdalena screamed.

Between the two men, they wrestled him to his chair and strapped him in.

When Franz presented no further threat, Lawrence spat his tobacco into Franz's lap and brought a foot between his knees, tipping the chair precariously backward.

"Some good water therapy will do just the trick." Lawrence leaned in with a sneer.

"Leave my patients." Magdalena stammered. "Now. Get out."

When they left, Magdalena stepped into the procedure room and poured a basin of water. She slipped in the lye soap and created a lather before scrubbing her throat and face. The linger of the attendant's touch stayed long after the redness disappeared.

This must be how Dr. Talbot felt. Dirty.

As much as she'd tried with all the hard work, she hadn't forgotten about him.

She was a weak, pathetic little thing. How dreadful it was to be alone.

She looked at her reflection in a scarred mirror, the distortion equaling her inner turmoil. Why must things be so impossible?

The door to the basement crashed open, and the storming of feet across the stone floors held a warning.

Magdalena gathered the tattered remains of her courage and prepared for the inevitable conflict.

Mr. Fallon charged into the procedure room, face scorching red and contorted with rage.

"You," he shook his finger at her, "have cost us an attendant." His mustache blustered over the force of his words.

"It wasn't my fault." She felt a thread of embarrassment fill her. "That man had every intention of having me."

Why was it that victims, not the tormentors, often felt the plague of embarrassment?

"Nonsense. You will be reduced to one attendant." He bellowed. "Have you any idea what this has cost me?"

"One? That's impossible."

"Putting flowers in purgatory doesn't make it any less of a—" It appeared decorum made him stop short.

"You have made no difference," he spat. "Two weeks. Two weeks and I will take it all back, returning it to how it was."

Regret and pain were simple motivators, and if there was anything that was her call to action, it was her great love.

"I will fight." She stepped toward him slowly, swallowing back any dignity. She would beg if necessary.

"You would fight for nothing." He matched her quiet volume.

"They are not nothing." She ground out. "Luce, she speaks. Yes, entirely in Latin, but she speaks, and I feel she understands. Ellington is large and intimidates others because he doesn't understand his own strength. He loves animals, and he loves to smile and laugh."

"And Franz?" he taunted.

Magdalena met his tone. "That attendant pinned me to that wall and would have taken everything had Franz not thrown him away from me. There is something in Franz's eyes that tells me he is still in there. If he understood I needed saving, then can I not save him too?"

Mr. Fallon tightened his lips. "You will not have time."

He turned, walking toward the stairs.

"One attendant," he reminded as he closed the door.

You are alone, yes. It felt like she was gasping for air. Dread sat in her chest, willing her to give up. Why was it that every time she grew closer to accomplishing anything at all, it was snatched from her? Her apprenticeship, the basement. Even if she saw the possibilities in these patients, there was no guarantee anyone else would see the same.

The door opened once more and softer, more hesitant footsteps crossed the hall. Luce shrieked at them, and Ellington chuckled. Someone new.

"Ms. Trudeau?" a woman's soft voice called.

"In here." Magdalena masked her fatigue and hurt with a smile, as she often did, and stepped into the hall.

"They sent me to you. I—" Mara Spillman swallowed hard, her discomfort evident. "I'm afraid they are willing you to fail."

Magdalena could have laughed in this moment, though inappropriate. A woman. They had sent her a woman.

Had it not been this particular woman at this particular time, when she was most desperate for a friend, she might have been angry. This was her confidence, knowing fate fought with her.

"Then shall we..."

She stopped and faced Mara, knowing and sensing this was exactly what destiny intended.

"Then shall we be certain we do not fail?"

Chapter Twenty-Eight

Ezra

"Welcome to Bethlem Royal chaos. Walker may take your coat and cap?" The patient at the door's brows puckered in confusion over the choppy introduction.

When had the speech changed? Ezra found it strange, but he hadn't the time for oddities. No one visited Bethlem for the sheer choice of it, and neither did he. Roland was pushing for his opinions, and knowing Arthur was back in London was enough motivation to avoid lingering in the laboratory. There was no guarantee the man wouldn't show up again uninvited.

A month. It had been just shy of a month since he'd last tended to Franz. And nearly a month since he'd cut ties with Ms. Trudeau.

Her face swam across his memory. Don't go there.

But no matter how many times he reminded himself not to, it was where his thoughts strayed.

Ezra held his breath as he twisted the key in the basement door.

Preparing internally for the scent and the eyes, he didn't postpone lighting a lantern and opening the door. Get in, get out. Speak to President Fallon. Leave.

Yet when he turned the handle, the door hardly creaked but rather lurched from his coat-covered fingertips and slammed into the wall. Recently oiled, the door was sloped and uneven on its tracks. Perhaps it was why he felt immediately unbalanced.

But the imbalance continued. His mind, prepared for one vision, staggered in confusion, delaying the understanding of what he looked at. Ezra lowered the lantern to his side, unable to stop the slackness of his jaw or the rapid blinking of his eyes. He'd have turned and looked back up the steps to be sure of where he was had the door not closed behind him.

Light filled the basement, and the scent, though still musty, had been upgraded to a cleanliness comparable to his laboratory. No eyes turned toward him, no shrieking nor rustling of chains to suggest he was even in the same space.

On wooden feet, he stumbled past a series of empty cells and paused beyond the bars of the mad woman. Now, her mess of black hair was twisted into a plait, and she was no longer restrained to the floor by a thick chain.

"*Creo quia absurdum est.*" She shrugged, turning the page of a book with caution and reverence as if it could crumble.

I believe because it is absurd, his mind translated. He didn't want to believe her Latin words. Part of him wanted to ask who'd returned her soul, but he feared this mirage might shatter if he looked too closely. Impossible things couldn't happen, and this was full of daydreams.

"Mm." He tugged his cravat.

Further down the hall, Ezra blinked in wonder at the flowers lining the walls in vases and the charcoal depictions of plants gracing the walls.

In another cell, he saw the large patient seated comfortably on the floor with a large feline stretched across his lap. He giggled boyishly with garbled sounds, much like a toddler trapped in the body of a man.

And Franz? His knuckles gripped his medical bag. What of Franz? He had received written word via courier as he often did regarding this patient, but the query was puzzling.

"There has been change. Can he return home?" it read. Ezra's initial reaction was to laugh, but now—no. He shook his head. Whatever occurred with these other two couldn't be replicated in Franz.

He stopped just beyond the wooden door with its barred cutout at the top, flooded with doubt and confusion. Another small emotion, minuscule and hardly present at all, threatened to spark.

It is only anticipation. He denied any other possibility.

Soft voices pricked his ears and he stood to the side, cast in shadows as he watched through the bars.

"I have a sister—you remind me of her. She's fascinated with trains and can tell nearly anything about them. Everyone has a skill, and you, Franz, are an excellent artist."

A woman lay sprawled across the floor on her stomach with a writing tablet in front of her.

Her.

He knew her voice like he knew his own name. The way it trickled down his shoulders and settled peacefully in his chest was foolish. Ezra was torn between seeing her or closing his eyes and letting the sound of her seep into his mind like a balm.

But no, it couldn't be her. She wouldn't subject herself to this.

The thought sobered him.

Franz propped against the wall on his bed with a writing tablet of his own across his knees. The man was unrestrained and appropriately covered in clothing. This was all too much of the impossible.

"All right, mine is finished." The woman pushed herself up to sit and turned her tablet for Franz to admire.

A shy smile tugged at the patient's lips, and a garbled laugh escaped.

"Well now, Franz, I've done my best." She had an air of mock disappointment before chuckling herself. "Let us admit, drawing is not my strength."

Tight golden curls spilled out of a twist at the back of the woman's head, and an impractical yellow dress hugged a soft and warm figure. Ezra wasn't accustomed to noticing such things. He wasn't sure why he seemed to like that there was a softness to her, and the absence of sharp angles made his head swim.

His heart lurched in his chest turning to pleasant nausea in his stomach.

Nausea isn't pleasant, he argued silently with the sensation.

"Go ahead and finish your drawing. I thought I heard someone come in and I'd best see who it is."

She turned toward the door, swinging it open with her glittering eyes and perpetual smile, then froze.

It was her—Magdalena.

A touch of panic gripped him.

As he watched, her eyes dropped their shine and a shield settled over her gaze. The tilt of her lips remained but it was painted on like a mask.

"How ..." Her breath caught in her throat, and her words tumbled out softly. "... may I help you?"

She should yell at him, he knew. Lash out at him in some way. And when she didn't, it leached away the feeling in his gut and replaced it with gravel.

Hate me, he wanted to demand. Hate me so I can leave you be.

But words failed.

"Don't look at me like that," she whispered.

"Like what?" He choked out, thankful it sounded gruff and accusing and not like he'd just drank in the sight of her like a man who'd never tasted water.

"In the eyes." A little puff of air slipped between her lips like a voiceless laugh. Her shoulders squared and her chin tilted, but she refused to look back at him. "You're here for Franz?"

She stepped back into the room, holding the door open for him slightly.

"Mm." He nodded and cleared his throat.

"Franz, it's the doctor. May he come in?"

Franz looked down at the unused restraints attached to his bed and looked at her as he lowered his drawing pad to the bed beside him.

"S-stay?" Franz reached for her.

Ezra braced himself with the door frame. Franz could speak.

He had so many questions, required some sort of logical explanation. How? When?

Magdalena only nodded, seeming a bit resigned to staying in the room with her former instructor.

With a smile just for Franz, Magdalena nodded and climbed atop the bed beside him and reached for his hand.

The young man took it and rocked back and forth nervously, eyeing Ezra warily.

Ezra set his medical bag down and began a quick examination.

He reached for the shirt tucked in Franz's waistband until a familiar tug at his elbow stopped him.

"Ask," Magdalena mouthed the word.

It was this simple reminder that put Ezra in his place, and he felt his nostrils flare in annoyance. Distance had been created for a reason; he'd see it through now.

"Franz," he muttered. "The shirt?"

Franz reached down and pulled up his shirt, revealing the scar across his abdomen.

After ensuring the proper healing, blanching, and return of blood flow around the incision, Ezra nodded curtly.

"Looks well."

He dropped the shirt and stepped away, running his palms along his trousers. His narrow gaze landed on the patient. "Who sent you here, and when do they visit you?"

"What?" Magdalena blurted.

"The name," Ezra repeated more harshly, fastening his eyes on his patient and not her.

Franz's rocking increased and he hummed, low, quiet, somehow soothing himself with the vibrations of a wordless tune.

"That's quite enough." Magdalena rose from the bed.

Ezra noticed the drawing pad beside Franz and reached for it. "I'll bring it back."

He tucked it into his pocket, returning his stethoscope to his bag.

Franz wailed and closed his eyes, brushing Magdalena away.

"I'll see him out and be back, Franz," she murmured.

He heard her follow him out.

"What are you doing?" she demanded when the door shut behind them.

"Someone sent him here," he replied evenly, looking past her at the pitted mortar between bricks. "They continue to pay me to check on him monthly, which suggests they are wealthy enough to have him remain a private pay patient with a private physician. If he speaks and is in his relative mind at present, what prevented it before?"

Ezra stepped closer, backing her into the wall behind her. He'd done it to intimidate her. It hadn't been meant to make his pulse race.

Did her heart do the same? Was this reaction isolated to him?

When his eyes foolishly searched hers, it wrenched the air painfully from his lungs. He'd not have recognized the whisper of fear that passed through her had he not felt it himself before.

Dread sunk in his bones. Something had happened to her. Leaving her hadn't kept her safe.

"Who?" Venom coated his tongue and he reached for her, stopping when she flinched ever so slightly.

Ezra retreated, giving her space to step away from the wall.

Magdalena's forced swallow confirmed his suspicions.

"Did he hurt you? Franz?"

Moisture shimmered in her eyes for a moment, but she blinked it away.

"You may want to tuck that back in," she said evenly, stepping around him. "Your humanity is showing, and we simply can't have that."

Magdalena jerked her chin toward the exit. "Ask someone else your questions."

"*Astra inclinant, sed non obligant,*" the woman by the door called out.

"What was that, Luce?" Magdalena brushed the back of her hand under her eyes and pasted on that counterfeit smile.

The stars incline us, they do not bind us, he thought. But he wouldn't tell her. Luce didn't repeat it.

Strange name it was for a madwoman.

"There is no fate, only the will to survive," Ezra muttered when he passed her cell.

"*Timendi causa est nescire*," she retorted.

Ignorance is the cause of fear.

Ha, in his experience, mankind was the cause of fear. Witty little woman she was, though. Latin and all.

For the past month, Ezra hadn't spent much time in the laboratory. But now, he headed there straight away.

He'd grown tired of looking at the empty wingback chair—Magdalena's chair—and taken it to the alley, where he paid a lad to light it on fire. Mrs. Keene had given him a look of disgust but wisely kept her mouth shut. Now the empty space taunted him.

Ezra sighed and lowered himself to his desk chair, dragging a palm across his face. The drawing pad peeked out of his coat pocket, and he reached for it, thumbing through it as a distraction.

Fallon had been entirely useless when Ezra questioned him. The president knew very little about his asylum and closed up quickly when Ezra mentioned the rumors. It wasn't a surprise he didn't want to speak of it.

As a youth, Ezra had worked with his father for a few years, and between that and his experience in the police courts, it had made him prone to distrust. Ezra knew when someone was lying, or at the very least hiding something, and Fallon was abysmal at feigning ignorance.

Ezra's fingers hesitated over one of Franz's drawings. It was a well-done depiction of a flowering plant, the details near perfect in the shading. A wide, smooth, veined leaf with pointed tips. The flower petals formed a pinwheel shape.

The next page was a foreign, spiky object that appeared to be splitting into four equal parts filled with round orbs. He didn't recognize it either.

The next page wasn't quite finished, but the illustration was clear. Magdalena had been permanently imprinted across the page, sprawled across the floor with a soft smile on her face.

Without thinking, he carefully tore the picture from the notebook and smoothed it over his lap, hesitantly dragging his thumb across her face.

Touch me? His throat went dry over the memory, over how soft her hair had been when his fingertip had hardly brushed against it. She'd meant it to be some sort of manifestation of hope, that was all ... hadn't she?

"You are a sick man, aren't you, Ezra Talbot?" he muttered.

Yanking open the drawer of his desk, he buried the paper inside and slammed it closed.

"What sort of symptoms this time?" Mrs. Keene carried in a jostling tray and set it in front of him.

Ezra jolted, clearing his throat as heat tinged the tips of his ears. "Nothing."

"Nonsense, I've hardly seen you at all in a month. If you've been ill, perhaps you require a physician?" She crossed her arms and raised a critical brow.

"I am a physician." He pinched the bridge of his nose, trying to get rid of the beginnings of a headache.

"Then humor an old gal." She leaned against his desk a bit too close. "Pity there isn't a chair," she said stiffly when he moved a bit farther away from her.

He sighed and leaned his head back, closing his eyes. He could just tell her no, but then she likely wouldn't go away.

Perhaps she had some sort of insight that was beyond him.

"If you laugh, you will no longer be employed." He blew out a tired sigh, waiting for her nod. "Do you ... look at people?"

He nearly groaned at his own question.

Mrs. Keene looked at him like he was an idiot. "Of course I look at people, Ezra."

Wonderful. She'd used his given name. Propriety and professionalism may as well have been thrown into the street.

"I mean, have you felt urged to watch someone simply for the sake of it?"

She sniffed. "I am not a peeping Tom, if that is what you are suggesting."

He grimaced and shook his head. This was all wrong.

Ezra sighed and threaded his fingers through his hair. "Do you ever catch yourself simply looking at someone because they are ... pleasant to look at?"

A snorted laugh caught in her throat, and she clapped a hand over her mouth.

He glared at her. "Out with it, Mrs. Keene."

"Do you mean attraction?" She all but cackled out the last word. "I find myself looking at that Mr. Cain with rather appreciative eyes." She fanned herself with her hand. "He's a real charmer."

Attraction? Now it was his turn to laugh. Absolutely not. There was no attraction between himself and Ms. Trudeau.

Right?

He knew only what he'd heard of and this... whatever he felt, was kinder, softer than he'd heard Thaddeus or other men crudely suggest.

"What would your dead husband have to say about that?" He glared at her.

Mrs. Keene brought her fingertips to her chin and drummed them along her jaw.

"Have you ever seen a mangled cat so ugly it was cute? Well, that was my Milton." She sighed happily.

"You wed an ugly man?" His brows shot toward his hairline. "For what purpose?"

"For love, you dolt! Attraction takes many forms." She put her hands on her hips. "One can be attracted to a mind, a heart, security." She shrugged. "Now and then, a handsome man comes along, and I think it's natural for him to capture my gaze. I'm only human. Besides, Milton has been dead nearly ten years now. As you have so wretchedly told me, the brain is one of the first things to turn to mush. I don't imagine he has opinions any longer."

He hadn't considered this. If Ms. Trudeau were truly pleasant to look at, perhaps he'd feel less ashamed about appreciating it. Natural, human instinct and all.

"And if it is less ... loud?" He asked.

"Then perhaps one ought to consider if it is more than attraction."

"More?"

"Yes, Ezra. More." She smiled. "It is difficult to explain." Mrs. Keene pondered something for a moment. "Attraction makes for a pretty face. Something fleeting that fades with time." She paused. "That something more, it shines. A man can't miss it when he sees it."

He froze. The description was far too close for comfort. Attraction, he could perhaps come to terms with. This something more? He shook his head.

"Mm," he nodded. "That is all, Mrs. Keene."

He waited until she was gone before retrieving the drawing from his desk drawer. Cautiously he folded it before tucking it in his pocket.

Ezra wasn't a pervert. He simply wanted to be sure of what he felt ... for science.

Chapter Twenty-Nine

Ezra

It had been a few days since Mrs. Keene suggested the possibility of Ezra being attracted to Ms. Trudeau. More times than he'd like to admit, he'd attempted to self-assess a mirror. It felt a terrible thing for an ugly man to fancy an acceptable woman. He couldn't be sure if he fit that description, nor could he ask his secretary after her last display of unprofessionalism.

Ezra wasn't sure what one did with attraction or how to get rid of it. Did he need to find someone else to look at? The idea made him feel dirty.

Could he be attracted to her for a short time, or was this a permanent affliction?

If anyone knew, it was Thaddeus, which was why he'd come to the morgue. That and simple distraction.

"Thaddeus?" He called out, his boots sounding against the stone floor of the morgue.

"Ezra, that you?" The coroner responded.

He stepped into the theatre and looked over his friend's shoulder at the open chest cavity before him.

"Bit swollen." Ezra pointed to the heart.

"It is." Thaddeus wiped his hands on a linen cloth. "Marked down as congestion of the heart."

He stepped back, allowing Ezra a closer look.

"Mind if I open it?" Ezra gestured toward the organ.

Thaddeus looked a bit strained, grimacing. "I have it right, Ezra."

Ezra just looked at him expectantly.

Thaddeus sighed "Have at it, I suppose. Close things up when you are through. I've already filled out the report, so don't make me change a single thing."

He shook his finger at his friend with a tight smile.

Thaddeus moved on to another body and the pair worked in silence for a time. Ezra knew it wouldn't last long. Thaddeus couldn't handle the quiet.

"She did well for you." Thaddeus started with the worst topic he could have possibly mustered.

Ezra removed the heart from the male cadaver and set it on the table. Using a long scalpel to filet it open, he divided the ventricles in half.

"What is this one?" Ezra ignored his comment, pointing to the lack of a name card at the table he worked on.

Thaddeus breathed out a heavy sigh. "You raised your voice over them just last week."

"Since when do you listen to me?" Ezra muttered.

"I don't," Thaddeus chuckled. "In truth, I simply forgot that one. It seems without her here, there is no one to keep us human, aye?" He held up the name card beside the body he worked on. "Or are we simply half human?"

His smile didn't quite reach his eyes.

Ezra had come to speak about her with his friend, but not like this. This was nearly a serious topic, and those were uncomfortable. He continued to distract himself by examining the constriction of the heart muscles and the visceral quality of the congealed organ.

"Aptly done." He nodded toward Thaddeus, returning the heart to its center before replacing the ribs and suturing the incisions.

Thaddeus gave an audible sigh of relief and the tenseness in his shoulders released. "You had me in for quite a concern. You're in a bit of a mood."

Ezra ignored that as well, approaching to aid in the final autopsy. When he went to say something, only air and noise rolled around in his throat, earning him a bewildered expression from the coroner.

"What is the matter with you?" Thaddeus eyed him.

Ezra elbowed him in the kidney, eliciting a satisfying grunt. "I came here with a purpose."

"Which you will share when?"

"I need to know something." He ran his tongue over his teeth. "Am I ..."

Oh, for the love of logic, why was he here? Thaddeus would never let him hear the end of it.

"Spit it out, Ezra. Are you what?"

"Acceptable to look at?" He choked out, nearly plunging the needle into his own hand and not the soft tissue of the body in front of him.

Thaddeus snorted and rolled his eyes. "Wait, are you serious?"

Ezra looked away.

"You are!" He guffawed. "All right, let's have a look at you."

He gestured with bloody hands for Ezra to spin.

"I am not doing that. I'm leaving." Ezra grunted and moved toward the washroom.

"Oh, come on, Ezra!" Thaddeus chuckled until realization unfurled. The mirth died in his throat. Thaddeus knew it was an impossible thing if it were true.

"Magdalena?" Thaddeus asked softly.

Her name alone made Ezra's jaw clench.

"Of course not," he scoffed. The lie left a bitter taste in his mouth.

"Very well." Thaddeus didn't push it. "In any case, you're hideous. She is far too lovely for a dog like you."

Blast it, she was conventionally attractive. To his knowledge, Thaddeus had remarkable taste.

And the something more? He ignored the thought.

Ezra sniffed. "Says the man with a bullet hole in his forehead."

"I'll have you know—women love scars." The coroner wiggled his brows.

He snorted outright. If that were the case, Ezra would have more women than Henry VIII, regardless of his condition.

He went down the hall to change his shirt.

"You are in desperate need of a haircut," Thaddeus called after him with a laugh.

Ezra knew he should wait until he possessed some sort of inner fortitude, but evidently he was just as weak in resolve as he was in mind. He intended to return Franz's journal and that was all, yet for reasons he refused to consider, he took a few extra minutes to tie his cravat in front of the mirror.

"You are a fool." He glared at his reflection.

Shoving away from the washstand he put on his top hat and ducked out into the hallway.

The road to Bedlam wasn't long, but it felt arduous until the growler slowed in front of the asylum.

He clambered down before it fully stopped and let the door slam behind him, ignoring the driver's scowl as he took the steps two at a time.

Just before the landing, a scream split the air, stopping him in his tracks.

Instinctively he covered his ears and searched, seeing nothing until he looked up.

Above him, a woman clung to the third-story window with her hands braced against the casement.

"Mrs. Lewis!" An orderly inside shrieked.

The panic appeared to make Mrs. Lewis smile, a twisted and sadistic grin, before she turned up her chin and stepped into the air.

Time permitted no calculation or probability for saving her. Human fallibility in the end is cause for many a man's demise. There was nothing he could do but watch as she seemed to reconsider mid-fall before landing haphazardly across the steps mere yards away.

Ezra was beside Mrs. Lewis almost immediately as she gasped and choked over the inevitable internal bleeding. Crouching next to her, he found her pulse with one hand and pushed back her eyelids with another. Her pupils were massive, nearly blown with dilation beneath their lids. He sucked in a sharp breath, feeling her pulse pound beneath his fingertips as the heart attempted in vain to push blood through fractured pathways.

"That naughty bird," Mrs. Lewis gasped. "He's taken things too far."

She coughed as blood filled her mouth and dripped down her chin, flailing at the lapels of his overcoat.

Don't touch me. He flinched away.

"Don't dr—" She garbled.

And then she was gone.

Her eyes stared unseeing into the distance as the pulse racing beneath his fingertips slowed into nothingness.

He released his hand on her throat and withdrew his pocket watch.

Death was a part of life, he knew. This, however, was unexpected, and it troubled his mind.

Ezra felt his cravat tighten slowly, felt the scratch of the cloth against his throat, and he imagined it was himself lying broken on the steps.

Mr. Fallon ran haltingly to his side, his face red with horror.

"It cannot be." The president staggered beside her mangled body, clutching his chest. "Not her!"

"Send for the chief inspector," Ezra demanded.

"No!" Fallon shook his head, sending his gray hair tumbling across his forehead. "This will ruin me."

"You." Ezra directed an orderly, "Go to the Thames Police Court and fetch Roland Hugh. Now."

Ezra's glare alone seemed to propel the young man into a traumatized nod before he sprinted away.

Ezra called for a sheet, then lowered it over Mrs. Lewis's body, trying to ignore the faces pressed to windows and the eyes watching him.

"Go inside unless you intend to fail your own heart." Ezra ordered Fallon.

Fallon obeyed, muttering as he stumbled indoors.

It wasn't long before the horse-drawn police van slowed just beyond the steps.

Ezra rose to standing. He should have known precisely who it was when the rider within didn't wait for the horse to pause entirely.

The man stepped out, permitting the door to clatter closed, and placed a tall hat on his graying head. When recognition wrapped its fingers around Ezra's consciousness, he turned in vain to find a hasty retreat.

But Arthur Talbot had eyes for one purpose.

He stooped beside the body, tugging the sheet from its frame.

"Time of incident?"

"Just before eight." Ezra felt his mouth moving in response.

"You are a witness?" Arthur pulled out a notebook and jotted a flurry of notes.

"Mm."

"Name."

"Surname is Lewis. That's all I know."

"I meant your name." Arthur's tone was laced with annoyance.

Ezra chuckled as anger bubbled deep within. The detective hadn't paid any mind at all with whom he was speaking or he would have known.

"Ezra Talbot," he muttered.

Arthur's pen froze above his paper and his head snapped up, eyes connecting with Ezra's face. His father was one of the few who didn't look him in the eyes. That he'd given up on long ago.

Had Ezra ever pictured this moment, it wouldn't have looked like this.

Arthur's dark brown eyes drank him in from the top of his head to the polish of his boots.

Ezra's, meanwhile, did nothing. They simply blinked away sunlight and memories.

"Hello … son." Arthur cleared his throat awkwardly, adjusting his notebook and pen.

Emotions he'd tried to kill flooded Ezra like they'd been released from a fractured dam. Why after so many years, when this man had broken him beyond belief, did he still feel this urge to please him, to weasel his way into Arthur's non-existent affections? Why did the word "son" fill him with a poisoned longing?

"Don't." Ezra held up a hand bitterly, then motioned towards the notepad in his father's hand. "Next."

"You have grown into quite a man." Arthur paused. "Gone off to war and all, I've heard?"

He's followed up on you. Ezra buried the thought six feet under, where it belonged.

"Nearly fifteen years it has been. We will not have this conversation."

As though remembering the body, Arthur coughed, blinking back emotion from his eyes. Emotions he didn't deserve to own.

"Mm. Yes. What did you see?"

"She was in the window when I arrived. She screamed, appearing to jump at her own will—what she had of one."

"What ailment?"

"Delusion." Ezra crouched back beside Mrs. Lewis, checking the rigor of her body. "Specific to the Queen's parrot, Lory."

"I need you to complete the autopsy."

"I won't be doing that." Ezra stood back up, dusting his hands on his trousers.

"Bethlem Royal Hospital is, from this moment onward, under lockdown." Arthur Talbot took an intimidating step toward Ezra. "You are not going anywhere."

His demand sparked confidence in himself and doubt within his son, as his demands always had.

"Why have you any concern for a suicidal mad woman?" Ezra ground out.

"You know of the rumors, don't be a fool." Arthur leaned in closely. "Do the autopsy, Ezra."

"No." Ezra shook his head, attempting to step around him.

"Constables!" Arthur bellowed toward the two accompanying him. "Arrest this man."

Finnian Bulcroft's face blanched as he looked between father and son.

Ezra lost all the wind from his lungs.

"On what grounds?" he rasped, feeling the blood leach from his face.

"Contempt." Arthur smiled sadly. "By the time you can argue your cause, you will have been exposed to God knows what in the prison. Or—you can stay. Do the autopsy. The choice is yours."

Arthur held out his palms toward the sky as if he ought to be thanked for this great solution.

"Sick and twisted as ever." Ezra spat out. "You could not leave me to live in what little peace you did not destroy."

Ezra was far too upset to recognize the remorse that clouded Arthur from the moment he arrived. Even if Ezra had seen it, he was under no obligation to care. "You are a tragedy," He muttered.

Taking the steps, Ezra offered one last retort over his shoulder.

"Bring me Thaddeus Cain and I will stay."

His throat and lungs burned with emotion; his pulse beat a rapid crescendo enunciated by short, shallow breaths.

Once inside, Ezra didn't know where to seek solace. He paced in the foyer, and the smell of the hospital began to creep in. Was it any wonder in such circumstances that his feet led him to the only familiarity in this prison?

His steps were quick, his vision blurred full of stress and uncertainties.

Unbuttoning his coat, he tugged it off his shoulders as he walked and loosened his cravat.

Perhaps there was no safety in being alone, or else why would his instinct have been ... her.

CHAPTER THIRTY

Magdalena

Magdalena sat at the foot of Luce's bed. Fallon enjoyed reminding her that her time was nearly up. She didn't know what could be done for her friends in the basement, but she was not above reaching over the president's head.

The cellar door slammed against the brick wall followed by the sound of hasty footsteps. She ignored the visitor. Mara didn't let the door crash, and she'd learned quickly the term visitor was an oxymoron. Anyone dumb enough to follow her into the basement was either present against their will or motivated by morbid curiosity.

"Luce—lux?" Magdalena grimaced under Luce's pinched expression. "I'm sorry, Luce. I don't know the translation of your name."

Exasperated, Luce snapped her book closed with a glare. Her eyes drifted toward the open cell door behind Magdalena.

"*Persona non grata*," Luce groaned.

"I certainly don't need to know Latin to know that was not a kind phrase."

Magdalena chuckled, standing, and turned to face the source of Luce's distrust, then froze.

"Dr. Talbot?"

She stared at his disheveled appearance.

Gone was his general proper exterior. His cravat hung loose around his neck like a scarf, and his hair was mussed.

With chest heaving he let the coat he held in his fist drop to the floor as his eyes stole over her like a bandit. He looked half panicked and half starved for affection.

"Light." His words were ragged. "Her name means light."

She'd never seen so many conflicted emotions flicker through his eyes, but he was too overwhelmed to stop them.

She'd hold him if she could, pull the pieces of him together and assure him he'd be all right, that he could trust her.

Lies drew a man to pain. Some were told by others, but most, Magdalena knew, were told by himself. There was hope, cure, and endless possibility for someone else, but never himself. It seemed kindness was free unless he was looking in the mirror.

She knew the feeling well.

"What are you—?"

She watched his shoulders sag in silent confusion like he knew he'd not have the answer to anything she asked.

He passed the cell, disappearing further down the hall.

"Light." She turned to the woman and caught her face between her hands. "How perfect is that, Luce?"

Luce gave her an awkward pat and smiled faintly as she often did when Magdalena called her by name.

"I'd best see to him."

Magdalena stepped out of the cell and latched it behind her.

From the doorway of the procedure room, she watched as Dr. Talbot frantically washed his hands. Over and over, his hands glided atop what had been a fresh bar of soap.

He doesn't like you, Magdalena, she reminded herself. He doesn't like himself either.

Someone had better stop him.

"Dr. Talbot?" She blew the wayward hair from her eyes.

"Mm."

His hands went still. Glancing at them briefly he cleared his throat and rinsed them. Magdalena silently handed him a clean towel and gestured toward the basket at his feet.

Just as he seemed prepared to speak, the basement door crashed open once more against the stone wall. That blasted door. It drove her mad.

Perhaps it was instinct, or simply fate, but with an agitated growl she stepped back into the hall, locking him into the room behind her.

Ah, things were beginning to make sense.

She watched as Mr. Fallon scurried through with rounded limbs, dread etched across his brow, as a stern Detective Talbot scowled behind him.

Her jaw quirked in annoyance, and she crossed her arms over her chest. Whether a gesture of defense or defiance, either would do.

Were they coming to remove her? It hadn't been a month. She had a few days remaining. If Fallon wouldn't permit her patients to move upstairs, she could send them to Staffordshire Hall. She knew Olive would never go against Frank, but perhaps Charity or Zebulun would help.

The men stopped paces away from her, and Mr. Fallon awkwardly cleared his throat.

"This is Ms. Trudeau." Mr. Fallon told the man and scratched at his nose. "She, ah, rents the basement."

Mr. Fallon avoided looking at her but glanced nervously toward Franz's cell.

"Ms. Trudeau, this is Detective Talbot; I'm afraid there has been a grave incident. For the time being, no one will be permitted to leave the premises."

"What?" She blinked dumbly down at the short little mustached man.

"A patient has died under ... suspicious circumstances. There will, of course, be an investigation."

Mr. Fallon swallowed and shifted on his feet. The man was pitiful at hiding his fear of the basement.

Magdalena huffed out a sigh of relief. He wasn't there to send her away.

"Blessed Fate," she muttered, causing Mr. Fallon's eyes to widen in horror. "Oh, goodness. I meant what a tragedy."

She laughed when she was nervous, and what a terrible moment it would be to giggle.

"We do hope it won't be long." The detective gave a tight-lipped smile. "Just a few routine questions and everyone will be off."

His brows furrowed as he studied her, as if unable to place why she seemed familiar.

Seriously? They had met only once, but she expected to be more memorable.

Offering him a dainty hand, he begrudgingly took her fingertips in his and gave it an awkward shake.

"Why, detective, we are ever so grateful that you are here to sniff things out."

She tightened her grasp around his hand and leaned in close for a steady inhale.

Detective Talbot's eyes hardened as recognition dawned.

He shook loose her hand. "Trudeau? What did you say your given name was?"

"I didn't." She turned up her nose.

There it was again, the tugging threads of memory he prompted. She brushed it off.

"Now unless either of you intends to pay for a room, I suggest you take your concerns up those stairs before my patience gets a little unruly."

"That was not proper grammar." The detective grunted.

"It may take you just a moment, sir, but you will find that it was indeed, intentional."

"Ms. Trudeau!" Mr. Fallon sputtered, embarrassment seeping into his tone.

"We will speak about this later," he hissed her way, ushering the detective back the way they'd come.

Luce shrieked at their backs as the door closed behind them.

"Good riddance," she muttered under her breath.

Tongue in cheek, Magdalena slid open the procedure room door to find Dr. Talbot.

Composed, his hands gripped the sides of the water table. His dark curls were returned to some semblance of order, and his cravat had been returned to its place. Put together on the exterior, a disaster on the inside, she reckoned.

"Care to share what is going on?" Her tone was brusque.

Dr. Talbot sighed and shook his head. "Chaos."

"Why, thank you. That cleared things up."

"Mrs. Lewis is dead," He turned toward her, pushing his hands into his pockets.

Regret slipped in. "How?" While she hadn't known Mrs. Lewis well, she still mattered.

"She leaped from the third-story window."

His eyes settled on the top of her head, his words stiff and to the point.

Magdalena shuddered. "This should not be notable in any way to the authorities. Inevitably it will be a very brief hold, just as he suggested."

"There is more to this." He shook his head.

"The rumors?"

He nodded. "If they are connected, Arthur will draw this out for the sheer misery of it."

"You must also stay?" Surely the detective wouldn't confine his own son.

"Don't act surprised. You've met the man."

"What are your plans?"

"Thaddeus should be arriving shortly. We have an autopsy to conduct." He nodded curtly. "Cause of death is already well known. It won't take long."

"Yet what caused her to jump?" Magdalena shook her head, dismissing the ease of this idea.

"She was very delusional in her last breaths. There is no justification in madness."

"You were a witness?" Her breath caught. He'd watched her die and then been forced to face his father?

You aren't supposed to lend him your heart.

But that was the thing about her. She'd trade her broken heart a thousand times over if it could put someone else back together.

Her voice softened. "Are you all right?"

If his jaw were clenched any more tightly it would splinter, but she couldn't forget the expression he wore when he'd entered the basement. He'd been somehow ... comforted.

"Perfect." His word was clipped but his lips flickered at the corners. "Utter bliss for a Tuesday morning."

Extending an olive branch. Magdalena turned away before he could see more than she wished.

"It's Wednesday," she chuckled.

"Mm, of course it is." He pushed his thumb and forefinger over his eyes. "Wednesdays are for dying, are they not?"

He remembered. It shouldn't matter when it was something as silly as her decrepit sarcasm, but it did. There were few things mightier than someone recalling a minuscule, everyday moment.

Slow down.

But she never moved with leisure. She was a tornado of disaster and affection.

"Well, I'll be off then." She clapped her hands together and ducked past him.

"Where?" He sputtered. "He will not be persuaded into letting you leave."

It should be obvious.

"The third floor." She shrugged and unlocked the basement door as he followed.

"More than time," she called past him toward Franz and the others. They knew what she meant by the words.

He grimaced and brushed his hands across his ears.

"*Amor est insania*," Luce shot back.

It always made her smile to hear Luce speak, to know she often reserved the words for her or had them at all. She was a reminder that hope lived.

"What did she say?" Magdalena held the door for him.

He coughed and hurried up the steps intentionally, she assumed, ignoring her question.

"Love is madness," he muttered but didn't look back.

Neither said anything more until they made it up the third flight of steps. He followed her. He didn't have to, yet there was no denying his curiosity.

"Why do you suppose he cannot complete the interviews outside the institution?"

Forty-seven steps were about all she could muster before the silence got to her.

"It is punishment."

"Unlikely." She frowned. "Despite being an absolute badger, he is intentional and calculated. It's still morning, and if someone caused her to jump, it's possible they're still here. We can immediately rule out everyone in the basement—yourself, Mara, and I."

"Badger?" His brows shot up. It was a wonder he had any left with how many times she evoked the expression.

"I called him a skunk the last time. I tired of the comparison."

"You called Arthur a skunk? To his face?" Dr. Talbot looked unconvinced.

"If I am going to insult a man, it will always be to his face." Magdalena rolled her eyes.

"What—how did he respond?" He sputtered.

"I don't recall." They reached the top, and she shrugged, turning to face him. "I slammed the door in his face."

"You ... why?" He pushed his hands through his hair and paced a few steps. "Why would you have done that?"

"For you, you idiot."

She glared at him. How he could be such an intelligent imbecile was beyond her.

The doctor blinked and looked past her.

Magdalena turned to see what his eyes took in. Any words she had premeditated died in her throat as she took in the sight of the third story.

It seemed the closest comparison to Staffordshire Hall she'd witnessed. Its beauty comparative to her cherished painted room. The glass dome of the ceiling shot up above them like a cake tower with creeping vines twisting their way toward the sun. Despite winter's approach, it was warm and humid in the greenhouse. Short pathways ran between potted plants and raised garden beds were filled with greenery and flowers in a kaleidoscope of color.

"Would you look at that." Her jaw dropped. "Franz would love this."

She nearly turned to haul Franz up the steps at once.

The space was empty in the wake of the incident, though no one yet stood guard or sought evidence. A window lay propped open, and she stepped toward it, looking far down onto the steps below.

Shuddering, she moved back quickly. If one was to take themselves out, this didn't seem a surefire method.

"She jumped?" Magdalena swallowed back the horror. Mrs. Lewis hadn't been alone and for that, she was grateful. "Thank you."

"You still thank me for useless things," He sighed. "She couldn't be saved."

"I say thank you when something matters to me." She felt compelled to stick out her tongue. "It matters to me that she didn't die alone."

Dr. Talbot studied the window and the surrounding area. "There's nothing here, and it smells wretched. I'm leaving."

She scrunched up her nose. "You would find the scent of flowers unappealing."

"It doesn't smell like flowers. It smells like feet."

Magdalena made a face. "I smell nothing of the sort."

"Likely from your deviated septum. You once broke your nose." He shrugged. "It is why you are a mouth breather."

She'd never told him about her nose. Instinctively, she covered it with her hands.

"Ah, yes, let us immediately begin with the insults when you haven't apologized for the last ones."

The words slipped out before she could stop them, and his shoulders stiffened.

"I will not be apologizing," he said coolly. "Thaddeus is here."

He turned and left her standing there yet again, watching him leave.

"You big ninny, just when he was coming back around," she muttered to herself before hurrying to catch up.

Dr. Talbot didn't make knowing him a simple task. He made it a maze full of distorted distractions.

If only he didn't feel like fate wrapped in flesh, perhaps then she'd be capable of caring for him a little less.

Chapter Thirty-One

Magdalena

B y the time she'd managed the near-endless steps and made it to the foyer, Thaddeus Cain was already there speaking with the detective and Mr. Fallon. Dr. Talbot stood to the side, not in the throes of conversation but close enough to observe.

"Mr. Cain, thank you for coming." Mr. Fallon shook his hand.

"I wasn't given much choice." Mr. Cain removed himself from the president's handshake and nodded toward the constables accompanying him. "Deliver my tools to the autopsy space, would you?"

"You could have sent a message explaining things," she heard Mr. Cain whisper low toward Dr. Talbot in passing.

"Hello, Mr. Cain," Magdalena said cheerily, capturing his attention.

"Magdale—Ms. Trudeau!" Mr. Cain stopped entirely and beamed, clapping a heavy hand on her shoulder. "The sun does indeed still shine in Bedlam."

Dr. Talbot and the detective simultaneously snorted in disgust. She scowled at them.

The abrupt rise of the detective's brows suggested he caught the slip of her name. It was a pity. She enjoyed holding something over his head.

"Do you know all of London?" Mr. Fallon grunted at her.

"So it would seem." The detective remarked. A slow grin stole across his features when his son glared at him.

The coroner extended his hand toward the doctor's father, who shook it firmly.

"Detective Talbot."

He smirked when Mr. Cain's eyes widened over the introduction.

The group held a brief standoff as each surveyed the other. They were an unlikely band of curiosities.

"Well then." The detective gestured toward the back of the asylum. "My men have transported the body into an empty room."

He led the group to the back. Mr. Fallon, face pale over the mere mention of the word "autopsy," opted to stay in his office.

"Is she ... necessary?" She heard the detective ask.

Dr. Talbot brushed past his father and into the room.

"If she makes you uncomfortable, stay out."

As though no time had transpired, Magdalena joined Dr. Talbot and Mr. Cain as they set out the autopsy supplies and prepared the body. She smiled, recognizing the fingers of fate fiddling with her future.

"Hello again, Mrs. Lewis." Magdalena tucked the wisps of gray hair behind the woman's ears, her voice cracking ever so slightly. "No more pesky parrots. Dr. Talbot and Mr. Cain, true experts are they. We'll get this all sorted."

"Does she always talk to the dead?" The detective's beard covered the upturn of his lips.

"They are not so rude as to pretend I'm not here." Magdalena gave a tight smile.

"Well then, Ms. Magdalena Trudeau." The way he said her complete name was smug, and he gripped the sides of the wooden table Mrs. Lewis lay on. "Would you do us the honor of the first incision?"

He wasn't looking at her, she could see. He was taunting his son.

Her temper sparked below the surface.

Dr. Talbot nudged her with his knee beneath the table, beyond his father's prying eyes, like he sensed a reaction brewing and wanted to warn her.

It shouldn't matter, but it did. He touched her.

With an emboldened tilt of her chin, she unclasped her shirt sleeves and rolled them up.

Mr. Cain and Dr. Talbot exchanged a wary glance.

"Ms. Trudeau." Mr. Cain spoke hesitantly. "I haven't drained the body. It'll be messy."

"Have you ever known me to shy away from messy situations or messy people?" She winked at him.

A shallow chuckle slipped past his mustache. "On the contrary, I think I find you further in the mud every time we cross paths."

He pushed the handle of a scalpel into her open palm.

For a moment Magdalena worried she wouldn't be capable, but as it often did under pressure, knowledge flashed through her mind. She recalled medical texts on autopsy before beginning her first incision.

Looking for some sort of confirmation, her gaze sought out the dark brown eyes of Dr. Talbot. He let her for a second, perhaps more. She didn't waste away the moment by counting.

He didn't say anything but raised a brow and nodded ever so slightly.

It shouldn't have been all she required, but his quiet confidence in her always made her try harder.

Magdalena ignored the slight ache in her chest, knowing how she missed him, and pretended she didn't—wondering if he thought of her at all, but understanding it simply wasn't how he was.

She must have taken longer than he liked, for the detective made a sweeping motion with his hand.

"Go ahead, men." He grunted. "We haven't got all day."

"Oddly enough, my schedule has been cleared." Ezra leaned against the wall, one lazy foot in front of the other.

"As has mine." Mr. Cain smiled broadly.

Magdalena made quick and silent work of fileting open the skin to reveal the ribs below.

The irritating man looked slightly less smug for a moment. Then a sinister smile crept across his face.

"You boys may want to roll up your sleeves." The detective recommended, mimicking his son's relaxed posture against the wall.

Disgust settled in her stomach. Somehow the detective knew Dr. Talbot didn't roll up his sleeves. He looked at his son with a blatant dare plastered across his arrogant face.

The look of hurt that flashed across Dr. Talbot's eyes took the breath from her lungs and turned it to rage.

Her voice was ice cold when she spoke. "They won't be necessary."

Yet. Eventually, her knowledge content would run out. What then?

"Detective, would you be so kind as to take a few notes?" She encouraged with narrowed eyes.

"But of course." He pulled out his notebook and hovered his pen.

Magdalena bent over the body and cautiously ran her fingers across the ribs.

"Hairline fractures to the third and seventh ribs on the left side. Every rib on the right side has been affected, suggesting she fell bearing more weight there. A comminuted fracture to both the third, fourth, and sixth rib on the right-hand side."

Magdalena paused as his pen strove to keep up with her tongue. "Shall I spell any of that for you?"

The detective cleared his throat. "No, I've got it."

"I anticipate a great deal of damage to the lungs and a significant amount of internal bleeding," Mr. Cain predicted.

Giving her the lead, the coroner aided as necessary in removing the ribs, further opening the cavity.

The detective didn't seem to be enjoying his taste of humility and kept silent.

Their game finished, Mr. Cain and Dr. Talbot joined her, examining the extensive internal trauma. Blood seeped through her apron and into the material of her dress, soaking her into regret as Magdalena gazed down at the body.

This wasn't a toy to be used as a pawn—this was a woman. She had a name. And names mattered.

"Cause of death is internal injury." Mr. Cain shrugged.

They had all expected as much.

Dr. Talbot's presence beside her and Mr. Cain's across from her warmed her heart. The doctor took in a ragged breath under his father's watchful eyes.

It was unfortunate the detective knew his son well. Perhaps it was because they were so similar.

"I'm curious, Ezra. What will you do next?" his father mocked.

Resentment rolled from Dr. Talbot in waves.

Magdalena nudged him with her knee just as he had encouraged her earlier.

Frustrated, he looked at her face, not her eyes. He seemed to trace the curve of her jaw, the mess of curls that fell from their knot, and the slight deviation of her nose. A sheen of sweat on his forehead glistened in the light, but she couldn't catch his eyes.

If she could, she'd tell him he could do this, that he was strong and brave and kind.

Dr. Talbot swallowed, looking between her and Mr. Cain. Considering, weighing something for its value or acceptability.

"What will it be?" His father repeated with a smirk.

Magdalena's stomach lurched as Dr. Talbot turned to look into his father's eyes with a determination to prove him wrong.

The detective flinched.

But despite how uncomfortable she knew it made him, the doctor didn't waver. His own father expected him to.

Mr. Cain observed the standoff in an awkward silence of his own, holding his breath.

Ezra. Ezra will win.

Her heart sank to her toes. No, don't think of him as Ezra.

But it was too late. Perhaps it had always been too late for that.

Swallowing down the chaos of her wayward emotions, she held her breath as Ezra turned his eyes to her instead. This look was different, far from the one he'd exchanged with his father. It was intimidating with its slow blink as he pulled his cufflinks through the sleeve of his shirt.

Any moment he'd look away, she was certain.

But he didn't.

"Ezra?" His father cleared his throat, his voice laced with dread and perhaps a bit of regret.

Whatever it was that Ezra found in her eyes, it pushed him onward.

He slid his cufflinks into his pockets and rolled up first one sleeve and then the other. The silly little heart of hers could have soared for how proud she was of him.

Heaviness soaked into the atmosphere, spreading from the coroner and back to the detective.

At first, she misunderstood it, translating it to suggest that neither expected him to do it.

You're safe, she gave a small smile.

He lifted his chin toward his father with a smirk that seemed to shout, "Your move."

The detective looked away, defeated, as Ezra used a scalpel to withdraw Mrs. Lewis's stomach.

That was when she saw them.

Scars tangled their way up his forearms like a spider's web, the purples, whites, and reds crawling across the surface of his skin to disappear beneath his sleeves. Blessed fate, what had created such disfigurement?

The pulse in Mr. Cain's throat pounded with enough force to be seen across the table as anger and disbelief danced across his face.

He hadn't known.

Scars were an inevitability in this life, she knew. Most marred the mind or the heart, thickening the surfaces with a protective layer.

As a girl plagued by a nightmare, she had once burst into her aunt's quarters. The woman's sleeping gown had slipped off one rounded shoulder. There across Salomé's chest was a large, puckered scar.

"How did you get your scar?" young Magdalena had asked, climbing into bed with the woman and curling up beside her.

"That one? Oh, darling, that's the one that built me," Salomé had murmured, tucking the blankets around her charge before humming the whisper of a song to settle her off to sleep.

In that moment, Magdalena knew the detective had embarked upon this showdown for a reaction. Perhaps a substantial gasp of horror or weeping even.

Magdalena wouldn't give him the satisfaction. The only indication that Ezra was uncomfortable was the jostling of his knee beneath the table beside her. This she took extra care to make sure she blocked from his father's view.

Ezra slit the stomach and poured its contents into a basin.

"Have you ever seen a European badger?" Magdalena made conversation as she leaned over Ezra's shoulder. "In Wales, they call them *moch daear*, which translates to "earth pig," I believe."

Ezra's chin snapped up to study her quickly before dropping his eyes back to his investigation. He coughed over a threatening chuckle.

Success.

Mr. Cain played into the conversation simply enough, as if relieved someone spoke.

"Nasty little buggers. I've had to poison them out of my garden a time or two. Odd though," he remarked. "Isn't every pig an earth pig?"

"Couldn't we say the same about men?" Magdalena chuckled, watching as Ezra's knee steadied.

Mr. Cain pointed to something in the basin. "Breakfast contained what, do you suppose?"

They fell into a rhythm now in which the detective was the silent wallflower.

"Biscuit." Ezra used a pair of tweezers to sift through the debris. "Jam perhaps—difficult to say. Sausage is a possibility. Likely tea, not coffee."

"How would you recognize the beverage?" she asked.

"I'm not certain." He shook his head. "There is a fuller stomach content, and simple liquids may perhaps take twenty, possibly forty minutes before the body absorbs it or it is sent off to the bladder. But some remains."

She nodded slowly. "Breakfast is served precisely at seven-thirty."

"Dead by eight," the detective remarked. "We'll interview her attendant first."

It seemed Ezra played with something in his mind.

"What is it?" She asked for his ears alone.

"Nothing." He shook his head. "A time frame perhaps."

"Hypothetically speaking," the detective began, "if madness were to be replicated, how could it be done?"

Ezra's brow furrowed as though considering it. "A medication perhaps ... I'd need to see the symptoms to be sure."

"Why would anyone want to mirror insanity?" She shook her head in confusion.

"Ah, little M." Detective Talbot offered a sad smile. "There is wickedness in this world you couldn't begin to imagine."

She froze.

"What did you call me?" Emotion caused her vision to swim.

Ezra and his father exchanged a sharp glance.

"Magdalena," Ezra said quickly.

If it feels like a lie, sounds like a lie, and aches like a lie—that's precisely what it is.

Let it unravel.

No. That wouldn't do. Not with this secret.

CHAPTER THIRTY-TWO

Ezra

The cool water was a relief on Ezra's arms, though he could sense the crawling pity of Thaddeus's eyes on his back as he washed the blood from his skin.

Magdalena had gone off to borrow an orderly's dress, leaving the pair of them alone to hash out questions Ezra most certainly did not wish to answer.

"You had nightmares on the ship." Thaddeus was tense, a muscle clicking in his jaw.

Wonderful. Let's bring up every wretched thing at once.

"Did he do it?" Thaddeus jerked his chin toward the door, not looking at Ezra's arms any longer.

It ought to be a comfort, but it only suggested what his friend saw was too gruesome to view for long.

Ezra dried his hands and blotted over the scars before yanking down his sleeves and returning his cufflinks. Arthur hadn't caused the scars, though he had left Ezra at the mercy of Russel Breton, who beat for the pleasure of it and not just after a drink.

"No," Ezra sighed.

Thaddeus gave him a tight smile. "You could have said something."

After year one of their friendship or year six? Eventually, it seemed more insulting to bring it up. Better to leave it all unsaid.

"Leave it be," Ezra grunted.

"I'm ... sorry." Thaddeus reached for him, landing a heavy hand on his shoulder.

Don't touch me.

"You could have trusted me sooner."

Ezra shrugged out from under the weight of his hand. "If I wanted such a touching conversation, I'd have sought out a woman."

Thaddeus chuckled, dragging a palm over his jaw and holding up his hands in surrender.

"You are released from further inquiry. Though that woman..." Thaddeus sighed, eyes fluttering closed with a palm over his heart. "She is lovely, isn't she?"

Ezra rolled his eyes. "You have said the same about Mrs. Keene. I hardly believe that to be the highest compliment."

There was a tap at the door before it opened.

"The attendant is prepared for the interview." Magdalena stood just beyond the threshold wearing a gray orderly's uniform and nothing more than men's stockings on her feet. "And the detective has requested your presence."

"Where are your shoes?" Thaddeus's mustache twitched beneath his grin.

"Dirty." Sadness tinged her eyes before she covered it up.

Ezra wondered how often she did that, wearing the mask of a smile. An average woman would be embarrassed to trudge about publicly in borrowed socks. It wasn't proper. Then again, few women would have effectively conducted an autopsy. Or come here at all.

Why hadn't she reacted to his scars?

Her toes wiggled as she rocked back on her heels.

"Will we continue staring at my socks all day, or....?" She batted her eyelashes.

Embarrassment tinged the tips of his ears. "I wasn't ..."

"You were." Thaddeus disagreed with a nudge.

"Now it will really smell like feet," Ezra muttered, stepping into the hall.

He didn't care for feet.

Ahead of him, he saw Magdalena's shoulders slump as a woman scurried down the hall toward them, her eyes worried.

"Magdalena, what is all this?" The auburn-haired woman asked in a hushed tone.

"Mara," Magdalena murmured. "I'm afraid there's been an incident."

The woman's expression faltered.

"W-what?" Mara's hands trembled.

"There's been a death." Magdalena's voice was gentle.

"Who?"

"Mrs. Lewis passed on this morning, intentionally on her part. There is a detective here who is investigating what prompted it."

Mara seemed properly relieved.

"That doesn't make much sense to me." Mara shook her head.

"There must be more to it all," Magdalena sighed. "What do you recall of Mrs. Lewis before you came to join me?"

"She was always going on about that parrot. She had a strict routine, despite arriving just a few days before I saw the pair of you here."

Mara motioned in Ezra's direction, and Magdalena turned as if remembering their presence.

"Oh, I do apologize," Magdalena said. "These are my good friends, Mr. Cain, the coroner, and Dr. Talbot. This is Mara Spillman."

Mara looked at them both, guarded.

Thaddeus stuck out a palm and encapsulated Mara's hand in his own. He dragged his eyes over her with a wink.

His friend was a prat.

"I caution you—he could entertain the ears off a stone wall if it were a woman." Magdalena elbowed Thaddeus to release her friend.

"Well, now, I object ... I resemble that." Thaddeus chuckled.

"He's harmless," Magdalena reassured.

Mara gave a tight smile. Distrustful of men, so it would seem. Not that Ezra could blame her.

Loud footsteps sounded, followed by a bellow.

"Did I not send that blasted woman to fetch you?" Arthur rounded the corner, slowing when he saw them all gathered. "You just stand there?"

Ezra watched as Arthur's eyes traveled down to Magdalena's thick-knit stockings. "And you—you are absolutely ridiculous."

Annoyance pricked Ezra. Hadn't he thought the same thing? Yet somehow there was a difference between how he had begun to view ridiculous things.

"Ridiculously likable, ridiculously lovely ... by all means, please do complete the sentence." Magdalena smiled sweetly.

"It was complete," Arthur grunted. "Had punctuation at the end and everything."

Magdalena had a way with nearly everyone, and Arthur was no different.

The man brushed a palm across his face to erase the threat of a smile.

"I'd like the three of you to sit in on the interview," Arthur ordered.

It almost seemed as if Arthur were setting up moments where they'd be confined to the same space. As though it was something he wanted.

"Look in on the basements in ten minutes or so?" Magdalena squeezed Mara's arm. "I'll be down in a bit."

The interview was dull and the orderly particularly weepy. It didn't help that accusation often laced Arthur's tone.

Little of it mattered to Ezra. Being present only served to remind him of his youth when he'd worked with his father in the police courts.

"I cared for her," the attendant said tearfully. "It didn't matter that she would calm as the day progressed but return to her persistent madness every morning. I didn't care that she often accused me of consorting with that silly parrot, nor that she would on occasion strike me. It was my position, and I did not harm her."

"Walk us through Mrs. Lewis's typical day," Magdalena encouraged.

"She would rise at six, breakfast at seven thirty, gardens at eight. She was a bit of a wreck in the gardens, tended to frustrate the other patients, so we often kept her visits brief. Her digestion was never well." The orderly grimaced, as if uncomfortable speaking about her patient's bowel habits. "She would often pace or hide away until the afternoon. In the evenings she would have supper and read."

"That is all." Arthur waved a dismissive hand. "You are free to go."

The attendant scrambled away before he could change his mind.

Arthur looked at his son. "Ezra, when did you begin coming to the asylum?" He stood.

The rest of them followed suit.

"Beginning of September."

"And you, Ms. Trudeau?"

Thaddeus opened the door as they trailed behind Arthur.

"I first set foot in here a month ago. I've tended to my patients for just over three weeks."

"What do you recall in the beginning?" Arthur prodded.

"Mrs. Lewis greeted me when we came," Magdalena gestured to Ezra. "Very invested in the parrot. Seems she heard voices. I believed her to be harmless."

"And your patients?"

Magdalena exchanged a look with Ezra. "They were the violent ones."

Yet he had left her here. Ezra felt a pang in his midsection.

Arthur continued his long strides toward Mrs. Lewis's room with the unspoken expectation they follow.

"Why did you come back?" Ezra asked quietly, slowing his steps beside her.

"Their eyes." She hesitated. "I wanted to be hope when you said there was none."

Whereas Ezra sensed only the void in them, she'd seen humanity. There was still no cure for madness, yet she appeared to be the most illogical cure for broken souls.

He scrubbed his knuckles over his chest.

"Scars have a habit of trapping stories within them." She reached for his forearm and squeezed it. "Every untold story weighs something, and yours is heavy."

The pressure of her hand on his arm and her words in his head lingered, and he brushed a palm over his arm to rub away the feeling.

Ezra ducked around her, avoiding the tumultuous nature of his thoughts. Had he not considered himself to be reflective of the basement? Yet now, when it was full of light and warmth, what prospects did it suggest for him?

Was he fixable? Could she fix him?

Could he let her?

They followed the men into Mrs. Lewis's room, where his father rifled through drawers and overturned their contents onto the bed. There was very little—a hairbrush, hair pins, ribbons, a few letters, and three simple dresses.

Arthur slid open the missives and scanned them quickly.

"A madhouse divorce." He tossed the envelopes back onto the bed.

"Her husband sent her here?" Magdalena murmured.

"It's a tale as old as time," Arthur admitted with disgust. "A man marries an orphaned woman for her finances and sees to it she's sent away."

"She was the Queen's maid. That hardly constitutes a fortune," Magdalena said.

"Mm." His father shrugged. "Multiply her earnings several times over with however many women he chooses." He grimaced.

"Oh. Perfect." She scrunched up her nose. "How wonderful it is to be a lady."

"There is one simple protective measure," Ezra began. It wasn't often he felt compelled to offer anyone comfort, but this felt important.

She looked at him expectantly.

The answer was obvious. "Never get married."

Arthur chuckled. "Men are at just as much risk now as women since the reform."

Thaddeus was unabashed as he rifled through Mrs. Lewis's underthings on the mattress.

His father went back to searching the lining of a drawer using a knife to check the seams as if he were hunting a mysterious and well-bred criminal. Of course, Mrs. Lewis had been neither.

Nothing. There was nothing here.

Ezra ran a hand within the pillowcase and under the mattress as he'd been taught so many years ago. Instinct, so it seemed, never quite left, and working with Arthur was ingrained in him.

"What are we looking for?" Magdalena asked the hovering question.

"Any indication she was not a lunatic," Arthur suggested.

Ezra closed his eyes, remembering the woman's remarkably dilated eyes and the racing of her pulse. These were the only symptoms he knew of. It wasn't enough, not when both could be attributed to her impending death.

For a moment, he fought to determine whether he ought to let things be or ease his curiosity—opting finally to satiate the latter.

Ezra turned to Magdalena. "If you had something to hide, something that could prove your sanity, where would you put it?"

If anyone knew how to tuck in their oddities, it would be her.

Magdalena's brow furrowed as her hands went to the undergarments scattered about the bed, the place a man would not likely look at all. That is, unless their name was Thaddeus Cain.

"I would keep it close." She nodded slowly, thinking aloud. "I would always have it with me."

Ezra left them, retracing his steps toward the autopsy room.

It had been cleaned well, and Mrs. Lewis's clothes were stacked in a pile at the foot of the table.

He shook them out and searched through for the item that would have rested closest to her body. The chemise unfurled, and his fingers nimbly pinched over every hem, finally settling upon a lump just near the collar.

There.

Presumably, Mrs. Lewis had created a small slit in the hem and slid something within. He opened the hidden pocket and spilled the firm object into his palm … just as he sensed Magdalena's company behind him.

"What is it?" she breathed.

Ezra held up the most innocent, yet incriminating object—half of a broken shank button. A familiar one.

The memory settled over him, and he groaned internally. Indeed, they'd be stranded in the hospital for longer than he wished.

"A cufflink?" Magdalena asked.

"Mm." He closed his hand around it and tucked it in his pocket. "Magdalena..." He hedged. "Was Mrs. Lewis ever in the basement? When you arrived?"

"No, only the three—Luce, Franz, and Ellington." Magdalena looked confused. "She was always upstairs. Why?"

Ezra dragged a palm over his face.

"When we first arrived, there were two others. I recall it clearly. Not including Franz, and the one in the procedure room, there were three behind the bars."

The eyes. He had always dreaded the eyes.

"Three? What do you mean?" She paled.

"I mean that between the moment we visited together to the time you returned alone, two people left that basement."

"How?" Magdalena blinked up at him.

"Something happened to her down there." The idea made him sick. "Perhaps someone twisted her mind into madness before sending her up the steps." He was thinking aloud now as he paced the room.

"Yet they killed her in the end?"

"I don't ..." This was all too confusing. "I think her death was an accident. Human error."

He watched the pulse in her throat.

"We have to find the missing two." Magdalena was adamant.

The implication of the small accessory resting in his pocket suggested something far more sinister than he had predicted, and he berated himself for not sensing it.

Ezra growled low in his throat and struck the table with the heel of his hand in agitation.

"What's going on?" Magdalena placed a gentle hand on his arm. "Let me in on your frustration."

This was his fault. He could have prevented things had he come when Roland first brought the rumors to his attention. Timelines didn't lie.

"Mrs. Lewis didn't arrive a few days before we visited, as Mara suggested. She was in that basement long before we met her."

"Are you certain? Mara wouldn't mislead us."

"I am, and perhaps she wouldn't. Not intentionally. It's just as likely she didn't know." He pulled back out the cufflink and set it in her hand. "I removed the other side of this link from Franz's stomach not long after your near drowning."

Her eyes darted toward the hall beyond the door. "Who else was in that basement?"

That was the question, which when fully discovered would lead directly to the responsible party. How did the sane turn mad, and who else within the walls had been transformed along with Mrs. Lewis?

How could one separate the seemingly insane from those who were truly so?

"Is there not something to protect people from false allegations?"

Magdalena drew up a hand to nibble at her fingernails.

"There is." He nodded slowly. "Admission requires a physician's signature."

They hurried through the hall toward Mr. Fallon's office.

"I'm on my way out." Thaddeus stopped them in the hall. "Should I return this evening?"

"You're not on lockdown?" Magdalena mused.

"I was invited." He waggled his thick brows, puffed up his chest like a peacock, and strutted a few paces. "Thus, I can come and go at will. Also, death stops for no man," he admitted. "The police have another autopsy waiting for me in the theatre."

"Mm, bring me a change of clothes if you would?" Ezra asked.

"Please let Mrs. Keene know—she will worry." Magdalena sighed. "And my sister. Frank will be upset."

"Certainly." He gathered up his hat and coat. "Be safe."

He met each of their eyes to convey his sincerity.

"Have life." Ezra nodded.

They turned toward Mr. Fallon's office.

The man sat behind his desk looking particularly pitiful as he shuffled through Mrs. Lewis's file.

"Her admittance reports?" Ezra held out his hand.

"Your father has it."

"Of course." Ezra had nearly forgotten his father was here.

"You will tell the detective what we have found?" Magdalena inquired as they left.

Would he tell Arthur? He ought to, though there was a hesitation as he nodded.

"Ezra." Arthur barked from the end of the hall, shaking a fistful of papers as he stormed toward them.

Ezra tensed, hating the recoil of his muscles and the flinch as his father grew closer. How could so many years have repaired so little? Out of instinct bred from a childhood of fear, he searched for familiar signs.

He's sober, he reassured the fear in his mind. He only hit when he was drunk.

"What is the meaning of this?" Arthur shoved the papers into Ezra's chest.

"For goodness's sake," Magdalena said.

Ezra pulled the papers away from his body and shuffled through them, seeking the source of his father's anger. Not that the man had needed much source in the past.

"You acted as though you'd never met the woman before, yet here it is. Proof!"

Arthur's face contorted in fury, spittle flying from his lips as he shouted.

Ezra's eyes widened as he looked at the admittance paper, and his breath caught in his throat.

Magdalena gasped and snatched the paper away, scanning it. Then she sighed in relief.

"Such a fright for nothing." She put a hand over her heart and turned to Arthur. "This isn't Dr. Talbot's signature. Have you seen this man's handwriting?"

She knew it in a near instant after seeing it, yet his own father hadn't. It was a bitter feeling.

Nonetheless, there it was,—the name "Ezra Talbot" scrawled across the line of the document.

"You didn't sign this?" Arthur paused, faint relief flickering through his expression.

"Of course not."

Ezra's eyes scanned the paper hastily before the detective pulled it back away. Even the date written on the form appeared to be incorrect.

Magdalena's stomach erupted with a growl, and she had the decency to look mildly uncomfortable.

"I must check the patients in the basement and give Mara a reprieve. And this," she gestured to her stomach before giving each of them a pointed look. "This is nature's reminder to eat something so the pair of you do not kill one another before this is solved."

"You know something." His father accused when she was gone. "You've had that expression all your life when you have a secret."

"Don't patronize me." He turned away.

"Your name is on this paper. Who has something against you?"

He grabbed Ezra's forearm.

Don't touch me. His shoulder spasmed.

Arthur caught the motion, and guilt seemed to seep out of him like a saturated sponge.

"Did you recover?" Arthur's words tumbled out raw and rough. He searched Ezra's face. "It's been so long, surely you have?"

Good, let him hurt.

Ezra drew back his shoulders. "Tell me, how does one recover from their father trying to kill them? Precisely how does one tell their mind they do not need to fear human touch when the one person it was supposed to trust betrayed everything?"

The harshness of his words struck him. As they should.

"Ezra, I'm sor—"

"Keep those filthy words in your mouth," Ezra spat out. "And in answer to your first question. Supposing we are anything alike at all, it is likely there is a very, very long list of people who have something against me."

With that he stormed away, down the long hall away from his father.

"Be sure to eat," Arthur called after him, his words cracked with emotion.

It should have been satisfying to hear his father's pain. Instead, the words sank low in his gut.

Arthur couldn't change. Ezra knew that full well.

How unfortunate it was that a son still wished for his father's approval or affection—especially when those emotions should long be abandoned.

He hated that they weren't. Hated that it mattered to him.

A heart could not be trusted, and evidently, neither could a mind.

Chapter Thirty-Three

Ezra

An ear-splitting scream erupted through the halls, tearing Ezra from his tea. He covered his ears.

Frantic footsteps clipped through the otherwise calm. In an asylum, this alone wouldn't have made him pause, if not for the fact that the woman's voice was screaming his name.

Mara staggered down the hall, clutching at the walls to steady herself. The sleeve of her dress was torn, and her lip bloody.

"The basement!" She gasped, grasping at her throat. "They have come alive as monsters."

Arthur bolted into view down the hall and disappeared just as quickly toward the basement.

Find her! Save her! He knew Arthur would do so without being told.

Arthur had cared for Magdalena as a girl. Certainly he'd look out for her now.

Ezra dashed to the medical supply closet and grabbed a bottle of chloroform and a rag before hurrying down the stairs.

The madness within was evident from the moment the door opened.

Luce's screams were enunciated by the sound of pages being torn from the mangled book she cherished. The shreds scattered like bits of snow around her cell.

Ellington laughed and plucked invisible strands from the air as the cat skittered past in a panic.

Not Franz, he begged. But of course, that was where she would be. If he'd hurt her...

The thought terrified him.

Franz's cell burst open as Arthur stumbled backward, landing unceremoniously on his back.

"Franz—Franz darling. It's all right. I'm right here." Magdalena's voice trembled.

Ezra slipped silently around his father. Dousing the rag in chloroform, he turned his face away from the fumes.

Inside the room, Franz towered over Magdalena, who had scrambled backward on the floor until she was pressed, flinching, against the wall. She saw Ezra and shook her head gently, softly pleading for him to leave her.

But he couldn't. He'd made that mistake before. Twice.

"Shall we make some drawings together, Franz?" She pushed herself to stand. As she did, blood from a cut on her hand trickled down her fingertips.

Franz groaned and grabbed at his head. He shook it as if to clear a foreign haze.

Ezra was a head taller than Franz, though the young man was quite strong—he'd proven it before.

Quickly, Ezra stepped behind him, forcing the man's head into the crook of his elbow. He used the other hand to press the rag over his mouth and nose.

Franz gasped, struggling in vain to remove the hands that restrained him.

Bile rose in Ezra's throat as Franz grappled at his fingers.

Don't touch me. His shoulder snapped toward his ear. Ezra hissed through his teeth, unsure of whether he wanted to flee or crush the man's neck further.

He nearly released Franz in discomfort as his fingers burned and the familiar vice clutched his lungs.

"Badgers eat hedgehogs," Magdalena sputtered out, her eyes full of panic.

What? Badgers? She was mad herself. The distraction, while completely bizarre, pushed back the threatening fog.

Then Arthur was with him, catching Franz as the man's knees gave way. The pair dragged him to his bed.

Clipping the restraints into place, Ezra's anger was ignited.

"You." Ezra glared at Magdalena. "Stop trying to save the world when you cannot even save yourself."

"And you." He turned to Arthur. "If you say a single word, I will…"

Ezra tugged a palm through his hair, the adrenaline coursing through him and clouding his thoughts.

"Just don't," he muttered.

Ezra grabbed Magdalena's wrist and pulled her through the hall, past the other patients and up the steps.

He didn't slow down nor pause until he closed the supply closet door behind them.

He spun, prepared to give her a piece of his mind, to shout at her perhaps as the pounding of his heart recommended.

But all the rage drained from him when he saw the glistening moisture in her eyes. Shadows danced across her face from the lantern swinging overhead.

He dropped her hand and stepped back, horrified at this possibility.

"Did I hurt you?" he choked out.

A silent tear gathered enough boldness and rolled down her cheek as she shook her head and turned away. She pressed her forehead into the door, taking in a ragged sigh as she swiped at her face with her hands.

Ezra was many things, but he would never hurt her. He knew that now. At least not on purpose.

"No." Her shoulders rattled. "I'm not hurt. I'm angry."

Neither of them spoke as Ezra swallowed, his chest heaving until his heart slowed to a more natural pace.

"They are still here." Her voice was hard. "A monster in our midst."

She was correct, of course. They'd made someone nervous.

"Mm." He nodded.

She shifted and unhooked the sleeve of her dress, rolling it up to tend to the laceration across her knuckles as she searched the shelves for a bandage.

Ezra sighed and pulled down a wrapping, setting it beside the washing table. He took her hand, settled it in the bowl, and poured water over the wound.

"I can do it," she argued quietly.

"Can you?" He dismissed her words.

The laceration wasn't deep, more of an abrasion upon closer examination.

"He grabbed Mara." Her voice cracked. "It was terrifying—you should have seen his eyes. The pupils were large, unlike anything I've seen before."

She shook off the memory and withdrew her hand, taking the bandage from him and winding it twice.

She was distracting herself with this small task, and Ezra distracted himself with her comment. Mrs. Lewis's eyes had also been dilated to an extreme. It surprised him then too.

"They've all been drugged, not poisoned, nor medicated," he murmured, more to himself than to her. "There must be value in keeping them alive."

He should have seen it sooner. He tapped a fist on his forehead, willing his mind to process every seemingly trivial detail.

"When were they alone?"

"Just the short time I was with you before Mara arrived. Thirty minutes, forty at the most. They were in a terrible upset nearly twenty minutes after she went down there, but she didn't want to interrupt us. Somehow Franz's cell was unlocked, and I arrived as ..."

Her eyes met his.

"I always lock it," she whispered fearfully.

"Mm."

Mrs. Lewis had eaten breakfast at seven-thirty, mad by eight. The timing was nearly identical.

"We need a drug, one which reaches its potency in at most, forty minutes. Something discreet and managed with meals."

"Surely those options are limitless?" She was horrified at this potential.

"Not limitless." He shook his head. "It is here. We just need to find it."

Ezra opened the door and returned to the basement. She didn't need to follow him, and perhaps a part of him was surprised she did.

Magdalena was reckless, he realized. It seemed almost intentional how she inserted herself into the ugliest scenario. He wanted to ask why.

In the basement he went to Luce's cell first—close, but not close enough for her to reach him, which she did attempt with clawing hands. She didn't speak to him, and her eyes were nearly black from the size of her pupils.

He grabbed the woman's wrists as she stretched them through the bars, turning them over in his hands to find her pulse. Luce's face was scorching red, a symptom Mrs. Lewis hadn't possessed.

"Fetch my watch." He directed Magdalena. "Pocket of my vest."

Magdalena withdrew it and indicated the time.

"One hundred and thirty-one beats per minute."

He released Luce's hands just as she spit through the bars, narrowly missing the pair.

"So we have two side effects? Rapid pulse and dilated eyes." Magdalena tucked his watch back into his vest.

"More than two. Flushing of the face, dilation of the pupils, elevated pulse, delusions, paranoia, panic."

"How many patients are in Bethlem?" she asked.

Arthur stepped from the procedure room, holding a damp cloth to his jaw.

"One hundred and twelve patients. One hundred and fifteen, including these." His eyes narrowed. "Now what have you been keeping from me?"

Ezra and Magdalena exchanged a glance, and she gave him a reassuring nod. Irritating.

He pulled the half-shank button from his pocket and tossed it to his father.

"You can trust me," Arthur said as he caught it.

Ezra scoffed. Liar.

But his heart was a fool, wishing he could.

CHAPTER THIRTY-FOUR

Magdalena

"Are you all right?" Magdalena leaned in close and dabbed at Mara's bottom lip with a rag.

Mara nodded slowly, tugging up the shoulder of her torn dress.

"I think it would be best if you returned home until this passes. At the very least, until morning." Magdalena pinned the sleeve as best she could.

Mara nodded. The woman hadn't been here when Mrs. Lewis jumped. Surely, she would be permitted to leave.

"We have never discussed it but ... are you safe, Mara? At home?"

Magdalena hadn't pried into her friend's personal life but hoped she would trust her now.

Mara stiffened and looked away, nodding cautiously.

"Peter—he left me."

"What?" Magdalena couldn't hide her surprise, nor disgust. "When?"

"Last week." Mara gave a weak smile tinged with relief.

"I'm sorry," Magdalena said this small, half-truth.

Mara gave her a crooked grin and raised a delicate eyebrow. "Truly?"

Magdalena snorted and shook her head. "I met him once and it was more than enough."

"Sometimes I wish I could stop feeling," Mara whispered.

Magdalena shook her head furiously. "I know that that sounds wonderful, but it isn't. Life conditions us through pain to feel nothing at all, but then we miss out on the things worth feeling."

"Surely it would be better than this?" Mara fisted her skirts in her hand. "I think I've forgotten how to feel human or alive even. I can hardly look myself in the mirror, Mags."

"Then I will remind you every beautiful thing about yourself, lest you forget how lovely you can be through the eyes of another," Magdalena promised.

Mara seemed perfectly in control of every emotion as she stood and hugged her friend.

"I hope his black heart kills him in the end," she murmured.

A knock sounded at the door.

"We need you, Magdalena," the detective snipped.

"I will return tomorrow morning." Mara gave her a parting pat and opened the door, chuckling as she did. "Perhaps bring you some shoes."

"Women." The detective muttered as Mara squeezed past.

"—are fantastic," Magdalena finished for him, tucking her hand into the crook of his elbow.

Arthur looked down at her, entirely confused by her interaction, which of course encouraged her to make him even more uncomfortable.

"You called me Magdalena?" She wiggled her eyebrows up at him.

"What are you doing? Stop touching me." He shook her off.

"Why? Do I make you uncomfortable?" she asked, humor shining in her eyes.

"Of course you do," he muttered.

"Perfect." She clapped her hands together. "What is it you need?"

"I don't need you," he clarified. "Ezra needs you."

Highly unlikely.

"He would never admit it." Arthur voiced her thoughts.

"Of course not," she clipped. "You Talbot men are a stubborn breed."

He cleared his throat and gestured toward her hand. "Are you all right?"

"Ah, yes." She nodded. "Just a minor accident."

"He's angry with you."

"With me?"

"Mm." He nodded, looking at her in his peripheral. "You should not be here, so it seems."

"What does it matter to him?" She planted her hands on her hips. "And what business is it of any of yours where I go or what I do?"

She shook her finger at him, adding, "Do not think of letting me go home and not him."

Detective Talbot chuckled and scratched at his beard, a nervous habit.

"And," she added, "do not dare go about projecting your feelings as his. You are a skunk and a badger—do not add lying to your misdeeds."

The last retort stung just a bit and his smile slipped. She'd feel a bit worse about it had he been anyone else.

"Indeed," he said softly.

She found Dr. Talbot in the foyer beside an uncomfortable-looking Mr. Fallon as patients lined up in a queue with attendants stationed every few paces.

The doctor checked the first patient's pulse with eyes on his pocket watch before scribbling down the number and completing his evaluation. The woman in front of him seemed to pass his assessment, and he moved on to the next.

"It will take days at this pace. You have some medical knowledge?" The detective asked.

She rolled her eyes—she had nearly autopsied an entire body in front of his eyes.

"No, I am only for decoration."

With that, she unhooked his pocket watch from his vest coat and joined the doctor.

Ezra gave her a curt nod as she did.

Magdalena's patient had an acceptable pulse, no ruddy complexion, and average pupil size. She sent him on his way.

They were nearly a quarter the way through when Ezra interrupted her evaluation with a thrust of his chin toward the man in front of him.

"Denton Cole, forty-one years of age."

He spoke low in her ear, his breath toying with the fine hairs that escaped her braid.

"Good afternoon, Mr. Cole." Magdalena smiled into the man's distant eyes.

Pupils distended, flushing of the complexion, pulse racing. She looked at Ezra.

"Who is his physician?" Ezra asked, calling Mr. Fallon over. "What medication does this man take?"

Mr. Fallon sputtered. It was evident he did nothing but fill a chair and take home a stipend.

"Useless," Ezra muttered.

"Find out," the detective demanded, throwing his hands up in irritation.

Mr. Fallon scampered away toward his office.

Magdalena waved over an attendant. "Please take Mr. Cole to the basement, there are several rooms available."

She tried to offer Mr. Cole a warm smile.

But Mr. Cole erupted into a fit of sobs.

"I did nothing wrong." He wailed, grasping at Magdalena's collar. "Please, don't send me back to the basement!"

His speech was slurred and his steps uneven.

The detective untangled the man's arms from around her and pushed her toward his son.

Instinctively, Ezra's hands closed around her shoulders to steady her as two attendants pulled Mr. Cole off down the hallway, failing to console him.

The remainder of the line erupted into shrieks and wails as the patients in the line seemed to feed off his terror.

Their eyes traveled down the line of patients stretched through the foyer and down the halls. Nearly seventy remained left to sort through.

"Can't do a thing until the rest are calm. Panic will mimic the symptoms we seek." Ezra pushed a frustrated palm through his curls.

Their efforts would have to be postponed.

Finnian and the other constables rushed to help.

"We'll take them from here." The detective offered.

She watched Ezra's eyes dart around at the chaos. His chest began to rise and fall rapidly.

It was too loud, she realized.

He buried his hands in his pockets as his lips moved silently with whatever his means of distraction were.

"Let's go." She smiled up at him, looping her arm through his.

"Where—" His words were cut off as she tugged him through the halls and out a side door.

"You haven't any shoes!" he argued when they were outside in the crisp autumn air.

She shushed him, enjoying her secret adventure.

She didn't release him until they stood on a bridge over a small, shallow pond.

He cleared his throat and shook off her hand.

Withdrawing a scone from her pocket, she tore it in half and offered it to him, which he declined with a look of disgust.

"It's not for you, Doctor. It's for them." She looked pointedly at the geese.

With a heavy sigh, she pushed it into his hand when he didn't reach for it.

"Like this." She demonstrated, tearing off a piece and tossing it to the birds.

Seeing there were treats readily available, nearly every bird in the pond veered in their direction.

Ezra stared at the bread in his hand like it was poison.

"If they are drugging the scones, I wonder what it would do to the geese."

His lips twitched into a true smile, the first she'd seen in over a month.

She gaped at him. "I've just drugged a goose!"

She searched for her victim in the spattering of birds to no avail.

"We'll just wait about thirty minutes, and it will be the goose who fears the water," he joked, tearing loose another piece and tossing it to the birds.

"That's awful!" She reached for his bread with a gasp, intent on stopping him from potentially victimizing more geese.

He held it out of her reach and chuckled.

The happy sound was beautiful, and she wished she could offer him the permission to do it more often—even if at the expense of hearing his dark humor.

"Stop." He raised his hands in surrender, eyes still twinkling. "It's not likely to be the scones."

She sighed and leaned on the railing. The chill of the autumn afternoon radiated through her stocking-clad feet.

Her eyes drifted toward a solitary goose on the opposite end of the pond. Poor thing—he ought to get at least a small morsel.

She tore off a small chunk of bread and offered the other end to Ezra.

"Distract them?"

She tugged off one stocking and then the other before pushing them into her pocket. He did as instructed, surprisingly, and continued tossing bits into the water.

Magdalena slipped quietly from the bridge, her toes squished in the mud at the pond's edge as she tiptoed closer to the solitary goose at the far end.

When she got closer, she saw the poor bird was rather maimed. One eye appeared to be functional, but the other was gone entirely, a nasty scar covering its face.

Scars. Even animals carried stories they couldn't share.

Magdalena made a gentle kissing sound, garnering its attention, and just as she thought it would fly away, she tossed the scone.

It hesitated just long enough to notice the morsel, snatching it up before any of the others could get a chance.

"Be a good little bird," she encouraged before trudging back through the mud.

"Why do you do that?" Ezra asked softly when she approached.

"Even birds get hungry."

"That's not what I meant," He blinked out at the water. "Why do you care about things that don't matter?"

"Everything matters, Doctor Talbot. It simply depends on who you ask."

"I'm asking you." He leaned his forearms on the railing and looped his fingers together. "What matters to you?"

She didn't quite know how to answer him. Drying her feet on the hem of her dress, she tugged on her stockings and then lay flat on her stomach looking over the bridge and into the murky water below.

"What are you doing?"

"Looking for things that matter to me," she said over her shoulder.

The planks of the bridge shifted as he crouched beside her and peered into the water.

"Fish?"

"Shh, look." She pointed. "Right there."

"I don't see anyth…"

His words trailed off, and she watched his reflection narrow its brows and glare at her as he caught sight of himself on the surface of the water.

His face disappeared as he stood and walked a few paces away.

"Why?" he asked. "Why do you chase the broken things? I've seen you seek them out almost unknowingly. Instead of running away, you run toward them, like some twisted addiction."

Magdalena chuckled and sat up. "You believe yourself to be my addiction?"

It was likely he wasn't wrong, though she wouldn't admit it aloud.

He shook his head. "You are playing a game you do not know how to win."

"That's the thing." She scrambled to her feet. "I get to decide if I win this game. I made the rules."

"I don't even know what we're talking about anymore."

He flicked up his collar, ducking into it.

"What happened after you left me here all those weeks ago?"

He didn't turn to look at her.

"Did you think of me once? Did you feel even the slightest bit of regret?"

"You will never hear me say the words you seek." His words were dark and bitter.

They stood in silence for a time with the heaviness of unspoken remorse pouring off him.

"That's the thing ... I don't need to hear the words to offer my forgiveness."

"Keep it."

Magdalena shrugged apologetically. "I already gave it to you."

"That's a terrible choice. When someone wrongs you once, they'll do it again."

"It's impolite to refuse a gift." It broke her heart to see him struggle with something so simple.

"There are things I have not told you." He began to pace. "Things you would never overlook. I have misled you, I have shouted at you, I have been willfully unkind. You shouldn't be here."

He closed the distance between them.

"Clearly, you were raised as an only child. If the worst thing my brothers and sisters ever did was tell me to shut up, it was a particularly good day."

"I need you to go home, to bring yourself away from me," he pleaded.

Her eyes narrowed. "Now listen closely, Dr. Talbot. I am not this weak and shallow thing you believe me to be. You do not get to tell me where to go or what to do. You do not get to hurt me in some method of trying to protect me from yourself. Why do you keep pushing me away? Why do you want me to leave?"

"Because everyone leaves!" He snapped. "Because you do not listen, and I am trying to tell you that being near me will bring you nothing but pain and I—I don't want to watch it unfold."

The empath she was, Magdalena felt his anguish as though it were hers.

Salomé would have known how to put him back together, but she was gone, and Magdalena wasn't her. Dr. Talbot's words hurt her, though likely far less than they hurt him.

Did he truly know her so little? That he would think simple things would make her run away?

"I don't care," she said stubbornly.

"You don't—" He huffed out a humorless laugh, throwing up his hands in frustration.

"I don't care," she repeated. "You could show me the vilest parts of yourself, and I would still be here."

"If you knew half my fear, you would shatter."

"And if you knew a fraction of my melancholy, you would drown. But what if we could fix both? What if—?"

Hope leaped in her throat. Perhaps she had been about things all wrong. Perhaps this was not an independent journey, but one they were destined to take together.

"No." He shook his head. "Neither will be cured in our lifetimes."

"So what? We can build on the steps that already exist. We can prepare for future generations. This is hope—can you not feel it?"

"You are mad if you believe this, Magdalena."

Dr. Talbot shook his head, but she saw the wheels spinning behind his insult.

"Then be mad with me." She clasped her fingers beneath her chin. "We're already halfway there as it is."

"What about the rest?" He gestured to himself. "Did you hear nothing I said?"

"You will tell me in your own time, and it will change nothing."

"That is not a guarantee."

"There are no guarantees." She grinned. He was wavering.

He shook his head. "I'll think on it. I don't know what this sort of study would remotely resemble."

"The unknown is my favorite." If he were anyone else, she would throw her arms around him.

He held up a palm. "Whatever it is you're thinking, don't."

"Someday Dr. Talbot, I'll put you back together, and when I do, I'll expect a kiss."

"Magdalena!" She heard the dramatic cry of Mr. Cain interrupt from the lawn.

She turned to see him gaping with a theatrical hand over his heart.

"I leave you but a few hours, and you turn to him?" He wilted in feigned betrayal.

Of all the wretched timings. She chuckled.

"It was not as it sounded, Mr. Cain."

"I certainly hope not."

Dr. Talbot's ears were red. She'd seen them do that when he was embarrassed before, and now, it struck her as oddly familiar. Endearing.

Mr. Cain approached them.

"The detective filled me in when I arrived. He requested we divide and conquer the remaining patients before they are put to bed."

Ezra cleared his throat. "There isn't much time." He glanced at the lowering sun in the sky.

"We'd better run." Magdalena smiled.

"I don't run." Ezra shook his head.

She raised a brow, challenging him.

"Ever." His shield was firmly back in place, the word stilted and stubborn just like him.

There. It was another secret. She grasped it and held it tightly.

CHAPTER THIRTY-FIVE

Magdalena

"That's the last one," Mr. Cain remarked, pulling the door closed behind him. "Shall we have a quick meal before I turn back?"

Dr. Talbot grimaced. They were all tired, and it hadn't helped that they'd not found the remaining patient. Constable Bulcroft had agreed to watch the basement until Magdalena bedded down there for the evening.

"Mm, tea perhaps." Dr. Talbot nodded.

The detective was off, pulling orderlies for interviews one by one. He'd not be stopping any time soon.

Magdalena stepped into the kitchen to request a pot of tea and some semblance of supper.

The cook wasn't friendly with the late intrusion and pointed her in the direction of some rustic bread with cheese to tide them over until the morning.

When she returned, Mr. Cain reached for the tray Magdalena sat before them.

"What are tomorrow's plans, then?" he asked. "Surely, he cannot keep everyone here much longer, there will be mutiny."

Ezra inspected his cup before gulping down his tea.

"We will likely complete the interviews tomorrow. There was a bit of an incident this afternoon that delayed things a bit."

"What happened?" Mr. Cain poured himself a second cup as the doctor hesitantly tore off a chunk of bread.

Magdalena nibbled on her morsel, her eyes growing heavy in the wake of the day's events. Nothing had gone quite as she intended. Ezra's eyes drifted toward her, as if gauging what to share.

She sighed. "Someone drugged the patients in the basement, willfully we believe, considering that they were relatively well in the last week or so."

The coroner's fingers tightened into a fist as he seemed to notice the bandage on her hand. "Who was it?"

"Mr. Fallon doesn't seem likely. He may know something he should not, but he is no great mastermind."

"I meant who hurt you?"

"My friend." She dismissed his concern. "It wasn't his fault."

Mr. Cain gave a tight smile.

The men carried on their conversation as she thoughtfully stared off into space. Mr. Fallon hadn't been pleased to have her in the basement. While he had an apparent love of money—many do—that alone didn't make him vicious enough to drug the sane into madness. Did it?

Seeing the pair were finished, she gathered up the tray and returned it to the kitchen.

Cook was none too pleased inside.

"You got the wrong tea, Miss," she seethed, setting about making another pot. "That was the medicine."

"What?" Magdalena felt the blood drain from her face.

"The medicine." Cook pointed to the teapot on the tray she'd returned. "Every evening, we make the tea and let it steep for the next morning. Now I've got to do it again."

Magdalena turned toward the stove, where there was a separate kettle—the one she should have retrieved.

"What was in it?" Magdalena shouted, her mind racing. She hadn't consumed any tea, had she?

Just a sip—but Ezra and Mr. Cain had had at least a cup. Maybe two.

"Huh?" Cook crossed her arms.

"What is the medicine? What's in the tea?"

Magdalena snatched up the linen sack on the counter and poured some of the contents into her hand; the tea leaves had been cut with small oval-shaped seeds she didn't recognize.

"Tell me what this is." Magdalena held up the foreign kernel.

"How should I know?" Cook snapped. "I am a cook, not an apothecary. It is delivered for those three—er, two—and I make the tea. That is all I know."

Magdalena grabbed a fistful of the blend and pushed it into her pocket.

"What other patient?" Her simple meal lurched in her stomach and her lips pinched.

Now the cook seemed to sense Magdalena's urgency. "Mr. Levitt, second floor. Room 209 of the men's ward."

"Do not make the tea for tomorrow, just this once. Make them a regular pot."

Magdalena ran from the room in a panic.

"Doctor!" Magdalena shook his shoulders.

As he turned it was clear. She was far too late.

His pupils were beginning to expand, and an uncharacteristic pinkness tinged his cheeks. Mr. Cain, so it seemed, was at a further point, and he grinned at Magdalena as if she were a jester.

"Mm?" The doctor asked.

"You need to vomit, immediately." She pulled his arm. "You too, Mr. Cain. They have drugged the tea."

"I knew it smelled a bit like feet," Dr. Talbot muttered.

"What did you say?" Magdalena froze, midway between looping Mr. Cain's arm over her shoulder.

Of all the times for the halls to be vacant.

"It smelled like feet," The doctor hissed, shaking a finger at her. "I thought we were friends."

If he didn't look entirely pitiful, she could have laughed.

"Quickly now, Dr. Talbot." She gestured toward him. "Give me your arm. We'll get you to the basement before you both lose your minds entirely."

"I do not like the basement. It's cold."

"I'll get you a blanket," she promised.

"I am perfectly capable of walking by myself." He shrugged away from her offered hand and sauntered in the wrong direction.

"Mm, no." He stopped himself, full of logic, and twisted toward the correct direction.

"This is the way." He nodded to himself.

This was quite possibly the most ill-timed incident. The drug was quite literally at hand, and if Dr. Talbot's ramblings held any merit, the scent could be traced to the greenhouse on the third floor.

Perhaps Mr. Fallon was to be blamed after all.

They managed to enter the basement without much incident, where Constable Bulcroft rushed to her side.

"Ms. Trudeau!" He gaped at her, seemingly flabbergasted by the scene unfolding.

"She is lovely is she not?" Thaddeus ran a palm along the constable's jawline.

Magdalena snorted. "Mr. Cain, that is the constable."

She said it loudly as though the volume would help him understand.

"Very sorry, sir." Thaddeus bowed, pointing toward an empty cell. "I shall go in there."

She looked around. "Doctor?"

He was gone.

She found him rifling through his medical bag tucked away in the procedure room. He withdrew a small sachet of something and pulled it to his lips.

"What are you—stop that." She reached for it but he spun away.

Goodness knows what the man was trying to ingest.

"Activated charcoal," he muttered. "If you are trying to kill me, I won't let you."

Charcoal, she recalled, would coat the stomach and potentially prevent complete absorption of the drug.

A black powder coughed out of his mouth as he gagged and reached for the pitcher of water. He gulped long and hearty swallows to wash down the consistency of chalk.

Magdalena smiled. It would seem nothing could take away the doctor's sanity.

She took the remainder of the paper sachet, mixed it with a cup of water, and hurried it to Mr. Cain.

She turned to Constable Bulcroft. "You must find me several things. Someone has been providing the kitchen staff with drugs for three patients, Mrs. Lewis, Mr. Cole—," she gestured to the cell beside Thaddeus, "—and Mr. Levitt, second floor, room 209."

She held Mr. Cain's chin and poured the liquid into his mouth, forcing it closed to prevent it from gurgling out.

Mr. Cain swallowed with a grimace.

"You must notify the detective, then find me a plant in the greenhouse that has an unpleasant smell. Like ... like feet."

"Will you be all right here?" The constable gestured to Mr. Cain sidling up to a broom, caressing its straw hairs.

"He's a bit occupied." Magdalena nodded, biting back a smile. "Just in case, give me your belt."

"My belt?"

Magdalena stretched out her palm.

Constable Bulcroft turned scarlet, and she nearly pitied him as he struggled with the clasp and pulled it through its loops.

"Thank you." She took it from him and strapped the coroner's wrist to the bars of his cell. "He'll be fine until he has some sanity. We'll all be fine, go quickly."

She hesitantly handed him the key. He'd need it to get back in.

"And find Mr. Fallon, for goodness' sake." Magdalena had a question or two for that irritating man.

"Miss!" Thaddeus wailed as the constable hurried away. "She was so beauti-ful."

"How is it that you have hardly changed at all under the influence?" She rolled her eyes.

"I've been influenced?" He whispered with a roguish grin, extending a hand toward her.

"Nope." She brushed his hand away and gave him a reassuring pat. "You keep those to yourself."

"Doctor, come along here and have a rest." She called to him, turning down the bed.

"No," he responded defiantly from the procedure room.

"I'll be right back," Magdalena reassured Mr. Cain, who was entirely indif-ferent and had resumed his flirtations with the cleaning equipment.

"Don't take my cigarettes," he chirped after her.

She sighed and rubbed her temples. So much for a night's rest.

She took the last sip of the charcoal concoction just to be safe. She wouldn't benefit from joining them in their temporary insanity.

Magdalena mustered up enough energy to talk the doctor into being obedi-ent for once.

She pushed the door open and gasped at him in horror. "What are you doing?"

Clothing littered the floor. His boots were strewn carelessly in the middle of the room. The socks peaked out from beneath the bed and his vest lay slung across the washstand.

"I'm in an oven." He groaned. His hands moved to his cravat and tugged it loose, dropping it at his feet.

"Sir, you cannot." Magdalena's eyes went wide as he began on the buttons of his shirt.

She grappled for his hands. "That's quite enough."

To her surprise, there was no flinching away at her touch, no ragged breath-ing, nor any lifting of his shoulder. It was as if the drug forced his mind to abandon its efforts at self-protection.

Dr. Talbot pushed her hands away and gestured toward the door. "You. Out."

Perhaps it was indeed best if she let him remain in there for the night. He did seem insistent on it, and his agitation was becoming a bit alarming.

He swayed and staggered toward the door, an apparent dizzy spell sending him stumbling for support.

As he did, he leaned into the procedure room door, inadvertently closing it.

Magdalena watched all of this, not sure whether she wanted to laugh or cry.

Ezra collapsed against the door, turning to have it at his back as he lowered himself to the floor. Closing his eyes, he thrashed his legs out in front of him like a toddler in a tantrum.

When his eyes opened, he looked surprised to see her still standing there.

"I thought I told you to get out," he muttered.

Her lips were thin as she spoke. "I can't, Doctor."

"Can't?"

"It seems you've locked the door."

He huffed. "You have the key."

Magdalena laughed outright because it's what she did when she panicked.

"I do not."

She shook her head. Surely Mr. Bulcroft would return with her key and all would be well. It was simply a matter of time. But just how much time, she couldn't be sure.

"Stop that," he snapped. "Restrain me."

He crawled toward the bed at the far side.

"Absolutely not. I tied Mr. Cain to the bars because he was canoodling with the mop,"

She shook her head. There was a significant difference between the two men.

He glared at her. "Just listen, for once in your life."

"You won't hurt me." Her smile faltered.

"You can't know that." He sat on the bed, head in his hands. "Everything is spinning. My mouth is so dry I could drink the contents of the well and then some."

He groaned, leaning back onto the bed where he looped a leather restraint around his wrist.

"And my arms are on fire."

"They hurt?"

She hesitated to move closer to him. He was right. There was no guarantee how one would act under this influence. It seemed Mr. Cain was quicker to fall, and his inclinations appeared to be simply an exaggerated delusion of who he already was.

With this logic, who would Ezra become?

"Mm." He nodded, and then he was silent. One leg outstretched on the bed and one knee propped up.

Magdalena searched through the contents of his bag, finding several vials. She opened each, taking a cautious sniff before settling on the one that smelled a bit like licorice. She turned it in her palm and read the scrawl across it—burns. This must be it.

She sat beside him on the bed, swallowing hard.

"Dr. Talbot?" She nudged him. "I have your oil if you're ready."

Ezra thrust his arm haphazardly across her lap with a grunt.

When he didn't open his eyes, she unfastened his cufflinks and rolled up his sleeves, exposing the scars on his forearms. Willing her nerves to calm, she opened the vial and poured it into her hands, rubbing them together to warm the mixture before she hesitantly rubbed it into the tightness of the skin. Gently, she went around the restraint he seemed convinced was necessary.

He didn't flinch.

It smelled familiar ... like what they had administered at the foundling home. Certainly this was why he had journals detailing the combination and how he knew so many of its uses.

Her fingers traced the ridges of each scar. Some spaces were smooth and others were gravelly and bumpy, puckered by flame and then healing. He would never have permitted the proximity, nor the pain she felt in her chest over seeing them. Respectfully she turned back down his sleeves and returned the vial to his bag.

You could tell him about yours...

She buried the idea. Winter was coming, and winters were for—well. They were for something nearly as wretched as Wednesdays.

Not knowing what else to do, she picked up a spare blanket and stretched it out on the floor, far from the doctor.

She hesitated before blowing out the lantern. It thrust them into near darkness, and she felt unsettled in the few moments before her eyes drifted closed.

The doctor shifted on the bed before everything was still, nearly peaceful. The illumination of a lantern in the hall offered only shadows and glimpses through the barred cutout at the top of the door. Something about his nearness was comforting.

She was nearly asleep when a voice spoke through the darkness. It was one she nearly didn't recognize.

"Miss?" It whispered.

She sat upright, taken aback by the sound in the silence.

"Miss, are you in trouble, too?"

"Wha—?" She began, startled by Ezra's form.

She blinked against the shadows, squinting to make out his shape. The doctor's knees were drawn to his chest with his arms wrapped around them. She recognized the posture—it was the same way he'd sat in his flat the night his father returned.

She hesitated. "What do you mean?"

"It's all right. Don't be afraid," he reassured her.

The tone wasn't his own. It was his voice, but warped and soft as though he'd changed into someone else entirely.

"My name is Ezra. What's yours?" He asked sweetly.

She couldn't be more alarmed. This must be a dream.

"Magdalena," she whispered, her heart clenching.

She shouldn't entertain this conversation. He'd be upset later. Yet there was a burning question, a hunch perhaps, which pushed her on.

"Ezra ... how old are you?" His name in her mouth felt foreign, and the simple syllables tripped out awkwardly.

"Nearly eleven years now," he admitted.

Magdalena rested her head on the stone wall behind her. "Ezra, we ought to get some sleep."

He sniffed. "I understand. We wouldn't want him to hear us." He cleared his throat, his voice manipulated by emotion and a childlike pitch.

Her curiosity did indeed get the best of her. "Are we … are we at your home?"

"Of course not," he scoffed. Apparently this reaction was just as natural for the child as it was for the man. "This is the Breton School for Boys."

Chapter Thirty-Six

Ezra

The lady in the cellar was quiet. Her being here didn't make much sense. How had she come to be at Breton's? What wretched thing had she done that they'd punished her, too?

Russel Breton had been real mad when the kitchen help let it slip about the fire. He rubbed his arms through his sleeves, thankful the new skin didn't hurt quite so bad today.

Ezra shifted uncomfortably on the narrow bed, trapped by a leather strap on one of his wrists. That was new.

The woman didn't say anything else; she just lay back on the floor.

He lowered his head toward the restraint so he could cover his ears. Sometimes silence was loud too.

"Are you cold?"

Her words were no more than a jagged whisper through the palms covering his ears, but they startled him and he flinched. She seemed nervous, and it made him want to be a bit braver.

"No, miss."

He lowered his hands from his ears, noticing it was his left hand they'd chosen to strap. Breton must have done that on purpose. Ezra had always felt a bit left-handed by nature.

"Are you?" He hesitated before pulling the blanket from beneath him and stretching it toward her.

"Ah." She cleared her throat and stood, cautiously, almost as if she were terrified of him.

The idea made him smirk just a little bit, and he was happy for the dark.

She carefully came closer and sat beside him on the bed, mimicking his posture. He didn't see girls much, but it felt a little strange she'd sit like a boy.

"Shall we play a game?" she asked.

He could only just make out her features in the dark. He imagined she was quite pretty. Her hair caught bits of light filtering in.

"A game?"

If she were asking, it must be that she wanted to play, and he ought to just for the sake of it.

"You can ask me any question, and then I can ask you any question." She nodded excitedly over the idea. "We are required to answer with only the truth."

He would hate to upset her by not playing along. Perhaps just a few turns wouldn't be any harm.

"You start." She clasped her fingers together and nodded reassuringly.

Ezra had many questions—like, did the cold air bite everyone's skin or only his? Did objects have hidden eyes and was that why they had the power to make his skin crawl? Did the silence make her ears hurt as it did his? Did too much noise make her sweat and want to run away?

"Have you a favorite color?" Safe words.

"I do!" She clapped her hands together cheerily as if it were the best question he could have asked. It made his stomach feel funny. "Blue. It is the color of the sky, and I know lots of people who live up there. What's yours?"

Maybe she didn't have any good ideas for questions, either, so she had to use his.

Ezra shrugged. "Yellow." Perhaps it was, though he didn't feel much confidence.

"You are supposed to say why." Her smile caught the light.

Maybe he was just dead, and she was the one who greeted everyone when they died. That should have made him scared, but she was nice, and he didn't feel that way.

"I like the sun, especially how it glints over water in the early morning. Turns it sorta gold." He pointed. "Like your hair."

In that moment he knew he'd been right. Yellow was his favorite color.

She giggled, a silly sound for an adult, and he would have been embarrassed if it were anyone else. If she were the sky, he was happy to be the sun.

"Next question." She nudged him.

This was more difficult than he thought. "How did you get here?"

"Well..." She smiled. "I have some friends down here."

Ezra looked around the small stone room. It had only a wash table, a chair, a black bag, and a small mirror.

Something clicked in the corridor, like a fine clasp opening and closing. It distracted him for a moment.

"What are their names?" He'd accidentally asked two questions in a row—maybe she wouldn't notice.

"Well, there is Franz, Luce, Ellington, Thaddeus, and you." She listed them off on her fingers, yawning ever so slightly.

"You must not make very good friends if they're all in trouble," he admonished, ignoring that she'd called him her friend. He couldn't be friends with a lady.

Too late, he realized his words were impolite. "Sorry, Miss."

He tried to scoot over just a bit, but the strap would only let him move so far. Saying sorry made him shudder. It was a silly word that never made a difference. He'd mess up again later as he always did.

"You said sorry," she murmured.

He shrugged. He hadn't meant it. Saying sorry was the biggest lie he'd ever heard.

The lady blinked at him. "Does this hurt?" she asked, her hands brushing against the leather at his wrist.

She fumbled with the buckle.

"You shouldn't do that," he insisted.

"It's all right." She reassured him. "I'll return it in the morning if it would make you feel better."

He rubbed his wrist after she removed it, and they sat in silence. She was odd, and he felt like he should know her.

"Where were we?" She dusted off her hands. "What is your favorite kind of cake?"

Cake? He did recall having a slice with Papa when they had gone to the city. Cider something, was it? She took his thoughtful silence as not having a proper answer.

"For your birthday, what sort of cake would you like?" she encouraged.

Ezra felt his fingers close into tight fists and his breath caught in his throat. He didn't think he was in the cellar anymore. This felt more like the attic after one of his father's incidents. Things faded away, spinning until they settled, and he was left feeling cold.

"Ezra?" She settled a gentle hand on his arm.

He flinched away. If only he'd behaved just a bit better, if he hadn't been bad, Papa wouldn't have been so angry with him. How did she come to be here, too? None of this made sense at all. The attic was dark, and his stomach didn't feel so good. He must have gone without supper again.

"Don't let Papa hear you talk about birthdays." He groaned and held his head. "I mustn't celebrate that day with cake."

"Whyever not?" She tried to keep her tone light, but she was talking too loud, and Papa would surely come upstairs if he heard her.

Ezra clapped a hand over her mouth silencing her.

"It was the day I killed my mother."

His throat burned at the revelation.

He hated her, Eliana M. Talbot. He'd seen her name in the graveyard just outside. There were times Papa didn't drink, and he'd take him to town or bring him fishing. Those times he'd talk about how Ezra's mother had been kind and beautiful and every good thing. Times when Papa seemed himself, Ezra nearly made the mistake of thinking he'd changed.

But then Papa would go thinking about that woman too much and start all over again. He clenched his fist.

Magdalena's expression fell and her breath caught for just a moment.

Ezra's heart ached over having revealed this most painful secret. Why had she kept pushing? His eyes felt heavy and full of threatening tears, and he willed himself to push them away. Boys didn't cry, especially him. Papa got even more angry when he saw those.

"I didn't mean to." His voice cracked as he lowered his hands.

"Bollocks," she muttered, and after a huff of a growl she did the silliest thing.

She reached for him and all but hauled him into her lap. She must be a very tiny woman, because he didn't fit very well, but it felt like coming home. Not home how he'd known it, but home like he'd heard in storybooks.

It made him want to cry more.

"You are the bravest boy I've met in all of my life," she whispered gruffly into his ear.

No one had ever called him brave before. It seemed she knew, somehow, that he didn't like faint whispery touches. Her arms tightened around him.

"But I'm not." He shook his head. Her hair tickled against his cheek, and he scratched away the feeling. "I'm scared all the time."

He buried his face in her neck, breathing in the faintest smell of lilacs. He loved lilacs, Papa planted twenty-seven lilac bushes in the back acres, one for every year Mama had been alive.

"Everyone is frightened of something, Ezra." She pressed a kiss to his forehead.

"What are you scared of?"

"Long winters." She laughed but it seemed sad. Winter seemed such a silly thing to be afraid of. "When I was scared as a little girl, my Aunt Salomé would take my hand and draw pictures on my palm for me to guess."

Tentatively he held his out for her. Magdalena's fingers were soft and warm as they drew in his hand. "Sometimes they were simple things."

She moved her fingertip.

"A flower?"

"Well done." She squeezed him, almost like she wanted a reason to hug him again. He liked that. "Let's try something a little trickier."

She drew something with sharp lines and angles, making his brow furrow.

"A star?" His palm tickled and as though she could tell, she brushed it on her skirt for a moment before beginning again.

"When I got a bit older, she would write me a message. Can you read?"

"A little." He ducked his head, focusing on whatever she was about to write.

"Tell me the letters," she encouraged.

"S, A…" He looked at her when he couldn't guess the next.

"F." She smiled.

"E." He finished.

"What do you suppose that spells?"

"Safe," Ezra whispered, reaching for his tight throat.

He felt like he was on a ship with everything rocking and spinning. How did he know what being on a ship felt like?

"Let's get you a drink," She untangled herself from him and crossed the room. When did Papa put a wash basin in the attic? This was wrong, all wrong.

A cool tin cup was pushed into his hands. Water. His mouth was terribly dry, and his tongue was thick and heavy as he gulped it down.

"Slowly," she instructed, but he had already drained the cup.

She set it aside with trembling fingertips, and he had the strange sense she was nervous again.

"Come back?" He reached for her, worried if she were too afraid, she'd run away, and he didn't ever want her to leave.

"I'll always come back to you, Ezra." She promised. "That's how fate works, isn't it?"

He blew out a relieved sigh when she sat back down beside him and tugged his hand into hers, tangling their fingers together in a web. He stared at them in silent awe.

"How old are you?" he blurted out.

She leaned her head back on the wall and laughed. "Twenty-six. Now, if you keep me talking much longer, I'll spill all my secrets."

She shushed him, and he tentatively lowered his head to her lap.

"I like your secrets," he whispered into her skirts.

He was tired, and his eyes grew heavy the moment he lay down.

"Then I have one more for you," she said softly. "But you must promise to never forget it, even in the morning."

"Mm." He nodded, eyes drifting closed.

Her fingers wove their way through his hair, scratching against his scalp in a curiously wonderful sensation. He was nearly asleep, but he wanted to hear her secret.

"The secret is, Ezra, that you are the only one who can decide that you are tired of living in the dark. Light the match, darling. I'll still be here no matter what the light shows."

It didn't make much sense to him, and he felt the soft rustle of fabric being tugged over his shoulder.

She couldn't possibly be real, but he hoped she would still be here in the morning.

CHAPTER THIRTY-SEVEN

Ezra

The sound of metal clanging against stone shattered through his sleep-hazed mind, and oh, how it resonated. Ezra moaned, reaching for his head and gripped it between his palms, attempting to stop its pounding.

Lurched into sitting by a familiar, accusatory laugh, he chanced opening his eyes, squinting and blinking over the brightness of lantern light held in front of his face.

Arthur? Shards of memories filtered back in confusing pieces that didn't quite fit together. There had been tea and Thaddeus. And then...

Ezra swayed to his feet and stumbled away from the bed.

No. No. No. His stomach roiled dangerously, threatening to overturn completely, and he swallowed back the acid in his throat.

His skin crawled, not fully recalling the sequence of events in any order but knowing without a doubt that she had touched him.

Magdalena groaned and arched her back, stretching out the kinks born of a sleepless night sitting.

Socks, where were his socks? He felt dust beneath his bare feet, and few things could unravel him as quickly.

Ezra stooped and overturned his vest and boots as panic settled in. What had he told her? What had he done?

"Pleasant morning, so it seems?" Arthur chuckled toward the constable at his side.

"Socks," he mumbled. "I—I need my socks."

Magdalena shifted her way off the bed, reached beneath it, and withdrew his socks.

"Let's, ah, give them a minute. Shall we?" Arthur gave Finnian a tight smile and Ezra a nod.

His father knew how pathetically he could crumble, and Ezra hated it.

"I'm sorry for the delay, sir," Finnian acknowledged. "We were set back with some unexpected information."

Stockings and boots on, Ezra roughly yanked his vest over his shirt and buttoned it with shaky fingertips. Without a solitary coherent word to direct toward her, he stayed silent as he tried to tie his cravat in the mirror. Between the trembling hands, spinning room, and panic in his chest, he couldn't manage it. He tugged it back through his collar with a growl.

"Here we are." Her hands slid up his back and rested on his shoulders before she turned him around. "Give me that."

Her hair was down. Blast it, why had she taken it down? The curls hung down around her shoulders and rounded her soft face.

At just the sight of her, the memory of her, he couldn't breathe.

Ezra clenched his eyes shut and steadied himself with the wall as she made quick work of his cravat. Being unable to tie his neckwear was the greatest reminder of how entirely useless he was.

"Ready?" Arthur was back in the doorway.

"No," Magdalena mumbled, shouldering Ezra out of the way so she could tend to her hair.

She scooped it up in one palm, exposing the soft curve of her pale neck as she twisted and pinned bits.

His mouth, which had already been overwhelmingly dry nearly turned brittle, from lack of moisture.

Idiot. The first person to touch you in nearly fifteen years and you suddenly think you are attracted to her.

Instinctively he knew—perhaps this was the something more Mrs. Keene had mentioned. So much more.

He scoffed. Attraction was relative. He'd heard of a man in Scotland who was rumored to be attracted to sheep—this was nothing. He owed her the common decency and respect to ignore it entirely.

"You look terrible." He grunted, wincing internally over the insult.

"Then you are like looking in a mirror," she muttered angrily.

Why was she angry? He poured himself a cup of water and gulped it down too quickly.

"Ms. Trudeau," Finnian cleared his throat. "There seems to be a bit of a problem."

"What time is it?" She huffed out a sigh.

"Just before four, Miss."

"Yes, that is a problem." She turned a glare toward the constable, who gripped the back of his neck sheepishly. "No one, and I mean no one, should be up before the birds."

Tension crawled through him, his stomach seizing around the limited contents. Had he eaten more the day before, symptoms may have been less severe.

"That's it, might as well get married now." Arthur smirked.

His mouth released a sudden influx of saliva as his abdominal muscles contracted on their own volition. Ezra was going to vomit. He brushed past them and into the hall.

Thaddeus intercepted him en route to the water closet holding his backside.

"Ezra," Thaddeus warned, face twisted in discomfort as the unearthly sound of his flatulence erupted in the hall. He shuddered. "Please, that was just a warning."

He scurried past him and claimed the coveted solitude.

Ezra began to heave just as Magdalena pushed a basin into his hands and gave him a gentle push back into the procedure room.

"Close the door!" he rasped.

Neither Arthur nor Finnian asked any questions, and the door clanged behind them.

"Clean up after yourselves," Magdalena demanded from further down the hall.

Lowering himself to the bed, with a basin between his knees, he wanted to curse. Everything smelled horrid, including himself.

Or so he thought until the scent of his oil seeped through his sleeves. How?

Magdalena. She had played him. Like some little pity game, chased him like one of her broken things.

No, if anyone was angry, it should be him.

He pushed a palm through his tangled hair, and a spot near his temple tingled with a memory.

She kissed me.

No, he shook his head. Magdalena wouldn't have.

Looking at his fingers he remembered something more, how her pale hand had looked in his.

Ezra slammed the basin down and staggered to his feet. No more. He would ask her precisely what happened and be done with it.

He could hear her down the hall, her voice echoing even though she spoke softly.

"Shall we get you changed, Luce? Don't you worry about your book. I'll find you another copy."

No one was this kind. Her affection and naivety were a farce.

Ezra rapped on the door to be let out. It swung open quickly.

"Are you all right?" Arthur reached for him but had the good sense to lower his hand.

"Perfect."

Thaddeus too, stepped out beside them.

Magdalena looked between the two of them, clearly fighting a smile at their misery.

"Don't you dare say a word," Thaddeus muttered.

"Oh, I had no intention of it," Magdalena said breezily as she moved into Franz's room.

The door partially closed behind her—and then a scream erupted so loud it could have dislodged a loose brick.

His first instinct was to clutch his throbbing head. The second was to rush into the room.

Magdalena was frozen in the doorway. Beyond her, he could see Franz on his bed, rocking back and forth, with silent fear etched across his face.

And there, on the floor of Franz's cell, was Mr. Fallon—a very dead Mr. Fallon.

Blood seeped around him onto the stone floor, and the weapon of choice protruded from his carotid.

It was a charcoal pencil.

Franz's pencil.

Magdalena hurried to Franz's side and brushed back his hair, plastered with sweat to his forehead.

"Don't touch him," Arthur barked.

She ignored the detective, her hands on the young man's face.

Ezra stooped to check the rigor of the body and evaluate its temperature. The incident had undoubtedly occurred in the night. Rifling through the man's pockets, he ran flat palms down each leg, across the trunk and arms—just as he'd seen Arthur do as a youth.

His father joined him, removing the man's shoes and shaking them out. A scrap of paper fell to the floor and he turned it over in his palm.

"Bank numbers?" Ezra asked.

"Mm." Arthur nodded, tucking the slip into his own pocket.

Finnian looked chagrined. "Well, I suppose that solves why we couldn't find him. Sort of."

"Franz didn't do this." Magdalena shook her head. "He wouldn't."

"He was drugged, Magdalena." Thaddeus shook his head apologetically.

"He's prone to violence as it is, or he wouldn't be here," Arthur agreed. "Don't concern yourself with this. The mad have very little consequence."

"That is not the point. Any accusation, any conviction would keep him here for the rest of his life." She shook her head. "I will not stand by it."

"You may not have a choice," Arthur warned.

Storm clouds crept across her face as she clenched her worn, gray dress in her fist.

"Then we lie," she demanded. "No one knows what happened in this room. No. One. Knows." Her words warbled. "No one needs to know."

The men were silent.

She was speaking to a detective, a constable, a coroner, and an affiliate physician with the courts. The odds were against her.

Ezra didn't like it.

"Fallon doesn't have a key." Ezra stood, scrubbing his palms across his thighs. "I checked."

Arthur divided his attention between the blood spatter on the floor and Franz's relatively pristine clothing.

"I need the science," his father ordered, gesturing with his hand.

It was familiar, how Arthur barked out demands and how responses were so abruptly at the tip of Ezra's tongue.

"Blood is transported through the carotid artery at a higher velocity. Direct puncture to this artery will cause a spray between six and eighteen feet."

Their eyes followed the arcing spurt across the floor, up the wall, and where it staggered over part of the stone ceiling.

"More." Arthur pushed.

Ezra blew out a ragged exhale and crouched once more beside Fallon. "The pencil has an upward trajectory, suggesting it entered from below. Per such an angle, blood would have shot outward rapidly, covering anything in its path."

Arthur's gaze fell to the floor, where a gap existed in the blood spray. "Mm."

"With that logic, Franz would be covered in blood," Ezra finished.

Magdalena's statement made sense.

With the men appearing no less convinced, she pushed on.

"I told you about the tea," she argued. "Mr. Fallon knew of it. This was his fault. If someone must be blamed, can it not be him?"

"You cannot blame a man for his own death." Arthur shook his head. "Not when it looks like this."

Franz began to hyperventilate, gasping against the volume in the room and the situation before them.

Ezra remembered the incident the day before when Franz had been uncontrollable. Magdalena had insisted the door to Franz's cell had been unlocked even though her routine in locking it was ironclad.

"What was in the tea?" Ezra stood. "What drug had that potent of an effect?"

Magdalena reached into her pocket and withdrew a fistful of tea leaves spattered with a familiar seed.

"I saved some. I assumed it would come in handy." She shrugged.

Ezra's mouth went slack. He knew that seed.

Quickly he left the room, searching for his overcoat. Finding it, he reached into the pocket and withdrew Franz's notebook.

Hurriedly he flipped through the pages until he found what he was seeking.

The bell-shaped flower on the one side and the pine-cone-shaped seed pod on the other.

There.

If he wasn't mistaken, Franz had drawn the very seed used to drug them.

Ezra returned to Franz's cell. Magdalena still held the seeds in her palm.

He placed the drawing beside her hand as he looked between the two.

"It's the same," she remarked.

He released her arm and stalked toward Franz.

"What is this?" He thrust his finger into the drawing.

Franz whimpered and turned away.

Ezra inhaled sharply. "I said, what. Is. This?"

Each word he enunciated with a jab on the paper.

"That is not the way." Magdalena tucked the seeds and tea leaves from her palm back in her pocket and dusted off her hands.

She tugged the notebook from Ezra's hands and sat beside Franz.

"Franz, darling. It's quite all right." She sat between Franz and his view of the body on the floor. "You must have been terribly frightened."

He nodded hesitantly, eyes darting between her and the men.

"Shh, don't look at them. Just look at me." She smiled and set the notebook in his lap. "I know you love flowers a great deal. Tell me about your pictures."

She gestured to the men to step farther away.

Franz hesitantly opened his drawing book and riffled through, finding the one Ezra asked for.

"G—garden." He hurriedly turned the pages of his book searching. He settled on a page with the faceless drawing of a man that had been slashed by a streak of blue paint. "H—home?"

Tears filled his eyes, and Franz began to sob.

"Shh." Magdalena rubbed his back. "Let me get you something to eat." She stood. "I'll be right back."

Ezra filtered out the rest of their conversation as things were tidied and the body was prepared for removal.

"He likely did it. There is no way out of his room unless it's opened from the outside," Ezra overheard Finnian whisper to Arthur. "And it was his pencil."

His father shrugged off the idea, watching as orderlies aided in cleaning the floor. It seemed he trusted Magdalena, which was surprising. Arthur generally didn't trust so simply.

He watched as Arthur stopped beside Franz's door and crouched close to the locking mechanism. Fidgeting about, the detective pulled a pen from his pocket and used it to loosen something from the notch.

Ezra stepped closer and stooped to see what it was.

"Tampering," Arthur grunted. "It is possible..." he trailed off.

"Mr. Fallon came in without a key, or he entered with someone who had one?" Finnian asked.

"Or he knew a key wasn't necessary," Arthur added.

The possibilities were nearly endless. Franz either did it, or he did not. If Fallon came in alone and Franz killed him, why wasn't Franz covered in blood? If Franz were innocent, the only other potential was for Fallon to have entered the cell with someone else—someone who knew precisely how to get in and out undetected.

His father motioned for Ezra to join him back in Franz's room where he closed the door.

He leveraged his foot in the crevice beneath the door and gripped the bars in the cutout window, lifting his toes he pulled the door inward.

The door opened silently with very little effort.

The pair looked at one another, understanding this could offer small doubt in Franz's favor.

"Bulcroft," Arthur addressed Finnian. "Do not take so quickly to the easiest possibility."

Finnian looked chagrined, pulling a pair of tweezers from his pocket and settling down beside the lock to finish what Arthur's pen had not been able to do. He pulled and twisted until a small, folded tin was retracted.

Finnian passed the tin across Ezra to his superior, as if he could redeem himself from his earlier mistake.

Before passing it to Arthur, Ezra took it for a moment without thinking and brought it to his nose. It smelled a bit like rust, dirt, and tobacco.

"And just what took you so long to return?" Magdalena entered, giving Finnian a pointed look.

She settled a tray on Franz's lap.

"When we couldn't find Mr. Fallon, we interviewed the cook, who had some incriminating things to say about Mr. Fallon and the tea." The constable glanced at his superior.

Arthur nodded, giving him permission to continue.

"Which led us to the families of three separate patients—and a bank. Seems someone's been funneling away a large sum."

"We have that account number now." Arthur patted his pocket, crinkling the paper he'd tucked inside.

"Everything points to Fallon. Or so we think?" Finnian confirmed with the detective.

"Mm." Arthur shrugged. "Perhaps. It also seems Fallon had plans to flee to Spain."

"He has relations in Spain," Ezra remembered.

"A brother-in-law who retired," Magdalena added. "He was the president before Mr. Fallon, if I remember correctly."

"So Mr. Fallon gave the tea to Cook, who drugged the patients." Thaddeus raised a brow. "Why?"

"Money is a powerful motivator." Arthur folded his arms.

"As is fear," Ezra murmured.

Constables entered, heaving Fallon onto a stretcher and carrying him away.

His father turned to Thaddeus. "Take the body to the morgue but stay alert in case we send for you."

Arthur left Franz's room ahead of the coroner.

"Have life." Ezra gave his friend a quick nod.

Magdalena slipped out as Thaddeus left. He had a hunch she was playing detective. If recent events were an indicator, it wasn't safe for her to be alone.

Trailing her down the hall, he bypassed Denton Cole's cell. Arthur had rolled up his sleeves to his elbow and shed his vest and tie. He didn't say anything further to Ezra as he settled himself in beside the man Ezra had found in line the day before. Arthur's back was hunched and his hair in disarray. Ezra could see the slight tremor of his hand as he moved. Yet another interview.

It shouldn't bother him, the fact that age didn't appear to be treating his father well.

But the thought worried Ezra, and worry interfered with apathy.

CHAPTER THIRTY-EIGHT

Ezra

Ezra found himself taking the stairs to the third story. If he knew Magdale-na, and he was beginning to think he did, she'd be there looking for the drug. Trying to prove Franz's innocence and likely a bit enraged over mankind's seemingly endless cruelty.

The space looked empty aside from the whisper of skirts. She wasn't wearing shoes, as he recalled. The early morning hum of rising patients and bustling orderlies had not yet made it up the steps.

He followed the sounds until he heard something different, the intentionally quiet tapping of a second pair of feet crossing the tiled floor. Ezra had spent many a night tucked beneath a bed, hiding from the vilest sort of predator. And this he knew.

Magdalena wasn't alone.

Either she was someone's target, or someone else had every intention of finding the drug before she did.

His heart naturally increased its tempo, and he quickened his own silent gait.

Thousands of little hairs all over his body tingled with anticipation, and he softened the sound of his breathing. Magdalena stepped out in front of him, and he covered her mouth with his hand, pushing her backward with quick, sure steps until her back rested against a wooden pillar.

Magdalena's eyes were wild with fright, filled with the sheen of panic as she struggled with the fingers over her mouth. His stomach lurched at her touch, and he choked back a growl as he fought against his mind.

Badgers eat hedgehogs. It was entirely useless information.

Soft.

Hedgehogs were not soft? No, but her lips are.

He shuddered and jerked his hand away, rubbing it on his trousers.

Mind having caught up with her vision, she blinked up at him, eyes full of accusation, looking fully prepared to tell him off. He brought a finger to his lips and stepped into the shadows of plants with her.

Too close? There it was again, a question in his mind, not a demand.

The footsteps that had been following made a hasty retreat, no longer caring to obscure their sound.

She bit her lip, shaking her head.

Don't you dare, he warned himself. Like a magnet, his eyes pulled toward her heart-shaped mouth. Released from her teeth, they were moist and pink. How could such a simple feature cause his heart to stagger in his chest?

She was going to be the death of him, one way or another.

"I am not the only one following you. You need to go home," he muttered in her ear before pushing away from the wall and away from her.

"As do you." She glared, straightening her skirts and brushing her mouth across the forearm of her dress where his hand had been, like his hands were dirty.

He scowled.

"Don't act like your hands are any cleaner than my mouth," she scoffed, storming down the walkways of the greenhouse.

"Of course they are." He crossed his arms over his chest. "When did you last wash your lips?"

"Wash my—?" She threw a look over her shoulder. "I rinse my face every day, thank you very much."

"Wash, not rinse."

"With soap?" Her brows pinched and she stopped on the path with hands hooked over her hips.

Hips ... hips are nice, he choked. Hips were hips, they connected legs to the core.

"With soap." He nodded curtly.

"Well ... I don't ..."

There was a sinking feeling in his stomach. He wasn't certain where he'd anticipated this conversation going, but he had a hunch it was about to take a rather poor turn.

"Is that something you do?" She gestured toward his mouth with her features pinched. "That people do? Wash their lips with actual soap?"

"Of course." A strangled sound caught in his throat. "Are you telling me that in twenty-six years of life, you have not once intentionally washed your lips with soap?"

"Well pardon me for not knowing this was a thing people do."

"I—" He paced a few steps away and pointed to her face incredulously. "I put my mouth on that."

"I was nearly dead." She growled back. "I didn't ask you to."

Would she? He couldn't, obviously, but it brought up other questions.

Had she thought of him as attractive?

Was he?

Stop!

He threw up his hands in surrender having had an entire conversation with only his conflicted emotions.

"It's all right." He sighed. "Honestly, this is truly a benefit to my situation."

He pinched the bridge of his nose. He couldn't maintain attraction for her if he found her lack of hygiene repulsive, right?

"My not washing my lips disgusts you and that aids you in what manner, Dr. Talbot?" Her jaw clenched and he should have taken it as a warning.

"You touched me last night," he accused, tongue in cheek. "If you can't maintain professionalism, you'll need to keep your distance."

She stomped her foot. "You say another word about it, and I will pull your spleen out of your nostrils, do you understand me?"

She closed the distance between them and pushed a finger into his chest. "There is nothing I would not have done to take away your fears."

He wanted to catch her fingers and tangle them with his own, like he'd dreamed of.

As though she could read his thoughts, she snatched back her hand.

"What is wrong with you?" she demanded, but the sharpness was stolen from her words and replaced with something he couldn't quite interpret.

"Nothing." Everything.

He looked away from her, down the path where soil spilled across the stone.

"It's gone." Ezra realized. "Someone is removing loose ends."

"Dirty rat," Magdalena seethed, following his gaze.

"While those most likely do reside here, rodents are not the sort of culprit we are looking for," Ezra said dryly, needing to put some familiar distance between them.

They checked the rest of the greenhouse to no avail. Whatever evidence had been there was gone now.

Magdalena's stomach growled and gurgled unhappily, cutting through the silence.

"I think it's speaking to you," Ezra whispered.

Odd it was how toying with her tended to make him smile. He didn't like it and forced his face into submission.

Magdalena curled up her lip at him and scrunched her nose.

"It is," she snapped. "So you should not be."

She stormed away from him and down the three flights of steps to the kitchen, him trailing behind.

He watched as there she procured a mighty breakfast feast. One void of any tea, he noticed.

Finnian and Arthur soon arrived and situated themselves across from her in the dining hall. This left only one option, and he wasn't entirely certain he was prepared to risk any further wrath from her.

"You have already slept the night in my lap. Stop considering whether you can sit beside me at the table," she snapped without looking up.

Using a socked foot, she pushed out the remaining chair.

Arthur cackled and reached for a strip of salt pork from her tray. She swatted at his hand and took it for herself.

"Get your own." She hunched over her breakfast like a vulture over a fresh cadaver.

Ezra hesitantly sat beside Magdalena. Aside from the sound of her chewing, which was horrific, he appreciated the lull in her conversation. He had never witnessed a prompter turnaround in behavior.

As her appetite was satiated, she sat up straighter, the sparkle returned to her eyes, and an apologetic smile crossed her face.

Never trust a woman whose mental stability is severely impacted by food.

CHAPTER THIRTY-NINE

Magdalena

Ladies weren't supposed to drink coffee. Somehow this fact made it taste better. Every sip made her think of Mother and how the woman would be horror-struck to know it was Magdalena's morning beverage of choice.

She took a lengthy swig and tipped her mug toward the invisible, lurking shadow of Lenora Trudeau.

"You're quiet," Constable Bulcroft acknowledged.

"Ah." She nodded, turning her attention back to the table. "There's a lot to think about."

The young constable's eyes looked heavy as he nursed his coffee, and the detective did the same. Ezra leaned back in his chair, one knee jostling under the table ever so slightly.

He'd eaten very little the day before and nothing sat in front of him now.

She excused herself from the table, returning her tray to the kitchen before gathering up a round bowl of porridge.

Cook glowered at her across the room, and Magdalena shifted under the woman's tired frustration. Inspecting the silverware, she opted to wash a spoon herself just to be sure before bringing them both to the table. Food was the simplest peace offering, and she'd made an epic fool of herself hiding deeper emotions behind her temper.

Magdalena pushed the bowl into Dr. Talbot's hands and sat beside him.

"I'm not—" He looked at the contents and a flicker of gratitude passed through his eyes.

"Yes, you are," she urged. "I washed the spoon myself."

He grunted but raised a bite to his lips. The restlessness of his knee gave way to a content stillness. She cleared the table, and by the time she returned, the men were pushing in their chairs, discussing the next course of action.

"Someone got to the drug before we did." Ezra brought up the incident in the greenhouse.

"Which suggests Franz is innocent." Magdalena chimed in. "A constable has been sitting with him during this time."

This made sense. Surely they could see that.

Arthur dragged a tired palm over his beard. "Either they know their way around the asylum well enough to stay out of sight, or I've failed to find them in the never-ending sea of interviews."

He leaned against the table with a heavy sigh.

"I'll start over."

"I don't think so." Magdalena shook her head. "An officer is covering the basement, we've found the drugged patients, and for the time being, they are safe. You two need sleep. Put the doctor and I to work."

Arthur looked lost in thought for a moment before giving a slow nod.

"You can look through Fallon's office."

She stood between Detective Talbot and Constable Bulcroft and tucked a hand in the crooks of their elbows.

Their lack of refusal proved just how exhausted they were as she led them down the hall and into Mrs. Lewis's old room.

She gave them a gentle push.

"Thi—this is the women's ward," the constable stammered.

"Women also sleep in beds." Magdalena closed the door firmly behind them, muttering, "When they're not lying awake regretting their life choices."

Dr. Talbot's hands were buried in his pockets, and though there was still a tiredness in his eyes, he looked better off having eaten. He didn't seem to want to talk, but she'd caught him watching her enough times this morning to have grown a bit leery of whatever was on his mind.

The two were let into Mr. Fallon's office by an officer standing watch at his door.

One wall was split by a towering bookcase to the ceiling with a row of cabinetry beneath. Labeling was poor, though there were some scattered markings separating patient records from literature. The desk she'd sat at nearly a month ago was positioned in the center of the modest room.

Wordlessly they tackled the desk first, sorting through drawers and shelves.

Finding nothing beyond scribbles and notes, they turned to the bookshelves, flicking through pages before tucking texts back into place.

Botany? Magdalena's fingers went still on a text and set it on the countertop.

The book fell open to where a folded sheet of paper acted as a placeholder. She pushed the paper aside excitedly.

"Look!" She gestured for him to come closer.

Datura stramonium. A simple weed, poisonous and certainly not recommended for recreational use considering the violence of its side effects. Vision changes, vertigo, urine retention, the overwhelming sensation of fever, high pulse ... it all made perfect sense.

"It's exactly as it was in Franz's drawing," she remarked.

The doctor picked up the paper and opened it, smoothing it out before muttering under his breath.

Where had she seen this flower before? Magdalena was nearly swimming in this tension and his refusal to speak. The man was marinating in his own misery, and she was being forced to join him by reciprocity.

"Now, this one is your signature. What is it?"

"Mm." He scanned the document. "Franz's surgery report."

Ezra sorted through patient records and withdrew the folders for the other two drugged patients. A familiar poorly crafted, fraudulent signature was scrawled across each admission form, and he held them up for comparison.

"Have you been in this office before?" She sensed something was missing.

"Mm." He nodded.

She looked around the room.

"Do you recall the painting?" She pointed, and indeed the nail that had held the image still graced the wall. "I do, simply because it was hideous. There was a horse and a flag and … it was terribly chaotic."

"No." He pinched the bridge of his nose.

"Headache?" She prodded. It seemed they were back to single-word communication.

He grunted.

Lovely. Next they'd be speaking through interpretive dance.

Silently, Ezra checked the tops of the bookshelves while Magdalena looked behind the armchair.

"Here." He withdrew a canvas from behind a beverage cart.

Returning it to the wall they both stood back and exchanged a grimace. At least he was looking in her general direction now.

"I think even I could paint a better horse than that." Magdalena attempted in vain to pull a smile from him.

"Fallon was either a very poor criminal, or he was merely someone's puppet."

Dr. Talbot pointed to the shirt sleeves in the painting.

Magdalena peered, absorbing what he saw. The shank buttons from the portrait were identical to the half Ezra had pulled from Franz's stomach and Mrs. Lewis's chemise.

"They're a match." Her brows knitted. "And while that is perhaps some clarification, it brings us no further to going home."

She pointed to the botany book lying open on the desk.

"If Fallon was simply a victim himself, who has been pulling the strings?" Magdalena arched her back, stretching out the tension. "Because it certainly wasn't Franz."

"Where is she?" A man's voice bellowed from the foyer.

A voice she knew.

Magdalena stiffened. It had only been a matter of time.

"Get out of my way," she heard him yell. He was restraining himself, she mused, considering there was an officer of the law standing guard.

"I won't be doing that," the officer argued.

"Magdalena, get out here. Now!"

She sighed, shoulders slumped, about to obey.

Ezra stopped her with a hand on her arm, jerking his head toward the door in silent question.

"My brother-in-law. Frank," she whispered. "He didn't know I was spending my time here until I sent word with Mr. Cain yesterday. He doesn't … like the hospital."

Frank must have had a terrible time getting in through the constables out front.

The doctor narrowed his eyes. Then, in what appeared to be some heroic act of masculinity, he stepped toward the door and tossed it open, blocking Frank's visibility.

"What do you need?" Ezra demanded.

Frank blinked, his face reddening and fists clenched at his side. "I am here to fetch my sister. Give her to me at once."

"Give her to you?" Ezra repeated, pushing his hands in his pockets. "Like, an object? A possession? Something that should listen without thought?"

He spat out the words. It wasn't a domineering posture, but it was one so wholly him—resolved, stony in his demeanor.

"Say it again and see if you like the sound of it now."

Oh—well then. Magdalena's jaw fell agape, and she was suddenly a bit flushed.

Frank stammered and tried to look around Ezra.

Ezra sidestepped, blocking him. "Try again."

"Magdalena, please." Frank lost his steam. "Come home."

"She doesn't want to." Ezra didn't turn around but simply leaned casually on the door frame.

Where was the man who'd spoken in nothing but grunts mere moments ago?

"You didn't ask her." Frank held onto his last fragment of decorum.

"Mm." Ezra closed the door in his face and stepped back.

Slowly he turned, rolling his shoulders, and she saw the tension, the worry and uncertainty he'd held at bay.

"Dr. Talbot?" She closed some of the distance between them.

He held out a palm, stopping her.

"I've told you what to do before." He didn't apologize, but somehow the feel of it lingered in the air. "I'm not sure you've listened a day in your life."

He shrugged, looking pained and confused.

"Do you want me to now?" she asked.

Ezra stiffened, dragging a hand through his hair. "Would you?"

"If you say please?" She smiled.

"No."

Her smile widened. "So you want me to stay?"

The pause was long and awkward, just as a pause ought to be.

"No," he huffed out a half-hearted chuckle.

"And if I choose to stay?"

"Something could happen."

"Some things I like, some things I do not." She smirked. "Could we be specific?"

"You drive me mad," he murmured.

"You're in the right place for it." She stepped closer, and the sounds and bustle of Bethlem Royal Hospital slipped away.

Ezra's throat bobbed, and his lengthening hair tumbled across his brow. Seemingly without conscious thought, he untucked his hands and one of his calloused fingers slipped through the tie of her apron tugging her closer.

Slowly, giving him enough time to back away, Magdalena brought her eyes to his.

"Aren't I supposed to stay with my physician?" she gestured between them.

"Yours?" he rasped out.

She nearly smiled.

"Mine."

"Yours." Ezra nodded slowly, half drugged, half wired.

His eyes, the brown she'd come to look forward to catching every once in a while, held hers, nearly drinking them whole.

CHAPTER FORTY

Magdalena

"Magdalena?" Frank called through the wooden door. "What'll it be?"

His words broke whatever the beautiful spell was, and Ezra staggered away, blinking and looking anywhere but her.

She smiled then.

"I'm your patient, after all." She opened the door. "I'm staying, Frank. But it was so good of you to stop by. Give my love to Olive, if you would."

"Patient," she heard Ezra mutter. She nearly laughed outright.

Frank was already shaking his head and shouldering his way past her. "You can't."

"Why do you care?" She fired back. "What is it about this place you despise so much?"

For the first time she felt emotion while looking at her brother-in-law as he sagged into a chair. He warred with himself in silence, and she watched the battle unfold. Magdalena felt curiosity and perhaps, if she were honest with herself, a meager amount of pity.

"I can't..." Frank closed his eyes, shaking his head.

Ezra, pushing off the utter confusion he must feel, cleared his throat.

"It was you who found me so easily after Magdalena fell in the river?"

"Yes, I—"

"You found me in less than a day's time." Ezra's eyes narrowed. "Which suggests you knew me before I saved her that day."

Frank's eyes widened, and it was all Ezra appeared to require.

"I don't know who you are, nor do I care," Ezra growled. "I won't even attempt to understand your family dynamics. But you are a poor cynic and an even worse liar."

In that moment, one by one, pieces of the picture fell into place.

It wasn't just one illustration but many, Magdalena realized. Images drawn with a charcoal pencil. One of lilacs, hidden beneath her pillow. Another of a faceless man marred by lines of blue paint—much like a blue tie. Both, in different places of London.

But both undeniably, she knew, done by the same artist.

Franz.

"You—you killed Mr. Fallon," she murmured, reality sinking in. "You monster!"

She dove for him, prepared to cause some sort of bodily harm, but came up short when a fist tightened around the back of her apron.

"Think of my sister!" she shrieked.

Frank's jaw went slack. "Fallon is dead?"

Her blood boiled. Was he lying? Or did he truly not know?

"I didn't kill Fallon." Frank shuddered. "What I did was worse."

He crumbled. There before her eyes.

This man, a man she'd come to dislike for simply existing, fell apart. And just like that her heart, the ornery thing, changed its mind all at once.

"Who is Franz to you?" Ezra demanded, loosening his grip on her apron.

Frank's chest heaved, and moisture flooded his eyes. "My son. Franz is my son."

"Your son? You've paid me in secret to care for your son? You have hidden him away in an asylum instead of caring for him in your home?" Ezra's expression was dark. "London's fathers are a tragedy."

"Magdalena," he pleaded. "Your sister. She doesn't know."

Obviously.

"I had a gardener about the house before I wed Olive." Frank swallowed hard, beginning his sordid tale.

"Franz's favorite space was the gardens, though he didn't care for the gardener." He stopped, eyes full of remorse as he looked at Magdalena. "I love your sister."

"Finish your explanation." The doctor waved him on.

"The wedding was drawing closer, and I still hadn't found the right time to tell Olive about him … when it happened."

His eyes drifted away. "Franz was alone in the gardens, and the gardener began taunting him a bit. I'd witnessed it before and warned the man, with the threat of his being released from his position if it happened again."

"This time, though, I thought Franz would kill him." Frank swallowed hard. "The man was hardly breathing by the time a servant came running into the house. Franz had his hands around his throat—he wouldn't listen no matter how loudly I shouted."

Frank's voice cracked with emotion. "That was when I was persuaded to send him away. It broke my heart, but what if he—he …."

Magdalena crossed the room and knelt in front of him, her heart winning despite her frustration. "You were trying to keep him safe." She rested her hand over his.

"What happened to the gardener?" Ezra pushed.

"He was released from his position and given a hefty severance for the trouble and his silence."

"What was the gardener's name?" The doctor asked.

"The only name I have is … Lory."

Magdalena and Ezra's eyes met, the weight of that single name hanging heavily in the air between them.

"Frank, go home and tell my sister." Magdalena stood, trying to clear her thoughts.

Frank shook his head. "I want to see Franz." He palmed a familiar key from his pocket. "Please."

"How did you get that?" She gaped.

"Not yet," Ezra brushed off her question and addressed Frank.

Her brother-in-law nodded hesitantly, but he gave a tight squeeze of her hand and left.

Magdalena sank into the chair he'd abandoned. It felt as though she'd nearly managed to complete a puzzle but somehow lost a piece or two.

Tugging violently on a loose curl, she stared at the wall, thinking, connecting pieces, hoping something might fit. Her eyes rested on a bust on the wall. She'd seen it before, but today it stood out to her.

"A cleft chin." She lurched to her feet. "Dr. Talbot, what was it you said about cleft chins?"

"Improper fusion of the—"

"Never mind." She shushed him and stood on the chair, removing the bust from the wall. "What do you see?"

Ezra's eyes hardly glanced over it. "I don't care much for faces." He shifted away.

"Just look." She held it up again.

He blew out a sigh and took the face in his hands, turning it over. His hands went still, and he brought it closer to the window, brushing over the cleft chin before moving onto the cheekbones and prominent forehead.

"The body in the barrel," he chuckled. "We've got three dead and the Queen's parrot to blame."

"The parrot's dead too," she corrected.

"The body was wearing clothes of poor quality. I'd have to compare more closely to be certain," Ezra warned. "His uniform was..."

He trailed off, reaching for the gray of her borrowed dress. "It's improbable."

She watched as Ezra scribbled a quick note to Mr. Cain.

"But possible," she smiled.

"Unless Thaddeus has fallen asleep, he should get the skull to us in an hour at most."

He tucked the note into an envelope and sealed it before swiping his hands across his trousers.

"I'll give it to an officer," she reached for it, trying not to brush against his fingers as he handed it to her.

He didn't have the same caution and closed the letter between their palms as he tugged her closer.

Magdalena stumbled awkwardly. If she didn't move, she wondered how long he'd linger.

"What are you doing?" She hedged, playing off how her heart skipped when he touched her.

"You." His thumb skimmed over the back of her hand. "Magdalena Trudeau, are remarkable."

She choked over nothing but the air in her lungs and fought watery eyes so she wouldn't cough in his face. Perfect.

She slipped, and her finger brushed against his wrist before he hissed and jerked away.

"What does it feel like?" she asked softly.

"Mm?"

"When you're touched?"

Dr. Talbot shrugged, pushing his hands into his pockets.

"No one has ever asked. I'm not sure I can ..."

"Please," she encouraged.

"Dread." He cleared his throat.

She ought to let him stop.

"Then the pain comes." A strangled sound slipped between his teeth. "It burns, or it aches. It is a hundred needles or liquid ice in my bones. There is no rhyme nor reason, no manner I can predict."

Yet he still became a physician?

"Your mind has twisted touch to mean pain." Incredible, really. She smiled softly. "It's self-preservation. I always knew your mind was fascinating."

"Have you heard nothing?" His brows reached beneath the dark curls splashed across his forehead. "There are monsters in my mind that have pre-determined everyone to be a danger."

"Everyone has a monster," she promised. "Some are just louder than others."

"No," he shook his head. "You don't get to do that. Don't attempt to convince me I'm not a lost cause."

"You can't accept touch, yet you initiate it. You've learned to tolerate some through textiles with a semblance of control. For goodness' sake, Dr. Talbot, you are a physician and a surgeon. I think you find solace in helping others when it is the only reminder that you are very much human. You bring healing when all you feel from others is pain."

"Magdalena—"

She had always heeded very little to caution. "Do you even want a cure, Dr. Talbot? Are you not exhausted from living in the dark for so long?"

"You think I enjoy being this way? You think I didn't want what every other man wants? A wife? A child?"

The last word was a solitary tremble away from breaking, and his eyes closed like the thought of never being a father was a far greater pain than he could bear.

"I think you're afraid," Magdalena whispered. "I think you're afraid to want, and without want, you have nothing."

He didn't say anything, refusing to look at her further as the muscle in his jaw tightened and released in a mechanical motion.

"With want I have nothing either," he said bitterly.

"Well then." She resigned. "Shall we go wake your father?"

She let him in front of her, passing the note off to the constable on guard. The thing about hope was that one had to claim it for themselves. Ezra needed to throw just enough caution to the wind to believe in unlikely things.

A familiar figure walked quickly down the hall and she groaned.

"Frank?" She called after him. "Frank!"

But he didn't turn.

"I've got to get my family out of Bethlem," she muttered

There was a wide hall dividing the women's ward where she stood and the men's ward, which housed the basement at its far end. She knew now that Frank loved his son, though it had been stupid for him to return. Magdalena had enough people to keep safe.

With a shake of her head, she stepped across the hall and haphazarded a glance toward the foyer.

And there, she saw him. A man with a mask shrouding his face.

Magdalena wasn't some fine constable with reactionary speed. She was an entirely average woman with a bit of recklessness poured in.

And now she froze, rooted to the spot, as the man in the mask stared at her. Then, slowly, he raised a gun and fired.

The bullet pinged off something behind her. Where were the officers?

He raised the weapon again, staring at her like he knew her, as though this were intentional.

She felt another brush of air whiz beside her head as someone yanked her backward, pulling her down the hall.

"I know you've had the urge to kill yourself before, but this would be a very messy method," Ezra growled at her.

Constable Bulcroft burst through Mrs. Lewis's door with gun drawn, Detective Talbot on his heels.

"Wait." Ezra's hand shot out for his father's arm. The weight of unspoken words hung between them as the doctor swallowed hard. "Never mind."

He dropped his hand and rubbed it on his trousers.

"Stay put." Detective Talbot jerked his chin. "Both of you."

More shots rang out as the men entered the dividing hall, but no sound of falling bodies followed.

A patient's door cracked open, and a woman peeked out across from them, looking both ways in search of the noise.

"Get back inside," Magdalena mouthed to her.

With a scowl, the patient listened.

Locks rested at the midline of each patient door. That patient had only been the first. Others would grow curious too. Someone would die.

The doctor, following her eyes, stepped in front of her and shook his head.

Offering only an apologetic shrug, she began at the far end and began clicking locks closed as quickly as she could.

Resigned in her attempt, Ezra followed suit and aided until they reached the mouth of the foyer, where he glared at her once more. He crossed the gap between them on silent feet.

The gunshots ceased with neither the detective nor constable anywhere in sight.

"They will die if they come out unexpectedly." She defended her choice.

"You will die." He held fast to her arm. "You cannot die."

"I won't." She smiled and shook loose his hand. "It isn't Wednesday."

Taking a deep breath, she covered her head with her arms and darted through the opening of the foyer.

A shot echoed behind her. She didn't stop to see where it was coming from. Instead, she frantically locked the patient doors one by one.

Footsteps followed down the corridor, and her heart nearly tripled its tempo. She hadn't the time to gauge who they belonged to.

The last room was empty, and there was no need to concern herself with it. She was so close she could nearly see the basement door.

Just then a body slammed into her back, and they tumbled into the empty room.

"You are categorically insane." Dr. Talbot silently closed the door, thrusting them into darkness.

She felt his hand on hers, tugging her toward the bed and pushing her beneath it.

"Whoever that man is, he knows you." Ezra accused. "And he acts as though he wants you dead."

"Have you never played hide and seek?" She hissed. "This is the first place everyone looks."

She shuddered as he forced himself beside her. Beneath the single bed, there was no possibility he didn't have various limbs protruding.

"When did you last look for a sane adult beneath a bed?" He ground out. "Will you fit in a drawer?"

"We'll be too close. It's too dirty."

"Yes, do point out everything that will cause me to panic all at once."

"You will have to come closer. He'll see you."

Her heart hammered in her chest. She needed him to be safe.

"Please." She tugged at his shirt . "I will stay between you and the floor."

"This is the stupidest thing I have ever done."

"Then I would say you've made it through life remarkably unscathed by poor choices."

Her smirk died on her lips as he rolled over the top of her. Dr. Talbot's knees pressed into the floor on either side of her own and he attempted to rest his weight on them.

Say something, anything to ensure he didn't hear her heart pounding.

"There is a certain benefit to this room having only one bed." For mercy's sake.

"I don't want to inhale your exhale, stop talk—"

The door cracked open, sending a sliver of light across the floor.

Magdalena muffled a gasp as the man stepped beside them, nearly stepping on her skirts.

Ezra's breath was ragged as he used his knee to drag her dress further into the dark.

The man tossed open the armoire, muttering under his breath before leaving the room. He left the door cracked in his wake.

Ezra filled her senses. His presence, his warmth, his scent.

It was overwhelming in the best way, but he couldn't discover that. The longer they remained here, the higher the risk became.

Magdalena moved to shift out from under him. The floor creaked with the movement, and Ezra shook his head. She felt it more than saw it in the shadows filtering through the windowless room.

"Don't be an idiot," he said low in her ear, lips brushing against her temple as he spoke.

Her body erupted into goosebumps, and she shivered too forcefully to pretend she hadn't.

I am fully willing to be threatened again if it means such delicious torture.

"What?" he whispered sharply.

Her face blanched. That was an in-your-head thought, not an out-your-mouth thought, Magdalena.

The darkening shadow of scruff across Ezra's jaw scratched against her cheek and his hair tumbled down across his forehead. His shoulder spasmed, and he nearly growled with irritation.

Overwhelmed by the terrible urge to do something reckless, something like kiss the poor man, she clenched her eyes closed.

Don't look.

Don't touch.

Magdalena was a child in a candy shop, and he was everything she wanted.

She lacked a compulsion against physical proximity and even she needed to get out from beneath this bed—quickly.

CHAPTER FORTY-ONE

Ezra

Four hundred and eleven seconds of torture.

It was nearly impossible to maintain the quarter inch of space between their chests. Every time the woman breathed, she'd get close enough to make the surface of his skin come alive in warm spidery tendrils. The average human heart beat between sixty and one hundred beats per minute. Presently his was near one hundred and ten and standing.

Could one die from this? It felt possible.

There were no further sounds of gunfire nor footsteps in the hall since the man's departure. A sinking feeling took over the warmth Magdalena had launched in his stomach.

Arthur was out there.

The constant push for the man to get what he deserved and the pull for his affections made Ezra's head spin.

"Your preference for avoiding unnecessary touching must be causing great affliction by now," Magdalena whispered.

"That ... is what you choose to say?"

She shrugged, shifting until her hands crawled up between their chests and fiddled with the buttons of his shirt.

A grumble settled in his chest. "Let's not do that."

His voice sounded like he'd swallowed rocks.

"I am ..." She blew out a peppermint sigh into his face and he shuddered. "I don't ..."

"What?" His brows furrowed, and he ducked closer to hear her mumble.

Her eyes widened and her chest went still. Why wasn't she breathing? Magdalena's gray eyes blinked slowly at him until they moved lower on his face, leaving a path of heat in their wake.

She took in a ragged inhale.

"I—I cannot do this any longer. Let me up."

She pushed against his chest, sending his back into the bedsprings above him.

"Just stop moving." He shifted and rolled out from under the bed, standing quickly and silently to his feet before dusting off his clothes.

Magdalena staggered out from under the furniture with so much noise he wondered whether she'd forgotten why they'd been under there in the first place.

"I'm going out." She peeked into the hall.

He was beginning to believe others were not simply at the forefront of her mind— they were her only thought. She held no regard for herself.

"Do you suppose he's already been captured?" She was talking quickly and fidgeting with her hair in jerky movements.

"Are you all right?"

Magdalena ducked away. "Don't touch me," she hissed.

He laughed a little puff of air at the irony.

"I'm going to find your father." She paused. "Or I'll go to the basement."

It seemed she wanted nothing more than to get away from Ezra, and he couldn't figure out what he'd done wrong.

"You shouldn't go down there." He felt obligated to say, knowing it wouldn't make any difference.

"What I should do and what I do are often two very different things." She shushed him and crept out the door.

Clearly, this attraction he felt had turned him into an imbecile because he followed her through the quiet hall and down the stairs toward the basement.

"The officer isn't standing guard." She gave him a worried look. "I don't think I could bear it if anything has happened to them."

It was likely the officer heard the ruckus and joined his father.

"Things will be all right," he heard himself murmuring.

Grabbing a fistful of matches from the tin pail hanging beside the door he tucked them into his vest pocket before taking up the lantern.

The first thing he noticed when they entered the basement was the dark. It immediately set him on edge.

Magdalena quickly unlocked Luce's cell and tugged the woman into an embrace. Arching away from her, Luce looked confused.

"Luce," Magdalena whispered.

The way she said names was like a caress, how it melted over them and made them feel wildly important.

Luce tucked her forehead against Magdalena's and nodded.

"If things turn poorly, Luce, you must take the others and lead them out," she urged. "Do you understand?"

Luce nodded. Ezra couldn't be sure if it was simply a response or if she truly understood until she gripped Magdalena's chin and muttered, "*Semper fortis.*"

She clicked her caretaker's nose with this unregistered accolade.

Always brave. The phrase tickled through his hazy memory.

"You are the bravest boy I have ever met in all of my life."

The words flashed through his mind. Had Magdalena said this?

Ezra kept his laugh in his chest. Kindness and truth were two very different things.

Magdalena unlocked Franz's cell and pocketed the key. Frank and his son sat on the bed looking at one of his drawing books as though nothing had happened at all. With a relieved sigh, she took Ezra's lantern and blew it out in exchange for Frank's.

"Have you heard anything?" Magdalena spoke at full volume, stretching to relieve the tension.

"The constable went upstairs just a bit ago. Nothing since." Frank looked skeptical.

"You were told to go home," she reminded.

"Yes, but as I was leaving, I could have sworn I spotted Lory." He looked apologetic.

"Lory? You should have told an officer." She chided him.

None of this mattered now. Lory had every constable in the asylum looking for him. Gunshots had a habit of drawing attention.

Ezra stepped into the room also. "What does Lory look like?" Little good it would do playing keep-away from an unknown character.

"Thin, mid-build, dark hair," Frank described. "Prone to the unsightly habit of chewing tobacco."

"There was a tobacco tin used to jam the lock in Franz's cell," Ezra told Magdalena.

She turned to look at him, mouth open, and he could almost see the recognition click in her mind.

"There were only two men who knew this basement well," Magdalena said slowly, as if piecing it all together. "Franz hated one ... and Fallon ... was very upset when ..."

The blood drained from her face.

"Tobacco." Magdalena sat up straight and looked Ezra dead in the eyes.

He saw it clearly—she knew who it was.

"We all need to get out," she croaked. "Now."

The sound of a revolver being cocked just behind them resonated through the cell.

One look at Frank and Ezra knew who stood in the doorway.

"Hello, princess." The voice was familiar, as was the odd little pet name.

"Hello, Lawrence," Magdalena said softly. He watched a shudder ripple through her. "Or should I say, Lory?"

Ezra turned to see a man, his gun pointed directly at Magdalena. He looked vaguely familiar and Ezra remembered—the orderly. The one who was always so cruel to Franz.

Lawrence. Lory. Had he viewed the employment records, perhaps he could have discovered this sooner. Or perhaps not. Names had never mattered much to him.

Lory stepped into the room and tugged down the face covering he wore. A slow grin covered his face as he lapped up the sight of Magdalena in all her fear.

"Shall we pick up where we left off?" He drawled before sending a trail of chewing tobacco careening toward her feet.

"Let them go." Her voice trembled.

Of course she was trading herself at the expense of everyone else. Ezra tightened his jaw and loosened the hands in his pockets. It wasn't abnormal for him to feel like hitting someone, but the desire to follow through tempted him now more than ever.

"What fun would it be without an audience?" Lory smirked, stepping closer to her and dragging the barrel of the gun along her jaw.

Ezra snaked a hand out of his pocket and wrapped it around her waist, pulling Magdalena's back flush against his chest. Sweat beaded along his collar and began an uncomfortable trickle down his spine.

Adrenaline was a peculiar thing. Lory undoubtedly felt it coursing through him, just as Ezra did.

What one did with it, though, could make all the difference.

"Do you know how much money you've all cost me? The life I had just begun to lead? I started here when Frank over there kicked me out. Fallon was a stupid little man. Hardly knew anything about his patients, but he sure did like the money coming in, especially from people like you." Lory sneered at Frank. "You pay well for your dirty secrets."

"It was the greatest opportunity when I was transferred to the basement. I saw the wretched underworld and just knew if I could replicate it, there was money to be made."

His eyes narrowed on Ezra's hand pressed into Magdalena's stomach.

"It's like that, is it?" Lory gave a careless shrug.

No, it wasn't like that. Keeping Magdalena close was intentional. Give her the reassurance she required in exchange for her rational silence, and in turn no one would get shot by the lunatic.

Magdalena's fingers wrapped around Ezra's forearm. Instinctively he squeezed his arm tighter as a shudder rippled through her.

"Make the mad madder, terrify everyone enough to stay out." Lory waved the barrel of the gun around his temple in a swirling motion.

The smells rolling off the man's body turned Ezra's stomach.

"Fallon wanted no part in my little scheme." He feigned a pout. "That is, until his brother-in-law croaked while they were drinking liquor in the office to celebrate his retirement."

Lory laughed, a pungent and hot cackle across Magdalena's face. "The old goat died naturally enough, I think."

"You misled him?" Magdalena blurted. "You let him think the death was his fault?"

"Of course." Lory winked. "Money was enough motivation for me. Fallon required a little ... fear."

Ezra nudged her. He shouldn't be all right with how close they were, yet somehow, it seemed just close enough.

"I gave him one of my uniforms and put the body in a barrel of his favorite Spanish whiskey." He flicked a sardonic smile toward Frank. "Promised I'd stay quiet about his little indiscretion if he ignored mine."

"And the plant?" She pushed. "That was you in the greenhouse?"

Lory chuckled. "I had a great little fling with Frank's garden, learned a lot. Not even the pests would go near those weeds. I bought 'em off a colonist just to mess with Frank." He gestured with his unencumbered hand. "They smell terrible, but a little trial and error with Franz in the gardens, and there I had it. The perfect distribution, and the best place to hide it. I'd get them good and mad and send them upstairs when I had it just right. Not too much, not too little. No one cared."

Lory dragged his dirty gaze over Magdalena.

"Until you. I bet you thought you made such a difference when I had to leave, what with their madness seeming to get better. Turns out your charity was all for nothing. It certainly made it more challenging. Keeping this up from the shadows with nothing but Fallon's words to go off. But I enjoyed keeping a close eye on you."

Lory ran his tongue over his dry lips.

Magdalena stiffened and attempted to step away, her breath ragged and angry.

"Stop," Ezra ground out close to her ear.

"I worked the rumor mill from the streets. Fallon worked the front desk." Lory's voice took on a prideful, cheery lilt. "Word spread fast that people could pay a small percentage of their winnings and keep up their game."

A second and third weapon clicked from the door.

"There were six shots in that gun, boy. You've used four." Arthur's voice was cold. "There are two of us, and by the time you get off a single shot, you'll be dead."

Lory laughed a dirty and gritty sound, taking in the scene before him.

"Ahh. I do believe this is your son."

He lunged for Ezra.

Ezra ducked and shoved Magdalena toward the bed just before Lory wrapped his clammy arm around Ezra's neck and pushed the barrel of the gun into his temple.

Ezra flinched. Don't touch me.

Lory turned him to face his father.

Arthur's arm stretched out in confidence. It didn't waver as he pointed his weapon.

"I take it you have no children," Arthur said steadily. "If you did, you'd have the good sense not to threaten a man's son. For that, you will not walk out of this room alive."

CHAPTER FORTY-TWO

Arthur

SPRING 1831. SEVENTEEN YEARS PRIOR.

Arthur's heart pounded in his chest. This was his favorite part of a chase—the capture.

But this wasn't just any apprehension. This was Burnes, Theodore Burnes, secondhand to L'entraineur. His arrest would be the highlight of his career, and if it led to the arrest of L'entraineur, Ezra would be set for life with the reward money. Arthur could leave London more quickly than he planned.

The thought made his chest ache and caused a bitter taste to rise in his mouth.

"We have twenty-three constables, armed and at the ready." Roland blew his cigar smoke into a cloud before brushing it away.

The man was an idiot, a rubbish inspector well on his way to a chief inspector with all the politicians he kept in his back pocket. The smoke clinging to his suit would be enough giveaway when they slipped in through the warehouse in a few moments.

Arthur made a mental note to let him go in first and stay far from his stink inside. He fought a sheepish smile; Ezra was rubbing off on him.

"Is that enough?" Arthur wasn't convinced that twenty-three was sufficient. Twenty-three constables, half of whom had never held a gun, let alone shot one. With any luck, they'd shoot Roland.

"If you doubt me, someone dies today," Roland barked.

Why had he gone and said a fool thing like that? Arthur wasn't a man of such petty thought, but the words irked him a bit. It was an ordinary Wednesday, and nothing in the spring air suggested otherwise.

"Leave the boy here," Roland scoffed, looking at Ezra who sat alternately covering his ears and turning the page of an autopsy text in the corner. "Disturbing."

The inspector gave a mock shudder.

His blood boiled. Ezra was coming. There was nothing wrong with his boy, and he'd bring him even if just to spite Roland.

Arthur smirked and tipped his hat. "See you at the warehouse."

He stood and grabbed his gun off his desk. "Time to go, Ezra."

"Yes, sir." Ezra ducked around him to grab his jacket from the rack.

"No coat, son." He said it stiffly, suddenly aware of all the Bobbies watching.

Ezra's hands paused over the outerwear. He blinked a few times like he wouldn't listen. A snicker passed around before Arthur had a chance to look up and see who it was.

"No coat," he repeated.

Arthur didn't mean to snarl, but his son had an audience.

Gripping the back of Ezra's neck a little too firmly, he steered him from the safe house and pushed him ahead of him into the street.

Ezra didn't defend himself. It worried Arthur how gentle he was. When life should have made him hard, he'd somehow managed to stay kind. People abused that sort of thing.

The pair slipped silently around the back of the warehouse leading his horse. By a small stand of trees in the back lot, he extended the muddy lead toward his son. Ezra hesitated before nodding and silently taking the reins.

Arthur felt a moment of remorse. That was why the boy had wanted the coat, to hold things. He mentally kicked himself. He'd let him wash his hands after this.

"Don't tie him. We may need him in a hurry," Arthur whispered, withdrawing his gun from his holster. "No matter what you hear inside, do not come in. Do you understand me?"

"Mm." Ezra swallowed. "Yes sir."

Bobbies flooded the side street, and some lined the rooftops. Roland ducked toward the side door and Arthur followed him at a crouch, silencing his footsteps on the loose stone beneath his feet.

They crept in through the door, following the sounds of barking dogs. Not a great sign. L'entraineur, also known as The Trainer, kept many dogs at his disposal, using their expert instincts to conduct all sorts of illicit affairs.

The air inside was stagnant and reeked of canines and Roland's smoke. A row of dog kennels stretched on either side of them. Shepherds lunged toward them with dehydrated foam seeping from their mouths.

"Dear God," Roland muttered up ahead. "It's a…"

Arthur hurried to look. Inside one of the kennels was a sleeping toddler, no more than three years at best, with its little brown ringlets and toffee-colored skin.

Arthur tried the latch, but it was locked.

"We can't leave her here," he argued, but Roland kept walking.

Arthur cocked his chin but followed bitterly. If the chief inspector died, he'd take a hit for it himself.

Set up in the center of the mostly vacant warehouse was a painting on a stand, set specifically to capture the light filtering through the high windows.

He'd never seen Roland look afraid, only ignorant, but his steps slowed the closer they came to the painting. It was a portrait of a man who looked eerily like him.

The inspector coughed out a laugh born of fear and whirled around looking through the shadows for someone who likely wasn't there. Burnes knew they were coming—it seemed the Thames Police Court had a rat.

"Theodor Burnes!" Roland's panic was poorly masked as he screamed up at the rafters, spinning in frantic and deranged circles. "I will find you!"

Arthur ducked back down the row of dog kennels. The child. She was the only thing that didn't fit...

But she was gone. No.

A simple distraction.

L'entraineur was not above the use of children, no matter how sick and twisted it seemed.

Backtracking, he saw the flash of a blade glint in the sunlight and dove across the floor for Roland's feet, taking them out from under him moments before the knife buried hilt-deep into the painting.

Rupturing some hidden compartment within the illustration, the perfectly aimed dagger lodged in the portrait's chest, spraying red, bitter air into the room and stealing their breath.

"Get out." Arthur grabbed the shocked Roland beneath the arms and dragged him outside, choking and coughing over whatever had just been deposited into their lungs.

A window shattered and the scream of a horse filled the air just as Arthur collapsed into the dirt beside the inspector. Gunshots filled the air.

But only one thought raced through his mind.

"Ezra."

He grappled with the hands of a constable who loosened Arthur's collar.

"The horse is gone, sir." Someone answered. "We don't see him."

"Find my son. Find Ezra."

He pleaded before the burning haze took over his vision, and he lost consciousness.

No one touched Ezra without consequence, not even him. If Burnes had laid a finger on his son, he was going to die.

CHAPTER FORTY-THREE

Ezra

Lory's chest heaved into Ezra's back, and he felt himself begin to spiral.

His airway constricted, shoved into the crook of the man's arm, and he tilted his chin to hiss in a breath.

"I should have killed Fallon when the rumors started."

"But still, you did in the end." Arthur pushed.

"He misplaced his fear," Lory admitted. "Seems he shifted it to you and your investigation."

His father exchanged a look with Finnian.

"He was a fool!" Lory shouted.

Ezra could feel the spray of Lory's tobacco on the back of his neck.

Get it off. Get it off. Get it off. Ezra's hands closed around the man's arms as his face contorted into a grimace.

He felt the pounding of Lory's heart hammering. The man was losing composure.

And so are you. Fear warned. What good will you be then?

An image of Theodore Burnes flashed into his mind with a little girl tucked under his arm like she was nothing. The reins had been muddy. He'd tied them up for just a few seconds while he scrubbed the film off his hands at the well.

That had been all the time Burnes needed to take the horse and to …

His chest heaved as he looked at Magdalena, using her body to cover Franz like she was a human shield.

"Then there's this doctor." Lory spat out. "Franz got Fallon in a headlock one day and he lost a button. This doc had to be a little too good and found it in the lunatic's stomach. That was trouble. The only choice was to frame it all on a doctor. Surely it would be the doctor who didn't care a lick about anyone but himself. He'd be one who'd lie on a few little admission forms."

Lory shrugged as his grip on Ezra tightened.

"See, that's where you lost me." Magdalena piped up, so full of sunlight and innocence.

She'd never lost that, he realized. Somehow even after seventeen years apart, she still looked like she believed in better tomorrows.

"Your dates didn't line up. The signatures were all wrong. You may have been just bright enough to pull off a fraction of this, especially considering you are illiterate," she goaded. "But if I must choose your weakest link, it would be right there."

No. Stop, Magdalena.

"Oh, shut up!" Lory snapped and the gun pressed harder into Ezra's temple.

Had not Ezra told her the same thing? Two words, and there were worse words. Yet they sounded furiously insulting and he hated them, hated them coming from this man's mouth, especially hated that they were directed at her.

Ezra's composure flickered.

"So you lured Fallon into Franz's room?" Finnian asked.

"Fallon was smarter than I gave him credit for," Lory admitted. "I had the bank account in his name." His voice shifted with rage. "But he took the account number and wouldn't tell me where it was. And I didn't kill him! He fell. I swear to you, he fell on that pencil!"

"You pushed him. You pushed him." Lory chanted under his breath. "So much blood."

"Let go of my son and I'll give you the number," Arthur said.

It had to be a lie.

"You have it?" Lory stiffened.

"Mm."

"Then put down your weapon, unless you want his brains painting the walls," Lory demanded.

Arthur wouldn't. He'd never trade what he felt was right for the sake of his son. Nor would he now trade Ezra for a madman.

Ezra laughed humorlessly. What a way to die. Looking his father in the eyes as he went.

Lory tightened his grip on Ezra's throat, cutting off his airflow for a moment.

"Lory ..." Magdalena started, prepared to bargain for him.

The man was coiled with jerky movements. He wasn't safe.

"How is that left arm?" she asked softly. "I know Franz hurt you."

Her tone sounded nearly as though she truly cared, and it distracted Lory into loosening his hold.

Left arm. The arm wrapped around Ezra's neck. It was a hint Magdalena was giving him, not concern for the man.

Ezra took a deep breath. He calculated and weighed the odds.

Then in one swift motion, Ezra took a step, pushed his back into Lory's chest, and crashed his head backward.

Connecting with the man's face, Ezra gripped the left arm and yanked with a twist. He heard a loud pop as the joint disconnected from its socket.

Lory screamed.

It was unfortunate that the weapon was already cocked, and his finger remained on the trigger.

A shot erupted, and the bullet ricocheted beside the door. He hated that his first reaction was to see if his father was hurt.

But it was Finnian who dropped. Blood seeped out from a wound in the young constable's shoulder.

"Drop it!" Lory screamed at Arthur, pointing the gun once again at Ezra's head, holding his left arm close to his body.

There was an apology in Arthur's eyes, a regret surpassing the moment they faced.

And then the hands, hands that had always been so forceful and unrepentant, went limp. Arthur lowered his gun, resigned to this consequence, as he pointed it at the floor.

"What do you want? I can get you out of London," Arthur promised.

"I had a lovely little thing here." Lory wiped a smear of blood from his lip where Ezra's head struck him. "Fallon was in the palm of my hand, and we were pulling in more money than you could imagine. You'd never believe how many people are willing to pay to put away their loved ones. Drop your gun and kick it over here." He instructed. "Constable's too. Let's be quick about it."

Arthur did as he was told, but Ezra knew his father. He had every intention of using other forces, and there was one bullet left.

Just as the guns skittered across the floor, Ezra dropped, snuffing out the lantern and pitching them into darkness.

Lory shrieked, Franz wailed, and Ezra frantically brushed his palms across the floor, searching for the other weapons.

"Ezra!" Magdalena gasped.

He froze.

She did many things, things without thinking. She was inappropriately bold, she pursued hurt people and hurt things, she chased darkness without restraint, and yet it never seemed to diminish her own light.

But she had never—in any moment save in his delusion—called him by name.

"That's right." Lory chuckled. "Nice try."

Ezra's heart clenched in his chest, understanding fully that Lory's words meant he had her. He had failed her again.

A swatch of material brushed across the back of his hands, and he willed himself to focus. It had been the feel of skirts against his skin, and there was only one other woman besides Magdalena in this basement.

A woman who had been directed to get everyone out safely.

"Lory ..." Ezra swallowed. "The thing about the dark is that the more time you spend in it, the easier it is to recognize the faintest bit of light."

He reached into the pocket of his vest, fingers brushing against the wooden matches within.

He pulled one out, carefully, willing it to ignite on the first attempt.

"That's enough of your philosophy," Lory barked. "I am getting out of here and I won't be letting her go until I am. If I let her go at all."

"See that's the thing," Ezra whispered. "I think I need her."

Ezra braced the tip of the match against the sole of his boot.

"Fiat Lux," he murmured just as he struck the match.

In the second the match ignited into flame, Luce lunged for Arthur's gun and held it up to Lory's forehead.

The match flickered out and a gunshot sounded.

Magdalena's screaming was the only consolation he required. He struck a second match, scrambling for the lantern, lighting it and scorching his fingers in the process.

Ezra's pulse roared in his ears, his breath caught in his throat, and he sought her out as light refilled the room.

Magdalena had dropped to the floor, blood splattered across her face, with Lory crumpled beside her. She was still screaming, even when he crouched beside her and grabbed her shoulders in a gentle shake.

"It's over," he promised.

He wanted to pull her to his chest and never let go but people were watching, and what good would it be if she couldn't embrace him back?

Her screaming turned into pitiful whimpers, and a relieved and inappropriate chuckle escaped as he pulled her up to stand.

She turned to see the aftermath, but he stopped her with a look, shaking his head.

"It's not something you need to see." He dropped his hands as she breathed in panicked gasps.

"What'd I miss?" Thaddeus's voice rang out.

Ezra looked up to see his friend pop his head around Arthur.

His father crouched to evaluate Finnian writhing in pain.

Of course, there was never a moment's pause. Blasted Finnian.

"Nothing, why?" Ezra muttered sarcastically.

The coroner shoved the skeletal head into Arthur's hands and stepped over the constable.

"My word, Mags." Thaddeus wrapped his arms around her, unfazed by the blood on her face or the fact he should avoid going about touching people. "Are you all right?"

She oozed into him like a puddle. Stupid it was how Ezra's nerves felt on edge. Even more so because he knew this was what she needed.

"There is a dead man there and a dying man here. May we save him?" Ezra snapped.

"I'm dying?" Finnian sputtered, holding a hand over his wound as blood seeped between his fingers.

"Not likely," Ezra muttered.

"Constable!" Magdalena gathered enough gumption to find the strength in her limbs and gave Thaddeus a parting pat before she hurried to Finnian's side. "Are you all right?"

She held his face. Ezra realized she tended to do that when she really wanted someone to look at her.

"Not particularly." Finnian grimaced as Arthur helped him to his feet.

"Procedure room?" she asked Ezra.

"Mm." He nodded.

The others left him there. With his father. One of the last places he wanted to be.

"Son." Arthur stopped him with that lone word. "You've done well."

Arthur swallowed and clapped Ezra on the shoulder.

Don't touch me.

His heart was a treacherous thing, prone to betrayal as it did in this moment, fluttering its pathetic little wings in response to any accolade his father offered.

"I've got to help the constable." Ezra shrugged off his hand, ignoring the pained look on his father's face.

"She's something, isn't she?" Arthur opted for what he perhaps felt was a safer subject— it wasn't.

Magdalena Trudeau was the farthest thing from a safe subject.

"You haven't told her, have you?" Arthur's question held an air of accusation.

"That I killed her parents?" Ezra said bitterly. "No. I haven't found that golden opportunity."

"We talked about this." Arthur shook his head in dismay. "If you hadn't pulled her from the carriage ..."

Ezra didn't want to look into his father's eyes. To feel memories he wished didn't exist. Magdalena wasn't a common name, and at first, he had pretended she could be any Magdalena in the ever-growing population of London.

Of course, when she'd mentioned her parent's untimely demise he'd known it was her.

Ezra was a far cry from the person she likely didn't remember at all, and he'd not mentioned it. This either felt irrelevant or too relevant.

Irrelevant because it had been so long ago, and terribly relevant for the fingers it pointed at her cherished fate.

"Leave it be." Ezra shook his head.

CHAPTER FORTY-FOUR

Ezra

In the end, Finnian had little more than a flesh wound, a clear through and through that required little more than cleansing and sutures.

Thaddeus offered to knock him out if he kept up his bickering, and Ezra nearly asked him to follow through. Arthur gave Finnan the bullet casing from the door as his very own memento of the occasion, and all were able to go home.

Magdalena clomped beside Ezra on the wide path out of Bethlem. The borrowed shoes she wore were two sizes too big, even with the men's socks covering her feet.

Thaddeus had taken Lory's body out, and Frank had gone home with the promise to return for Franz.

Luce and Ellington had been moved to the high-need corridors, and as luck would have it, the wretched basement was soon to be no more.

There was a spattering of food carts along the path, and Magdalena stopped beside one, purchasing two potatoes and accepted the steaming spuds into a pair of handkerchiefs. She gestured toward a bench and sat, waiting for him to join her.

He would … but it was a familiar bench. The one he'd sat on as he said terrible things to her over a month ago. While it shouldn't matter, it did.

"Sit," she grunted. "I can't eat unless you take one of these."

"Not ... that bench." He looked away.

She glanced around and sighed, stood, walked a few yards, and sat on the next with a groan.

"Better?"

He exhaled and sat too, medical bag across his knees as she handed him her offering.

Magdalena took a bite of her potato and closed her eyes, relishing the moment of quiet. Her golden hair was in complete disarray with soft tendrils falling across her face.

She's beautiful.

The idea surprised him. He'd not admitted as much to himself before. Had she always looked so perfect with her slightly crooked septum and cleft chin? Had her cheeks and the tip of her nose always turned pink in the cold? Did everyone else see it too? Surely, they could, and he looked around to be sure they appreciated it.

"I hear you are in need of an apprentice."

She could have been addressing the clouds for all the acknowledgment she offered him as she folded up her handkerchief and tucked it into her pocket.

He hesitated. There were worlds more he wished for, but had stopped dreaming of long ago. He didn't want her to simply be his apprentice, he realized. He wanted her, in every capacity or shape. In the mornings before she had properly eaten, or in the evenings when she was bleary-eyed and handsy.

He rubbed at his chest. It felt like it was on fire, but the best sort of fire.

With all of this in his heart, he knew in his mind none of it was fair to her. She'd come alive when she'd been able to touch him, full of spark and energy. To say yes would be a willful agony, to have her close but never more. Magdalena Trudeau needed a man who was kind, strong, and brave. Someone who could protect her and tell her she was lovely without choking on the words.

"I have conditions, you understand?" She elbowed him.

"Conditions?" He looked at her, confused.

"Your apprentice," she reminded him patiently. "I would like to start over. I didn't meet you under circumstances that I wish to repeat, and I would like you to be fully aware of what you would be getting into. Also, I have no intentions of being run off again."

He didn't answer.

"Hello. My name is Magdalena Trudeau," she began. "I have been told I make terrible tea and I talk too much, often without thinking. I don't listen well. I speak of my aunt often and it may drive some to frustration. I pretend to know what I'm doing until I do. I am mediocre at best regarding anything of feminine value. I suffer from melancholy at times, and I don't like to be alone because my mind is an unkind place to stay. And I may become irate when I haven't eaten."

"Any redeeming qualities?" The corners of his lips twitched.

All of them. He wanted to answer on her behalf.

"I love people I have never met. Oh, and I can sing the bones of the body from top to bottom in a toe-tapping rhythm."

"That one doesn't count."

That song was perhaps the most mentally invasive sound he'd ever heard.

She paused, her brows knitted together, and she drew her bottom lip between her teeth.

"I do believe a warm embrace can fix the broken places in someone's heart. After all, Aunt Salomé could do it. And finally, I believe in logic, but I also believe in fate."

She shrugged.

It could not be possible this woman believed she possessed only four redeemable qualities, two of which involved what she could do for others and only one of which felt realistic in any manner.

He was not prone to making observations in a person save medical ones, but every part of her, every memory, would be ingrained in his being for as long as he lived. In this moment, the sparkle in her eyes flickered, and pain met him there.

He realized she didn't know. Magdalena didn't know the impossible things she had accomplished. That every little miraculous thing that had unfolded in the months he'd known her were all because of her.

She didn't simply believe in hope—she was hope.

Pushed on by this bizarre and illogical revelation, he mumbled out an awkward response.

"My name is Dr. Ezra Talbot." He sighed. "I don't like people. I think they are dirty and lack proper intelligence. It physically pains me how dull they can—"

Magdalena cleared her throat.

"Mm. I do like to be alone." He said the words, but for the first time, it felt as if they did not ring entirely true. "Things must be tidy."

His voice was strained, and a trickle of sweat dripped down his collar.

"I'm blunt, often unkind, and I have only two—three people who can tolerate me. I intentionally work myself to distraction."

He looked at her, she was chuckling as though he weren't near dying over the conversation.

"I will spare you further unless you have any redeeming qualities." Magdalena's eyes danced with laughter as she slipped her fingers into a pair of gloves.

"You think you did not make a difference in the basement."

The words surprised him as they blurted from his mouth. He sighed because now he must finish what he'd begun.

"You have tricked yourself into believing what he said. That they only improved because they were no longer being drugged after Lory left. It's a lie."

Her jaw went slack.

"When I was ... influenced..." He loosened his cravat. "You were safe, you were kind, and I trusted you."

She blinked back things he couldn't read in her eyes before she rose to her feet.

"Do we have an agreement?" She extended her gloved hand.

He had never been able to sense such a tangible change in an atmosphere or felt as though the earth itself tilted in a curious alignment. This was different from the luck or favor he felt often swayed far from his grasp.

For the slightest instant, logic collided with the possibility that he was supposed to take her hand.

In the moments it took him to consider, Magdalena tugged his hand from his pocket and shook it vigorously, pumping his arm like she was operating bellows to usher oxygen into a dwindling flame.

The effect was the same, and he ground his teeth over the awareness of her gloved hand in his.

A blasted furnace ignited in his chest.

"Hope is always tested," he murmured.

"Aunt Salomé used to say that hope swims." She released him and fiddled with her seventh button. "Prepare to tread water."

Tempus omnia revelat.

Time reveals all things.

Epilogue

DECEMBER 1848. LONDON, ENGLAND.

It had been several weeks in the wake of Bethlem, and though it seemed such a short time, so much had changed.

Olive had been nervous to meet her stepson, and Franz, too, in some ways feared returning home. But the two of them, as Magdalena had known, became fast friends. Frank seemed a bit less dull, and the estate felt ever so slightly more like home. Mara split her time between being Franz's new caretaker and keeping an eye on Luce and Ellington.

"Are you certain you don't want a growler?"

Ezra shook his head. "It's near."

"Very well then." She tucked her black bag under her arm and shifted through her pocket, searching for a peppermint candy. She took one out for herself and offered him one, knowing he'd decline.

"Do you intend to pout all day?" She clapped a hand on her hip and turned toward him.

"I'm not—" His eyes narrowed, and he tucked his chin into his collar.

"You are."

He let a frustrated sigh slip around his gritted teeth. "You could have tended to the babe yourself."

He'd begun giving her a few simple cases.

"I didn't want to go alone … in case something happened."

Shh, he mustn't know about winters. Magdalena forced a smile.

They approached the tenement house across from the foundling home as a few icy spatters of rain descended from the clouds above and a loud clap of thunder shook the structure before them.

Magdalena squared her shoulders and opened the door.

The doctor did despise the lack of cleanliness here, though he said it was better than it had been upon his first visit. The idea of it being worse at any time made her grimace as she wiped her palms on her skirt.

They tended to the baby quickly and left, ducking beneath the roofline as Ezra waved down an approaching growler.

Her ears were pricked over the sound of whispering in the alley between tenement houses. Angry whispers.

"I'll be right back." She stepped away from the boardwalk and into the shadows.

It wasn't uncommon for young boys to slip into the alleys and experiment with things they ought not. She'd caught more than her fair share of youth sneaking the occasional cigarette or even strong drink. On one particularly poor day, she had found a pair with an opium pipe. She'd been mortified, and they'd been lost in the clouds.

"Come on out of there, the both of you," she called out.

The whispers ceased.

"Shall I come in there and get the lot of you? Your mothers would be ashamed." She growled when neither came out of the shadows. "Very well then, I'm coming. And if you are from the foundling home, Mr. Mansley will have your hides."

As she rounded toward the back, an arm flashed out in an instant. There was a flurry of retreating footsteps and a pinch at her side, a pinch followed by burning—a fierce and wretched burning that captured her breath away at once.

Magdalena looked down, gasping and fighting back shock. The immediate flushing of adrenaline overwhelmed her.

There, buried in her coat, slicing past her clothes just between her right hip and floating rib; rested a blade; hilt deep in her side. She could hardly swallow the confusion that threatened to cloud her judgment and she staggered away from the rear of the tenement building.

"Magdalena," Ezra's voice called from the street. "The growler is waiting."

She turned and fled the alley, stopping in front of him, grasping the handle of the blade in her hand.

"I wouldn't go in that alley," she sputtered.

Ezra's eyes read her face before traveling down to her side.

His eyes widened as he pulled away her hands. It took longer than it should have for him to say anything.

He generally did so well under pressure.

"Don't touch it," he finally insisted.

Ezra tugged his scarf from around his neck, used it to cover the knife protruding from her, and ushered her into the carriage. He must have instructed the driver. It jolted off, jostling the blade and making her wince.

"What happened?" Ezra dropped the scarf and began tearing her cloak and dress away from the wound, methodically and focused.

Her flesh was puckered around the knife. Blood seeped out and trickled down toward her hip.

"I was stabbed," she murmured bleakly, followed by an awkward little laugh.

Ezra's breaths came in short, choppy inhales. He captured her wrist in his hand and counted her pulse. His brown eyes met hers, fearful.

She understood.

"You've always said kidneys are finicky things."

Her body began to shake on its own accord as if she had been exposed to inclement weather.

"No." Ezra's hands trembled. He switched to the seat beside her, reclining her against him. "We haven't any idea how deep it is. Things will be all right."

His voice lied.

His hands never trembled under medical duress, his voice rarely wavered, and not once had his eyes ever radiated the dread emanating from them now.

"I'm sorry, I—"

The growler slowed and the driver shouted down. "Can't get to that address, there's a police van in the road."

A police van? Of course.

She heard Ezra shout back at the man, giving him the address of Thaddeus's morgue. The carriage redirected and continued a new path, one that would take no more than ten minutes but would undoubtedly feel much longer.

She tried not to, but she wilted against him then. She wasn't near faint, but the grimness of reality was warning her.

She was going to die... and on a Wednesday.

Must everything terrible happen on a Wednesday?

Acknowledgements

On April 4, 2023, I lay in a tent at the edge of Lake Jocassee and scribbled down an idea for a romantic comedy. A neurodivergent physician would be forced into marriage with a member of the Ton after saving her life. As I began to write, I quickly discovered Ezra and Magdalena didn't want to get married and they wanted no part in a romcom. Ezra demanded the use of anesthesia, messing with the timeline entirely, and Magdalena kept trying to die. From there I became the character's voice for a story that simply went off the rails.

It wasn't until the first draft of *Wednesdays Were for Dying* was complete that I realized it was more than a novel. I had unintentionally given these fictional beings the traits I liked least about myself. I wanted them to be happy, to find joy and contentment in themselves. This novel became a love letter to myself: August, you did it.

To my husband, Brandon: I am not a damsel, but I'm often in distress. Thank you for being the hero of my story. You have handed me tissues, money, and at times, my sanity. I love you always.

To H and G, my children: Thank you for sacrificing your time with me in the evenings. May this show you that dreams are meant for chasing. You give me hope for even greater tomorrows.

To my mothers, the one who gave me life and the one who gave me her son: You were the first to read my novel and tell me I had something special, then you never let me forget it. Thank you for cheering me on.

To Jenae Perry, my friend through every season: Thank you for giving me advice from querying to the size of a standard novel. You are the only person I'd stand in the rain for to meet Stephanie Garber. Ew David. Now it's your turn.

To my team, Beverly, Donya, Diamond and Erin: Thank you for sharing my excitement. It wasn't goodbye, only see you later. Don't worry, I'll be sure to practice my autograph in your books. You read illiterate writing best.

To my editor, Jessica Brodie: I'm glad I wrote down your email at that writer's conference. Thank you for not judging my chronic passive voice and the horror that is my grammar. You made this readable.

To Katarina @nskvsky, my cover designer: Thank you for not blocking me. Not once did you make me feel less-than as you taught me things I should have known but didn't. I gave you an odd idea, and you made my dream come true.

To my photographer, Scarlet Kasperbauer of Peaceful Springs Photography: Without you, everyone would know about my scoliosis .... Whoops. I guess they know now.

Lastly, to my Savior: You are the beginning and end of this book and its writer. Thank You for listening to me whine when I didn't see Your vision. I'm sorry I was a big baby; it'll probably happen again.